SAMUEL

MORONI'S YOUNG WARRIOR

A NOVEL BY

CLAIR POULSON

*To my wife Ruth
and my children*

Covenant Communications, Inc.
American Fork, Utah

Printed in the United States of America
First Printing: August 1993
93 94 95 96 97 98   10 9 8 7 6 5 4 3 2

Samuel: Moroni's Young Warrior
ISBN 1-55503-553-1
Library of Congress Catalog Card Number: 93-70859

Cover design: Amy A. Floyd and Roxanne R. Bergener
Cover illustration: Mathew Judd

Covenant
Communications, Inc.

PROLOGUE

Deep in the heart of Nephite lands, only a few hours travel from the great capitol of Zarahemla, lay Gilead, an obscure, sleepy village surrounded by fertile forests, lakes, and streams. Gilead was many miles upstream on the Sidon River from the thriving Zarahemla. Gilead's peaceful inhabitants did not anticipate or prepare for a Lamanite attack.

The city of Shurr, more vulnerable to Lamanite invasion, had been fortified—enclosed by casting high mounds of dirt around the entire city and topping that bank with tall timbers. However, even such fortification failed to save Shurr against the armies of two Nephite traitors who sought to destroy the freedom and claim the lands of the peace-loving Nephites. Jacob, the eldest, captain of an army of 2000 Lamanite warriors, led the merciless attack that brought Shurr under Lamanite control.

After participating in the overthrow of Shurr, Jacob's brother Antium, even more bloodthirsty than Jacob, swept down upon the sleeping village of Gilead with his men.

Most of the men of Gilead, including a courageous man named Latoni, were away fighting for the nation's freedom in the borders of the land. They served under Captain Moroni, the powerful and righteous leader of the Nephite forces. The unsuspecting village was defenseless. Antium ordered his cutthroat band to kill every man, woman, or child who resisted the midnight raid.

Nearly half the citizens of Gilead died that tragic night. Antium and his brutal men plundered the village and drove the survivors like cattle through the wilderness. So cruel and treacherous was the march from Gilead to the city of Shurr, that many women, old men, and little children died. Those hundred or so who survived the trip were locked in small houses—held captive along with that city's survivors, in the most inhumane conditions.

Antium boasted boldly of his evil work, and word of his murderous attack on Gilead reached the Nephite armies. Captain Omni, one of Chief Captain Moroni's most trusted leaders, was ordered to go north and attempt to reclaim the city of Shurr and free the prisoners held there.

Latoni pled with Captain Moroni to allow him to lead his 500 men as part of Omni's rescue force. Because of Latoni's personal interest in the lives of the survivors of Gilead, Moroni granted his request.

So it was that Latoni marched forth, praying that his wife and three children would be among the surviving prisoners in besieged Shurr and asking the Lord's help to successfully rescue them.

CHAPTER ONE

A GENTLE BREEZE STIRRED THE STALE AIR OF THE LITTLE room giving tantalizing hints of fresh, moist grass and flowering shrubs. The room held four miserable, depressed captives. Samuel shuffled over and inhaled a refreshing breath of the fragrant air that entered through the small barred window. Samuel, fully six feet tall though he was only sixteen, stood at the narrow window as he gazed at the high, timbered wall of the city. The wall was only a few feet from the pathetic house where he and his family had spent the past few weeks in utter misery.

As Samuel stood there, a husky young Lamanite warrior strode confidently into view on the catwalk attached to the wall of the city. Instinctively Samuel stepped backward from the window. He felt the anger boil up inside him at the sight of the breechcloth-clad young man whose bronze skin glistened in the sun. Samuel had noted with envy the finely carved wooden bow that the warrior carried. If only he had the quiver of arrows or even the crude sword that was hanging from the Lamanite's muscular waist!

Curious, Samuel looked out the window again. The young Lamanite stretched his stocky frame to peer over the wall to the grassy stretch of land beyond the city. Samuel pictured the solid mass of dark green forest that stood beyond the meadow, wishing he could be free of his loathsome prison.

Samuel guessed the Lamanite to be about nineteen years old, only three years older than he was. Samuel swelled with pride at his own height, knowing that he could have seen over the sharp pickets of the wall without any effort at all. Lost in his thoughts,

Samuel suddenly felt a sharp jab of fear when he realized that the dark Lamanite eyes were staring from beneath equally black eyebrows, down a wide nose, and piercing Samuel's own. He could feel the hate that boiled behind those enemy eyes. The young Lamanite would rather see Samuel dead, his eyes said, than guard him alive.

Samuel tried to square his shoulders and shoot a look of courage back at the dark eyes of his enemy, but he faltered and his eyes darted, unbidden, to the ground. When he glanced up, the young warrior was carrying his hate, born of generations of lies, boldly out of sight. Samuel's gaze trailed after him, and for several minutes he stared at the bright blue sky, his thoughts creating fantasies that only a reckless young mind could conjure up.

"Sam." Sarah's gentle voice pulled him from his daydreams and away from the window. "Please, son, you must quit thinking of ways to escape," she said, surprising him as she so often did with her uncanny ability at reading his thoughts. "You will be the death of us all if you try something foolish," she admonished. "We must be patient and wait and pray and hope. Captain Moroni and his armies will deliver us soon."

But his mother's voice broke, stealing conviction from her words. Fear and fatigue were etched on her careworn face. She tried to smile as she gently squeezed his hand, but he jerked away. "And you think they won't kill us someday if we don't get away?" He spoke in anger but instantly felt ashamed as tears slowly streamed from his mother's gentle dark eyes.

"I'm sorry, Mother," he said lamely. "But what if you're wrong? What if no one comes to save us? What will happen to Oreb and Nonita? Mother, Oreb's barely eleven and Nonita's only six. Somebody must do something for them. Look at them," he pleaded, glancing beyond his mother at his little brother and sister, napping fitfully in the hot, stale air near the door.

"But, Sam, what could you possibly do? You're just a boy yet. Look around you," she begged, wiping the unwelcome tears from her face with her slender hand.

"You just won't let me grow up, Mother," Samuel muttered. "Well, I don't know what I'll do, but I'll think of something! I can't just let our enemies, these Lamanites," he said, jerking his arm toward the window, "get away with this. We've got to fight back."

Despite his tone, Samuel dropped his eyes when his mother gave him one of her rare looks of determination. "I won't let you make things worse for us, Sam," she said.

Samuel stepped back to the window. He thought of his father, whom he hadn't seen for months and whose fate he did not know. Oh, how he missed him! He wondered what his father would do if he were here. But he *wasn't* here, Samuel thought resolutely, and that left their safety in his hands whether his mother liked it or not. But what could he do?

Something!

His father would not just sit idly and wait for someone else to rescue him if he were here. And neither would Samuel!

Despite Sarah's goodness, Samuel felt she didn't understand his need to take action and not just accept the plight they were in. To her, he would always be her little boy. Well, he'd show her he was a man now.

He surveyed the cramped room again with its small wooden table and two benches whose seats generously gave tiny slivers to anyone who dared to sit on them. The children were lying on one of the rough mats woven from the tall grass that grew in marshy areas of the land. A stench came from one corner of the room, where a faded woven blanket hung from the ceiling to hide the large earthen jar that served their personal needs. A smaller jar stood by the low door in the wall opposite the window, half full of tepid water. It wasn't fit to drink, but it was all they were given. Like it or not, the prisoners forced it down just to sustain their lives.

His eyes fell on the four empty gourds that had contained their meager, distasteful breakfast. He felt like retching. It wasn't right that the Lamanites could make his family suffer so. He couldn't sit idly by and watch his family wither away in captivity.

Samuel pushed angrily on the door as he had done dozens of times the past few weeks. He thought of Ophera, whose family was imprisoned in the room across the hall. Samuel had always known Ophera, but recently he had begun to see her as more than . . . well, the girl from across the road. He wondered if she ever pushed on her door as he did his. Maybe one day the guard who brought their food and changed their water would forget to bar it and . . .

His mother's quiet sobs interrupted his thoughts. It seemed that he was always saying something to hurt her tender feelings lately. But, he thought stubbornly, he was right and she was wrong.

A shout outside drew him again to the window. An older Lamanite warrior approached the fierce young man on the cat-walk. Samuel observed both of them with anger, wishing he could reach between the bars and hurl them over the wall.

"Gadoni," the older Lamanite said, "a messenger has just brought word that more prisoners will be arriving soon. We are to prepare for them." Samuel looked at the young Lamanite warrior. So Gadoni was his name, he mused.

"Why don't we just destroy these Nephite pigs?" Gadoni sneered. "I didn't join the army to spend my time guarding a flock of trembling women and runny-nosed children. I want to fight—to take back the lands that are rightfully ours!"

The seasoned warrior shook his head warningly. "You mustn't talk that way, Gadoni. You will be punished severely if you disobey orders given by Captain Jacob. Even though his skin is the color of theirs," he swept his well-muscled arm toward the cluster of grey houses, "he knows of their treachery and how best to fight and conquer them."

Gadoni sneered again and said, "Fight! This isn't fighting. This is old women's work!"

"Enough," the older man said abruptly. "We have our orders. These Nephites will be of use to us later. Jacob has plans for them . . . then they will die!" At his tone Samuel felt a chill go up his spine. "Meanwhile, we must keep them alive. Now, carry on, and no more of this dangerous talk. If you do your job well, you will have the chance later to kill as many Nephites as your heart desires," he concluded and moved away, the afternoon sun reflecting on his glistening brown back.

Samuel slapped at a fly that was orchestrating an irritating buzz in his ear and looked toward his mother. Had she heard the warrior say that they would all die?

"What did the mean men say, Sam?" Samuel hadn't noticed his

dark-haired sister move to his side. Her quivering little chin was upturned, an innocent, questioning look in her round brown eyes. Nonita, not yet seven years old, was still pretty, but the long weeks of captivity had dimmed her sparkle. Angrily, he wondered how they could do this to such an innocent child.

"More Nephite prisoners will be here in a few days," he finally said. His hand trembled as he patted her dark head.

Samuel knew that Nonita adored him and he certainly felt the same about her. Even with her long hair matted and her thin face badly in need of a proper scrubbing, he saw there a beauty that would someday turn the head of any Nephite boy—if she lived through this.

"How many more prisoners will there be, Sam?" This time it was Oreb—impetuous, good-natured, but quick-tempered Oreb.

He was the middle child. Like Samuel, he had brown hair and a medium complexion, but his eyes were different. They gazed at him, alive with intelligence and determination. Samuel couldn't help wishing his brother were older. Although Samuel knew Oreb would blindly attempt to do anything he asked, he could be so much more help to him if only he were about fourteen instead of eleven.

Samuel could only answer Oreb's question with "I don't know. They didn't say."

Sarah brushed her hair from her tired face and spoke words that sobered Samuel. "However many there are, it may mean less food for the rest of us. But we must have faith. We will be delivered," she said.

Samuel thought her voice lacked conviction. Unable to restrain himself, he added, "Only if we help ourselves. Father always said that God would only help those who help themselves. I'll think of something."

"I'm with Sam," Oreb said bravely, his eyes coming alive at the prospect of an adventure. Sarah shot an angry glance at Samuel.

Their discussion was cut short by footsteps in the narrow hallway beyond the door. The bar grated as it was removed and the door squeaked open. A frowning Lamanite guard threw in a few pieces of stale dried meat and hard, dirty fry bread, then shut the door with a bang. Samuel and the others hungrily attacked the meager offering as only starving people could.

The silence as they ate gave Samuel a chance to think about escape. He had tried to talk to the old men and other boys during the single hour each afternoon when the captives were herded into the yard for the only exercise and sun they were allowed. They, like his mother, told him he was foolish and would get them all killed if he didn't stop dreaming.

The visits to the yard, a small fenced area near the cluster of houses, had not been entirely unproductive. Samuel had carefully memorized every detail of the city that was visible from there. The tall, timbered wall surrounded the entire city and would be a formidable barrier even if they were to escape from the house that served as their dingy prison. Samuel had puzzled many hours over how to get beyond that imposing wall. Captain Moroni's design for well-fortified border cities had been inspired, but now the Lamanites used this one, and probably others, to their advantage.

Only one gate cut through the mighty walls way down in the southwest corner. It was tall and made of heavy timbers. From the yard, Samuel could barely see it. Every few feet above the catwalk were square holes, designed for soldiers on the wall to fire arrows through to defend the city.

The city was square, about a mile in each direction, Samuel judged. At each corner, Moroni had caused a great tower to be erected so that soldiers could see approaching enemies for great distances in all directions.

Samuel didn't know how many homes were in the city, but he guessed there were over fifty. The industrious Nephites who had occupied them had planted several large vegetable gardens, which now lay trampled and neglected. The invading Lamanites, accustomed to a meat diet, had not developed a taste for the nourishing vegetables and let them go to waste.

Most of the dwellings were clustered near the house where Samuel and his family were held. The stables and corrals were on the far side of the city. Of special interest to Samuel were the nearby freshwater springs that gathered into one stream and meandered diagonally through the city. He was sure it must feed into a large river somewhere beyond the walls, a river which in turn would empty into the East Sea. An idea began to form in his mind.

Samuel munched with effort on the dry meat and bread, swatting at the flies that buzzed around his meal. The flies were not in the least intimidated by his broad shoulders and tall, muscular frame. Their noise in his ear made it difficult to concentrate on a plan to escape. Samuel tried to ignore them as his mother did, but like Nonita and Oreb, he kept swatting.

After washing his scanty meal down with stale water, Samuel dropped on his mat and stared at the ceiling. Thoughts of freedom filled his mind. Suddenly, he jumped to his feet and stepped on one of the rickety wooden benches. Reaching for the ceiling which had always looked solid to him, he pushed on a certain board. It moved!

"Mother, look, there may be a way out through the attic," he exclaimed. Without waiting for her to thwart him, Samuel pulled the table beneath the hole and scrambled up onto it. The additional height allowed him to poke his head through the ceiling. It took a minute for his eyes to adjust to the darkness of the attic. A few slender shafts of sunlight shone through the narrow cracks between the logs that formed the walls of the house.

He began to pull himself up when Sarah whispered sternly, "Get down, Sam, the guard is coming."

He dropped onto the table and hurriedly pulled the board back into place as the guard removed the bar that bolted the door to their room. He took a step backward, placing his weight on the corner of the table. It overturned and sent Samuel sprawling to the floor where he cracked his head with a loud *thunk* just as the door swung open.

"What goes on here?" the guard demanded, jerking his cruel sword from its sheath.

Samuel lay still, the breath knocked out of him, his head swimming with pain. Sweat formed on his body like an unwelcome mist. His mind churned for an excuse for his ridiculous position, but the pain made it hard to think.

"Answer me, white boy," the angry warrior shouted, pressing his sword against Samuel's exposed stomach. Something warm and moist trickled down his bare skin. He tried to force words out of his mouth, but none came.

"Please, don't hurt him," Sarah pleaded, approaching the Lamanite boldly while the younger children cowered in the corner. "He was angry with me because I gave more dried meat to the younger ones," she said, surprising Samuel with her sudden burst of inspiration. "He shoved the table in anger and tripped over that," she lied, knowing it was the only way to save her son's life. She pointed at the bench Samuel had failed to move when he pulled the table under the hole.

Samuel began to emerge from the fog caused by the bump on his head. Still, his mother's words were like a dream. He made no effort to speak—he'd let her get him out of this one.

"Look," Sarah continued, "there's the meat." She pointed to a few pieces scattered on the floor, fragments so small they would have generated little interest even for a mouse.

A half smile creased the guard's thick lips as he studied Samuel and the meat. Samuel glanced at the ceiling and discovered that he had not replaced the board exactly right over the hole he had crawled through. A tiny crack betrayed his only hope for freedom. He felt the sweat start to pour again and forced himself to look away so as not to alert his tormentor to his discovery.

With an effort, Samuel spoke, trying to confirm his mother's attempt at a cover-up. "I'm starving," he croaked. "I'm bigger than they are. They don't need as much to eat as I do. I should get more, shouldn't I?"

The Lamanite gave a high-pitched chuckle. "Just like a white boy. Greedy all the time, just like your greedy forefather Nephi. Want everything for yourself, don't you? You'd let the rest of them starve so you could have all you wanted!" The idea thoroughly amused him.

Oreb, not one to be left out of an adventure, smugly pitched a final convincing line. "See, Sam, we need food as much as you do. Even the Lamanites know that, so you better share more after this."

The Lamanite laughed heartily and withdrew the sword from Samuel's trembling stomach. "I came to see if you needed fresh water, but I don't like to interfere with a nice little family fight, so

I won't stay," he said, chuckling at his attempt at a joke. He departed, leaving the tepid water undisturbed.

Sarah rushed forward and examined Samuel's bleeding stomach. Using a little of the water they would have to tolerate for another day, she cleaned the wound as best she could.

"I thought I was a goner," Samuel said cheerfully while she scrubbed.

"You almost were," his mother scolded. "You won't listen to me, will you? You could have gotten us all hurt, son."

"I'm sorry, Mother. You're pretty fast with your wits," Samuel said teasingly, "but I'll be more careful after this."

The wound was small and not nearly the bother that the rapidly swelling knot on the back of his head was. Samuel struggled to his feet, but an attack of dizziness hit him and he felt the nasty food boiling around in his stomach. He was afraid it was about to make a return appearance. Over an hour passed before he felt well enough to attempt an exploration of the attic space.

Sarah protested, as he knew she would. "Just like your father, aren't you, Sam? Once you get an idea in your head, no power on earth can get it out." But there was fondness in her voice, and Samuel couldn't help but feel pride at the comparison. He grinned as he scooted the table back under the hole. Soon he was searching the dark space above their room while the others listened at the door and watched out the window to avoid any more unpleasant surprises.

The attic was cramped and terribly hot. His body was soon drenched, but he was determined to explore every inch. There were no loose logs nor was there any other way to the outside. Discouraged, Samuel was almost ready to give up when he discovered a dusty box in a far corner.

He reached into it. With a gasp of delight, Samuel produced a large knife in a leather sheath. He held it up to a shaft of light and discovered that the handle was shaped like an exotic bird with folded wings and the blade was of fine steel and sharp enough to scrape the hair off his arm. A wide leather belt with a gold buckle to match the knife handle was embossed with a bird's head. Samuel dove back into the box with vigor. He pulled out a beautifully crafted leather vest and a skin water bag. The vest had tooled on the back the majestic head of an eagle.

"Mother, look!" he said, handing the things he had just found down through the ceiling.

Sarah shook her head. "What possible good are those things to us? Do you think you can bribe our release with them?" Her voice betrayed dismay. "And don't get any ideas about using that knife. You could get us all hurt."

"Don't you believe the Lord has provided these things for us, Mother? I do. We must have faith, you said."

With an idea growing in his stubborn head, Samuel put his treasures back into the attic. He replaced the loose board carefully. He had no intention of losing the precious things which had been delivered, like a miracle, into his hands.

In the late afternoon, Samuel and his family were herded into the yard with the other captives, including several new ones. Of the captives from Gilead, Samuel had been one of the few young men. He knew that to escape, he would need help. He was pleased to see a striking young man of about twenty with a bold and fearless countenance. Samuel introduced himself, "You're new here. I'm Samuel."

"Jashan," the other fellow said and frowned.

"When did you get here? I heard more prisoners were coming, but I didn't realize they were here yet."

"I'm a soldier," Jashan said, looking at Samuel with contempt.

"Hey, that's great. I'm working on an idea. I think we can get out of here. I'm working on a plan and you could really help . . ."

Jashan cut him off. "Listen, Sam. You're just a kid. I'm not helping you do anything. Furthermore, I don't need your help. I can think of my own escape plan." he said contemptuously.

"Well, I just thought . . ."

"Don't think. Leave that to the men," Jashan said, and walked away.

He won't be any help, Samuel thought to himself in discouragement. He would have to go ahead without this new fellow. He surveyed their prison house from outside. The log walls looked solid, but that didn't dampen his spirits—he had a knife now. He looked over the city again, taking special note of the nearby stream and the position of the dark green trees and large clumps of shrubbery. The tall grass waved invitingly and the neglected gardens made his mouth water.

"Sam." A musical voice interrupted his thoughts. At the sight of Ophera, Samuel took a deep breath as he always did when he saw her. She was thin, and her face was streaked and dirty, but a little smile tipped up the corners of a perfect mouth. Ophera stood out in any Nephite or Lamanite crowd because of the color of her hair. It was long and blonde and fell across dainty shoulders. Ophera watched him intently.

"What was all the commotion in your room awhile ago? It sounded like you were having a fight or something," she said. Her voice raised little bumps that made Samuel's skin tingle.

He swallowed hard and tried to think of something to say. It was always hard to come up with words when confronted with Ophera's graceful beauty.

Waiting for his answer, her gentle smile broke into a grin that scattered rays of sunlight. "And what was the noise in the attic? I would have sworn somebody was up there."

"Shhhh," Samuel said in alarm.

Ophera looked startled. "I just wondered. You don't have to get mad."

Samuel found his voice at last. "I don't want the guards to hear. I almost got caught earlier." He fingered the tiny wound on his stomach.

"Sam, you're hurt!" she cried.

"Keep your voice down, Ophera," he said sternly. Despite his tone, his head swam with delight at the concern in her voice. "It's nothing. I just had a little run-in with the guard, but it's all right."

"What happened?" she pressed. Her eyes were wide, and she had an expectant look on her face.

"I found a little box in the attic and . . ." he began.

"Then you *were* up there!" she whispered with excitement. "I thought so."

Samuel looked around. He didn't want to talk too freely. Other people were close and the guards were standing in little clusters around the fence. "I'll tell you about it later," he said.

"Who was that man you were talking to?" she asked, looking past him.

He turned. Jashan was watching them from across the yard. He frowned at Samuel, but smiled at the sight of Ophera.

"He says his name is Jashan," Samuel said. "He's a soldier. He thinks he's too good for the rest of us."

"Oh, I don't know. He looks like a nice person," Ophera mused.

"That's what I thought, until I talked to him. He's not."

She looked back at Samuel and the light faded from her eyes. "What's going to happen to us, Sam? I hate it here. Sometimes I feel like I'll never see my home again." Although the day was warm, she shivered.

"We'll be all right, Ophera. Trust me. I have an idea." He hoped he conveyed more confidence than he felt. He had to admit to himself that he was afraid. If only Jashan would help.

Looking at Operha's thin but still beautiful face, and at her pleading eyes, Samuel felt committed to action, despite his fear. He couldn't let her down.

Over the next two days, Samuel's ideas came together in the form of what he desperately hoped was a workable plan. The knife became useful in a way its creator would never have expected.

Samuel selected a corner that was not visible to the stern Lamanites who diligently walked the catwalk. There he whittled a hole through the rough wooden floor. Painstakingly, he cut the boards in a diagonal fashion so that when loose, they could be put solidly back in place. After several hours of whittling, Samuel had a hole large enough to let himself through and he immediately set about exploring the damp, musty space beneath the house.

The cracks between the logs allowed enough light to shine through to make exploration possible. Carrying his knife in his hand, he worked his way through the dead, dry grass the house had been built over.

Suddenly, an almost imperceptible breeze stirred the hairs on his hand, and the deadly head of a poisonous lizard struck the hilt of his knife, just missing his hand. Instinctively Samuel attacked with such blinding speed that he instantly severed the head of the lizard from its body. In morbid fascination, he watched the dead body writhe in the dim light, then lie still on the dry grass.

Trembling, Samuel made his way cautiously back into the room. Sarah knew something was wrong. "What is it? You look ill."

Trying to control the trembling in his voice, Samuel described his narrow escape.

"You see," Sarah said, "you're only going to get yourself killed with this foolishness of yours."

"But, Mother, I've got to do something."

"I don't know, Sam. I still think we should be patient and let Captain Moroni . . ."

Samuel pleaded, "He may not even know about us, Mother. We'll die if we stay here much longer. Can't you see that?"

Without waiting for an answer, Samuel grabbed one of the planks he had cut from the floor and lowered himself through the hole again. He swept it back and forth in front of him as he explored the entire space beneath the house. He didn't stop until he was satisfied that the dead lizard had been a hermit.

Samuel tested every log with the tip of his knife. He selected the one he thought was softest and began to carve away at it. After hours of painstaking work over two days' time, he finally managed to cut out two short lengths of log which, when shoved out of the way, would create an opening to the outside world.

The day he completed his carving, Samuel again approached Jashan in the yard. Samuel thought Jashan might listen to him now that he had a solid plan. "I've got a way figured to get out," Samuel said. "But I could use . . ."

Jashan turned away rudely. "I told you before. I don't need a child telling me what to do. I'll figure out my own escape. Who do you think you are, anyway?" he said arrogantly.

Samuel looked at him for a moment. Jashan, though older, was a good inch shorter than him and did not weigh much more. "Hey, I may be younger than you, but I'm no smaller," Samuel said in anger.

"You'd do well to get out of my way before I trim you down to size." Jashan clenched his fists.

"Fine, I'll carry out this escape without your help," Samuel said as he spotted Ophera's blonde head. Without bothering to say good-bye, Samuel joined Ophera. He could feel Jashan's eyes on his back as he and Ophera talked.

"You've been arguing with that new man, haven't you?" she asked, her curiosity evident.

"I tried to talk to him and see if he would help me, but he won't. What kind of a Nephite is he anyway? I'll do it by myself. Everything will be all right. Just trust me."

"What are you going to do?" she asked.

Samuel looked away. "Oh, nothing," he said evasively.

"How can I trust someone who plans to do nothing?" she teased. "You asked me to trust you. Can't you trust me, too?"

"Okay, I'll tell you, but don't mention a word to . . ." he began. He stopped short when he saw Gadoni sneering at them from the catwalk. When his dark eyes turned to Ophera with a glint in them, Samuel felt a surge of fierce anger.

Ophera shuddered. "He frightens me, Sam."

Samuel responded with reckless courage. "That's all he better do to you," he said and then felt his face burn as she gazed at him with a look of profound respect.

When Samuel looked up at Gadoni, Gadoni was grinning. For a fleeting moment, the dark glint in his eye was gone and Samuel wondered . . .

CHAPTER TWO

ON DARK NIGHTS SAMUEL HAD SLIPPED OUT OF HIS HOUSE to make quick trips to the nearby gardens to bring back a few pithy vegetables for his grateful family to eat. Those brief escapes from captivity had gone well, and he even thought he had discovered how he might get out of the city. "Tonight . . .," he thought. "I'll try tonight."

"Sam," his mother protested after he told her his plan," even if you do get past the walls, that's no guarantee that the rest of us could do it."

"I'll worry about that when I see if it's possible. I'll be back in a few hours. The guards never check the room at night, so they won't miss me."

"All right, son. You become more like your father every day. Go . . . and I will be praying for you."

With his new knife and skin water bag secured to his belt, Samuel replaced the logs and slipped away from the house. He paused and listened to the constant croaking of frogs in the stream and the pleasant, high-pitched chittering of crickets. A soft wind was blowing, rustling the grass and leaves. Finally, he heard the sound he sought, the light patter of moccasined feet as a Lamanite guard tread softly along the catwalk.

Dark clouds hid the moon. Samuel was glad. He waited until the guard on the catwalk had passed again before crawling on his belly through the grass toward the stream. He had not gone very far when he heard the muffled sound of moccasins again.

The moon broke through the clouds and Samuel saw a warrior

standing on the catwalk facing him. The guard must have seen him! His heart pounding, Samuel drew his knife and prepared for the inevitable fight. But to his amazement the Lamanite fell forward into the darkness. With a burst of desperate courage, Samuel jumped to his feet and ran toward him. A flash of lightning revealed the man on the ground, face down in the grass, an arrow protruding from between his shoulder blades.

Suddenly there were men running toward him. Samuel yanked the dead warrior's sword from his side and ran. Cut off from the house, he was forced toward the stream. The moon revealed Lamanites everywhere, many of them scrambling onto the catwalk and firing their arrows over the wall. The city was under Nephite attack!

Samuel dove into the dense shrubbery and trees at the edge of the stream, expecting warriors to dive in after him at any moment. None came, and gradually his pounding heart slowed down. He sat and listened to the sound of shouting men and clanging swords. After several minutes, he parted the branches ahead of him and peered out. The clouds had thinned and moonlight lit the city. Samuel saw a few Nephites soldiers making it over the walls, most of them dying before they made it to the ground.

Hundreds of Lamanite warriors now lined the catwalks and they continued shooting arrows from the wall. The screams of dying men made Samuel shudder and he felt sick to his stomach. It brought back vividly the night that Antium and his men raided Gilead and spread death so freely in that quiet little village. Samuel had seen enough of the battle. All he wanted now was to get back to the house and get inside. He was content to let the Nephite army do the fighting and free the prisoners.

He steeled himself and ran for the houses. He was almost there when he felt a sharp pain in his shoulder.

Terrified, he dove for the space between his house and the one next to it and crawled forward until an arrow struck the wall just beyond his face, halting him abruptly. Looking up, he saw a warrior running toward him, wielding a sword. Samuel lay still until his enemy was almost upon him. Then, ignoring the pain in his shoulder, he leaped to his feet and engaged the warrior in a desperate struggle. Samuel slashed with the sword in his hand, shocked when he felt the sword enter the soft body of his fierce opponent. He jerked the sword back, the blade dripping with blood. The Lamanite warrior slumped to the ground.

Another warrior appeared and Samuel stumbled backward, passing the hole that led into his house. The Lamanite sprang toward him, and Samuel heard Oreb's cry at the same moment the warrior's feet suddenly flew out from under him. In the blink of an eye, Samuel saw the heavy stick Oreb had used to trip the soldier, then he turned his attention back to the soldier, who lurched forward onto Samuel's outstretched sword. The force of the warrior's weight carried him forward, wrenching the sword from Samuel's hand.

"Sam! Into the house!" he heard Oreb call.

He glanced at the Lamanite's body, lying grotesquely on its face with the point of Samuel's sword sticking out above him. It had been driven clear through the body.

"Hurry," Oreb called again.

Samuel scrambled into the hole and Oreb helped him place the chunks of log back in place. Once they were safe, Samuel's legs gave way and he collapsed on the ground and cried. He had never killed anyone before. He felt horrible inside. He felt sick.

Oreb didn't know what to do or what to say.

They both sat trembling in the pitch-blackness of the space under the house. When Samuel finally found his voice he said, "Oreb, go tell Mother I'm okay. I'll be along in a minute."

His shoulder throbbed, and his head ached. It was several minutes before he found the strength to crawl up into the room where he collapsed on the floor. In the darkness, Sarah washed the wound in his shoulder.

"You must have been grazed by an arrow," Sarah said, her voice breaking. "I shouldn't have let you go out again."

"I'm okay, Mother" Samuel groaned.

"But you could have been killed."

Samuel pulled himself upright. "But I wasn't," he said. "I'll be okay."

For the next hour, they listened to the battle raging outside, hoping beyond hope that the Nephites would win. They were dismayed when they looked out the window after the sounds of war had faded. Lamanite warriors still lined the catwalk. The Nephite attack had failed.

In the golden dawn, Samuel and his family gloomily watched as Lamanite warriors carried the dead and wounded away from the catwalk. They saw more Nephite casualties than Lamanite.

Later, as they sat on the floor talking softly, Oreb said proudly, "I tripped that man who was trying to kill you. I helped, didn't I?"

Samuel looked at Oreb with surprise. He had been so involved in the battle that he had forgotten Oreb's role. "Yes, Oreb, you saved my life. I owe you a big one for that, little brother." Oreb beamed, but Samuel found that he could not smile in return after the night of his first real battle. He was still shaken by it.

Samuel had a hard time sleeping that day, but he finally managed to get a few hours of rest before darkness. As soon as the sun slipped beyond the horizon, he belted on his knife and water bag. "Sam, what are you doing?" Sarah scolded with alarm.

"I'm going to go find the army. If I can get out, they can get in," he said. To his relief, Sarah said nothing, and he kissed her lightly on the cheek, hugged Nonita, tousled Oreb's hair, and slipped beneath the floor.

Outside, he looked around. He shivered. Despite the confidence he tried to show his family, he was afraid. So much depended on him, and the terror of the past night had left him unsure of himself. Still, he had to go.

There was very little light outside. Dense clouds hid the moon and didn't seem to be clearing. There was enough light, however, for him to find his way, although he doubted there was enough for the Lamanite guards to spot him.

The shadowy figures of an unusually large number of guards milled about on the catwalk. Samuel was sure they feared another attack, and he was grateful for the distraction. The more the guards concentrated on the area outside the city, the less likely they would be to see him moving about inside.

Samuel's first goal was to reach the stream again. It flowed diagonally toward the southeast corner of Shurr, just east of him. He did not dare make a run for it as he had the night before. He decided it would be safer to crawl through the hundred feet or so of trampled grass and shrubbery to reach it, working his way slowly from tree to shrub. His eyes darted about him and he strained to hear any sound that might betray movement in the darkness around him.

The dense growth of the stream bank soon stood directly in front of him. With relief, he pulled himself into the welcome protection and rested. After satisfying himself that no one was near, he slipped into the cool stream. He was sorely in need of a bath, and the waist-deep water felt wonderfully fresh! He moved slowly with the slow flow, letting the water guide him.

The trees and shrubs at the sides of the narrow stream furnished comforting protection, and the tension in his body began to relax. At a point where the water slowed, Samuel stopped and drank some of the clear, clean water. How good it tasted after weeks of nothing but the stale liquid from the earthen jar! He slipped his leather water pouch from his belt and filled it.

After strapping it back on, he started down the stream again. He had only gone a few feet when something brushed his leg beneath the water. He reached down but recoiled when his hand touched the rough skin of a snake. With blinding speed, the deadly serpent wrapped its rope-like body around Samuel's legs. Frightened, Samuel grabbed at his knife as the snake lifted him off his feet and plunged him headlong into the stream.

Desperately slashing at his unseen enemy, Samuel struggled to get his head above water and gulp in a deep breath before being mercilessly drug beneath the surface again. Thrashing about violently in the water, Samuel began to panic as the long body of the snake moved from his legs to his upper body. With strength born of fear, he struggled with the creature. Just when he doubted whether he would survive, he felt his knife enter the body of the snake.

The giant serpent's stranglehold relaxed as the knife worked its way through the thick body. Finally, nearly severed, the long body relaxed in death, and Samuel wiggled free. Gasping for air, Samuel worked his way to the grassy bank to recover.

Aching and bruised, he breathed a silent prayer of thanks as he listened for any sign that the drama had attracted attention.

19

Satisfied that it hadn't, Samuel drifted down the stream again.

The stream turned around a bend just when he was beginning to wonder if he would ever reach the point where the stream flowed from the city. Suddenly the shadowy city walls rose ahead of him. He stood in the water and took in the sounds of the night, listening for any danger lurking ahead in the darkness.

Suddenly he heard a faint splash followed by the unmistakable rasp of a man clearing his throat. Samuel sank down in the water to his chin and strained his eyes until he spied a shadowy figure on the bank. A moment later, a second figure appeared, and the low murmur of voices drifted his way. He waited, the tension building until he was ready to burst, but the pair appeared to be in no hurry to leave.

Samuel almost held his breath, taking care not to make even the slightest sound. He could hear their voices clearly.

"I wish they would attack again tonight. The fight last night is the only fun I've had since they sent me to this city." Samuel recognized the voice of the speaker. It was Gadoni. He went on, "Well, actually there is one other thing."

"And what's that?" his companion asked.

"That pretty Nephite girl, Ophera. Even if she is white, she's a beauty. I think I make her nervous, though," he said with a light laugh.

"You probably make that Nephite boy nervous. He seems to have an eye for Ophera, too, I've noticed," the other man responded.

"You mean the one they call Sam? The one who looks down his nose at us? Ha! He'll never get her. I'll see to that," Gadoni said with venom.

"Dream on, Gadoni. What do you want with a white girl? There are plenty of pretty Lamanite girls at home just waiting for us to return with tales of our bravery in conquering the Nephites," the second man said with a chuckle. "I can hardly wait."

"She is pretty, though, don't you think?" Gadoni asked his friend.

"No doubt about that, Gadoni."

Samuel had heard enough. He was bristling with anger. With fierce determination, he promised himself that he would protect

Ophera from Gadoni at any cost. He could hardly believe what he was hearing from the man's lips. Gadoni was full of evil thoughts and desires. Then again, perhaps his attraction to Ophera was not so strange. She was the most beautiful girl Samuel had ever met. But Gadoni was a Lamanite and Lamanites enjoyed fighting and bloodshed. Samuel would never let Ophera fall into his evil hands.

Unlike Gadoni who seemed to want to fight, Samuel shuddered when he thought of those men he had killed and seen die. Even though they were his enemies, the very thought of their dying horrified him. Death didn't seem to horrify Gadoni. Gadoni wanted to kill the Nephites. That made him a savage, didn't it?

In that moment, Samuel felt a peculiar feeling. As he thought of the anger and hatred he had felt in the past toward Gadoni and all Lamanites, he was now surprised to discover that he was no longer angry. He realized that he would have to fight and kill to preserve his life and freedom, but he swore that he would never take joy in it. He just wanted the world to be a place where everyone lived together in harmony.

As Samuel slid silently into the water, well beyond Gadoni and his friend, his thoughts turned to the mighty wall ahead. The water flowed faster and was more shallow as he drew nearer. The banks rose high on either side where the stream cut through the imposing mound of dirt upon which the walls were built. He hugged the bank while, above him, the shadowy figure of a guard passed by on the narrow catwalk. He drew a deep breath, savoring the sweet fragrance of the flowering vines that crept up the steep banks. He listened to the water splashing and rippling just beyond him. The noise was comforting, muffling the pounding of his heart and providing security as he approached the heavy grate that filtered the water where it flowed beneath the towering wall.

Samuel examined the thick, sturdy logs of the grate. Holding his breath, he dived and groped for the bottom. As he had hoped, the force of the water had eroded a space beneath the grate that might be large enough for him to force his way through. He resurfaced and took several deep breaths, smelling freedom mixed with the sweet fragrance of the blossoms. Then, holding a deep breath of the delicious air, he dived to the bottom of the stream and squirmed beneath the grate. It was a tight fit, but he was making progress until the strap of his water bag caught on something. He struggled to free himself, but the strap held fast. He tried to wiggle backward but couldn't move an inch that way. Again and again he lunged forward with all his strength, scraping and bruising himself on the gravel beneath him and the rough logs above. He tried to reach the strap but couldn't.

A searing heat filled his lungs as they cried for air. He fought the powerful impulse to breathe, knowing that he would only draw in water and drown. At the very moment when he was ready to give up, the strap mercifully slipped free, and Samuel mustered every ounce of energy and forced his way through the hole, bursting to the surface. He gulped great breaths of life-giving air. Never had anything felt so good. He leaned weakly against the grate, too tired to enjoy the freedom that was now within his grasp.

The sweet air soon sent new strength flowing into his limbs and cleared his foggy head. In a few minutes, he was almost as good as new. He tightened the strap that had nearly cost him his life then moved cautiously downstream again. He knew that he was not out of danger yet. The guards were watching for an invasion, and he was now in the area where they were watching for movement. He stayed tight against the bank of the stream under the heavy foliage that draped nearly to the surface of the water. Most of the time he was able to travel completely hidden by thick branches and broad leaves.

Behind him, the faint silhouette of the wall receded into blackness. He stayed in the stream for a few more minutes before pulling himself out. The long time he had spent in the cool water had him shivering, and the hot, muggy night air felt good.

He figured it had taken him over an hour to come this far. He was anxious to find the army, discuss his plan with them, and return to the confines of the little house with his family.

Samuel studied the sky. He was thankful that the clouds had cleared, for he needed the light of the moon and the guidance of the stars. Latoni, Samuel's father, had taught him to read the position of the stars and find his way using them as a guide. He had no fear of getting lost as long as he could see the stars. He planned to go into the trees and circle the city in ever wider circles until he found the army.

Samuel ran through the dense forest, walking only when he couldn't be sure what lay ahead. He had always loved to run long distances through the forests and in the mountains. He was a good runner, with powerful legs and great endurance, although his captivity had decreased his stamina.

For over an hour he ran, straining to see his way in the dim light. Suddenly, he saw dark silhouettes just ahead of him. He darted, but was overpowered and wrestled to the ground. He struggled desperately, but two strong men were on him. A shout rose in his throat, but before it sounded in the dark forest, a cloth was shoved into his mouth. Another was tied around his head, holding the first firmly in place. He gasped through his nose, trying to get enough air to lend strength to his winded body. Before he was able to breathe normally and feel the strength return to his limbs, his captors had bound his arms tightly behind his back and blindfolded him. Without a word, they pulled him to his feet and shoved him roughly through the forest.

Samuel felt hot tears beneath the tight cloth. How could he have been so careless? Now his family would suffer even more when his absence was discovered. With regret, he thought about his mother's warnings. Had she been right all along?

For several minutes, Samuel and his silent captors passed through heavy timber. He could hear the breeze rustling the leaves overhead as they hurried along. He soon stumbled into a clearing. The pungent smell of smoke from smoldering campfires entered his nose. He could hear the snores of sleeping men all about him and sensed that he had been taken into the midst of an army of slumbering soldiers. Cold fear gripped his heart, and he broke into a sweat. Could there be an army of Lamanites this close to the city, he wondered?

He was pushed forward until he was sure he must be in the very center of the encampment. He was halted roughly near the heat of a small fire. He stood trembling, wishing they would take the blindfold from his eyes. He felt desperately helpless when he couldn't see his silent enemies.

One of his captors spoke. "Sir, we caught this man passing

near the camp. He seemed in a great hurry." The voice was distinctly Nephite!

A surge of relief rose in him when he heard, "Remove the blindfold and gag. He's a Nephite." The strong, deep voice leaped at Samuel. He knew that voice as well as his own!

No sooner were the gag and blindfold removed than Samuel, tears streaming down his face, choked weakly, "Father, is it really you?"

A moment of intense silence followed, and then Latoni, the mighty Nephite soldier, leapt to his feet and Samuel found himself enfolded in the loving embrace of his father. Although Latoni was too moved to speak, the guards swiftly surmised that the captive was his son and loosed the bindings on Samuel's arms so he could return his father's embrace.

Neither father or son could find words for some time. Finally, Latoni said, "Sam, where is your mother? Is she all right? How did you get here? Where are Oreb and Nonita?" The questions flooded out, but before Samuel could answer, Latoni went on. "Oh, my son, my son. Thank God you're all right. Oh, how I have missed you. I was afraid you might be among those murdered by Captain Antium and his men." He paused, his eyes searching Samuel's face in the light of the glowing fire.

Samuel said, "Mother and the little ones are fine, but how did you know about Antium, Father?"

"Antium is a notorious braggart," Latoni said. "Word of his evil deeds spread rapidly, even to the Nephites. I had permission from Captain Moroni to bring my men with the army of Captain Omni to free the city. So far we haven't had much success. We lost a lot of men last night. We're not sure how we will attack it next."

"Father, I must get back or I'll be missed. But I know how you can attack and defeat Captain Jacob and his men. That's why I escaped and came in search of the army."

Latoni listened intently to Samuel as he unraveled his plan. Several other men listened as well, and one of them said, "It might work, Captain. It just might."

"I agree," Latoni said, placing a hand proudly on his son's shoulder. "You've done well, Sam. Your plan is sound. I'll awaken

Captain Omni, and we'll prepare. Now, you must be on your way. I'll send two men to accompany you as far as the stream. May the Lord go with you."

Samuel and his companions traveled swiftly. Too soon, he bid them farewell, slipped into the stream and began his wet and lonely journey, already missing the companionship of the soldiers. Before long, the walls of Shurr appeared, a dark silhouette in the waning night.

As Samuel waded, he chewed on a piece of dried meat. It was some his father had given him and it tasted vastly different from the stale stuff the Lamanites fed their prisoners. The food gave him renewed energy, and in practically no time he was again confronted by the stout grate.

He was apprehensive and cautious as he prepared to force his way beneath it. He removed his water bag and stuffed it between the logs, above the water. Then he submerged himself and spent a few of the precious remaining minutes of darkness clawing at the rocks and gravel under the grate. He soon had a hole large enough to allow his body to slip through with ease. He retrieved the bag and hurried up the stream.

Encountering no obstacles on his return trip, Samuel was soon back in the house. Sarah cried with uncontrollable joy at Samuel's message. Mother and son talked until the dawn threw golden rays over the captive city.

CHAPTER THREE

NONITA SAT WIDE-EYED ON SAMUEL'S LAP AS HE RECOUNTED in detail the events of the night before. She was full of questions about her father. When Samuel told her that their father was all right, Nonita smiled at him. "I knew Father was all right. Every night in my prayers I asked Heavenly Father to bless him, and I know God hears me when I pray." She leaned her head on Samuel's shoulder and added, "I prayed for you last night, too, Sam."

Later, Samuel spent an hour in the dark space under their house carving a hole in the floor to the room where Ophera and her family were being held. He was anxious to tell her the good news. Ophera squealed with delight and relief when Samuel's head suddenly appeared in their room. The noise of his carving had had them all on edge. Feeling a sense of adventure, she joined him beneath the house and rejoiced over the prospect of freedom. But she said very little after Samuel began speaking of his father. Ophera's father had left at the same time as Latoni and word of his death had come only weeks after his departure.

Samuel spoke briefly with her family through the hole he had made, but he did not enter their room for fear of being seen through their window. Lib, Ophera's aged grandfather, stared at the wall, and Samuel sensed the family's deep grief for Ophera's father, in contrast to the joy of his own family that Latoni was alive and well.

Samuel admired Ophera's mother, Kamina. A woman of great faith, even in captivity, she constantly taught and admonished

Ophera and her brother, Josh, who was nine, to be faithful. She took every opportunity to teach them to respect their elders, and her children showed deep reverence for her old father, Lib, as well as for Sarah.

After Samuel returned to his family, Nonita asked the question that was on everyone's minds. "Samuel, when will we see Father?"

Samuel smiled and said, "Keep saying your prayers and we will all soon see Father."

For two days in a row, the Nephite captives were deprived the few cherished minutes outside when they could mingle with their friends. Samuel spent the rest of the day sleeping. Not until evening of the second day did a guard finally come. Without a word, he threw them their food, replenished their water, and left.

Samuel had not had time to gather more vegetables before setting off to seek the Nephite army and he wouldn't have time to gather more before he left again to rejoin them. Oreb eagerly volunteered to gather vegetables. "I can go and get some food," he told Sarah as Samuel prepared to leave that night.

"No," Sarah said firmly. "It's enough to worry about Samuel and Father. I'm not going to worry about you getting caught, too."

"I won't get caught," he protested, with a scowl.

"No, you won't, because you're not going out. Now, I don't want to hear of it again."

Oreb started to say something, but a sharp look from Samuel changed his mind and he sulked in the corner of the room. Samuel spoke quietly to Sarah, telling her a little of what he hoped would happen that night, then he was gone.

The second trip on his belly through the matted grass to the stream went without a hitch. The Lamanites on the catwalk were still watching intently for a second Nephite invasion. Although their voices drifted down to Samuel, he could barely see their dark shadows. The moon was hidden by thick clouds and the night was black. When the guards spoke with confidence of repulsing another attack by the Nephites, Samuel smiled in the darkness. If only they knew how precarious their position was! But he was glad they didn't know.

As Samuel slipped into the cool stream, he thought of the snake he had killed the night before, but forgot it quickly at the sight of two Lamanites kneeling at the water's edge. In the light of the torch held by a third Lamanite, shadows danced over the water. After dipping water from the stream, the men turned and walked away. Samuel waited until the light of their torch faded in the distance.

Samuel made his way downstream steadily then melted silently into the foliage at the stream's edge at the sound of laughing Lamanite voices and splashing water. These Lamanites were coming upstream toward him! There was no time to climb out of the water and find a place to hide. Thinking quickly, Samuel sliced off a length of hollow reed, stuck one end of it in his mouth, and slipped below the water's surface.

Forcing himself to breathe evenly and slowly, Samuel clung to the river's edge under the water until the men had passed. As Samuel drew near the grate beneath the wall, he became anxious, for he could hear voices on the catwalk. With the reed in his mouth, he stayed below the surface of the water and made his move to the grate, took a deep breath, dropped the reed, and sunk to the bottom of the stream. He easily slipped through the opening, glad that he had enlarged it the last time through.

Samuel moved silently and soon the city walls were swallowed by the black night. He clambered out of the stream when he felt it was safe, forcing his way through the bulky reeds and bushes. At last free of the dense foliage, he began to run. This time he knew his destination, and in much less time than it had taken him the night before, he found the anxiously awaiting army.

Latoni embraced him, and a murmur of excitement surged through the ranks as word of his arrival spread. Near Latoni stood a distinguished looking warrior, who Latoni introduced to Samuel as Captain Omni.

"He's one of the chief captains who serves under Captain Moroni," Latoni said. "After I learned of Antium leading the raid on Gilead, I requested to come here with my 500 men and help free Shurr. I am grateful that he and Moroni allowed it. Captain Omni favors your idea and wants you to brief all the captains before we move out."

After Omni had introduced Samuel to the other captains, Samuel described the layout of the city. When he finished, he looked at Captain Omni who nodded his approval and then briskly gave assignments. Samuel was assigned to go with Latoni and one hundred hand-picked men. They furnished him with a bow, a quiver of arrows, a sword, and a battle-ax before Captain Omni motioned to Samuel to lead the way for Latoni and his men.

The moon found a hole in the clouds. Looking back at the soldiers, marching smartly, three abreast, Samuel felt proud to be part of this well-disciplined group of fighting men. They were so much better organized than the Lamanites with whom he was only too familiar. The Lamanites were motivated by greed and hatred whereas these men were fighting for freedom and for the protection of their wives and children. No wonder they moved so boldly into battle.

At Samuel's signal, Latoni motioned his men into the stream. There they moved single file, hugging the bank closely. At the wall, Samuel paused and listened intently until he was satisfied no Lamanites were in the water beyond the grate. As Samuel had expected, the guards above paid no attention to the stream, expecting another Nephite attack directly against the massive walls.

Samuel silently handed his weapons to his father and dropped to the bottom of the stream to re-enter the city. Latoni passed the weapons to Samuel through the logs of the grate before submerging himself in the stream. One by one, the rest of the company of soldiers followed, and in less than an hour they were all within the city!

Samuel wondered if so many men could travel up the stream without being seen by the enemy, but the guards on the catwalk were engrossed in their study of the shadows beyond the city walls.

When they reached the houses, Samuel and Latoni paused in the space between the first two and knelt by the opening Samuel had made. "I wish I could see Sarah and the children now," Latoni said longingly, "but that must wait."

They decided to hide two Nephite soldiers in each room. Two

by two, Samuel and Latoni escorted the soldiers to the houses. Excitement soon turned to astonishment as the plan was quickly explained. They carefully replaced the bars after the soldiers were inside to avoid arousing suspicion. All soldiers were to remain hidden throughout the hot day ahead.

Only one event marred the excitement of the night. When Samuel opened one of the doors to let the soldiers in, he discovered it was Jashan's room. The two soldiers who were to stay with Jashan explained what had taken place, and Jashan scoffed, "You don't expect me to believe this whole thing was Sam's idea," he said, pointing at Samuel. "This boy is afraid of his own shadow. And why do we have to wait until tonight?" Samuel ignored him and left without a word. Jashan was one man he would like to stay as far away from as possible.

Only after the last men were safely inside did Latoni get his wish to see his family. After a joyous reunion, he led them in a prayer of thanksgiving, petitioning God to help them defeat the Lamanites in battle that they might free the city.

The soldiers attempted to sleep throughout the hot, muggy day to be rested for the arduous night ahead. Samuel could not rest at all. His excitement to tell Ophera about how he had led the soldiers in was almost as great as his excitement for the night ahead. But Ophera, though there was now a hole in her floor, did not come to see him.

Sarah sensed Samuel's feelings and casually remarked, "I'll bet Ophera's grandfather is enjoying his visit with the soldiers in their room. He's probably keeping them spellbound with stories of his days in the army as a youth, during the reign of King Mosiah."

Sadly, Samuel responded, "More likely, it's the soldiers telling the stories and Oph—that is, the others listening to *their* heroics."

Latoni knew nothing about Samuel's interest in Ophera and said only, "Oh, I agree with your mother. Old Lib has seen plenty of action in his time."

Oreb, ever loyal to his big brother, comforted Samuel. "Ophera should have you tell her about last night. I bet those soldiers over there never did anything as brave as you did."

Samuel felt the balm of his little brother's admiration and said eagerly, "You don't know the half of it yet. When we get out of this mess, I'll tell you and Nonita the whole story."

"Tell us! Tell us!" Nonita tugged at Samuel's arm, her dark eyes imploring.

Latoni had quickly assessed the situation. Chuckling, he slapped Samuel on the back and said, "Ophera is a pretty little thing, but this is hardly the time to be worrying about girls, Sam."

Samuel stepped to the window and gazed out while Latoni spoke softly to Sarah, careful to stay out of sight of the guards that walked the catwalk. At that moment, Gadoni strolled by and met Samuel's eyes. As their eyes locked, deep hatred flowed from his eyes to Samuel's.

To Samuel's surprise, Gadoni shouted at him, "Hey, you! Sam, isn't it? Haven't seen you in the yard for awhile. Do you like it in the room so much that you want to stay there?" he laughed maliciously. "Well, you better like it in there because you won't be allowed outside for a long time to come."

Samuel said nothing, and Gadoni went on, "You can thank your mighty army if you don't like it. They made the mistake of trying to steal the city away, but they failed. Now Captain Jacob has ordered us to keep you all indoors, without a break."

Samuel had to grit his teeth, especially when Gadoni's last words before strutting on were, "I miss seeing pretty Ophera, though."

"That young man certainly hasn't had much of an upbringing," Sarah remarked after a moment of tense silence. "Someone needs to teach him to mind his manners."

"Yes," Latoni said sadly, "many of these young Lamanites could have been good men. The fault lies with their parents."

As darkness approached, the air began to carry the moist scent of impending storm through the little window. The loud thunder frightened Nonita, who ran to her father's arms in fear. Lightning tore through the sky like mad demons trying to bring back the departed daylight.

Latoni was worried. "If this keeps up, Sam, it's going to make things difficult for us tonight. We need darkness," he said as he strapped on his sword, "but there's nothing we can do except proceed with our plan. Captain Omni and the rest of the army will be in position beyond the walls soon. All must be in readiness within the city when they are ready."

The violent thunder and lightning ceased as suddenly as it had begun. Now it rained heavily, steadily. "This is better," Latoni observed in satisfaction as the water beat loudly on the roof. "The rain will cover the noise we make. It's time we get busy. If the guard would just come now," he said anxiously.

He got his wish. A Lamanite entered the little house, unlocked the door, and stepped into the room, promptly receiving a hard blow to the back of his head from Latoni who had been standing behind the door. The guard fell, and Latoni and Samuel quickly bound him, depositing him beneath the floor.

"Oreb, he is your responsibility now," Latoni instructed his younger son, patting him affectionately on his head. "He is your prisoner. Don't let him move." The night's mission had begun.

Samuel and Latoni ran swiftly from house to house, releasing the soldiers and locking the doors behind them. The tense prisoners were assured that it was for their own protection and that they would soon be free.

Working in pairs, the soldiers moved quickly through the center of the city. A few Lamanites stumbled upon them in the darkness and were quickly captured, their cries unheard in the pounding rain. The Lamanite army was camped at the south end of the city, and the Nephites circled wide around the large encampment. There they waited, hidden in tall flowering bushes and behind heavy trees whose thick, leafy branches brushed the tall grass beneath them.

One by one, the guards on patrol were taken by surprise and carried, bound and gagged, to a stable that had been pressed into service as a makeshift jail. While the Lamanite army awaited the call to defend the city from attack, the number of those who might have made the call was dwindling.

After the two men who stood guard at the great gate of the city were safely bound and gagged, and all the guards on that end of the city had been captured, the Nephite soldiers removed the heavy timbers that secured the gate and swung it open. A courier ran into the night, and within minutes, Captain Omni and nearly 3000 soldiers marched into the city to reinforce Latoni's men around the camp of the sleeping Lamanite army.

In the meantime, as the rain continued to pour, Latoni, Samuel and a few others searched out the last of the guards on the catwalk in the extreme far corner of the city. One of Latoni's men started to pull himself onto the catwalk, but slipped on a wet, broken board. As he fell, he brushed against another Nephite soldier, knocking him to the ground. Hearing the noise, two Lamanite warriors ran toward them, crying for help. Four more Lamanites came quickly behind them.

Samuel, Latoni, and several other Nephites ran forward. Swords clashed and bodies fell to the ground. When the fight was over—it had seemed like an eternity to Samuel—three Lamanites lay mortally wounded, another was critically injured, and three more were bound and escorted to the stable. But not only Lamanite men had been hurt.

Samuel's head was spinning. He could not see for the pouring rain. "Father," he cried. There was no answer.

"Sam, over here," a voice called. "We need your help." Samuel shook his head, fighting off nauseous fear.

With horror, Samuel saw that a sword had passed clear through the thigh of the wounded man on the wet ground before him. It was too dark to see the man's face clearly. The soldier wiping the mud and blood from the man's face motioned for Samuel to remove the sword while he treated the head wound. Samuel grabbed the sword by the hilt and leaned backward as he pulled. As the weapon came free, the soldier cried out in pain.

It was Latoni!

With trembling hands, Samuel pressed a palm on the wound in his father's leg to halt the bleeding, his tears mingling with his father's blood. He called for help, and more soldiers responded. Two helped him carry Latoni while others carried the other injured Nephite out of the storm and into the houses. The wounded Lamanite was also carried, no less gently, inside to be cared for.

Samuel knelt beside his father as his mother cared for him with tender hands and a heavy heart. The room was lit with a smoky yellow light from a torch. Outside, Nephite soldiers took their places on the catwalk, and Captain Omni's men tightened their circle around the Lamanite army. Although Samuel knew that victory would soon be theirs, his heart felt a pain he had never before known. As he helped his mother, he earnestly prayed for his father's life.

"Is Father going to die?" Nonita sobbed.

"No," Samuel said with resolution. "We won't let him die. There must be someone who can help." Samuel pressed his father's limp hand and left the building, slipping from house to house, asking if anyone could help his father. At last he found a woman who knew how to care for injured people. She knew of two other women who were similarly knowledgeable. He took the woman to his father then went to find the two others, sending them to care for the other wounded men. This time Samuel left the doors unlocked, warning those within the houses that the battle was not yet over and to stay indoors until further word.

Returning quickly to his father, Samuel found him conscious and looking a little better. Samuel knelt on the floor, his face near his father's, who said, "Well done, my son. You're a brave man and a good soldier. Don't worry about me. I'm almost as tough as you." His smile was weak but it comforted Samuel enormously.

He squeezed his father's hand and stood up, unable to speak. His father's words kept ringing in his ears. "Well done," he had said. Samuel had been ashamed of his fear and weakness but he felt reassured by his father's words. He would be stronger the next time he faced danger and tragedy.

He held Nonita tightly. "Father is going to be all right, little sister."

"Sam." A hand touched his shoulder and he turned to see Ophera, her hair shining in the light of the torch. "I'm sorry about your father," she said, wiping away a tear. "But I'm proud of you." Her voice broke and she fled across the hall to her family's room.

Knowing his father would be all right, Samuel felt compelled to see how the wounded Lamanite was being treated. The man may die, the nurse told him, and he found it hard to hope that he didn't.

And yet, as Samuel stood watching the warrior, something stirred within him. It was as if he knew this man. He leaned down and looked closely at the Lamanite's face and suddenly recoiled as he recognized Gadoni, whose eyes had been filled with hate whenever he saw him.

For several minutes, Samuel fought a different battle. It would be easy to hate this man and wish him dead. But Samuel remembered his father's words, that it was the fault of Gadoni's forefathers that he was so full of hate—that he had been taught to hate just as Samuel had been taught to love. Gadoni did not know that all men were God's children, but Samuel had been taught this. He knew he should wish and pray for him to recover, but he didn't want to. Gadoni was the enemy—wasn't he? As Samuel watched him lying helpless and dependent upon the kindness of those he believed were his enemies, Samuel felt the battle within him subside. He found himself wanting Gadoni to recover.

Later, just before dawn, Samuel returned to check on Gadoni, fearful that he might find him dead. As Samuel gazed down on him, the dark head moved slightly. Samuel knelt beside him and watched his face closely. Gadoni's eyes flickered open, then shut. A long minute later they opened again, and Samuel saw the glimmer of recognition as the black eyes blazed with hatred and the swollen lips moved soundlessly.

Samuel said carefully and clearly, "Gadoni, we're going to help you. You will recover from your wounds. You are a great warrior and fought a brave fight. Please, don't hate me. I don't hate you. I really don't." Samuel imagined that the glow of hatred dimmed a little—he hoped it did. He hesitated, then said, "We could be friends, you and I. We really could. Whatever you do, please remember that I want you to live, and I'll help you if I can."

Gadoni's eyes closed, and Samuel rose to his feet. After the long night, he felt weary. It was strange, he thought to himself, this kinship he suddenly felt for his enemy. He had always been taught to love his enemies but, until this moment, he hadn't really understood what it meant. Now, with the force of the unrelenting rain, it struck deep in Samuel's young heart. It was possible! He knew now that he could love his enemies.

Daybreak arrived as the storm gave a last, feeble burst of rain. Captain Jacob surrendered when he discovered that the reason none of his guards had returned during the night was because the Nephites had captured each small party of men Jacob had dispatched. The former Nephite swore that he would get revenge someday for this humiliation. Word had spread that it was a Nephite boy named Samuel who was responsible for this humiliating defeat. That young Nephite, Jacob boasted in his anger, would pay dearly. But, for now, his better judgment prevailed and further bloodshed was mercifully avoided.

Shurr was free!

CHAPTER FOUR

CAPTAIN OMNI WARNED THE NEWLY FREED NEPHITES THAT a return to their homes in Gilead would not yet be possible. It would be dangerous to travel because Lamanite armies remained in the area, not the least of which was the one commanded by the very man who had been the cause of their captivity: Captain Antium. Rumbling threats against the newly-freed people had been heard as the captive Lamanite soldiers were escorted away. Because of the danger, the people did not protest; they were too weak to travel anyway. The wounded needed to be cared for and the sick nourished. Wisdom dictated several weeks delay before their return trip.

A busy life for the freed captives followed. The remaining prisoners of Captain Jacob's army had to be closely guarded until Captain Moroni could send troops to escort them to another city which held other Lamanite prisoners-of-war. In the meantime, the prisoners and the army of Captain Omni needed food. The Nephites would not feed their captives a diet of stale, dry meat, and tasteless pottage, so the Nephite women were asked to prepare nourishing meals for their former captors.

Hunting parties were sent to find fresh meat. Some were sent into the forest in search of nourishing wild fruit, roots, and edible plants while others were assigned to harvest the neglected gardens.

Latoni and the other injured Nephite soldiers healed slowly despite the most tender care any soldier could ever hope for. Under the direction of the nurses, plants and roots with healing powers were gathered and a concoction made for them to drink several times a day in addition to their dandelion and herb tea. The main healing ingredient was cayenne pepper, prepared by crushing the fruit of the cayenne pepper plant, found in the Nephite gardens. Compresses containing the mashed leaves of plantain, a common herb, were kept directly on their wounds to cool the inflammation around the deep cuts and punctures. After a few days of expert care, the patients gained strength enough to voice their complaints about the nasty, burning cayenne mixture.

Even though Gadoni was given the same treatment for his wounds, his progress was slow. He had lost a great deal of blood from the deep puncture in his side. The old women pulverized the dried root of the *hon-kos-kao-ga-sha* plant and mixed a generous amount with plantain. A compress of the powerful mixture to Gadoni's wound had halted the bleeding.

Gadoni's fever continued to rise even after several large doses of fiery cayenne tea. Regular baths with cool water had no effect. After a few days, Gadoni became delirious, and the Nephite nurses shook their heads sadly over him. The old women asked for barley, a grain used commonly by the Nephites, and prepared a strong drink from it. At last, Gadoni's fever dropped.

Samuel was kneeling at Gadoni's side when Gadoni came out of his feverish delirium. "Feeling better?" Samuel asked. He had taken a special interest in Gadoni and visited him almost daily. "You gave us quite a scare."

For a moment, the old hatred was evident in Gadoni's eyes. Then, he surprised Samuel by speaking. "How long have I been here?"

"You've been sick for a full week now, but you've had good care," Samuel nodded toward the old women who had taken turns caring for Gadoni night and day.

Gadoni said gruffly, "Lamanite women would have had me on my feet and fighting by now."

"Maybe," Samuel responded evenly, "but there weren't any here in the city."

"Why?" Gadoni asked, his eyes appraising Samuel. "I am your enemy. Why didn't you let me die?"

"Because you are our brother. We want you to recover and be strong again." Samuel was sincere but Gadoni glared at him.

"You want me to be strong again! Ha! You want me to be strong so that you can make me a prisoner and a slave. I would rather be dead!"

"I want to be your friend," Samuel said quietly. "Maybe when you are well you could teach me how you hunt."

"Never! You hunt your way and I'll hunt mine." Gadoni paused a moment, then added bitterly, "If I ever have a chance again, that is."

Samuel said nothing. Gadoni's outburst had depleted his limited strength, and his eyes closed, his mouth set in a hard line. Samuel rose to his feet and left him lying there.

As he returned to his temporary home, Samuel was pleased to come across Ophera. Her face flushed when she saw him. Suddenly the world seem brighter to Samuel. The afternoon sun seemed to shine in Ophera's sparkling eyes. Samuel's heart fluttered.

"Hello, Sam," she said, her voice softly musical. "How is the Lamanite today?"

Samuel still found it hard to talk to Ophera, but he could talk about her question. "He's doing better. His fever's broken now so he's rational at least. We had a pretty good talk. He tries to sound tough, but I think he's mellowed some."

A frown tipped the corners of Ophera's delicate mouth.

"Aren't you glad?" Samuel asked, surprised by her look of displeasure.

"I don't like him, Sam. When it's my turn to care for him, I hate it. It makes me shiver to touch him." Ophera's chin lifted.

Samuel didn't know what to say. "Ophera, he's not such a bad person. We need to give him a chance. When he gets well . . .," he began.

"When he gets well, he'll be off to join the other prisoners, and I'll be glad!" she said. "You can trust him if you like, but don't be surprised if he tries to kill you. He's a Lamanite, remember. I would think you'd be smart enough not to trust him."

"I didn't say I trusted him. I just meant that maybe someday we could be friends. All Lamanites aren't bad. Maybe he'll change and . . ."

Ophera angrily cut Samuel off. "Some soldier you'll be, Sam!

You can't even tell who the enemy is. Well, the Lamanites killed my father, and I know they are our enemies, even if you don't!" She stormed away.

Samuel watched her long hair flowing like fine, fluttery wisps of gold. He certainly hadn't set out to make her angry. "What in the world did I say?" he wondered.

He couldn't understand how she could be standing there so pretty that his heart was all a-flutter one moment and then leave him with a knot in his stomach the next. He caught a last wistful glimpse of her as she flounced out of sight. When he started to walk away, he saw Jashan lounging lazily against the corner of the house. Samuel despised the leering grin on Jashan's face. No doubt he had witnessed the fiery exchange and took delight in it.

Not many days after his meeting with Ophera, Samuel awoke with the knowledge that today was his seventeenth birthday. He was now old enough to join the army, and as he lay on his mat in the room he shared with Oreb, he wondered if he should do so. His family needed him until his father was better. Later, if the war was still raging, maybe he would join Moroni's forces and show Ophera the kind of soldier he could be. For now he would try to put away thoughts of Ophera.

He gently shook his sleeping brother. Oreb rubbed the sleep from his eyes and sat up on his mat. "What did you wake me up for, Sam? It's still early and I don't have any chores to do," he protested sleepily.

"Sure you do, Oreb. You are going to help me gather some fruit and vegetables for Mother while it's still early so we can have time to take you out and teach you to shoot an arrow." Then Samuel added teasingly, "Unless you don't want to."

"Let's go!" Oreb shouted, jumping to his feet, the sleep gone from his eyes. "Right now."

Oreb had pestered Samuel for days to teach him, but Samuel had been too busy. Now that he had made the offer, there would be no holding his little brother back. Samuel wanted an excuse to practice himself. He could shoot fairly well but was not as skilled as he needed to be to be a good hunter.

But first there was work to do. Samuel and Oreb dug vegetables and picked fruit near the west wall. When Samuel began pulling weeds and cultivating the soil, Oreb was quick to join him. He was not about to ruin his big chance by being slothful!

Samuel explained that Captain Omni had asked that they make the gardens more productive. He had spent time every day in fulfillment of that command.

With arms full they returned home to join Sarah and Nonita at breakfast. The boys were delighted with the meals their mother prepared. After the long weeks of pottage and stale, dried meat, their mother's cooking tasted like manna from heaven. As they ate, Sarah spoke sadly of Latoni. "Your father is much stronger, but he may never be able to walk very well again because of the deep wound in his leg."

"You mean he'll be a cripple?" Oreb asked.

"Well, his leg will get strong, but it will always feel stiff and that will slow him down. Still," Sarah brightened a little, "that means that he will be able to stay home with us since he can't fight. We are blessed to get him back whereas poor Ophera and Josh . . . their father won't be coming back."

Samuel winced at the mention of Ophera's name. "Father will still be able to work with the horses, won't he, Mother? He is one of the best blacksmiths in the whole Nephite nation," he said, looking at Oreb.

"Oh yes, he'll make shoes for horses. His injury will not stop him from doing the work he learned from his father and does so well," she said with a smile. Latoni had indeed learned his trade well. Before the war, many of the wealthy men of Zarahemla and Manti traveled to Gilead for his services in caring for their horses. The people would be glad to have him back there.

"Oh, Sam," Sarah exclaimed suddenly. "It's your birthday today. You're a man now, and I'm proud of you." Her eyes glowed with the love she felt for her son and the pride she felt at his part in regaining their freedom. When she smiled at him, Samuel realized that he had almost forgotten how pretty his mother was when she smiled.

He blushed when she came around the table and hugged him. "Oh, it's no big deal, Mother," he said.

"Maybe not to you, but it is to your mother. You are my first-born and have grown to be everything a mother could ever want in a son. I am truly proud of you, Sam."

"Me, too," little Nonita bubbled as she wrapped her little arms around his waist. Samuel kissed her affectionately on the cheek, bringing a smile to her young face. He marveled at how quickly she had regained her strength and energy.

Samuel turned to Oreb. "We have some practicing to do with my bow. Will you get it, Oreb?"

Samuel didn't have to ask twice. Oreb returned in a moment with the bow and quiver of arrows that the army had given to Samuel, but as the boys started out the door, Sarah said, "Not so fast, Sam. Your father asked that I send you in to see him right after breakfast. And he said I was to give you a present from him."

Samuel stared in disbelief as she walked to the corner of the room and picked up Latoni's superb bow and quiver of arrows. "He wants you to have these, Sam. He won't be able to use them much anyway, with his injuries, and he wanted you to have the best," she said.

Samuel reverently touched the beautifully designed steel bow. His grandfather, Latoni's father, had made it especially for his son when Latoni was a young man. There wasn't a finer bow in all the land. It had served Latoni long and well both in hunting game and in the field of battle.

"Thank you, Mother," Samuel said. "Here, Oreb. It looks as if I won't be needing this." He handed his other bow to his little brother.

The look on Oreb's face showed that he could not have been more delighted if Samuel had given him ten limnahs of gold. He held his new possession reverently and said, "Someday, Sam, I will be as good a shot as you are."

Samuel laughed. "Probably better, little brother. Probably a lot better. Let's go thank Father, shall we?"

Samuel spent much of the morning teaching Oreb how to hold his bow, how to place his arrow on the string, and how to shoot accurately. Oreb was a good student and practiced faithfully until he could hardly lift his arms. Samuel was amused that Oreb didn't suggest quitting, nor did he complain about the sore muscles or the fresh blisters on his fingers.

"You have a natural talent, Oreb," Samuel said as he set down his bow. "If you continue to practice, you'll soon be one of the best marksmen in the land."

Oreb beamed happily. "Thank you, Sam," he said humbly. "I want to be just as good as you."

Samuel smiled. He was surprised at the way Oreb had handled the big bow. He really believed what he had told the boy. "We'll do this again in the morning, all right?"

"And the next and the next and the next," Oreb coaxed.

"It's a deal," Samuel said. It was fun to spend time with his little brother. It sure beat trying to figure Ophera out!

After lunch, Samuel and Oreb climbed a huge mangrove tree tall enough that they could see over the city walls to the east. They trembled with excitement as they watched the army approaching the gates to the city. In front of his marching men, Moroni was mounted on a magnificent white stallion that held its great head high and lifted its feet grandly with each step. It was as if Moroni had chosen the proud steed to exemplify the pride he had in his countrymen, for no leader loved his fellowmen more than Captain Moroni.

After the army had entered the city, Samuel started down the tree. He reached the grassy ground first and was several steps away from the tree when Oreb screamed. He turned just in time to see Oreb hit the ground with a crack. Samuel dashed to Oreb's side.

"Are you all right?" he asked anxiously, his hands exploring the boy's outstretched limbs.

For a long, agonizing minute, Oreb couldn't speak. The wind was knocked out of him. Samuel continued to search for broken bones, but his young brother seemed uninjured. Samuel rolled him gently over. A broken, dry stick lay where Oreb had fallen.

"Must have been this stick that I heard crack," Samuel said hopefully, holding it up for Oreb to see.

Finally getting his breath back, Oreb grinned and said, "I'm okay Sam. I just slipped."

"Are you sure you're not hurt?" Samuel asked, doubtfully.

"I'm sure. I'll show you," he said as he stood up, an impish look on his round face. "I'll race you to see Father," he cried and was off like an arrow.

Oreb was so excited that the words tumbled from his mouth as he reported the day's activities to his father. Samuel listened quietly for a few minutes before winking at Latoni and slipping away to see Gadoni.

The young Lamanite warrior was awake and turned his head to look at Samuel as he stepped through the door. Ophera and her mother, Kamina, were helping the nurse change Gadoni's bandages. Samuel waited in silence while they finished. He tried to read the mood of the wounded man but his face was like stone. Gadoni's eyes shifted from Ophera to Samuel. No emotion showed in their black depths.

After the bandages were in place, Ophera and the others walked to the door. Ophera's eyes met Samuel's. She seemed about to say something but then abruptly dropped her gaze and whisked by him without a word. He followed her with his eyes and, despite himself, his heart skipped a beat as she left.

"She's a beauty, isn't she?" Gadoni said. Samuel jerked around in surprise at Gadoni's words and felt the heat rise up his neck as he blushed.

"She's okay," Samuel replied flatly. "How are you feeling today, Gadoni?"

"Better. With a nurse as pretty as Ophera, any man would get better," Gadoni goaded, a faint trace of a smile on his dark face.

"You don't know her very well," Samuel countered. "She's just another girl."

"I think that you're the one who doesn't know her very well. I wish she would look at me the way she just looked at you," he said with a sly smile.

"You really are feeling better," Samuel said soberly, shifting the unexpected conversation away from Ophera. "Is there anything I can get for you?"

"No," Gadoni said, the rare smile vanishing. "But I do hope that I can soon return to my people. What's all the excitement? I thought I heard someone mention Moroni. Is he here to take my people away?" Gadoni asked, the bitterness creeping back into his voice and hostility again shooting from his dark eyes.

"Yes," Sam said firmly. "But I wish we could all be friends and your people could return to their homes in peace. There is plenty of room for all of us to live. We have no need to fight."

"That's easy for you to say, Sam. Your people have not been wronged as mine have. Captain Jacob told us all about the greed and hunger for power of the Nephites," Gadoni said with venom.

"Jacob is an evil man, Gadoni. He is trying to hurt his own people and yours as well. He and his kind are the ones who crave power. They don't care who they hurt or how, as long as it gets them what they want. They left my people because they wouldn't obey our laws and weren't willing to support our government. They will be your friends only as long as you do what they say." Gadoni stared at him for a moment, then said, "How do I know who to believe? Nephites are liars."

"Watch what we do and how we act," Samuel said. "If I didn't want to be your friend, do you think I would visit you like this? I don't have to, you know."

At that moment, a Nephite soldier stepped into the room and asked Samuel to come with him. "Captain Moroni wants to see you immediately," he reported. "He's waiting for you in front of the house where you're staying."

As he followed the messenger from the room, Samuel caught one last glimpse of Gadoni. His face looked puzzled . . . questioning. Samuel smiled to himself and asked the soldier, "What does Captain Moroni want of me?" He couldn't imagine why so great a man would want to see an obscure, seventeen-year-old boy.

"He didn't tell me, but we must not keep him waiting. He's a very busy man," the soldier said impatiently, as if he, too, wondered why the captain would waste his time with a lowly boy like Samuel.

Samuel's knees were shaking, and he hoped his legs would not fail him. A crowd had gathered, and the most famous man in all the land was visiting with them like they were his best friends.

Samuel paused at the fringe of the crowd. Seated on the weather-checked steps of the house was Lib, Ophera's old grandfather. He laughed and slapped a bony knee in response to something Moroni said. Samuel's eyes caught the golden gleam of Ophera's long hair. Josh stood shyly beside her, half hidden behind his mother's dress. His eyes were big as saucers as he, too, watched and listened in awe. Little Nonita, arms folded reverently across the front of her ragged blue dress, stood between Josh and Sarah. Her face showed that she understood that she was in the presence of greatness.

Samuel's eyes rested on the man whose call he was answering. Moroni was large in stature. He was heavier but not much taller than Samuel. The muscles of his arms and legs bulged. He was a handsome man with a broad, clean-shaven face, intelligent brown eyes, a strong square chin and light brown hair held away from his face by a gold headband. His voice was deep and strong, and Samuel could feel a great spiritual strength flowing from his person, inviting all to share his faith in God.

Samuel heard running footsteps behind him. He turned his head and saw Oreb stampeding toward the crowd. When he neared Samuel, Oreb skidded to a careful walk, trying for all he was worth to look much older and more dignified than his eleven years.

"Here is the young hero now," Samuel heard Lib say when the old man's eyes fell on him. "Don't be shy, Sam. Come over and say hello to Captain Moroni."

Samuel stepped timidly forward. He felt awkward with everyone's eyes on him. Moroni's smile was kind as he saluted Samuel. He held out his large hand. "So you are the young man I've been hearing so much about. I'm Captain Moroni."

Samuel took his hand and, shaking it, said awkwardly, "It is an honor to meet you, sir." His head was swimming with excitement. He bit his lip until it hurt, trying to keep from fainting dead away.

"Young man, I've come to thank you," Moroni said, his voice booming so all could hear. "You're a credit to the Nephite people." He let go of Samuel's hand, which was numb from Moroni's stone-breaking grip. "Your courageous actions and brilliant military strategy has resulted in the freedom of many prisoners, the recovery of one of our cities, and the capture of the traitor Jacob and his entire army. He and his men have been a scourge to our people for many months. I'm grateful to you, Samuel, for bringing them under our control. Jacob's actions, and those of his brother, Antium, have led to the death of many Nephites, including women and children. Some of them, I understand, were your friends and neighbors in Gilead."

Moroni put his hand out expectantly to the soldier at his right who dropped something into it. Then he announced, holding up a gold chain and pendant, "This is the Medal of Valor. It is presented only to those brave soldiers who risk their own lives to save others in the most trying of circumstances. Never before has it been given to one so young or to one who was not actually in the army. But, Samuel," he said, looking the stunned young man directly in the eyes, "you have earned it as much as anyone who has ever received it. It is with great pride that I present you with this Medal of Valor for actions far beyond the call of duty." With that, he slipped the beautiful gold medal over Samuel's head, lifting the wavy locks of brown hair at the back of his neck. The pendant gleamed on his chest and looked as though it belonged with the rich, tooled leather vest he had worn constantly since the day the town was liberated.

"Now, young man," Moroni said, the formality gone, "would you show me to your father's bedside? And please, invite your family to come with us."

Samuel beckoned to his mother. She latched onto Nonita and Oreb. Samuel stole a glance at Ophera as he walked away. Her eyes glistened as they met his, and her hand reached up to wave at him shyly. Despite his best efforts to ignore her, Samuel felt his heart grow lighter.

A few moments later, Latoni greeted Moroni with a weak salute. Moroni took Latoni's hand in both of his. "I'm truly sorry that you were injured, Latoni. How are you feeling now?"

"I'm getting better, but I'm told that my leg will remain stiff and numb. And how are you, Captain?" Latoni asked.

"I will be much better when we have established peace in the land," he said. He told Latoni of the progress of the war and then of the Medal of Valor he had given to Samuel. "You are as good a father as you are soldier. You have a fine family." Moroni visited a little longer with Latoni and Sarah before saying to Samuel, "Would you please take me to see the Lamanite prisoner that is being treated for his wounds?"

47

"Yes, sir," Samuel responded, wondering why the famous soldier wanted to see Gadoni. He was concerned that Moroni would tell him that he had to be moved with the other prisoners. His concern prompted him to ask a question that he would otherwise never have dreamed of asking. "What do you need to see him for, sir?"

Moroni said, "A young lady, I believe she said her name was Ophera, told me that you have been trying to make friends with him. She says she's afraid of him, but that his attitude seems to be softening. I thought I might be able to help. I feel, as Ophera says you do, that it's better to make friends with the Lamanites than to fight them. They often refuse our friendship, but it's always worth a try."

Samuel was surprised, both that Ophera would mention it to Moroni and that the leader of the army of the Nephites would take the time to befriend a Lamanite prisoner. His admiration for the captain grew.

As they approached the house, Samuel said, "I hope you *can* help, sir. I believe that, deep down, Gadoni is a good person. This is where he's being taken care of, sir."

The guard at the door saluted Moroni smartly when they entered the room. Gadoni lay on his side, facing away from them.

"Gadoni, it's me, Sam. There is someone here who would like to meet you." Gadoni rolled painfully onto his back and looked first at Moroni and then at Samuel. His black eyes registered surprise. Samuel said, "This is Captain Moroni, the chief captain of the Nephite armies. He would like to talk with you."

Gadoni's eyes narrowed to hostile slits. Moroni smiled and said, "It's a pleasure to meet you, Gadoni. I've heard a lot about you. Are they taking good care of you here?"

Before answering, Gadoni regarded Moroni warily. His face mirrored surprise that the chief captain would visit him. Samuel knew that the only things Gadoni had heard about Moroni were from traitors like Jacob and Antium, but Moroni's face showed kindness, warmth. Finally, Gadoni said with a hint of a sneer, "I am treated well enough. But what do you plan to do with me when I have recovered?"

"That, my young friend, will be up to you. We have no desire

48

to cause you further injury or harm of any kind," Captain Moroni told him, "but you will have a choice to make. You may either make a covenant of peace with us or you may go to a prisoner-of-war camp. I believe that you are a man of honor. If you promise never to take up arms against the Nephites again, we will allow you to depart to your home in peace. Or you may live with our people if you desire. However, if you choose to remain an enemy to the Nephite people, then we will have no choice but to see that you remain a prisoner until the war is over. And in case you are wondering, I will make the same offer to the rest of your people who have been captured. Of course, that does not include the white traitors."

Gadoni lay quietly, staring at the ceiling. Samuel's heart raced. How he hoped that by some miracle Gadoni would choose peace. When the young Lamanite finally spoke, he said, "I am a Lamanite warrior. I believe that I should choose to remain one." He paused then said, "But I would like a little time to decide, if that's possible. I must know if you are being honest with me or if Captain Jacob speaks the truth about you and your people."

Samuel wiped the perspiration from his forehead and looked anxiously at Captain Moroni. The great man said, "You must choose, but you have until you are well to do so. I hope that you will carefully consider my offer. You have my word of honor that if you swear with an oath that you will never take up arms against us, you will be allowed to go free."

"What if I take the oath, and your people come into our land and try to steal it from us? Could I not then defend myself?" Gadoni asked earnestly.

"If my people were to act in wickedness and make you their enemy, then you would be released from your oath. I hope that will never happen, but I would ask no man to give up the right to defend his home," Moroni said.

Gadoni nodded and said, "I will think on your words."

"Thank you for listening to me, Gadoni." And with that, Moroni and Samuel left the room.

As Samuel walked beside Captain Moroni, he could see that he was deep in thought. There was a lot he wanted to say, but he waited for Moroni to break the silence. "You know something,

Samuel? There are none more dangerous than those who have tasted the sweet and then chosen the bitter—men like Jacob and his brother Antium. Your friend, Gadoni," Moroni shook his head sadly, "has the tradition of lies told by generations of forefathers. Yet, when it comes to making a decision of peace, he is torn between my words and the words of evil white men. I believe if it were not for Captain Jacob and his brother, you could win him over. But, as it is, he may not be an easy man to persuade to take the oath, although his chances are better than many I have spoken with."

"I hope he will take the oath, Captain," Samuel ventured.

"It may well be up to you, Samuel. You have certainly had an effect on him. It's worth the effort to keep trying, you know." Moroni reached out his hand to Samuel and said warmly, "It has been a pleasure getting to know you. I hope that we'll meet again sometime. I have a son who was very much like you when he was your age. He's older now, but you remind me of Moronihah. I hope that you two can meet someday." As Samuel turned and walked back to his family, Moroni's eyes lingered on the majestic eagle tooled on the back of his leather vest.

That night, as Samuel lay in his room listening to Oreb's even breathing and the gentle sounds of the night that drifted in the window, he was deep in thought. Sleep had refused to come as thoughts of Moroni and the important lessons he had taught that day kept stirring his impressionable young mind. He had learned that great men like Moroni are not so different from men like his own father when they shared the common bond of love for their fellow men and for God. Samuel now had two great examples to follow: his father, Latoni, and Captain Moroni.

CHAPTER FIVE

Samuel awoke to the shouts and laughter of thousands of men breaking camp. Captain Moroni was to lead his army and part of the army of Captain Omni toward the East Sea later in the day. With them would be all the Lamanite prisoners except Gadoni. None, when offered an oath of peace would accept, so Moroni ordered them all to be held. He left a small force of men under the command of Captain Omni to defend the city of Shurr and led the others out before noon.

Captain Omni sent a message for Samuel to meet with him that afternoon. Omni was waiting in the shadow of the synagogue when Samuel arrived. Omni got right to the point. "We are short-handed and need your help, Sam," he began. "It's my hope that we can build up a supply of food in the city. Game is scarce near-by and it'll be necessary for us to hunt in the mountains." He swept his arm toward them.

In the distance, Samuel could see the majestic blue peaks rising above the clouds. He wished that he could be there himself. He loved the mountains with their beautiful green forests, clear crisp air, and abundant wildlife.

"Would you accept an assignment as one of the hunters, Sam?" Omni asked.

Samuel could scarcely believe what he had just heard! "Yes, I would be glad to help," he answered, trying not to sound too eager.

"You will be careful? Remember you are hated and could be hunted by the Lamanites. I don't want anything to happen to you after all you have done. I wouldn't ask you to put yourself in such danger if your help weren't needed so badly," Captain Omni said sternly.

"I understand," Sam said, his excitement causing the captain's caution to slip past as quickly as he had heard it.

"Start getting ready then. You'll be leaving soon," Omni said. "We'll let you know when the others are ready. It shouldn't be more than a day or two."

Two days later, the hunting party passed through the city gates long before the sun had made its daily ascent of the rugged mountains they were bound for. Samuel's heart was light as the small group of men hurried along. This was adventure, and he was going to enjoy it to the fullest. He hoped to bag the largest animal to send back to the city.

Many hours passed before they found signs of plentiful game. They were deep in the jungle, still several miles from the foothills of the mountains Samuel longed to hunt, but the leader of the party ordered them to make camp for the night. "We'll hunt here in the morning," he announced.

Samuel had hunted in the jungles near his home before. Experience had taught him what to look for and where he would find it. The men all found and killed game. Samuel's first contribution was a small, grey tapir which he shot easily as it fed on the fresh green leaves of a low-hanging branch at the edge of a small clearing. The men hunted for a couple of days and succeeded in accumulating a large amount of game that needed to be transported back to Shurr.

Samuel was assigned to return to the city and bring a party of soldiers and horses to transport the meat before it spoiled. He left before dawn and covered the miles in just a few hours, running most of the way. Shortly after dark he returned with the men and horses. They departed with the quarry early the next morning, and the hunting party moved on into the mountains where they sought bigger game.

One day, Samuel came across tracks so enormous that he believed he was following the largest mountain sheep in the whole region. He stalked the elusive animal, climbing higher and higher up the steep mountain. Occasionally, he caught fleeting glimpses of its shaggy coat, sending his blood racing through his veins, spurring him on with great vigor. He ignored the ache in his muscles and the cramp in his side from the strenuous climb. His fingers became sore from pulling himself over rocky ledges as his pursuit took him into the sure-footed ram's favorite stomping ground, but that did not dampen his enthusiasm.

Samuel had to stop often to gulp in the cool, thin air and give his aching body time to recover. He began to wonder if he would succeed in bagging the superb beast he pursued. The sheep seemed to sense that Samuel was tiring, and it romped leisurely ahead of him, stopping frequently to graze on clumps of grass protruding from tiny cracks in the rocks.

Finally, Samuel rounded the bottom edge of a sheer cliff that towered above him so far that thin white clouds shrouded the grey peaks near the top. There he spotted the ram, poised on a tiny shelf ahead. Its head was turned toward him, bearing the largest horns he had ever seen on a mountain sheep. Dark green eyes gazed solemnly at him, no fear in their somber depths.

Bracing himself carefully, Samuel notched an arrow on the string of his bow and slowly pulled it back until it was taut. Breathless, he took careful aim. The majesty of the huge beast seemed to pierce his very soul. It never moved, challenging him to shoot if he must. Something came over Samuel, and he relaxed the tension of his bow and watched in awe as the great mountain sheep shook its mighty head as if in thanks, then slowly began to inch its way toward the lofty peaks above.

A feeling of peace came over Samuel. He would probably never get the opportunity to shoot another animal so beautiful—the finest of its kind. But as he watched it ascend out of sight, he felt the same feeling as when he first spoke with Captain Moroni. He had enjoyed the rare privilege, once again, of being in the presence of greatness. To kill such a royal beast didn't seem right.

He returned to camp empty handed. The other men had all brought meat back that day, and they chided him for his failure. He took the kidding in good spirits, choosing to say nothing of the magnificent animal he could have taken. They would not understand why he let such a grand prize escape when it had been within his power to slay it.

During the days that followed, Samuel made several long trips to Shurr and led the transport party back to the mountains for meat. After three weeks, the hunters returned to the city for a few days rest.

Gadoni was healing quickly and Samuel feared what his decision would be. He had tried to learn the young warrior's feelings whenever he had visited, but Gadoni had always answered him evasively. He was convinced that Gadoni wanted to depart with an oath of peace, but that his pride stood in the way. While Samuel couldn't say that he had won Gadoni's friendship, there was one thing he felt sure of; he had succeeded in tearing down some of the barriers between them.

Latoni was much better now and had moved in with his family. They cared for him with great affection, and he was soon able to walk around the house with very little aid. His injured leg was stiff and numb, but it was improving.

Samuel told Latoni of his experience with the great mountain sheep. As he had expected, Latoni understood. "I've had those same feelings, Sam," he said. "If you ever reach the point that you can take the life of wild animals for fun, you shouldn't be hunting. You did the right thing in letting that animal live. I can see that you will be a truly great hunter."

Samuel spent several hours with Oreb. He was amazed at the skill the boy was gaining with his bow. Never had he seen anyone so young who could shoot so accurately and with such power. Oreb beamed with boyish pride at Samuel's praise.

The final evening before embarking on another hunting mission had arrived. Samuel lay on his back in the grass beneath a huge tree. He was searching its sprawling branches for the source of a noisy squawk that told him a blue and yellow macaw was there. He was so intent in his search that he failed to hear Ophera's light footsteps approach.

She stood quietly near him and watched as he peered into the leafy heights. He finally spotted a splash of rich yellow and said, "So there you are. What's all the racket about, anyway?"

He jumped when Ophera said, "You talk to birds, do you?"

He turned his head toward her, a sheepish grin on his well-tanned face. The macaw stopped its squawking at the sound of their voices. "Noisy things, aren't they. Can you see him?" he asked, sitting up and pointing at the brightly colored bird.

She sat down close to him and tried to follow the path of his pointing finger. His heart raced when her long hair brushed his arm, and he quickly lost interest in the brightly colored parrot. She was so close that he could feel her warm, sweet breath on his face. Awkwardly, he asked, "So, how have you been, Ophera?"

"Fine. Why haven't I seen you since you came back?" she asked, her large, blue eyes searching his face.

"I've been busy," he said, admiring the fine lines of her mouth and the silky smooth texture of her skin. He basked in the glow of her radiant smile and wondered about the change that had come over her.

"I've been busy, too," she said in a soft lilt. "I'm helping cook for the soldiers since the wounded men no longer require so much attention. I'm even learning to prepare wild game." She paused, looking past him, then said, "They say you're a very good hunter."

"I'm learning," he said modestly, starting to feel a little more at ease. "We've had a good time, and I'm becoming friends with the other hunters."

"What do you talk about at night?" she asked, her eyes gazing at him again. They were warm and appealing.

"Oh, lots of things. Mostly the other men talk about the battles they've fought and things like that."

"Do they ever talk about their wives or girlfriends?"

"Oh, a little. Not much, though," he said, feeling ill at ease again, staring at his feet.

"Sam, I've been unkind to you," she said abruptly.

"No you haven't," he said without looking up.

"Yes I have! And you know it, Sam. I had no right to be angry with you for trying to be nice to Gadoni. When I told Captain Moroni about it, he said that he wished more of the Nephites felt the way you feel about the Lamanites. He said that you were right in what you were doing," she admitted.

He continued to stare at his feet. "Look at me, Sam!" she commanded. "I'm trying to tell you that I'm sorry."

He lifted his eyes, embarrassed at her flash of anger. She looked away, giving him time to collect his thoughts. Samuel was afraid to say the wrong thing now for fear she would either flounce away or begin to cry.

At last he said, "I don't blame you for what you said, Ophera. I was just as afraid of Gadoni as you were, and I still can't trust him. And it looks like you were right. He'll always be a Lamanite warrior, full of pride and anxious to join his people." Her eyes urged him to go on. "I spoke with him today. Moroni offered him a chance to take an oath of peace, but he won't say he will . . . and yet . . ." He stopped.

"What, Sam?" she pressed.

"Oh, nothing." He didn't think she would understand about the bond he felt with Gadoni and was relieved when she let the matter drop. Samuel feared that the young Lamanite would soon be in a prisoner-of-war camp and he would never see him again.

Together, the young couple walked through the city and Samuel finally worked up the courage to take her small hand in his. The sun glowed brightly over the west wall before it faded gradually away, leaving only the faintest memory of pale color around the edge of a few high clouds.

As he felt the sweet miracle of her presence, Samuel wondered what it was about this girl that made him feel so good. He had forced himself not to think of her the past few weeks, but he knew that the memory of Ophera would accompany him the next morning as he left for the next hunt.

During the next few days, Samuel hunted as if in a dream. He imagined Ophera gliding before him in the trees. When he bent to quench his thirst at a clear mountain spring, he saw her radiant smile and eyes dancing on the surface of the water. Often at night, as he lay beneath the stars, he could hear the musical ring of her laughter drifting with the wind currents overhead.

After several successful days of hunting, Samuel turned toward Shurr to meet the transport party. Thoughts of Ophera filled his mind, and he was less cautious that he should have been. Too late he saw a band of Lamanite warriors emerge on the trail ahead of him. He dove in a panic into the trees, only to be confronted with more warriors there.

Threatened with their weapons, Samuel backed slowly onto the trail, his heart pounding so hard he thought his chest would burst. At least twenty Lamanites, their faces painted grotesquely, advanced menacingly toward him. He recklessly considered fighting, but his better sense prevailed. He stood meekly, shaking in fear as they stripped him of his precious steel bow, arrows, and jewel-studded knife. After binding his arms tightly behind his back with rawhide cords, they pointed him north, toward a distant mountain range.

The warriors laughed and ignored him when he asked them where they were taking him, chattering nonchalantly with each other as they propelled Samuel through the jungle. They traveled many miles before the sun descended in a panorama of color which gradually gave way to dusk. Only then did they stop to make camp on the shore of a stagnant lake, deep in the jungle. They bound Samuel to the gnarled trunk of an ancient broad-leaf tree whose roots twisted and turned through the grass like a den of snakes. One warrior thrust a piece of dry meat into Samuel's mouth. He chewed it and tried to swallow. Only after he begged for several minutes did they finally give him a little tepid water to wash the meat down with.

Sleep that night was nearly impossible with his hands behind his back, pressed tightly against the protruding knots of the tree, the hump of one of the twisted roots digging at his hip. Mosquitos helped themselves to a liberal portion of blood from beneath the most sensitive parts of his exposed skin. When leaving, their bellies distended and red with stolen cargo, they each paused a moment to play a nerve-racking tune in Samuel's defenseless ears.

At some point during the night, he was alarmed to discover a huge, six-legged creature scaling up his bare stomach. Despite his best efforts to shake it off, it found its way to his chin. He puffed tiny streams of air at it, but it climbed, undisturbed, past his pursed lips. It paused to study his left eye in the near darkness. Samuel promptly shut his eye until the gargantuan insect grew bored and advanced upward, bedding down snugly at the base of a thick lock of his hair.

By the time morning arrived, Samuel was so cramped and sore

that he didn't think he would be able to walk. His wrists were chaffed and bleeding where the rawhide had rubbed unmercifully with his every movement during the long night. He longed to have his hands free long enough to scratch where the mosquitos had tormented him and help the unnamed insect find its way out of its bed in his hair.

One of Samuel's captors surprised him when he called him by name. "Samuel," he said, "I am Tarshi, leader of this brave band of warriors. You are a terrible enemy of the Lamanite people. We know of your treachery and evil deeds. Because of you, one of our brilliant captains was murdered by your Captain Moroni. We lost a brave leader and you are to blame."

Samuel's throat was dry and his head throbbed. A desperate fear, cold and clammy, crept under his skin. "How can you know who I am?" he rasped.

Tarshi leaned so close to Samuel's face that the caustic aroma of his breath nearly gagged him. "Following the hanging of Jacob, a few of his loyal soldiers escaped. They found the army of Captain Antium, and from them we learned of your treacherous acts. We also learned of the love that Captain Moroni has for you. He regards you as a son, they say. We plan to offer you in exchange for the freedom of our imprisoned warriors. We will see then how valuable you are to Moroni."

Samuel's thoughts raced. He was not surprised to hear that Lamanite warriors had escaped. If a young untrained boy like himself could do it, as he had done from the city of Shurr, then surely cunning and experienced warriors could do it as well. His life must not be in danger yet, but it would be after they heard from Moroni. He wondered how much time he had to escape from his captors. He did not want Moroni to be forced to choose between his life and those of so many Nephites who could die if the Lamanite warriors were released.

As if reading his thoughts, Tarshi said, "Don't even think of escape. You won't get that opportunity. We do not know how you left the walls of Shurr to help the Nephite soldiers, but you will be watched every minute, even when you sleep."

Samuel was silent. Now was not the time to talk and Tarshi was probably not the one to talk to. Maybe he could learn something later from one of the younger warriors.

As they resumed their journey, they no longer wandered toward the mountain range but moved in the direction of the East Sea. Samuel judged that they were several miles north of Shurr. However, the Lamanites, wherever they were taking him, were not in any hurry. They traveled slowly, stopping to rest often and spending much of the time lounging lazily in the trees.

Samuel, though he feared for himself, was even more troubled to think of his parents. They were people of great faith and would call upon the Lord for comfort, but they would be sick with worry.

He thought of Ophera. Would he ever see her again? A few days ago he would have denied that she was important to him, but now he ached to see her, to talk to her and hold her hand. Would she miss him, too, or did she have so many friends among the soldiers she cooked for that she would have no time to think of him? He felt a sharp prick of jealousy as he thought about all the young men she was around each day, especially Jashan, who looked at her like he owned her, although he did not think she had done anything to encourage him. He must try not to think about her—it was too depressing.

What about Gadoni? Without Samuel to encourage him, he almost certainly would not make the oath and instead would be taken to a prisoner-of-war camp. What irony it would be if Gadoni was one of the prisoners he was offered in trade for.

Little did Samuel know that, even as he thought about Gadoni and Ophera, they were involved in an intense drama of their own.

CHAPTER SIX

GADONI'S BODY WAS HEALING FAST. HE WAS AMAZED AT the strength he felt in his limbs. A guard was posted in his room now, and as he paced about in his cramped quarters each day, he conversed with the guard on duty. He had told each of his guards about Captain Moroni's offer. He had not told them that he was going to accept it, but he had succeeded in making them believe that he would, for he wanted their trust. For several days he had been devising a plan.

One guard, about Gadoni's own age, had shown himself to be especially friendly. On the day Gadoni had planned to escape, he came on duty at noon. Gadoni joked with him about the young man's girlfriend back in Manti. Gadoni visited with him for an hour, pretending to speak casually, before he made his move. Suddenly, he seized the young Nephite guard around the neck, shutting off his air supply. In a matter of seconds, the soldier quit struggling and drifted into unconsciousness. Gadoni stretched him out on the floor, pulled the man's sword from its sheath, and hoisted it into the air above the hapless young man.

For several seconds, Gadoni stood with the sword poised over his enemy. Then he sadly shook his head and lowered the weapon and laid it on the floor. Taking the guard's belt, Gadoni found that it held not only the sheath for the sword, but also a short, very sharp, double-edged knife. Gadoni buckled the belt around his waist, wincing when it pulled tight over the still-tender wound in his side. He shoved the sword into the sheath before he bound and gagged the guard and slid him into a corner.

The Nephite regained consciousness, his eyes terror-stricken as he watched Gadoni waiting behind the door for whoever entered next. The wait wasn't long.

Carrying Gadoni's lunch, Ophera looked around the room in surprise when she didn't see the guard in his usual place. When she spotted him, lying helpless in the corner beyond the door, she gasped and started to back out of the room. In a flash, Gadoni sprang from behind the door and grabbed her, knocking the tray to the floor. His strong right arm pulled her tightly against his chest, and he clamped his left hand over her mouth.

It took a moment before he realized whom he had taken hostage. Ophera didn't usually bring his meals. Gadoni felt a pang of guilt for having handled her so roughly; she had never mistreated him, and he knew of her feelings for Samuel, who had tried so hard to be his friend. But he hesitated only a moment. He was a Lamanite warrior and must not weaken. Though his hatred had been softened, his pride drove him on.

Ophera struggled briefly but Gadoni held her tightly. When she relaxed momentarily, Gadoni said, "If you scream, I will kill you." Slowly he removed his hand from her mouth. Although she was trembling, she remained silent. He pulled the knife and held it to her throat.

Gadoni knew he could never take her life, but she was the means to his escape so he had to make her think he would. "You are to do exactly as I tell you, or Samuel will never see you again," he hissed with all the viciousness he could stir up. "You and I are going to take a walk across the city to the gate. If anyone tries to stop me, he will be responsible for your life, so you better cooperate. When we get there, tell them to open the gate, and we'll go out. After I'm a safe distance from the city, I'll release you, and you may return so you can be here when your beloved Sam comes back from his mighty hunt. Do you understand me, Ophera?"

"Yes," she said quietly. "I'll do as you say." She began to weep softly.

Gadoni wished she wouldn't cry. He pushed her roughly through the door. "Let's go."

In the narrow hallway outside the door, he found a bow and a quiver of arrows. He hadn't counted on them being there. They must belong to the guard, he thought. They would certainly be useful.

The first person they met outside was Oreb. When he saw them, his mouth dropped open in alarm, and his eyes almost popped from their sockets.

"Oreb," Ophera said quickly, "he won't hurt me. He just wants to go back to his own people. Don't tell anyone and I'll be okay."

His eyes indicated doubt, and Gadoni could see his little mind furiously at work. He knew how much Oreb adored Samuel and Gadoni hoped Oreb wouldn't try to be a hero for his older brother now. To Gadoni's relief, Oreb asked, "Are you sure, Ophera? I'll help you if you want me to."

Gadoni rudely responded, "Do you think Sam will be happy if you get his girlfriend killed?"

"No," the boy replied bravely, "but if you hurt her, Sam and I will come after you, and you'll wish you hadn't."

"You stay put, Oreb," Ophera said. "I'll be back in a little while." Gadoni thought her voice lacked conviction, but Oreb agreed. "Okay, I'll stay here, but you better not hurt her, Gadoni."

They met others as they crossed the city, but none were willing to risk Ophera's life to recapture one Lamanite prisoner. They passed in safety to the gate.

Captain Omni met them there, ordering, "Don't do it, Gadoni." "Let her go."

"Get out of the way," Gadoni shouted, "unless you want to explain to Sam how you got his girl killed." A few weeks ago, this whole thing would have been so easy, even to kill this girl, but now his heart was pounding. He had to remind himself that he was a proud warrior and must not falter. Deep in his heart, he knew that if Omni did not let him and Ophera through the gate that now stood open, he could not use a knife against her. Rather he would shove her aside and make a run for it. At least that way, he would die a brave warrior when the Nephites filled him with their arrows.

Ophera pleaded with Omni. "Please, let us go. He will release me after a while and I'll return to the city. And please, don't let anyone come after us."

Omni let them pass, and in a few minutes they were a mile from the city, entering the shady forest. Gadoni was moving as quickly as he could, but Ophera slowed him down. Still he didn't want to release her too soon because he knew that as quickly as she was in sight of the city walls, soldiers would come after him.

"When are you going to let me go?" she pleaded after they had gone some distance into the forest. She was breathing hard, and her usually bright eyes were shadowed.

"Not for a while," Gadoni growled, still angry at himself for his weakness where this girl was involved. No Nephite deserved to live and yet he knew he would not have killed her even for his own life.

"But you *will* let me go, won't you, Gadoni?" she asked. "You said you would."

"I am a man of honor. But if I release you too soon your people will come for me, and they will not take me alive again." Gadoni watched Ophera as she stumbled along beside him. He experienced a curious feeling of sorrow when she looked up at him, her face wet with tears. He thought again how beautiful she was for a Nephite girl. For a fleeting moment he envied Samuel and said, "Okay, you may go now." He didn't want to release her this soon, but he didn't want to see the hurt in her pretty eyes anymore.

She looked at him with deep relief. "Thank you, Gadoni." But rather than turn back toward the city, she found a moss-covered, rotting log and sat down.

"You better get on your way," Gadoni ordered her. "You don't want to be out here when it gets dark."

But Ophera did not move. "Why did you do it, Gadoni?" she asked sadly.

"I'm a Lamanite. There was no other choice for me," he said, averting his eyes from hers.

"But Sam said that you were given a choice. You could have taken an oath and returned to your home in peace." Her voice had taken on a sharp edge of disappointment.

Gadoni looked at her and saw anger in her eyes. He couldn't explain to her why he had made the decision he had. He wasn't sure he understood it himself.

"Well, we sincerely tried to help you, Gadoni." She rose to her feet and started off in the direction she thought she had come.

"If you want to return to the city of Shurr, you'll need to walk *that* way," he said, pointing to her left.

She looked at him, fire still in her eyes, then changed her direction with a toss of her head and started through the trees.

"Ophera," he called.

She stopped but did not look back.

"Tell Sam that we are even now. Tell him I gave you your life in exchange for what he did for me—for what you and the others did for me," he finished. He walked away for a moment, then turned and looked back. She was watching him. He squared his shoulders and strode quickly through the woods. He didn't look back again.

Several miles away, Samuel stumbled along, his arms nearly numb from the rawhide bindings at his wrists. He expected to be brought into an enemy army camp at any time as evening approached. But when darkness began to settle over the forest, Tarshi ordered his men to stop. Samuel collapsed immediately. He was exhausted and weak. He looked toward the sky, hoping to see the stars so that he would at least be able to figure out their approximate location. Only blackness loomed above the tall pines. He had been too tired to notice the swollen, menacing clouds roll in earlier, but now he could smell an impending storm in the air.

Two of the warriors checked his rawhide bindings. He could have told them they were still secure, for his wrists were raw and bleeding. The men grunted in satisfaction and tied him to a small pine tree.

"Can't you at least let me lie down?" he begged. " You can tie me to that log if you want." He nodded his head toward a fallen tree a few feet away that was sheltered by the branches of a tall, bushy pine.

They grunted again and moved him. He was asleep before they got around to offering him more of their contemptible dry meat. He didn't wake up until the rain began falling in torrents from the ominous clouds. It rained for the rest of the night, and by morning Samuel felt terrible. He was chilled, feverish, and his stomach refused to accept the meat Tarshi offered.

Gadoni had a miserable night as well. He stumbled through the trees for many miles in the pouring rain. His wounds hurt and he was weak. He did not have the stamina he thought he had. Gadoni hadn't realized how much his injury and painful recovery had sapped his strength. Several times, in the last few hours, he had stopped to rest, the periods becoming longer each time. Finally, as the dawn thrust its way through the heavy clouds, he discovered a shallow cave. After crawling out of the storm, he slept.

By late afternoon, hunger drove him from his shelter in search of food. He had not eaten for nearly thirty-six hours, and he knew that unless he had nourishment soon, he would never live to find a Lamanite army.

Gadoni gathered a few mushrooms and pulled some roots, forcing himself to eat until he was full. The storm cleared, and the sun, though low in the sky, sent a few bright shafts of welcome sunlight through the trees. Gadoni sat with his back against a mossy rock and stared at a shallow pool of water. A small tapir wandered into the little clearing and dropped its homely head to drink. Gadoni pulled the string on his bow taut and let an arrow fly. Despite his weakened condition, his aim was true. The tapir only staggered three or four steps before toppling to the ground.

He cut into the little animal, stuffing the raw, bleeding meat into his mouth. Gadoni had grown up eating raw meat, but the weeks of eating the good cooking of the Nephite women had spoiled his taste. He gagged and spat it out. He tried again but could not chew or swallow it. Angrily, he drug the little tapir back to his cave where he built a fire and began cutting its flesh into long strips.

Using green branches, Gadoni fashioned a crude frame which he placed over his small fire. There, during that night and the following day and night, he rested while his meat dried. He cooked and ate the liver and heart, a little at a time, and he soon felt his strength returning. He also dried the hide near the fire. With part of it he made a bag that would carry his supply of meat. With the rest, he made a crude, but tight, water bag.

When Gadoni started on his journey again, he felt better and his spirits were high. The stiffness was gone from his muscles, and his wounds were only tender reminders of the fight in Shurr and the long weeks of recovery. He enjoyed his freedom, but something was bothering him, a nagging restlessness in his heart. He did not want to admit that maybe he had made the wrong decision and in so doing might never enjoy real freedom.

Although Samuel had become so ill that his captors did not dare prod him too much for fear he would die, they were too proud to carry him. He overheard Tarshi say that Captain Antium wouldn't care how long it took them to bring him to the camp of the Lamanite army. However, if they brought Samuel back dead, he would go into a rage and they would very likely end up dead themselves.

Tarshi knew something of the healing power of herbs. He prepared a tea made from bloodroot, garlic, and sarsaparilla. Constant doses of the foul mixture and long periods of rest made it possible for Samuel to travel a short distance each day.

Finally, five days after his capture, the Lamanites half-led, half-dragged Samuel into the disorganized camp of Captain Antium's army of Lamanite warriors. There he was shoved into a small, rank tent of dried animal hides. A guard stood outside.

An hour later, he heard the voice of Tarshi speaking to the guard. "Captain Antium is angry. He says that if we allow Samuel to die, we'll all be hanged."

The guard responded angrily. "I wonder about these white men who command Lamanites. If Ammoron were not king, white men like Antium would not lead Lamanites. I despise the king and all white men who call themselves Lamanites."

"That is enough. You talk treason. Say no more or you'll be the death of us all. Just keep a close eye on our captive and don't let him die," Tarshi said in a low, harsh voice. "If the Nephite dies, I'll personally turn you over to Captain Antium and let him do what he will to you."

Word of Samuel's disappearance had reached the people of Shurr, leaving them shocked and fearful. They had no doubt that

Samuel had been taken captive by the Lamanites. Latoni and Sarah feared he would be executed in retaliation for the capture of Jacob and his army.

While Samuel's parents bore their grief in silence, Oreb did not accept the fact that Samuel could die. "Sam will find a way to escape," he told everyone who would listen. And yet, in spite of his outward optimism, Oreb neglected his bow, ate little, and moped around his room. His parents tried to reason with him, but he would not listen. Nonita, as sure of God's care over Samuel as of his care over their father, tried to encourage Oreb, but to no avail.

In all the city, no one was more affected by Samuel's disappearance than Ophera. At first, following Gadoni's escape, she had seethed with anger at Samuel. If he had not tried to befriend Gadoni, she would not have been put through the harrowing experience that she had suffered. She had planned to really let Samuel have it when he returned.

Wise old Lib had counseled, "Ophera, my beautiful granddaughter, you have a lot to learn. If Sam had not befriended Gadoni, he would have taken your life as well as the soldier's who was guarding him."

"He didn't kill me because I did as he said," she argued.

"Oh, no. You don't know the heart of Lamanite warriors as I do. He would have left you dead in the forest. Only a softening of the heart, maybe something akin to respect or love, saved you."

"Then why did he leave?" she had demanded.

"I said that his heart may have been softened, not that it is completely soft. I believe that much of the hate is gone, but he still has his pride. He still is not sure if his people are right or if ours are. In light of that doubt, he did what most would do. He chose his own people. I still have hope that what Samuel did for him will work on his heart, and that he may yet lose his hatred toward us. But whether he does or does not, you must not be angry with Sam." Lib patted Ophera's hand.

It was not long after her talk with her grandfather that her mother told her the news of Samuel's disappearance. Ophera exploded with, "It serves him right!" then burst into tears and would not be comforted.

CHAPTER SEVEN

SAMUEL'S FEVER GREW WORSE BY THE HOUR. HE FOUGHT to stay awake, fearing that if he slept, he might not wake up. However, the raging sickness overcame him and he slipped quietly into unconsciousness. For three days, he was near death and Tarshi fought frantically to keep him alive. The Lamanite, knowing his own life was in jeopardy if Samuel died, tried every remedy he knew to combat the pneumonia and fever.

Fearing his sparse knowledge was inadequate, he sent men through the camp seeking someone who could save Samuel's life. Several came forward, suggesting various remedies. One of the white captains finally suggested barley tea.

They had a small supply of the popular Nephite grain which they had stolen in a raid on a Nephite village. Tarshi cleaned the barley corns and boiled them. In one of Samuel's brief periods of delirious consciousness, Tarshi helped him drink some of the tea. He added the roots and leaves of other plants to the tea as he was able to get Samuel to take more.

Whether it was the barley tea, the frequent dips in the water of the nearby sea, or a combination of treatments, something made a difference. Samuel's fever subsided and his racking cough gradually grew less violent. Samuel became aware of his surroundings and was surprised that he was still alive. A week after arriving in his feeble condition, he was finally able to stand on his feet, shuffle about inside his tent and assess his predicament. His first coherent thoughts were of escape.

Tarshi reported Samuel's improved condition to Captain

Antium and urged him to offer the young Nephite for ransom as soon as possible. Antium, not trusting the word of a native Lamanite, ordered that Samuel be brought before him. Tarshi obeyed, and Samuel, still pale and weak, was taken to the captain's big tent.

Never had Samuel experienced a look of such intense loathing as he received from Antium. Samuel studied him with morbid fascination. He was a large man, with muscular arms and legs, narrow hips and an ample but firm stomach. Dark brown hair hung in long greasy strands over his shoulders. His eyes were small and black, set close together beneath heavy eyebrows. A long, hooked nose dominated his face. Antium's mouth, partially hidden by his long, greying moustache, was permanently down-turned at the corners. His teeth, when he smiled, were crooked and yellow. Sweat poured off him like rain off an ant hill—small rivulets of water that left muddy streaks in their wake. He wiped his face with a soiled hand as he spoke. His voice was deep and gravelly.

"Jacob was a brave warrior and a great man. He was my brother, and because of you he was hanged!" he roared, shoving a long, bony finger toward Samuel's quivering face.

"Captain Moroni will either trade Jacob's warriors for you, or I will send him your head in a bag! You will pay, you dirty, sniveling Nephite. All of you will pay. The whole Nephite nation will pay! Now, get out of my sight before I change my mind and have you beheaded here and now!"

Samuel needed no encouragement to leave, and as he walked back to his tent, he fervently hoped he would never have to look at that repulsive face again. Antium was so angry about the death of his brother, yet it was he who had led the bloody attack on Gilead in the middle of the night. With men like Antium leading the Lamanites, it was little wonder they were so stirred up in anger against the Nephites. Samuel wished someone could deliver this evil man into the hands of Captain Moroni where he could be dealt with justly as was his brother Jacob.

"Why do you follow a man like Antium?" Samuel asked Tarshi. "Can't you see he only thinks of himself? He's only using you and your friends to help him vent his hatred for his own people."

"Quiet! It is not your affair." Samuel knew he had struck a nerve and was not surprised when the Lamanite muttered, "He'll pay someday. We are a proud people. He will not always be in power."

"Why do you wait?" Samuel asked boldly. "You're a better man than he is. These warriors," he said, indicating the vast field of tents with a nod of his head, "would rather follow you than him."

"He is a friend of the king," Tarshi said. "I cannot disobey the king." Angrily, as if he suddenly realized he was talking with a Nephite, he pushed Samuel into his tent. "You mind your own business. You have troubles enough of your own without worrying about ours."

At that moment a young warrior came running from the direction of Captain Antium's headquarters. "I have a message for you from Captain Antium," he said to Tarshi.

"I just came from there. Why didn't he tell me himself?" Tarshi demanded, his dark face betraying his anger and suspicion.

"He was upset. You know what a terrible temper the captain has. Anyway, he needs something of Samuel's to deliver to Moroni as proof that he's our prisoner."

Tarshi faced Samuel and said, "We have your weapons. Would Moroni recognize them and know they're yours?"

"I doubt it," Samuel answered truthfully. "I don't think he ever saw me carrying them."

"That vest that you're wearing is not something soldiers wear. Moroni would know it, wouldn't he?" Tarshi asked. "Give it to me."

Samuel was wearing the tooled vest he had found in the house in Shurr. Moroni had seen him in it. "He'd probably recognize it, but what will I wear instead?"

"We'll find you something. Now off with it."

Samuel shed his precious vest and handed it to Antium's aide who left on the run. Tarshi shoved Samuel back into his tent and said, "You'll have another vest shortly."

The one he was given a few minutes later was smelly and worn. He put it on. It was tight, but it would have to do.

For the next few days, Samuel was forced to spend most of his time in the tent. His attempts to converse with the guards were rebuffed. His situation began to look rather hopeless.

• • •

70

Gadoni stood atop a knoll and, sheltering his eyes with his hand, searched the forest below. For several days, he had searched in vain for an army of Lamanites. Twice, he had spotted fortified Nephite cities, but he dared not approach them; he didn't know if they were occupied by Lamanites or Nephites. Once he nearly blundered into the path of a massive Nephite army that was marching westward. Had the armies of Captain Moroni driven his people from the land?

He had decided to search for three more days and return home if he hadn't found any of his people by then. It was on the third day that he climbed to the top of the grassy knoll near the East Sea. At first, he wasn't sure but soon became convinced that an army was camped in the trees. He moved cautiously down the long ridge into heavy timber and crept near. When he spotted Lamanite sentinels guarding the outskirts of the camp, he felt like shouting.

He revealed himself to one of the warriors. "I am of the army of Captain Jacob," he said. "I escaped from the Nephites and seek a Lamanite army."

"I am sure you will be welcome here. Our chief captain is Antium, the brother of Jacob," he was told.

Gadoni was immediately taken to Antium's tent. He and his escort waited outside to be granted an audience. Gadoni recognized the deep, gravelly voice of Antium inside the tent. He had met Antium before and resented the way he so contemptuously ordered about the Lamanites who had been placed under his command as a reward for plundering the little Nephite city of Gilead.

"I want this message delivered to Captain Moroni and to no one else," Antium ordered.

"It will be done, sir. Where will I go to find him?" The Lamanite voice was subservient, placating.

"Go to the city of Bountiful. If he is not there, his people will know where he is. It will be your duty to insist that they take you to him. Here is a letter of introduction," the captain said.

"This letter explains that this is a matter of vital interest to Captain Moroni. Now I want you to go quickly. I cannot bear to have the one responsible for the death of my brother in this camp much longer." Antium's voice was full of scorn.

71

"I will leave immediately," the courier answered.

"This vest will give Moroni proof that we have the young boy in our power. And should you return to me without a reply, I will have your head right along with that boy Sam's!" Antium snarled.

So they have captured Sam, Gadoni thought. He felt surprisingly alarmed. It couldn't be another Sam. When the two men emerged from the tent, Gadoni's eyes fell on the vest held by the courier. It was the tooled leather vest that he had seen Sam wear so many times.

Antium stopped before Gadoni. "Who is this?" he asked the escort.

"This man says his name is Gadoni and that he was in the army of Captain Jacob. He escaped from the Nephites and desires to join with us."

Gadoni saluted. "I served under your brother. It would be a privilege to serve under you."

Antium did not answer but only turned to the courier. "You may go now. Do not delay. Your life depends on it!"

The courier sped away, holding Samuel's vest tightly under his arm. Antium turned his beady eyes on Gadoni and cleared his throat. "So you knew my brother?"

"Yes, captain," Gadoni answered, with a little too much emphasis on the "captain."

Antium said, "Come into my tent." Inside, Antium seated himself on a thick blanket on the floor and said to Gadoni, who stood there before him, "Tell me of your association with my murdered brother and of your supposed escape."

Gadoni seethed inside although he was careful not to show it. He did not deserve mistrust from Antium. He had come here seeking to serve again in the Lamanite army. "I was there, as you were when we overthrew the city of Shurr, and I was ordered to remain to defend it and guard the prisoners. When the Nephites attacked and regained the city, I was injured and taken prisoner. I was left behind when Captain Jacob and the others were taken from Shurr," Gadoni said.

"Why?" Antium asked suspiciously.

"Because I was too badly injured and too ill to travel."

Captain Antium was apparently not satisfied with Gadoni's

explanation. "How did you escape?"

"I overpowered my guard and . . ."

"You killed him, you mean?" Antium interrupted coldly, his cruel eyes looking steadily at Gadoni's face.

Gadoni was not sure just how to answer this bloodthirsty man. "Well, . . ."

Antium cut him off sharply. "Well, how did you kill him?"

"With his sword," Gadoni lied, fingering the long weapon at his side.

"Are you sure he died?" Antium growled.

"I stabbed him in the heart," Gadoni said, his voice rising. "That should have killed him!"

"Don't you raise your voice at me." Antium glared at him. "Just tell your story and tell it straight. What happened next?"

Gadoni collected his thoughts and plunged into a rather embellished story. "I grabbed a Nephite woman who brought my lunch. I forced her across the city to the gate, threatening to kill her unless they let me leave the city with her. She was strong and fought me all the way, but the Nephite soldiers knew I would kill her if they stopped me, so they let us leave the city. Then after . . ."

"And, of course, you killed the woman later," Antium broke in again, an evil, bloodthirsty glint in his dark, beady eyes as they peered past the great hook nose.

"Of course," Gadoni lied. "I left her body in the forest. I suppose they found it, for they searched for me for days. But I hid from them. After they quit looking for me, I found your army." As he spoke, he shuddered inwardly. Even though his words weren't true, it made him feel guilty to speak of such cruel and loathsome acts. He was surprised with himself. It was not long ago that he would have taken Nephite lives, such as the guard's and Ophera's, and not been troubled in the least.

Antium's next question forced still another untruth from Gadoni. "Do you know a young Nephite by the name of Sam?"

Gadoni thought rapidly. "I heard Nephite guards and nurses speak of a boy by that name. They said he escaped from Shurr and led the Nephite army back." His palms were sweating, and he could feel warm beads of perspiration on his forehead. He hoped that he wasn't telling Antium anything he didn't already know.

He didn't want to add to Sam's trouble. Still, it was important that Antium believe him so he would allow him to be part of his army.

"That's the one!" Antium bellowed in anger. "We have him here." He stopped shouting and said in a satisfied tone, "But he won't be here for long." His eyes gleamed with hate and the air rattled in his throat. He looked Gadoni over from head to foot, closed his eyes a moment, then opened them ever so slightly. "Who was the captain of the Nephite army that attacked Shurr and took my brother, Jacob, captive through the treachery of this murderous Nephite boy?"

"I heard them speak of one they called Omni." Gadoni was sure that Antium already knew that but was testing him further.

Antium stared hard down the length of his hooked nose and opened his mouth, exposing his yellow teeth as he shouted to the guard standing outside, "Gadoni is part of our army now. Take him to Tarshi."

To Gadoni, Antium said brusquely, "Tarshi has the responsibility to guard Sam. You will be under Tarshi's command. If all goes well, Sam will be gone soon, in exchange for Jacob's men. Then you will be with your friends again."

Gadoni couldn't believe this was happening. He would be guarding Sam. Troubled, Gadoni followed the guard. The words of Moroni and Sam kept coming back to him as he walked toward his new assignment. They had said that the white men who led the Lamanite armies were evil and conspiring men. Despite himself, he had to admit it was true. Never had he met anyone to whom he had taken a more instant and intense dislike than he had to Antium on this meeting. What a contrast he was to the kindly Captain Moroni. It made him doubt his own people. How could they accept the leadership of men like Antium? The Lamanites should be leading themselves.

His thoughts turned to Sam. He was an unselfish Nephite. He cared about others. Gadoni remembered telling Ophera that his debt to Sam was paid. But was it really? He wasn't sure anymore. Sam's words and deeds were affecting his own thoughts and actions. He would be guarding Sam until Moroni took him as ransom. What would he say to him? How would he treat him? Could he treat him any differently than Sam had treated him? He wasn't sure.

A thought came to Gadoni that caused him to shiver—what if Moroni wouldn't trade for Sam? Moroni, despite the great love he had for Sam, would not allow hundreds of men to go free without an oath of peace. To do so would mean the death of more Nephites, and Gadoni knew that Moroni would not allow that to happen. In that case, Sam's fate would be up to Antium, and there was no doubt that Antium would torture and kill Sam.

"Gadoni, this is Tarshi," Antium's aide said, cutting short his sobering thoughts. Glad that the man standing in front of him was a proud Lamanite, Gadoni saluted. "I'm pleased to meet you. I understand that I'll be with you and your men."

"Welcome, Gadoni. You can sleep there," he waved toward a dismal tent that looked like the hundreds of other little tents scattered through the forest.

Gadoni was now a real warrior again. That was just what he wanted—wasn't it? He wasn't sure anymore, especially if it meant accepting Sam's death. At that moment, he almost wished he had died in Shurr so he wouldn't have to face the uncertainties and tough decisions that lay ahead.

When Antium's Lamanite courier approached the city of Bountiful, he was taken captive by the Nephite soldiers who stood guard. Upon reading the letter of introduction from the infamous white Lamanite leader, they immediately ushered him before the highest ranking army officer in the city. The captain, an aging veteran of many wars by the name of Ahaz, explained that Captain Moroni was not in the city of Bountiful.

"Then take me to him," the Lamanite insisted. "There must be no delay."

"That is not possible," the white-haired captain replied. "You may give the message to me, and I will arrange to have it delivered to Captain Moroni."

"No, I must deliver it myself," the courier argued. "This requires an immediate answer to Captain Antium."

"Captain Moroni will send a response by courier if he sees fit," was the firm reply of Ahaz.

"No, you don't understand! Captain Antium ordered me to deliver this message in person," he said, angrily shaking the parchment in the captain's face. "I must go to Moroni, now!"

Patiently, the calloused old captain retorted, "No, you are the one who does not understand. Antium is a traitor and an outlaw—wanted for treason by the Nephite government. He does not give orders to us. Now, either hand over that message, or we'll take it from you, and you can return to your treasonous leader and tell him what I just told you."

The Lamanite courier could see that he was at an impasse and that nothing he could do would change the mind of Ahaz. "All right," he relented, handing over the parchment. "I see that this is the only way. But you must hurry. Captain Antium will have my head if I'm not back soon with an answer."

Captain Ahaz slowly read Antium's mandate. When he had finished, he looked up and said, "You'll be held until Captain Moroni sends his reply to this preposterous request." With that, he nodded to his aides who delivered the hapless Lamanite to a prison cell.

In the flickering light of a smoky torch, Captain Moroni sat surrounded by several of his principal captains. Although he was conducting a strategy session, at this moment he was listening to a scouting report on the location of Lamanite forces in the area.

"Captain Moroni, there's a courier here from the city of Bountiful. He bears a written message sent by Captain Antium's courier," one of Moroni's aides announced, interrupting the session.

"Antium!" Moroni said with scorn, but a moment later, his mouth tightened with anger. Looking up from reading the parchment in his hands, he said, "Men, I must leave at once. Put the army on alert. We may be marching soon. I'll be back after I have attended to this matter."

Moroni and several of his men rode hard through the dark night. A dim, yellow glow to the east promised a new day as they rode through the high wooden gates of the city of Bountiful. Leaving the others to care for his foaming white stallion, Moroni went straight to the army headquarters.

The faithful old captain greeted him with a look of surprise. "I'm sorry, sir. I had no idea that you would want to receive this message personally. I just . . ."

Moroni cut him off with a wave of his arm. "There's no way you could have known, Ahaz, my friend. The young man in the power of that old scoundrel Antium is a boy of extraordinary courage. He was responsible for the liberation of the city of Shurr and all the prisoners being held there. The brother of Antium was Captain Jacob, whose army was taken at that time. I had Jacob hanged. "Antium says he has captured Samuel and wants to trade . . ." His face wore a look of anguish. "But you already know what they want and how impossible that would be."

"What will you do about Samuel?" the aged captain asked.

"I don't know yet. Before I decide anything, I must meet the man that Antium sent. Will you get him for me?"

"Certainly."

In a few minutes, several soldiers returned with the Lamanite emissary. "I am Captain Moroni," the great man said solemnly. "I need to have a word with you regarding this." He waved the parchment containing Antium's message.

"I just need to deliver an answer to the good captain," the courier said anxiously.

Angered by his words, Moroni said sternly, "Don't call a demented man like Antium good! He is corrupt and bloodthirsty. Before I give you an answer, I must have proof that you have Samuel."

"Look in my bag."

Ahaz placed it on the table. The courier opened the ragged leather bag and pulled out Samuel's tooled vest and laid it with a flourish on the table. He did not say a word but looked Moroni in the eye, a smug smile on his broad brown face.

Moroni's heart sank. He had hoped that Antium was bluffing, but he would have recognized that vest with the proud eagle on the back anywhere. Sam was wearing it the day he presented him with the Medal of Valor. "I will need a little time," Moroni said, turning away from the courier to hide his emotions.

"I must hurry, Captain."

Moroni cut the courier off curtly. "You'll get your answer

when I'm ready."

"If you don't make the trade . . .." the courier began, but Moroni withered him with a look of rage, and the rest of the sentence hung in the air, unspoken.

"Take him away," Moroni ordered, and for more than an hour, he agonized over his decision. No matter how he tried, the answer didn't change. He could not free hundreds of Lamanite warriors to save just one person. The lives they would take in future battles did not justify it. Yet, to let Antium take the life of Sam was like letting him take the life of his own son.

Slowly, a strategy began to form in the captain's keen mind. He was not the leader of all the armies of the Nephites for nothing. He was there because he had proven that he could do the impossible, and that was what he intended to try now. He would send spies to follow the Lamanite and locate the army of Antium. Then he would. . . . A smile creased his tired face.

"Hold him until I return," Moroni told Ahaz. "Tell him I'll have an answer then."

"He won't like that," the grizzled captain said, shaking his head.

"No, I don't suppose he will, but that's the least of my worries," Moroni said soberly.

As he lay in his tent, Samuel was only vaguely aware of the morning sounds ouside, sounds that he usually found pleasure in. A deep, dark despondency had settled over him, and try as he might, he could not shake it. At any moment, he expected the guards to drag him from his tent and carry him to his death. He tried to pray, but it was difficult. He tried to picture Ophera's cheerful smile, but all he could conjure up were anxious, tear-filled eyes. Thinking of her or his family only intensified his depression.

He heard voices outside in front of his tent. The guard was being changed, as it was this time each morning.

"We have a new man here. He escaped from Shurr," one voice said. Samuel sat bolt upright. The voice went on. "His name is Gadoni, and he'll be standing guard with me tonight."

"So you have that Nephite, Sam, in this tent, do you?" The

voice was unmistakable.

Samuel's mind was in a whirl. How could Gadoni have found this place, he wondered? And how did he escape? Why didn't he take the oath of peace? These and dozens of other questions tormented him but soon the questions were replaced with a glimmer of hope that churned about in his tormented mind.

Samuel listened carefully as the guard pumped Gadoni with questions. His interest grew when he heard Gadoni say he had overpowered a guard. He couldn't help but wonder why Gadoni didn't mention taking the man's life. His companion must have wondered the same thing, for he pressed him on the point. Samuel thought that Gadoni's answer lacked conviction although the guard seemed satisfied.

Gadoni went on to speak of a girl he used as a hostage to get out of the city. Samuel noticed that again, nothing was said of taking her life until the other Lamanite questioned Gadoni more closely. Gadoni's details seemed to come unwillingly, and Samuel detected a note of aloofness. Something inside Samuel, a feeling deeper than conscious thought, gave him the feeling that Gadoni was no longer the cold-blooded warrior he had been— that he no longer delighted in the taking of innocent life.

The conversation drew to a close and the guard left Gadoni to watch the Nephite prisoner. Soon Gadoni entered the tent carrying a gourd containing Samuel's breakfast. Their eyes met, and Samuel tried in vain to read Gadoni's feelings. For a long moment, they stared at each other. Samuel wondered if Gadoni would call him by name or if he would pretend that he didn't know him. Samuel thought he saw a flicker of sadness in the young Lamanite's dark eyes.

Gadoni was trying to read Sam's feelings also from the look on his strained face. He could see a glimmer of pleading hope. He wanted to speak as Sam had spoken to him when he was the prisoner, but he wasn't sure what to say. He did not want anyone to know that he knew Sam. It was enough that they thought he knew *of* him.

Gadoni spoke first, in deliberately loud tones in case anyone was listening outside. "They tell me you're Sam, the Nephite who incited the overthrow of Shurr. I'm Gadoni. I was wounded and held prisoner there." His voice was cruel but his eyes were soft, and Samuel read in them a different message than his voice carried. "I escaped. Now it's your turn to feel the sting of captivity."

Not knowing when, if ever, he would get another chance to speak to Gadoni, Samuel asked quietly, but boldly, "They tell me that I'm to be traded for prisoners of Jacob's army. I know that Captain Moroni will never allow such an exchange. It would cost many Nephite and Lamanite lives, and he won't take that chance. He . . ."

Gadoni cut him off. "I'm not to speak with you about your problems. My assignment is to keep you from escaping and to keep you alive until Captain Antium receives word from your friend, Moroni."

Without another word, Gadoni loosened the abrasive bands on Samuel's wrists and allowed him to eat. Before he left, he tightened them again. As soon as Gadoni had fastened the tent flap securely, Samuel heard a voice say, "You did well, Gadoni. Tarshi says Sam will try to talk to us and get us to help him, so we should not speak to him at all."

"Very well," was all Gadoni said.

After the other guard left, Gadoni was left alone. As he stood there, a lone sentinel, he could hear Samuel's labored breathing inside the tent. The nearest tents were several feet away, and no one was in sight. A feeling of peace and tranquility settled over him. It was like nothing he had ever felt before. With the tender feeling came a single thought to his mind, almost as if spoken by an unseen voice, "Help him, as he helped you."

The still, small voice in his mind left him trembling. Then it came again, firmer and more distinct. "Help him," he heard as clearly as if it was spoken directly into his ear. At that moment, Gadoni made a decision, irrevocable and of lasting consequence, a decision that set his life's course in such a direction as he had never dreamed possible.

Looking around and seeing no one, he stepped close to the tent flap and whispered, "Sam, wake up." He had to speak of his new resolve.

Samuel stirred. He thought Gadoni was trying to speak to him. It must have been a dream, for Gadoni had been told not to speak to him again.

"Sam." It was Gadoni's voice beside the tent flap. Fully awake now, Samuel knew he was not dreaming. He shuffled toward the flap. It opened, and before he could say anything, Gadoni's head poked in. "Sam, I'll help you. I don't know how, but I'll find a way to get you out of here. I am your friend, Sam," he said softly and shut the tent flap.

Samuel's heart soared. He wanted to ask Gadoni a thousand questions, but Gadoni had stepped away from the tent. Samuel soon found out why. Footsteps were approaching, followed by Tarshi's voice. "Were you just talking to the prisoner?" Tarshi asked harshly. Samuel's heart skipped a beat.

"Yes," he heard Gadoni say. "He was telling me to loosen the bands on his wrists. He said I had tightened them tighter than the rest of you did." Gadoni laughed convincingly then went on, "I told him that he better stop complaining or I would tighten them even more."

A hearty chuckle from Tarshi told Samuel that Gadoni's story was acceptable. A short conversation followed and soon Gadoni was left alone again. He made no further attempts to speak to Samuel before he was relieved a few hours later. Samuel was left wondering how and when Gadoni would try to help him escape. He felt that it had to be soon, before Antium heard back from Moroni, for when he did, his terrible temper would flare and Samuel would be the object of his deadly actions.

Despite his worries, Samuel drifted into a peaceful sleep that night after offering a silent prayer of thanks to God for softening Gadoni's heart.

CHAPTER EIGHT

A SMALL MOUSE WITH COAL BLACK EYES, TINY AND protruding, came to visit Samuel regularly. At first the mouse was timid but soon became quite brave and scampered around the tent gathering up the crumbs that Samuel left from his scanty meals. Although the mouse provided some entertainment, Samuel watched anxiously for Gadoni to appear again. Two days passed without a word.

A gradual, but disheartening fear came over Samuel. He wondered if Tarshi had discovered the young Lamanite's true feelings. If he had, Gadoni himself might be a prisoner! Samuel began to pace endlessly with his shackled shuffle step in the cramped confines of his tent. The leather bindings rubbed his ankles raw as he paced. He didn't know which hurt the worst, his ankles, or his wrists which were kept tightly bound behind his back except when he was fed. Samuel's shuffling disturbed the mouse, and the creature quit coming, making his loneliness even more intense.

That night, lying uncomfortably on his filthy blanket, Samuel tossed and turned as he listened to a pair of guards talking outside his tent. Their words were muffled but he could understand most of them if he listened carefully. They were complaining and sounded as restless as he was. His ears perked up when one said, "Tarshi says that Captain Antium grows impatient. If the messenger he sent to Moroni doesn't return tonight, we move our encampment in the morning."

Samuel shuddered. He doubted that Antium would move him.

His fears were confirmed when the other guard said, "I'll be glad when we go. At least then we'll be rid of this pesky Nephite. I'm sick of guarding him."

The two guards continued talking, primarily of the fighting that lay ahead. Both believed that Antium would lead an attack on some poorly defended Nephite city in retaliation for Moroni's disregard of his proposed prisoner exchange.

Samuel, unable to catch any more information that seemed of interest, finally drifted into a fitful sleep. An indistinct sound near his tent awoke him. He sat up and listened. For a full minute, all he could hear was the distant rumble of the East Sea and the light rustle of the leaves in the trees, disturbed by a mild, rain-scented breeze. With a start, he realized that a knife was slowly slicing a long slit in the back wall of his tent from the ground up.

He held his breath, not sure what to expect next. In front of his tent, he could still hear the muffled dialogue of the two guards. He saw a head poke through the slit. "Shh. Sam, it's me. Gadoni."

The next thing he knew, the courageous Lamanite was beside him in the tent. Gadoni reached back outside and pulled a couple of bows and other weapons into the tent. Then, as he freed Samuel's hands and feet, he whispered softly, "I found your weapons."

Samuel had to restrain himself from singing out as he outfitted himself as silently as possible. He found it hard to work his stiff hands and raw wrists, but he managed, with Gadoni's help, to buckle on his knife and secure a quiver on his back. Not a word passed between the two while they worked.

A few raindrops struck the tent, followed shortly after with a steady pitter-patter as the storm intensified. Gadoni took advantage of the noise of the falling rain and whispered instructions in Samuel's ear.

Once Samuel was sure he understood what Gadoni expected him to do, he called out to the two guards. "Hey, I drank too much water. Can you help me outside for a minute?"

Both guards clambered into the tent, chuckling. Samuel and Gadoni sprang into action and shortly had the unsuspecting warriors bound and gagged. Once outside they moved silently, making their way steadily to the edge of the encampment. Only once did they meet anyone, a lone warrior standing beside a small tent, water dripping from his wet head and shoulders.

Gadoni spoke to him while Samuel stood a few feet away, his white face obscured by the misty rain and darkness. "Wet tonight, isn't it?" Gadoni asked amiably. "I hope it's better when we move out in the morning."

The warrior grunted in agreement, and the two young men passed on without incident. Soon, all that lay between them and freedom was a line of Lamanite sentinels that surrounded the camp. Fortunately they were watching for intruders from the outside and not paying attention to movement behind them.

With this advantage they were able to attack two guards, leaving them unconscious on the wet grass. In a matter of minutes, Gadoni and Samuel were well beyond the sleeping army, climbing the same long knoll that Gadoni had descended just a few days before.

Once out of earshot of the guards, they slowed their pace. Samuel was coughing and stumbling from fatigue. His body was weak from inactivity and not entirely healed from his recent illness. Gadoni suggested a short rest and found a mangrove tree whose thick leafy branches would shield them from the rain. Leaning against the trunk, Gadoni shared with Samuel the provisions he carried.

"Gadoni," Samuel said with unfeigned gratitude, "I thank you. You saved my life. I hope someday I can repay you."

Gadoni spoke slowly. "You saved my life as well. And even more, you gave me a new life. You taught me that hatred and killing and revenge are wrong. It is I who must thank you." Samuel couldn't see Gadoni's face for the darkness, but he felt the warm sincerity in his voice.

Samuel chewed the dried meat Gadoni had brought and asked, "But why didn't you stand guard after the day you spoke with me? I feared they were onto you and had taken you prisoner, too."

Gadoni chuckled. "No, Sam, the problem was just the opposite. They were afraid I was too angry with you. Tarshi was afraid I might harm you and, in doing so, bring the wrath of Antium down on him. He lives in constant fear of Antium, you know. He assigned me other tasks instead and ordered me not to go near your tent. It slowed my plans up, but as you can see, it didn't stop me."

"And I'm grateful. I feel some better now. Should we move on? When Captain Antium finds us gone, he'll be in a murderous mood. We can't let his men catch us."

Gadoni answered by scrambling to his feet and leading the way up the long ridge. They didn't stop again until there was over a mile between them and the sleeping army. Then they found shelter where both men could safely slip into a much needed slumber.

When they awoke, the sun was sending long streaks of bright orange light beneath the scattered clouds. They looked at each other in surprise as they caught the sound of shouting men and the metallic ring of many clanging swords in the distance. The young men sprang to their feet and dashed to the top of the knoll. From there they could see the terrible battle being waged below.

"Captain Moroni must have followed Antium's messenger with his armies and then attacked when he found Antium's army," Samuel said.

"I'm glad we got out of there when we did, though we've stayed too long here. You would have been killed at the first sign of a Nephite attack," Gadoni said as he led the way along the knoll. "We better get away from here in case the Lamanites retreat in this direction."

Samuel stumbled obediently along, following Gadoni into the forest of tall, broad-leafed trees of numerous varieties. They traveled several miles, the trees becoming thicker as they went. They discovered an area that was so dense with foliage that they had to crawl through, but after crawling several hundred feet, they entered a small clearing. They found the grass and ferns damp from the night's storm, so they crawled back into the dense underbrush where it was relatively dry. There they rested again, secure and well hidden.

Samuel did not know that the day before, Moroni had handed Antium's courier his written reply to Captain Antium and said, "Tell your commander that if he takes the life of my young friend, Samuel, I will hunt him to the very ends of the earth. And tell him that when I find him, I will hang him from a tree and leave his traitorous carcass for the vultures to devour."

The courier did not know that in the thick forest, outside the city Bountiful, Moroni's spies were hiding. As he began his journey back to the camp of Antium's army, he did not know he was being followed. Two of Moroni's spies saw the direction he was going and hurried around him at a safe distance, riding swiftly through the foothills ahead of him. They found the location of Antium's army, then doubled back and captured the courier.

Orders were sent to Moroni's great army, which was waiting. Moroni sent part of his force far to the west, around the Lamanite encampment, while more were sent behind them to thwart a retreat. The rest waited for a surprise attack at dawn.

His strategy was so well planned that the Lamanite army could only retreat toward the East Sea. With their backs to the waves, they fought like wild animals. Undaunted, Moroni's men swept down upon them, fighting from all sides.

Badly outnumbered, Antium's army suffered huge losses. At last Antium ordered his men to surrender but, fearing for his own life, he climbed into the high, dense branches of a large mahogany tree near the seashore and hid himself. From there he watched the disgraceful capture of his scarred and battle-weary army. His thoughts held little remorse for the loss of his men, but rather anger that Samuel had eluded his grasp. Only minutes before the surprise attack he had received word that both Samuel and Gadoni were missing. He swore that he would find them, and when he did . . .

Moroni, after the battle was won, ordered a search for both Samuel and Antium, among the living and the dead. Every tent was searched, but no sign of the prisoner or his captor was found. Moroni sent couriers to every city under Nephite control in the region and to all the Nephite armies with word to be on the lookout for Samuel and Antium.

Two days later, one of the messengers arrived at Shurr. The news spread rapidly through the city that Samuel had indeed been captured by the Lamanites but was now missing and unaccounted for. His family and friends received the news with mixed emotions. Some feared that he was dead, but his family held on to a renewed hope of his eventual return.

Samuel's recent illness, combined with his taxing flight into the jungle, left him weak and sick again. The next day, he and Gadoni were forced to stay in their hideout while Samuel recuperated. Gadoni provided food by killing small game, digging roots, and picking wild fruit.

The two friends spent the long evening telling stories from their widely divergent pasts. Samuel taught Gadoni about God and explained to him that a living prophet spoke with God and shared his will with the people. "He lives in Zarahemla and his name is Helaman," Samuel said. "He is a great friend to Captain Moroni."

Gadoni, like Samuel, recognized that Moroni was a remarkable man. Both Moroni and Samuel had befriended him and shown him an example of love and faith. Gadoni felt something stirring within him at the words of his young Nephite friend, something that was steadily growing into a mighty change of heart. He felt new faith, and still more reason to be thankful for what Samuel had done for him.

The next day the two friends began their trek back to the city of Shurr, falsely assuring themselves that since no one had appeared in their pursuit, they must be safe now. They moved from the valley floor up into the mountains where the air was not so hot and humid. It helped Samuel feel better. They also reasoned that a chance meeting with roaming bands of Lamanite warriors was not as likely there.

When they came to a rapidly flowing river, Samuel looked down at the churning water and looked questioningly at Gadoni, who agreed that it would be better to follow it rather than to cross. The second day they were delighted at the sight of a waterfall, which spilled from a mass of dense forest and cascaded over solid grey granite rocks, lined with dark green foliage. The water tumbled into a narrow gorge, then flowed gently into a deep, shimmering pool that was wedged between two high, vertical rock walls.

"Sam, we've pushed hard the past two days. Let's stop for awhile and swim," Gadoni coaxed.

Samuel was sorely tempted despite his anxiousness to return to Shurr. "All right. But just a quick dip."

From high on a cliff above the pool, Gadoni dove into the inviting water below. A full minute passed, then two. His worry deepening, Samuel dove into the water to find his friend. He opened his eyes underwater, searching frantically for Gadoni, until his lungs burst and he was forced to surface. As he sputtered and drank in the air, he saw the Lamanite treading water nearby as he waited for him.

"I thought you had drowned!" Samuel gasped. "How do you hold your breath so long? You must have been down there for three minutes."

"It's not so hard. You just have to train yourself," Gadoni replied as he began a gentle backstroke downstream to the point where the rocky ledge merged with the water.

"I hope I never have to follow you anywhere underwater. I would run out of air long before you needed any," Samuel said with a chuckle.

"Oh, you'd be surprised what you could do if you had to. Come on," Gadoni urged when they reached the bank, "let's do it again."

They trudged up the long, steep wall at the edge of the gorge until they were again standing on the spot they had dived from. "You first, Sam," Gadoni urged.

Samuel made a second dive, his graceful arc barely rippling the water's glassy surface. He forced himself to stay underwater as long as he could before he surfaced. No sooner had he filled his lungs with the sweet, clean mountain air than Gadoni let out a hoot and jumped from the cliff, feet first.

Despite his intentions for a brief swim, Samuel was reluctant to leave the peaceful setting and the two swam leisurely, unaware of the visitor who silently observed their every move as he carefully fitted an arrow into a bow. He pulled the string taut and loosed the deadly missile.

Samuel twisted in the water, the deadly arrow barely missing him as it sped within inches of his submerged face. Instantly, Gadoni was beside him, signaling for Samuel to follow, and they struck out for the dark rock wall on the far side of the pool.

Deeper and deeper they stroked, staying close to the vertical wall. Samuel could tell that Gadoni was searching for something and he wasn't sure how long he could wait to find out. His lungs burned.

Suddenly, Gadoni turned abruptly and vanished. He appeared to have merged with the ebony rock of the wall. Samuel reached toward the wall and found an unexpected opening. He entered the dark passageway and was relieved to see Gadoni swimming ahead.

Samuel's lungs screamed for relief and he gave a final push forward. Before he realized what was happening, his head shot out of the water and his lungs gulped the lifesaving air.

For several minutes, the two floated in the water, resting and studying their bizarre new surroundings. Many feet above them was a ceiling of moss-covered rock that swept in a giant arch in every direction until it merged with the shadowy water. The immense cavern contained a pool that was nearly as large as the one they had so urgently left.

Neither spoke while they gazed in wonder at the murky beauty that surrounded them. Filtered sunlight poured into the cavern from a hole at the far side of the pool. Instinctively, they swam toward it.

Once they had crossed the pool, Samuel began to tread water again and broke the silence, his voice echoing from the cavern walls. "What happened out there, Gadoni?" he asked. Startled at the ringing of his voice throughout the cavern, he spoke in a whisper. "I thought an arrow passed my face, but it couldn't be."

"It was, though," Gadoni whispered back. "Someone shot it from the ledge where we dove. I only caught a glimpse of him, but there was a man up there—a white man." He had a puzzled expression on his face as he thought for a moment. "There was something familiar about him, Sam. If I'd seen him better I may have recognized him."

"Well, I know one thing, Gadoni," Samuel said with a twisted grin.

"What's that?"

"He didn't come to join us for a friendly swim."

"That's for sure," Gadoni said. "I hope he thinks he hit you and that I drowned trying to save you."

Samuel agreed and then turned his attention to finding an exit. A dim light shone above. "Do you think we can get out the same opening the light is coming in?" he asked Gadoni

"We've got to try. Hopefully, our friend won't be able to see us when we do. Come on, Sam. It's only about twenty feet up to that opening," Gadoni said, swimming over to the edge of the pool.

The climb up the wall was slippery and difficult, and Samuel was still weak from his recent illness. He slipped on the moss and plummeted downward into the water.

"Are you all right, Sam?" Gadoni called down to him. "I'm nearly out now, and I'll look for something to help you up." Gadoni scrambled out the opening and reappeared a moment later. "Grab this," he ordered, lowering the end of a strong vine.

Samuel grasped it tightly and worked his way up the steep incline while Gadoni pulled, bracing himself in the opening.

In a moment, Samuel reached his friend's side and together they stepped into the bright sunlight.

"Let's see where we are," Gadoni suggested. He led the way through the thick growth of small trees, vines, and bushes that hid the opening of the cavern, keeping a sharp lookout for their unknown assailant. Samuel knew that he could be anywhere, but would most likely still be closely watching the area around the pool where he last saw them.

Samuel and Gadoni circled around the falls and crossed the river. From their elevated vantage point, they spotted a shadowy figure in the foliage at the cliff's edge. He was slowly working his way down the ledge, staying in the bushes as much of the time as he could.

Samuel could see their weapons on the rocks where they had left them not far from the crouching figure. Samuel wished he had them now. The man glanced uneasily behind him, as if he sensed Samuel's eyes upon him. Having a clear glimpse of his face, Samuel and Gadoni looked at each other in astonishment. It was Antium! Samuel could not imagine how he had escaped from the fierce battle they had witnessed or how he had found them here. But there he was, evil intent etched on his bearded face.

Samuel and Gadoni each grabbed a rock, the only weapons at hand, and started toward Antium and were nearly upon him when a monkey chattered in a tree overhead, protesting the invasion of his domain. Antium turned at the sound and saw them, his face a mixture of surprise and rage. He quickly reached for an arrow, but before he could let it fly, Samuel's rock hit Antium squarely in the eye with terrible force. He stumbled backward, grabbing at his eye, blood pouring down his face.

Disoriented, Antium stumbled and slipped. His bow flew to the ground in front of him as his arms flailed desperately in the air. His momentum sent him backward, and he plunged with an ear-shattering scream to the water below.

Gadoni angrily picked up Antium's bow, and with a powerful swing, he cracked it over a big stone, breaking it in two, and heaved it into the river. Then he led Samuel down the slope where they recovered their belongings. They spent the next hour searching along the stream for Antium as the sky grew dark with storm clouds. Unable to find any sign of him, they continued on their journey, convinced that he had drowned.

Some distance downstream, Antium, with one blind eye and a crippled arm, broken from a collision with a protruding rock during his fall, clung to the thick branches of a dead tree that lay across the river. He breathed shallowly, clinging to a branch with his one good arm, and saw Gadoni and Samuel pass by. They did not see him. He was not done with them yet, he vowed!

Samuel and Gadoni pressed on, jumping at every cracking branch, wishing that they could be sure Antium were dead and no longer a threat. When they spotted a cave on an open, rock-strewn ridge, Samuel turned to Gadoni excitedly. "This is one of the caves we used when we were hunting game after Shurr was freed. It's only about a two-day walk to Shurr from here. I could run there in a day if I weren't so weak."

Angry black clouds above them and dancing streaks of jagged lightning encouraged them to remain at the cave. Fortunately, a supply of wood left by the hunters awaited them inside. "It doesn't look like we can go any farther tonight. At least we can get dry and stay warm and then get an early start in the morning after this storm's over," Samuel said, trying to console both himself and Gadoni.

After building a fire, they explored the cave, using makeshift torches from the stockpile of wood. They spent an hour exploring the tunnels that led from the main cavern, safe from the terrible storm that raged across the mountain. In one tunnel, they could hear a deep, distant rumble.

"Since we're stuck here for the night, let's get some more pitchy knots and see if we can go back a little farther. I'd like to know what's causing the rumble," Gadoni said.

"All right," Samuel agreed, "but let's not be too long. We need some rest if we're to get started at daylight. I can't wait to see the walls of Shurr again," he said, thinking longingly of Ophera and his family.

Leaving their bows and arrows in the mouth of one of the tunnels well back inside the cave, and with several spare pitchy pine sticks tied to their belts next to their knives and waterbags they started into the mysterious, rumbling tunnel.

After winding several hundred feet into the bowels of the mountain, their tunnel forked. They followed the branch that echoed the ever-increasing rumble most loudly.

"It sounds like a waterfall," Samuel observed, as they got closer.

"There must be an underground river in here," Gadoni said.

The cave became increasingly narrow, and the ceiling lowered until Gadoni and Samuel had to crouch and then crawl on their hands and knees.

Samuel followed closely behind Gadoni. After a few feet the tunnel suddenly opened into an immense cavern where the roar of falling water was deafening. They were sprayed with a fine mist, and it took a minute before they realized they were standing behind a monstrous waterfall.

The mighty flow of water came from far overhead and plunged beyond them into the deep dark bowels of the mountain. They found themselves on a large, flat ledge and cautiously crept to the very edge of the precipice and listened to the echo of the water far below. They followed the wall to the right as far as they could go and found another tunnel that led back into the wall, away from the ledge. Samuel felt an uncomfortable feeling. "Let's go back now," he shouted. Gadoni nodded agreement.

Suddenly Gadoni shouted, "Look at this!" He waved his torch at several perfectly square holes that were cut into the wall about five feet off the floor. They were about eighteen inches square and seemed quite deep.

"I wonder what's in those holes. They look man-made, to me," Samuel shouted.

"I'll look," Gadoni answered and shoved his torch into the nearest hole, peering in. He barely had time to look when he jumped back like he'd seen a ghost.

"What is it, Gadoni?" Samuel hollered.

"Let's get out of here!" Gadoni muttered, badly shaken.

Samuel's look was as quick as Gadoni's. "There's somebody in there!" he shrieked.

"Used to be somebody, you mean," Gadoni roared back. "This is an ancient sacred burial spot. We shouldn't disturb the dead. Let's go."

They hadn't gone more that twenty feet when the ground began to tremble beneath them. The vibration was slight at first but rapidly grew more violent, knocking them down. They tried in vain to stand up as the shaking increased. Rocks fell from above them in a sudden torrent, and with a deafening roar, the ground parted in front of them.

Samuel and Gadoni pressed themselves against the wall as most of their ledge plunged into the mysterious depths below. For what seemed like an eternity, the mountain continued to shake. Samuel was sure that the whole mountain was falling apart—that he had just experienced the most powerful force in nature, unleashed with all its fury. He had no way of knowing that the damage outside was minimal. He and Gadoni were just unlucky enough to be deep in the mountain, near a small fault that had slipped. His greatest fear was that the tunnel which had led into the ancient tomb was damaged, trapping them in the heart of the mountain.

"Gadoni, are you all right?" Samuel called when the rocks had finally stopped falling.

There was no response, only dread stillness. Samuel found Gadoni, half buried in large rocks. He dug the rocks away quickly and pressed a finger to the large artery in Gadoni's neck.

Relieved that he was alive, Samuel examined his friend carefully. One leg lay at a queer angle, just above the ankle. Blood oozed from a wound on Gadoni's head.

Samuel fought to suppress his panic. He felt all alone and

Clair Poulson

terrified and didn't have any idea what he should do now. Remembering the teachings of his parents, he prayed for help, and as he prayed he remembered an impression that had come to him when he first entered the large cavern. He had been warned to turn back, but with the recklessness of youth he had disregarded the prompting. Now, on his knees, he sought forgiveness and promised he would never disregard that still, small voice again if God would save them from a dreadful death in this ancient tomb and allow him to be reunited with his family.

More at ease after his prayer, his fear subdued, Samuel was able to think through his plight. He knew that he could not leave his companion alone while he tried to find a way out. If Gadoni came to, he might crawl toward the edge of the precipice which was now only a few feet away, most of it having tumbled into the chasm. Gadoni wouldn't be able to walk, and he would be in great pain.

Samuel examined the broken leg again and decided that he should straighten it and put a splint on it while Gadoni was still unconscious. He thought of using one of their torches as a splint, but they were both gone—they had probably fallen into the gaping hole beneath them. The spares, tied to their belts, were too small to be used as splints. Finally, he realized there was only one thing he could do.

Shivering, Samuel removed his vest and cut several strips from it to use for cords. He gently wrapped the remaining leather around Gadoni's leg. After that, he groped in the darkness along the wall until he found the graves. He queasily selected several large bones and carried them back to the unconscious Gadoni. He felt a weird sensation as he worked with what used to be part of living, breathing people, but he knew he had to do it. Methodically, he lashed the bones to the broken leg until he had a strong and secure splint.

The abrasion on Gadoni's head had stopped bleeding, but Samuel reached for his water bag so he could wash some of the sticky blood off Gadoni's face while he waited for him to regain consciousness. His water bag was nearly empty, so he pulled Gadoni's from his belt. He used the small amount of water the two bags contained to cool and wash Gadoni's brow, and then

94

realized they badly needed more water to drink. Again he hesitated to leave his friend's side, but knew he would have to risk it. He crept cautiously along the much diminished ledge and felt his way around the back of the waterfall. There he located a small pool of water. He drank freely from it before filling both water bags with the delicious, cold liquid.

Samuel had started to make his way back to Gadoni when he thought about the tunnel through which they had entered the huge cavern. Quickly, he turned about and crawled over to check it out. Samuel felt along the wall discovering many large loose rocks, but he could not find the opening. The hair stood up on his neck as he went back over the same area again. Just as he had feared, the opening was gone!

At that moment, as if to punctuate the feeling of dread that had come over him again, there was another trembling of the ground. He rolled himself into a ball and waited for the rocks to come down and bury him as it had the opening to his tunnel, but the aftershock was mild, and not a single rock struck him.

Urgently, he hurried back to Gadoni's side with the frightening knowledge that there could be more such tremors at any minute. He started to pull Gadoni along the ledge to the opening they had found earlier at the far side of the cavern. He could only pray that opening would not be blocked and would provide an alternative route out of the cave. He was startled when he felt Gadoni struggle and resist being drug along the rough floor. Samuel dropped to his knees and leaned close to Gadoni's face.

"What happened?" Gadoni asked, shouting weakly, trying to be heard above the interminable roaring of the plummeting river.

"Earthquake," Samuel answered, his loneliness dissipating at the sound of his friend's voice. "I was just trying to get you out of here."

"Sam, something's wrong with my leg. It hurts like fire. I don't think I can walk." Gadoni strained to make himself heard.

"It's broken, but I put a splint on it. You'll have to let me help you," Samuel shouted in his ear. "Here, let's get you up."

But the blow to Gadoni's head had been a hard one, and he passed out when Samuel lifted him. Samuel eased him back to the ground and began to maneuver him along the wall. Before long, Gadoni came to again. This time, Samuel helped him sit against the wall, gave him some water, and waited until he felt a little better before trying to get him to his feet again.

Gadoni cried out in pain but didn't pass out when Samuel lifted him once more. With Samuel supporting him, Gadoni was able to hop slowly forward. By the time they reached the tunnel and got a few feet into it, Gadoni was exhausted and they had to stop.

The noise was not quite as thunderous in the tunnel and Gadoni was able to make Samuel hear him without shouting. "Where are our torches?" he asked.

"Over the edge, I think. Most of the floor of the cavern fell away. We're lucky we didn't go down, too," Samuel explained.

"Let's light one of the small ones we brought. This darkness is driving me crazy," Gadoni complained.

"We don't have any dry tinder and the knots are wet," Samuel said forlornly as he checked his tinder pouch. "I guess we will just have to get along in the dark until things dry out some."

"Sam," Gadoni said with a puzzled expression in his voice, "aren't we going the wrong way? Isn't this the big tunnel that we haven't been in before?"

"The quake closed the other one. We'll have to go out this way," Samuel said, trying to sound optimistic.

"We shouldn't have disturbed the dead," Gadoni wailed, after giving some thought to their predicament. "This would never have happened if we hadn't disturbed those graves."

The young men lapsed into silence. It was cold and they were both shivering uncontrollably. Samuel yearned for a fire as he coaxed Gadoni to his feet again. "We'll freeze if we don't keep moving, Gadoni. Let's move on."

The rock beneath their feet sloped more rapidly. It was all Samuel could do to support Gadoni while keeping his own feet beneath him. He tried to shuffle along slowly so he wouldn't trip, for he never knew what obstruction was ahead in the darkness. When they came to a fork, they stopped to rest again while Samuel decided which way to go.

Gadoni begged for rest and Samuel relented. The two huddled together for warmth, and before they realized what was happening, they had both fallen asleep. Some time later, a light rumble and trembling of the ground brought Samuel to his feet as another aftershock surged through the mountain.

When it had passed, he helped Gadoni up again. "We've had our rest, my friend," he said. "We're lucky we were roused or we might have sat right here and died. We better get going. Maybe with a little luck, this tunnel will start going up and connect with the one we followed in," he said hopefully.

"Maybe so," was Gadoni's somber reply.

They had started down the left fork. The ground continued to fall away before them. Obstructions arose everywhere, and it was very difficult maneuvering around them in the darkness. They felt encouraged when the tunnel widened out, but their elation soon ended—they appeared to be in a small dead-end cavern with no way out but the way they had come.

"We'll have to go back," Samuel said, after feeling his way around the walls.

"Let's try to light a torch first," Gadoni suggested. The tinder was still damp, but Samuel tried it anyway. He soon had a spark nestled in the ruffled bark in his hand and blew on it ever so gently. To his delight, it finally ignited, and they lit a torch.

The cave came to life with the flame. Shadows frolicked on the walls, and the light reflected off tiny, bright gems on the floor like glittering eyes peering at them in surprise. The space around them seemed to grow as the menacing blackness lost its stranglehold on them.

As if some magic power danced from the flame, the boys felt refreshed, stronger and more hopeful. Not so magic, but most welcome, was the heat of the flame. They huddled for several minutes around their tiny fire, soaking up the warmth.

"Where did you lose your vest?" Gadoni asked, when he noticed that Samuel was bare from the waist up.

"It's on your leg."

"Oh," Gadoni said, with a foolish grin. "I guess you had to use something to hold my leg together." He took the torch from Samuel's hand and examined his leg closer. "Aaaagh!" he screamed, recoiling violently, the torch bouncing on the ground.

Samuel picked up the torch before it went out.

"Bones!" Gadoni exclaimed. "You splinted my leg with bones! Sam, these are human bones! I can't wear these! Get them off

97

me!" He was shouting at the top of his voice.

"Calm down, Gadoni. I look at it this way: there was absolutely no other choice. Someone is helping you. You can't even move without a splint, and if you'll leave it on, I promise that I'll bury the bones properly when we get out of here. We'll splint your leg better then," Samuel reasoned calmly.

Gadoni finally gave in. "I guess you're right. There really isn't much choice, but I'll sure feel better when they're gone."

Samuel circled the small cavern holding the torch high. He found a good sized opening in the wall just above his head. "Gadoni, look up there. Maybe there's a way out of here without going back."

"But how will we get up there?" Gadoni asked practically.

"Here, hold the torch while I pack some rocks over," Samuel said in answer.

It took Samuel over an hour to find and carry a sufficient number of rocks that were loose enough to move. When he had a pile about two feet high, he clambered on top and tried to boost himself through the opening. He kicked and squirmed until he made it. Gadoni hopped over and painfully pulled himself onto the pile of rocks. Samuel reached down and laboriously hoisted his Lamanite friend up with him.

"I hope we don't have to backtrack after all this work," Samuel moaned as the two of them rested again. "Maybe we'll start to climb now and reach the tunnel we came in through."

After they had recuperated some, they struck out again. The floor of the tunnel leveled out and they made reasonably good time for awhile. Then, once more, they found themselves going downhill. The cavern twisted like a snake and forked several times. Twice they hit dead ends, and once they walked into a passage so narrow that they could not force their way through. Each time, they backtracked and tried again.

They rested periodically, and twice they took turns sleeping for an hour or two before going on. They lost all track of time and had no idea if it was day or night outside the mountain.

"Gadoni, can you hear that?" Samuel asked, after many hours of exhausting travel.

"Hear what?" his companion asked.

Samuel, though he was weak by now and feeling sick again, glanced at Gadoni, who clung heavily to his shoulder, and said, "You're about done in, aren't you? I can hear water up ahead. Do you want to rest here while I go on and see if I can find it?"

"Light me a torch and I'll wait," Gadoni said, sinking painfully to the floor of the tunnel.

Samuel lit another of the small pine knots. There was only one more left on his belt. When it was burned, they would be in the dark again. "I'll be back in a flash," Samuel said, with all the cheerfulness he could muster.

Relieved of his burden, Samuel made good time. The passageway grew wider, and the running water sounded nearer by the minute. The rock ceiling over his head was getting closer and closer as he walked. He finally ended up on his hands and knees, crawling for several feet. The water ahead of him sounded very close. It wasn't the thunderous noise that had tormented them in the large cavern where the fall was. Instead, it was more like the sound of a rapidly flowing river.

With the torch in his right hand lighting the way, Samuel negotiated a tight bend in the tunnel. He was almost on his belly, pulling himself ahead, when the torch slipped from his grasp and fell into a shallow pool of water, dousing the flame. To Samuel's surprise, a gray light still lit the tunnel.

With a shout, he splashed through the pool, rounded another bend, and stood, awestruck. In front of him was a mighty river flowing out of the mountain. He sat down, drank half of the water that he was carrying, and smiled. After a brief rest, he returned to Gadoni, lighting the last of his pine knot torches. Their escape was just in time, he thought with relief.

"You're back already?" Gadoni said, looking at Samuel with a forlorn expression. "Did you hit a dead end? I've been thinking while you were gone. I really wonder if we aren't deeper in the mountain. I . . ."

"No," Samuel interrupted happily. "I found a way out, Gadoni! Are you ready to go?"

Gadoni brightened, his dark eyes suddenly aglow in the flickering light. "Are you sure?" he asked.

"Positive," Samuel said, plopping down beside his friend.

"There are some rough spots ahead, but you can make it."

Samuel wisely refrained from telling Gadoni that the only way out was to swim the rapidly flowing river. Gadoni learned that soon enough for himself when they emerged from the passageway and confronted it.

"Sam," he blurted, "it's a river!"

"The same one that plunged through the cavern we were in, I suppose," Samuel said.

"We'll have to swim," Gadoni moaned. "I can't swim in this condition. What are we going to do?"

"We must swim, Gadoni. At least I must. I think that if we stay near the edge and you just let me tow you, we'll be okay. Just don't let go of me, no matter what."

Samuel was exhausted. He had been supporting most of Gadoni's weight and it had taxed his limited energy almost to its end, but he knew that he had to reach deep within and find a little more. With all his soul he willed himself to enter the river and swim.

The water was ice cold, and it soon numbed the pain in Gadoni's leg. By fighting to stay close to the edge, Samuel was able to tow Gadoni along. He was surprised when Gadoni began to swim on his own. "I'm okay," he shouted at Samuel. "I can't feel my leg, anyway," he gasped.

So, side by side, they swam rapidly through the gaping jaws of the mountain that had almost claimed their lives, and then swam on into the muddy waters of the lake. They swam to the nearest shore where Samuel worked his way through sticks and debris before boosting Gadoni out ahead of him onto the inviting, sun-drenched grass of the shore. Samuel followed him and stretched out, letting the sun luxuriously warm his cold and aching body. Warmth at last.

CHAPTER NINE

O RANGE FLAMES LICKED HUNGRILY AT EACH PINE BOUGH Samuel placed on the fire, but the heat they created disappeared rapidly in the same huge cavern where Samuel and Gadoni had sought refuge from the storm. Gadoni hunched miserably over the fire, his swollen, discolored broken leg packed in a plantain dressing. Sam fashioned a new shiny white splint from green, peeled boughs and hoped desperately that he had set the leg correctly.

Samuel's brow was creased with worry as he sat next to a tidy little pile of shavings that had accumulated from his whittling. He watched his Lamanite friend and wondered what else he could do to ease his pain and speed his recovery.

The soothing patter of falling rain drew Samuel's attention to the mouth of the cave. He rose to his feet and stepped outside. He stood for a moment, letting the soft rainwater drench his hair and run down his naked shoulders and back. He drew a deep breath as his eyes swept the panoramic view before him. Dark green, forested ridges and deep canyons spread below him for miles before being swallowed up in the grey mist of the storm.

His muscles still ached from the long, hard trek he had made from the river, carrying his friend upon his back as he returned to the familiar cave. He had been relieved to learn that the earthquake had done very little damage to the opening of the cave. He had kept his bearing and the cavern would make a good shelter and place of security for the two young men while they waited impatiently for Gadoni's bones to heal enough to allow them to complete their delayed return to Shurr.

"Sam." Gadoni's call sent him hurrying back to the fire.

"I was just standing outside, Gadoni," Samuel said gently.

"Find a sarsaparilla plant. There must be some on this mountain. Do you know what it looks like?" Gadoni asked, his voice weak and unsteady.

"Yes, it's a climbing evergreen shrub, but why do you want that? These pine boughs make good firewood," Samuel said, perplexed.

"The root. Get some of the root and dry it by the fire. Then you can brew a tea that I can drink to kill this pain in my leg. Please hurry," he begged.

An hour later Samuel returned with the ancient pain killer. After a few minutes he had strips of the root drying near the fire. As he worked, his stomach growled in protest of his neglect. All he and Gadoni had eaten in the two days since their swim to safety was some dried meat, a few roots, and some wild berries and mushrooms. Samuel had intended to hunt and kill some game, but the quake had sealed off the tunnel containing their weapons. He had been carving a long branch into a crude spear and set to work on it again. It wasn't much, but maybe he could kill something with it and provide Gadoni with the nourishment his injured body so badly needed.

By the time this latest storm had blown over and the sun glowed pinkly across the rolling forest, Gadoni was resting comfortably. A strong dose of sarsaparilla tea had lessened the pain. Samuel felt better just knowing that Gadoni's pain had subsided, but as he paced in front of the cave, an uneasy feeling tugged at him. At first he attributed it to his frustration at having his reunion with his family delayed, but it was more a feeling that some unseen evil lurked nearby. He stared into the fading sunset, willing its peaceful beauty to draw the anxiety from his mind.

By the time night fell, Samuel felt better. His relief was short lived, however, for when he turned his back on the forest, the hair rose stiffly on the back of his neck and an icy shiver ran the full length of his body. He spun around, but after finding the same peaceful scene spread out before him, he returned to the cave. Convincing himself that the dawn and a good hunt would settle the uneasiness in his stomach and drive away the haunting fear, Samuel settled down by the fire and slept.

Late in the night he awoke in a cold sweat, the image of Antium's repulsive face, contorted with rage, fresh on his mind. The cry of some unknown beast penetrated the stillness of the cave, strangely reminiscent of the wild cry of Antium as he plunged from the cliff, blood streaming down his face. Clutching his spear, Samuel crept nearer to the embers of his dying fire. Their dull glow seemed a sinister warning of danger lurking in the shadows. He piled several sticks on the fire and knelt to blow on the orange coals until a flame burst forth, casting a host of menacing shadows across the cavern walls. The whir of bat wings suddenly filled the air, hurling a hundred hideous, flapping phantoms along the wall.

Through the terrifying night, Gadoni slept, undisturbed and peaceful, but by the time the first grey light of dawn oozed over the mountain's crest and flowed through the mouth of the cave, Samuel's nerves were shattered. While he waited for Gadoni to wake up, he nervously brewed a fresh gourd-full of sarsaparilla by patiently holding it far enough above the fire to heat the bitter liquid without setting fire to the gourd. Sufficiently heated, he set it aside and fixed a bland breakfast, putting off waking his friend for as long as he could.

"Sam," Gadoni said, startling him, "is something wrong this morning?"

"I didn't know you were awake," Samuel said with a forced smile. "What makes you think something's wrong. The only thing wrong is that we don't have any meat, and I'm going to take care of that problem today," he promised, fingering his crude spear. "It may be difficult, but I'll get something with this."

"I'm sure you will, but I've been watching you for several minutes. You keep looking toward the entrance, and you're acting nervous. Is there something you're not telling me?" Gadoni asked with a grimace of pain, forcing himself into a sitting position and reaching for his bitter gourd full of medicine.

Samuel looked away for a moment. This man had become his best friend. They had each in turn saved the life of the other. Gadoni was dependent on him for food and protection, if protection was needed. He had no evidence that there was any danger around—just his own foolish fear.

"Sam. What is it?" Gadoni's plea was passionate.

"There's probably nothing to worry about. It's just that I have this feeling—this foolish fear that Antium is still out to get us. I think I've just let the sounds of the night get to me, but I'll be okay now that it's light outside. I guess maybe I was in the dark too long after the quake and that . . ." Samuel stopped speaking abruptly when he saw a look of unmistakable fear appear deep in Gadoni's dark eyes.

"I feel it, too. Maybe we better move away from here. It'll be terribly slow going, but maybe we could start working our way toward Shurr," Gadoni said, trembling visibly. "Maybe there's going to be another earthquake."

"No, that's not it. It's something else I feel. Let me help you farther back into the cave. I'll build a fire there and then I'll go find us some meat. We'll see how we both feel about things and decide what to do later, after we eat," Samuel suggested, irritated at the persistent uneasiness he felt.

Soon Samuel walked out of the cave and into the bright sunlight. The miles of forest-covered mountains and valleys beckoned invitingly, and he hurried down the mountain, crude spear in hand.

It was not a pair of eyes that followed Samuel's hurried steps into the waiting trees, but only a single, dark beady one. Its mate was blind, a mound of reddish scar tissue forming a repulsive cover over the useless socket. The good eye blinked rapidly beneath bushy, black eyebrows.

Antium peered from his hiding spot a short distance from the cave. He hunched between two tall, closely-spaced pines near the top of a long ridge. His evil mind was hard at work trying to unravel the puzzle of the two young men he hated so much. His bitter heart sought revenge, swift and final, but his military mind spoke caution. He had seen only Samuel, the white boy who was the cause of his problems, come and go from the cave high on the mountain in front of him. However, he had no doubt that Gadoni, that traitor Gadoni, was there somewhere—probably in the cave.

The dull ache of his crudely splinted arm made him wince and shift his position. It was hanging useless in a sling he had made from the skin of a snake killed with his own knife. This reminder of his injuries only served to further infuriate him, but he would bide his time. Until he was sure of the whereabouts of both of his enemies, he would not attack. When he did, it would be on his terms, in the dark of night, and even better, in the dark of the cave. His thin lips curled slightly in an evil grin. During the night he had approached the cave, but caution kept him from entering. Only when he was sure of himself would he make his move. Yes, he would attack when victory was certain. This time, Samuel and Gadoni would pay with their lives.

Hunting with the spear proved more difficult than Samuel had imagined. The beasts he stalked sensed his presence and darted to safety long before he was close enough to cast his spear. He finally succeeded in killing a large snake. Although the thought of eating its flesh did not appeal to him, he was becoming desperate. At least, it would provide nourishment.

With the serpent thrown over his shoulder, Samuel made his way wearily through the shady forest. He crawled over fallen logs, veered around dense stands of young trees, and forced his way through groves of bushy shrubs. As he left the last of the trees below the cave, his eyes froze on a patch of moist dirt. There, since yesterday's rain, someone had left the unmistakable imprint of a large sandal. All the terror of the past night returned. After quickly studying the print, he followed the mostly obscure path the sandal and its mate had taken. The tracks led to within a stone's throw of the cave. Then abruptly, the tracks led back down the hill.

Samuel raced up the last few feet of hillside and into the cave. Not until he saw Gadoni, sitting with his back to the wall where he had left him, did Samuel's heart lessen its wild pounding.

"What's the matter?" Gadoni asked as Samuel skidded to a stop and deposited the snake on the hard rock floor. Staring at the snake, he did not sense Samuel's anxiety. "I hope you weren't hurrying to bring me that fine piece of meat you so skillfully stalked. I guess I forgot to mention that I'm not overly fond of snake."

"You're feeling better, I see." Samuel was relieved to see

Gadoni in good humor and tried to squelch his own gloom. "I killed this magnificent creature. Now you prepare it for dinner," he ordered with a forced laugh.

By now Gadoni had looked up from the snake and the sparkle faded from his dark eyes. "You're not fooling me, Sam. Something's wrong out there, isn't it? Well, let's hear it. What happened, besides the fact that you couldn't get close enough to kill any real game?"

Samuel glanced inadvertently to the cave opening. "Someone is out there, Gadoni. The prints of his sandals are just a few feet from the cave. They were made after it rained. It may explain all the strange feelings I've had. We're being watched."

"Antium?" Gadoni said, pulling the knee of his good leg tight against his chest.

"I have no idea if it's Antium, Gadoni. What I do know is that he is an enemy and we must prepare a defense, just in case . . ." His thought lingered in the damp darkness of the cave.

Samuel carried most of the hunters' wood into the tunnel near their fire. Then, while Gadoni roasted some of the snake, he carried the rest of the wood into two other tunnels. There he prepared small piles, out of sight of the entrance to the cave, in both locations. Later, after darkness descended on the mountain, he would light them as decoy fires. He hoped that if their unseen enemy should enter, he would be confused as to their whereabouts, giving them time to prepare an appropriate greeting for his unwelcome visit.

After eating their fill of the offensive meat, Samuel and Gadoni prepared a couple more spears—nothing more than straight sticks with sharp, pointed ends. Then Samuel crept from the cave and into the forest, returning with several long, sinewy vines. In his absence, Gadoni had sharpened one end of several six-inch sticks. The sticks and vines were to be part of the surprise they planned for their enemy if he should choose to invade their sanctuary.

As soon as it was dark outside, Samuel ignited the decoy fires.

Antium shifted his broken arm, trying to make it more comfortable. He squinted his beady eye and peered from his hiding spot toward the cave. He cursed when he discovered that the usual fire just inside the mouth of the cave was not there this night. He decided they must have moved deeper into the cave. An owl hooted nearby, and a fly buzzed in his ear. Antium slapped at it furiously, sending it to his other ear. He slapped again. In revenge, the fly paid an irritating visit to the sensitive hairs in Antium's left nostril.

Antium slapped at his long nose so hard that it jolted his injured arm, sending an intense pain clear to his shoulder. The fly, discovering that it was in a rather nasty spot, turned around and, tickling the hairs in Antium's nose with its wings, made its escape. By then Antium was on his feet. When the fly, a split second later, began to drone in his ear again, Antium clubbed himself so hard on the side of the head that he lost his balance and stumbled forward, falling painfully on his broken arm. He emitted a piercing scream that shattered the peaceful calm of the night. The fly, frustrated but unharmed, left in pursuit of better hunting grounds.

"What was that?" Gadoni asked when a shrill, high pitched howl penetrated the deep recesses of the cave.

"I don't know. There must be a wild beast nearby. Maybe that will discourage our visitor out there," Samuel said nervously.

Both young men began to work faster. While Gadoni sharpened more sticks, Samuel was stretching vines across the width of the tunnel just around the bend from the fire. He secured the first one at each end with big rocks, the vine pulled tight about four inches from the hard floor. When he was satisfied with it, he placed a second vine about a foot behind the first. Anyone coming down that passageway without a torch would almost certainly trip on the tightly-stretched vines.

Samuel carried Gadoni's pile of sharpened sticks around the curve and placed them, sharpened ends up, on the near side of the vines.

"The trap is ready, Gadoni," Samuel reported after he had finished. "I'll go extinguish the other fires. Keep your knife handy just in case our visitor comes before I return."

Gadoni lifted the slender shaft of steel in his hand. It shined bright yellow, reflecting the flames. "I'm ready, Sam," he said grimly.

107

Samuel moved quietly through the tunnels in the darkness, pausing every few steps to listen for strange sounds. Only a chill silence met his ears. After extinguishing the decoy fires, he hid himself behind a large rock near his trap and settled in for a long, cold wait.

The hours passed slowly, the cold numbing Samuel's limbs and bare torso. He found himself shifting frequently to keep from becoming too stiff. His head ached from the constant strain of listening for sounds in the tunnel. Then, toward midnight, he heard a slight shuffling. At first, he thought he was hearing things, but a minute later he heard it again, closer. When he heard it the third time, it was accompanied by a high-pitched, raspy whistle, as if someone were having difficulty breathing. Samuel sensed the presence of evil.

The shuffle and raspy breathing seemed only a few feet away when the shuffle stopped and the breathing became more pronounced. Samuel itched to steal a peek from his hiding place but thought better of it as the reflection from the fire around the bend threw just enough light that the intruder might detect his movement.

Samuel held his breath and tried to still his pounding heart until, at last, the unseen enemy moved again. Samuel counted slowly to himself and tensed for the moment when the shuffling feet would meet the well-secured vine. He had only counted to fifteen when there was a thud followed by a hoarse scream of pain that reverberated through the rock passageways.

Gadoni hopped around the bend, a torch in one hand, his knife in the other as Samuel sprang upon their unwelcome visitor who lay sprawled, face down, on the ground. Samuel rolled the big man over and held a knife to his throat. He almost dropped it with surprise when he encountered the ugly scarred eye and hideous face of Antium.

"It's Antium!" Gadoni shouted.

Before Samuel could respond, a deep rumble erupted from the fallen man's throat. "You can't kill me," he said and began to struggle. Samuel, his initial shock gone, held Antium fast.

"You lie still, or you'll see what I can do," he warned, his youthful voice shaking.

"He's got two of my sticks in him," Gadoni said. "He's bleeding all over."

"Get them out of me!" Antium begged hoarsely.

"I thought you were brave," Gadoni observed wryly.

Samuel pulled one stick from Antium's shoulder and one from his stomach, pressing on the wounds briefly to staunch the flow of blood. With a piece of tough, flexible vine, Samuel bound Antium's good arm behind his back. Then he heaved the wicked man to his feet and shoved him roughly down the passageway toward the fire where, in the light of the flickering flames, he tended further to Antium's wounds.

"Well, *Captain* Antium," Samuel said when he had finished, "you aren't hurt too seriously. Other than the danger of infection from the filth all over your body, you should be okay. We'll be able to deliver you to Captain Omni fit for a proper hanging."

Antium grunted in protest and struggled to get up. Samuel firmly pushed him onto his back and bound his feet. Using vines, he secured Antium to a rock where the captive could uncomfortably spend the rest of the night. By morning, the captive's already sour disposition had deteriorated badly. He cursed and threatened them unceasingly. Gadoni, after taking all he could, stuffed a fistful of snake skin in Antium's mouth.

"There, we don't have to listen to you any more," he said.

Samuel was perplexed. He now had both an injured companion and an injured captive to care for. The sooner he could get back to Shurr, the happier he would be, but he knew both men needed time to heal. He also knew all three of them needed food and that to get food, he needed weapons. He secured Antium with more vines and left him in Gadoni's charge while he explored deeper into the cave to see if he could find a way to get back into the tunnel where their weapons had been left.

He spent the entire day searching, digging out partially blocked passageways and searching again. His effort paid off, for though it took the better part of two days, he recovered the weapons. The next day he killed fresh game, gathered more wild berries, roots, and mushrooms, and stockpiled more firewood.

Samuel was tempted to make the trip to Shurr and bring back help, but was afraid to leave Gadoni for more than a few hours at a time with Antium. His heart ached to see his family and Ophera, but he waited.

After four weeks had passed, Samuel could see that Gadoni's leg was healing well. "Do you feel like hiking out of here yet, Gadoni?" he asked.

"Sure. We'll have to move slowly, but I'm ready. I can't take much more of Antium's whining anyway," he said with a grin.

Antium's arm had knitted itself, although it was permanently crooked between the elbow and the shoulder. When told that they were beginning the trek to Shurr, he cursed and carried on with tirades of the most foul language. But he had no choice but to follow.

Samuel and Gadoni took turns escorting him as they hiked through the rugged mountains and down onto the valley floor. In spite of Gadoni's tender leg and Antium's constant attempts at malingering, the little group made good time.

A few miles into the valley, they came across the scene of a major battle that had taken place recently. The stench of rotting flesh seeped from the shallow graves of the dead. "Many Nephites died here," Antium gloated, although it was impossible to determine the victors. Hurrying from the repulsive place, the two boys tried vainly to rid themselves of the memory of the terrible odor. Antium was undisturbed by it. "His senses are permanently dulled," Samuel told Gadoni.

Antium laughed and sneered with disdain.

That night they camped in a grove of trees near a stagnant jungle lake. It was their second night since leaving the cave. "And it will be the last," Samuel said hopefully. "We're only a few hours from Shurr."

"Our arrival can't be too soon for me," Gadoni sighed, his patience with his vulgar former commander at an end.

By noon the next day, the trio walked out of the forest and faced the city of Shurr. Samuel's heart sank. Smoke rose from the smoldering ruins. The city had been destroyed!

Samuel fell to his knees, bitter tears burning his eyes. Antium laughed. "You see how your God watches over you and your people!" While he was still laughing, Gadoni swung a doubled fist with all the strength of his stocky body, sending Antium reeling to the ground. With all the pent-up fury from days of taking Antium's verbal abuse, Gadoni sprang upon him and choked him, shouting, "Don't you ever speak to Sam like that again or I'll personally string you to a tree and leave you for the vultures!"

Antium gasped and his good eye began to bug out. Not until his scarred face was turning blue did Samuel stop Gadoni. He took hold of Gadoni's arm and said, "Thanks, my friend. I think he got the point."

Gadoni shoved Antium's head to the ground, then stood and faced Samuel. "I guess I kind of lost my temper."

Samuel nodded sympathetically. "I have no fear but that Antium will be punished one day for all the evils he has committed. But for now I must see what remains of the city," Samuel said, leaving Gadoni to lead Antium as he ran toward the smoke and ashes.

Samuel stumbled over the high mound of dirt and through the charred remains of the wall. He stared in a stupor at the scene before him. Not a single house had been spared the torch. Even the synagogue in the center of the city was nothing but a smoking mound. Only a few sheds and corrals, stark and lonely, remained.

The familiar stench of death stung his nose. Samuel could see the bodies of many soldiers, both Nephite and Lamanite, strewn throughout the city. A terrible battle had been fought here recently, and there was no doubt in Samuel's mind who the victors had been. The Lamanite army had done this terrible thing, Samuel could see. Although they had taken time to destroy the city, they had left the bodies of the dead to stain the ground upon which they had fallen.

Samuel ran toward the remains of the house he had lived in for so many weeks. There he sifted through the ashes, looking for some remains of its occupants, but he found none. He went on to the next house and the next with the same result. His despair lessened with the knowledge that his loved ones had not been in the house when it had burned. He noticed, also, that none of the dead were women or children.

Samuel walked back toward Gadoni and Antium who had finally appeared at the top of the mound at the city's edge. Passing through the stream, Samuel lingered a moment to allow the pure water to wash some of the soot and ash off him.

Samuel spoke to Gadoni with effort. "Only dead soldiers lie here," he said quietly. "We can only hope that my people were gone before this happened."

Antium laughed again—a hoarse, evil laugh. Samuel angrily turned on him. "You and your kind will pay for all this one day. Your greed and hatred brings only death and misery to Lamanites and Nephites alike."

Antium stuck his great, hooked nose in the air and snorted his contempt.

"You have no conscience, do you?" Samuel turned from him. "Come on Gadoni, let's get away from here. The smell is more than I can take."

They camped a short distance into the forest. "Let's sleep on it tonight. We'll decide what to do tomorrow," Samuel suggested to Gadoni. He had no idea what he would do the next day, the tragedy and uncertainties of this day having left him shaken and bewildered.

They lit no fire that night for fear enemy eyes might see the smoke. They finally gagged Antium when he began shouting to attract attention.

They awoke with the rising of the sun the next day. The sky above them was bright, and the monkeys and birds in the trees kept up a constant, cheerful chorus, contrasting sharply with the dark, despondent mood the two young friends found themselves in. They chewed their dried meat as they talked quietly, not broaching the concerns that filled their minds.

They had removed the gag from Antium's mouth so he could eat, threatening to gag him and let him go without food if he shouted again. He was the first to vocalize the question the young men were avoiding. "Where do we go from here?" he asked, the familiar sneer ever present in his gravelly voice.

Samuel did not answer, his attention having been drawn suddenly to the unmistakable distant thunder of hundreds of marching men. Swiftly, Gadoni gagged Antium before he could make an outburst while Samuel sprinted to the fringe of the trees and stared out. Relief flooded over him like warm rain when he realized he was watching the orderly passing of a massive Nephite army led by someone on a magnificent white horse!

"Gadoni," he shouted, "bring Antium. It's Captain Moroni and his army."

Antium, understandably, wasn't particularly fond of their new plan to move him and resisted with all his strength. "Sam," Gadoni called and Samuel dashed to his aid. Antium planted his feet firmly on the ground, pointed his hooked nose in the air, and refused to take a step.

Samuel latched on to one arm, signaled for Gadoni to grab the other, and together they drug their mulish burden into the bright sunlight of the grassy, flat plain. Almost instantly they were spotted, and the figure on the white horse signaled his army to halt. A few minutes later, a dozen armed men approached them.

Samuel held up his hand. "I am Samuel. I seek Captain Moroni. This is my friend, Gadoni. He also seeks Captain Moroni." He dipped his head in the Lamanite's direction. "He wishes to take an oath of peace. And this is our prisoner, Captain Antium, of the Lamanite army."

At this the mouth of more than one soldier gaped open. One solider had the presence of mind to speak. "Come, we'll escort you to him." He ordered two of the soldiers to take charge of the prisoner, then led them toward the army.

Before they had covered half the distance, Moroni rode out toward them. Seeing Samuel, he leaped from his horse, tossing the reins to one of the men, and embraced Samuel as if he were his own son. "Where have you been, Samuel? I led my army to fight the army of Captain Antium, but you were not there. We have searched the country far and wide for you."

"Gadoni helped me escape," he explained.

"Gadoni. So this is the angry young man I met in Shurr." He reached a large, friendly hand toward him. "I thank you. You have done a service that cannot be repaid."

Gadoni beamed and shook his hand. "Sir, I'm ready to make an oath of peace if it is still possible for it to be accepted."

"Very well. Gadoni, do you swear that you will never make war against the Nephite people again?" Moroni asked.

"Yes, I promise," Gadoni responded.

"Your covenant is accepted. From this day on you may come

and go as you please among my people," Moroni told him. He started at the sight of soldiers dragging Antium toward them. "And who is this?" he asked Samuel.

"He's a little hard to recognize," Samuel laughed. "This is Captain Antium. Twice he tried to take our lives in the wilderness. So Gadoni and I captured him. I promised him that I would deliver him to Captain Omni. Since he's not here, we would be glad if you would take him. He's been quite a nuisance to us in the wilderness."

"I'll be happy to take him off your hands," Moroni said, staring evenly at the unholy wrath evident in Antium's beady eye.

"Captain," Samuel began again, his voice trembling.

Moroni looked at him and asked, "Is something the matter, Samuel?"

"Do you have any idea where my family has gone, sir?" he asked.

"Oh, so that is what's worrying you? A small company of soldiers is escorting all of the people of Gilead back to their homes. They left a few days ago. I left a small force in Shurr to take care of the affairs there," Moroni said.

"Sir," Samuel said, pointing in the direction of Shurr, "the city has been burned and the soldiers are dead. There are many dead Lamanite warriors, too."

A look of heavy sorrow creased Moroni's rugged face. "We fought and defeated a large army about ten miles that way," he said, waving a powerful arm toward the mountains. "Another army must have followed and attacked the city. We must find them before more cities are taken." He gave orders to his soldiers to call his scouts to his tent to meet with him, then turned back to Samuel. "What do you wish to do now?"

"Gadoni and I would like to find my people, sir, if it's all right with you, that is," Samuel said, glancing at Gadoni who nodded in agreement.

"Of course. But I would be pleased if you'd spend the night with us. We will camp here while scouts locate the Lamanite army. I would very much like to hear how two men, so young and inexperienced, outwitted a wily old bear like Antium," Moroni said with a smile.

"Thank you, sir. We would like that." Samuel said, relieved that his ordeal was finally coming to an end.

"But you young men must be very cautious on your journey to Gilead." Moroni cautioned. "I fear the region is full of Lamanites."

CHAPTER TEN

DAWN EXPLODED WITH A BURST OF GOLDEN RADIANCE between the lofty grey peaks on the eastern horizon. Latoni gazed in silent awe as the sun, a glorious, burning sphere, inched its way into the clear morning sky. Its appearance, after a cold and stormy night, brought hope of a new and better day.

Latoni sought moments like this to lift his spirits when they sagged and to give solace to his soul when it ached. He prayed that the feeling instilled in him during this peaceful respite would linger upon his return to camp where once more he would try to inspire hope in his fellow travelers.

The return to Gilead was proving to be more difficult than Latoni had imagined. Death and sickness had struck after little more than a week of tedious travel through a remote and rugged wilderness. Among the dead was old Lib, Ophera's dauntless, battle-scarred grandfather. He had slipped and fallen from a rocky trail, suffering broken bones and a serious blow to the head. Two days of travel were lost while they nursed him in vain. Kamina and her children mourned his tragic loss, placed his body in the hard ground, and gallantly moved on.

Other families grieved as more of the elderly succumbed to the strain and hazards of the difficult trek. Though death and illness did not stop the homesick company, it did slow them down. Now several lay on blankets burning with a fever. The soldiers assigned to accompany Latoni and his people grumbled that they, of all the Nephite fighting men, were the most unfortunate. To be forced to act as chaperones to a feeble group of civilians was bad enough, but to nurse the sick and aged was just too much. They spoke openly of their desire to return to duty with the regular army.

Experienced soldier that he was, Latoni detected the early warning signs of mutiny. Moroni had sent an honest but inexperienced young captain to direct the trek. The young captain knew of Latoni's record as a leader and called on him often for advice. However, the captain had never witnessed a rebellion and did not heed the older man's warning. "They just like to grumble," he had insisted, "but they'll do whatever is required of them."

"I hope you're right, but all the same I would advise you to be very careful," Latoni had cautioned him.

But Latoni's worries were shadowed by his concern for his beloved wife, Sarah. The loss of Samuel had been almost more than she could bear. He constantly reminded her that Samuel might yet return, and while they waited, she still had Oreb and Nonita to love and care for. He knew she tried to have a more positive outlook, but then she too was struck with the fever.

Wearily, Latoni traced the path of the sun as it rose ever higher above the mountains. He must get back. He was the informal leader of the group, and, with the help of God, he would see them safely back to Gilead. Grasping the fleeting solace he had received in this peaceful and secluded place, he limped back to join the others.

No sooner had he come into sight of the camp than he was beset by a very distraught Ophera. "Latoni, you must hurry! We can't find Oreb and Nonita!" she wailed.

Not anxious to have his hopes for a better day dashed so soon, he said, "Slow down, young lady. Both were sleeping soundly when I left for my walk a few minutes ago. They surely can't have wandered very far in such a short time. Had they eaten yet?"

"No, but . . . well, they chased after a monkey. I saw them go. They were laughing and running down the hill. They're always doing things like that, and it never occurred to me that they might get lost," she said.

"Well, they won't be far. Oreb's first concern is always his stomach. He'll come bounding back any minute, looking for some breakfast," Latoni reasoned with a smile.

Ophera was not reassured. "Sarah's too ill to get up this morning. My mother is fixing breakfast for you and your children. She sent me to find them and get them cleaned up, but they hadn't returned. I looked all around and some of the others helped me search. They're not in camp and they're not with the soldiers. Oh, what can we do?" she moaned.

A chill come over Latoni as he realized that his two small children might actually be in danger. He acted with decisiveness, organizing the camp and enlisting aid from the soldiers to conduct a thorough search of the area.

The children's tracks were located several hundred yards down the mountain but were soon lost on a large, rocky plateau. Hours of intense searching did not turn up a single clue. When it became too dark to continue, the search was postponed until daylight. Latoni returned heavyhearted to face his wife.

All day Sarah had been protected from this new worry with the hope that the children would be found. But now Latoni entered the little tent where she lay, unsure of what he should, or even could, say to her. Her eyes sought his face and he could see that she had guessed that all was not as it should be.

"What is it, Latoni?" she asked in a whisper. "What's gone wrong now?"

His heart ached for her. For eighteen years they had shared their lives. They had always agreed that nothing of concern to one should be kept from the other. Still, Latoni hesitated to add to her burden in her weakened condition.

"Latoni, please tell me. You have never kept anything from me. Just because I'm ill, don't start now," she begged, reading his mind with her usual uncanny accuracy.

"I don't want you to worry, my dear," he began hesitantly, dropping to his knees and taking one of her feverish hands in his own. "We haven't been able to locate Oreb and Nonita, but we soon will," he assured her, trying to convey a confidence he did not feel.

Sarah let out a despairing wail and started to rise from the rough blanket she was lying on, but Latoni pushed her gently back. She began to cry. "You must lie still, Sarah, so the fever will go away. We followed their tracks a little way down the hill, but we lost them in the rocks," he explained, alarmed at her sobs and the haunted look on her pale face.

Exhausted, she finally became quiet once more. "Who's looking for them now?" she asked.

"No one. It's too dark. We'll begin at the first light of morning and we'll find them. The soldiers are helping. Now lie back down. You must rest and get stronger, so we can be on our way again soon."

Meekly, she obeyed, out of sheer inability to do anything else. Latoni stayed at her side and tried to give solace. When Kamina came with some cayenne for her fever, he coaxed Sarah to take some of the burning liquid. She did and in a few minutes was asleep, but Latoni could not rest. His heart was filled with anxiety for his wife and children. He spent the night at Sarah's side, praying over her as he cooled her fevered body.

An owl hooted—a lonely, haunting call. Leaves rustled overhead as the evening breeze swayed the branches of the tall trees. Nearby, a cricket chirped as Nonita, trembling with fear, huddled close to her brother. The dark night sky was hidden from their view by heavy clusters of long, broad leaves that hung from the lower branches above them. Oreb had led his little sister into this dense thicket because he felt secure here, but the sun had not penetrated to the ground, leaving the sticks he had hoped to use to build a fire, hopelessly wet. It was too dark now to go in search of dry kindling, so he would have to comfort Nonita through the dark night without the solace of a flickering fire.

Nonita was so frightened. "There might be wild animals here," she sobbed.

"Don't worry, Nonita," Oreb responded bravely, smoothing her hair the way he had seen his father do so many times. "I have my bow and my arrows and my knife. We'll be okay until I can figure out how to get us back to the others."

"But the wild animals, what if they come in the dark?" she asked, scooting even closer to him.

"I'll wait until they are just a few feet away and then shoot them with an arrow. I won't miss," he said confidently.

"But how can you see them if it's dark? I can't even see you,

Oreb. I'm scared," she whimpered.

"We can see their eyes. Animal's eyes shine in the dark, and I will shoot right between their shining eyes," he said.

"Are you sure?"

"Of course I'm sure. I've seen them when I was camping with Father and Sam. When animals came near our fire we could see their eyes. So quit worrying," he said, blissfully unaware that it was the reflected fire that created the shine in their eyes.

Nonita's attention turned to her stomach. "I'm really hungry, Oreb."

"Go to sleep and I'll find us something to eat in the morning. I'll shoot an animal and pick some wild berries and even dig some roots," he promised.

Reassured, Nonita drifted off to sleep, her head snugly burrowed against her brother's shoulder. Oreb slept, too, his back against a tree.

The loud call of a parrot woke the children shortly after dawn. Oreb was startled at their surroundings until he remembered they were in the deeply shaded thicket. The parrot called again, a raucous sound. Oreb looked up to see if he could locate it. He spotted it a few feet above them. It was agitated and continued to cackle and screech as if it were trying to warn the children of something.

Suddenly, the parrot ceased its frantic chatter. The children were so unnerved by the unusual noise and then the somber, sudden stillness that they huddled tighter, their eyes wide with fright. The stillness was broken by a slight rustling to Oreb's right. He glanced in that direction and froze as his eyes fell on the huge spotted face and broad chest of a jaguar, only a few feet away from them. Sharp white teeth gleamed from behind curled lips. The cat's head was near the ground and its dark yellow eyes never strayed from Oreb's face.

As it inched forward, it made no sound, other than the almost imperceptible rustling of leaves as its huge paws propelled it toward the two lost children. Slowly, Oreb picked up the bow at his side and carefully fitted an arrow. The jaguar neither slowed nor hastened its pace as it slunk ever closer to its quarry.

Nonita had not seen the dangerous creature and was still looking up at the brightly colored parrot. When Oreb pulled the string taut, she turned her head, leaned around him and saw the sleek cat.

Simultaneously, Nonita screamed, the jaguar sprang, and Oreb released his arrow. The fierce creature fell in a heap at Oreb's side. His arrow had found its mark.

Both children leaped to their feet and backed away from the long spotted body. They were shaking, Nonita whimpering as she clung to Oreb. Wide-eyed, they watched the cat as its body writhed and twisted until its muscles finally relaxed and it lay still in death. Oreb stepped toward it, but Nonita backed away.

The still morning air was shattered again as Nonita cried out. Oreb whirled, expecting another jaguar. There on the ground beside Nonita was a small kitten, the cub of the jaguar that had died protecting it from a perceived enemy. The little cat must have strayed from its nearby den and wandered into the thicket where the children had innocently spent the night.

Oreb looked at the wild little creature and grinned. "Nonita," he said as he picked up the spitting cub, "I killed its mother. Now it has no one to take care of it but us. It's probably hungry, just like we are, so I better find it something to eat."

Nonita, still shaken, asked, "But what does it eat?"

"Meat, silly. I'll kill something to feed it. If I can kill a jaguar, then I'm sure I can kill something for a little baby to eat," he bragged as he stroked the fine little head of the creature.

"What about its father, Oreb? Can't its father feed it? You better put it down and we better get out of here before its father comes and sees what you did to its mother," she reasoned.

"No, Nonita. We don't have to worry about its father," he said, puffing his chest at his superior knowledge. "Only mother jaguars take care of the babies. Come here. It's getting tame already. Here, you take it and don't let it get away while I see what I can shoot to eat."

Oreb examined the huge body of the mother cat, then pulled his arrow from its chest with a mighty heave. As he led the way out of the thicket, Nonita followed, holding the little jaguar cub tightly in her arms.

Oreb soon spotted a young Brocket deer, only about fourteen inches tall, in a small clearing on the hillside below them.

Signaling Nonita to be still, he approached the buck, careful to stay downwind. When he was within range, he let an arrow fly. Oreb's aim was true and the little deer fell.

Oreb cleaned the animal, giving some of its raw flesh to Nonita for the cub. The cub snatched the meat and growled menacingly. After backing away from Nonita, it stopped about a dozen feet from her, gave one last warning growl, then devoured the meat. After it had finished, it carefully cleaned itself. Finally, its hunger satisfied, it curled up in the folds of Nonita's soft leather skirt and purred as she stroked its fine, spotted coat.

Oreb built a fire and soon had a large chunk of venison roasting over the flames. Nonita, the cat sleeping on her lap, watched hungrily but never moved until the meat was cooked and Oreb offered her some. The two children ate every bit of the roasted meat before storing the rest of the carcass under an outcropping of rock.

"I think we'll stay here, Nonita," Oreb suggested after settling down comfortably in the shade of the ledge. "Maybe if we quit moving around, they'll find us sooner," he went on, remembering his father's frequent lectures on what to do if he became lost. He built a small fire and they sat near it, more for security than for warmth.

As the morning wore on, the sky darkened in the west and a storm moved in. When it began to rain, the children and the little jaguar were able to keep dry by staying near their fire, toward the back of the outcrop of rock. With their stomachs full, they dozed. When Oreb awoke, the storm had increased in intensity, the wind howling and the rain falling in torrents. His fire had burned down to a bed of hot coals, forcing him into the driving rain in search of wood.

He gathered a large pile of wet branches which he stacked near the fire. He put several on it and blew until he finally had a small flame. Throughout the day he kept adding wood as it dried by the fire. When night fell again, the sounds of the dark forest spooked Nonita once more, but she kept her young jaguar close and told Oreb that they would be safe with the cat to help them.

Oreb awoke in the night and offered a small piece of meat to the kitten, encouraging it to stay near. Not once had it shown any sign of leaving them. It had already accepted Nonita as its surrogate mother. By the time another storm came with the awakening of a new day, Oreb was convinced that the orphan would stay, and he began to plan how he would introduce it to the camp when they were rescued.

Always the optimist, it never occurred to Oreb that they might never be found, but Nonita became more cross and less hopeful with the passing hours. Still, with the cub as a playmate, she was content to stay in the cramped shelter while Oreb tended to the chores of cooking meat and gathering wood.

When it stopped raining, Oreb ventured forth from the shelter of the ledge and looked around to see if anyone was coming to rescue them yet. Wild game had beaten out a trail that led to the right, down the hill, and out of sight in the forest two hundred yards away. He glanced down it and saw someone walking toward him. He didn't expect anybody from the camp to be coming from that direction, so he backed into the undergrowth at the side of the trail and watched.

The man was plodding along slowly, his head bent toward the ground. Oreb suddenly realized that the stranger on the mountain was a Lamanite. He watched him stop and look toward the side of the narrow trail, then start forward again. Oreb's heart pounded and sweat poured from his face. He thought of his pretty little sister and the danger she would be in if their enemy should find her. That disturbing thought prompted him to fit an arrow to his bow and pull the string taut. He took careful aim.

Oreb had never shot at a human being, and the thought of it made him shudder. He steadied himself, thinking of the danger that this Lamanite presented. He decided he had to shoot. At that precise moment, a white man joined the plodding Lamanite from the side of the trail.

Oreb hesitated, squinted, shook his head, dropped his bow and launched himself onto the trail and down the hill with a wild cry of surprise. "Sam! Sam!" he screamed at the top of his lungs, his stocky legs carrying him forward at breakneck speed and into the arms of his shocked, long lost brother.

Oreb was hugging Samuel and crying unashamedly in his strong arms when Nonita dashed into the trail and shot toward them, shouting, "Sam, you're home, you're home!" Tears streamed down her face as Samuel scooped her off the ground and pressed her to his chest.

It took Samuel a moment to find his voice. When he did, he asked, "Where are Mother and Father? Are they just up ahead?"

Oreb looked at him sheepishly and said, "No, we don't know where they are. We're waiting for them to find us."

"What! You mean you two are lost? How long have you been away from the others? I hope it hasn't been more than an hour or two. Why, Mother and Father will be worried sick!"

"We've been lost for two days, Sam," Nonita chirped with newfound confidence. "We knew that somebody would find us."

"Two days! You two must be starved," Samuel said with concern. "Here, I have some dried meat. You better eat before we look for the camp."

"Oh, we're not hungry, Sam," Oreb said.

"Oreb shot a deer yesterday, and we've been eating it," Nonita explained. Samuel looked properly impressed.

Gadoni had said nothing to this point but now he shouted, "Look! a jaguar cub in the trail. We better get out of here fast. Its mother may not like us getting so close to it. They can be fierce when their young are in danger, you know."

"Oh, that's just Snap," Nonita said hurriedly, revealing to Oreb the name she had decided on for the little cub. "His mother tried to get us, but Oreb shot her and we decided to keep him." She squirmed from Samuel's arms, propelling herself up the trail and scooping the cub off the ground.

Samuel watched the incredible scene with his mouth gaping. Oreb grinned and said, "Kind of surprised, aren't you, Sam? Didn't think I could shoot that well, did you?" His round eyes twinkled with childish delight.

"It is hard to believe," Samuel admitted.

"Well, I'll prove it. Come on, you and . . ." he stopped in mid sentence as he suddenly remembered the Lamanite and gaped at him. "You're Gadoni!" he shouted, as he recognized the stocky, brown-skinned young man.

"Yes, Oreb, this is Gadoni. He's my friend. He saved my life. Gadoni, you've seen Oreb before. Well, here he is. He's just like I told you, isn't he? Always full of surprises."

"You're Sam's friend? But I nearly shot you!" Oreb said in horror. "I'm sorry. I didn't know that . . ."

"I'm glad you didn't, Oreb," Gadoni smiled, reaching for Oreb's hand and shaking it in Nephite fashion. "I hope we can be friends, too."

"If you're a friend of Sam's, then you're a friend of mine," Oreb said.

They hadn't noticed Nonita coming back down the trail, the cub in her arms. "You're the man that stole Ophera," she observed gravely.

"Yes, I'm the one," Gadoni agreed. "I'm very sorry about all that. I hope everyone can forgive me. Is Ophera a friend of yours?" he asked.

"Yes, and a friend of Sam's, too. But she kind of likes Jashan now," the little girl said innocently.

"Jashan!" Sam thundered. "What's he doing with our people?"

"He's just one of the soldiers that are helping us."

"He hangs around Ophera a lot," Oreb agreed, "but I don't like him."

Gadoni wasn't through with Nonita yet and cut off the talk about Ophera and her friend Jashan with a question. "Do you forgive me?" he asked Nonita.

"For what?" she asked having already accepted Gadoni as Samuel's friend.

"For what I did to Ophera?" he pressed.

"Oh, that. If Sam likes you, so do I," she said and dismissed the subject by starting up the trail toward the ledge.

"We better find the others," Samuel said, still fussing to himself about Jashan. "Oreb, do you have a general idea which way we should go? I don't want Father or Mother to worry any more than they have to."

Oreb felt a queasiness in his stomach at the mention of his parents. "Sam, Mother is very sick," he said, choking back a sob. "She has a fever. She can't even get up. A lot of people are sick"

"Are the people camped, waiting for Mother and the others to get well?" Samuel asked.

"Yes. Father made them stop. Jashan and some of the other

soldiers didn't want to, but Father got angry and said they would just have to wait until the sick ones were well. He said too many people had died already, and he didn't want to have it happen to anymore."

Oreb quickly went on, reciting another problem. "Some of the soldiers don't like us, Samuel. Father says they want to go back with the army. Jashan is one of them. Right after Ophera's grandfather died, he told her there were too many old people. He wanted to take the rest of us and let the old ones come when they could. Father really got angry when he heard that. He told Captain Siron that he better straighten out the soldiers before there was trouble."

"Did old Lib die of the fever?" Samuel asked.

"Oh, no," Oreb responded. "He fell off the trail and got all busted up."

"How did he fall?" Samuel asked.

"The soldiers said he got too close to the edge. It was on a narrow trail, and Jashan said they tried to catch him, but couldn't."

Samuel looked suspicious, "Did anyone besides the soldiers see him fall?"

"No. They were the only ones that saw the others, too."

"Others!" Samuel exclaimed, casting a doubtful glance in Gadoni's direction.

"Yes, some of the other old people," Oreb explained.

Samuel shook his head angrily, then changed the subject. "How is Father?" he asked.

"Oh, he's okay. He walks kind of funny and slow, but he tries to keep everybody happy."

Nonita and the cub had begun to play under the ledge. Samuel rounded them up while Oreb collected the remainder of his meat and followed Gadoni, who had already started up the mountain. Several hours later they met a party of searchers, who greeted them happily. Oreb was surprised at how far he and Nonita had wandered.

"They have found the children!" someone shouted as they entered the camp.

"The children are found," someone else echoed.

Latoni stepped from his tent, looking haggard and worn. He

126

brightened when Nonita scrambled into his arms, and he hugged Oreb tightly. When he saw Samuel approach him, Latoni's face registered utter amazement.

"Sam. Oh my son, Sam," he choked and not another word made it past his trembling lips.

Samuel embraced his father and said, "It's good to see you again, Father. It's been so long." Nodding toward Gadoni, he went on, "This is my friend, Gadoni. You remember him. He rescued me from Antium and the Lamanite army."

The tired man smiled weakly and extended an unquestioning hand to Gadoni in friendship and welcome. Gadoni, with a look of profound relief, shook it firmly.

"So it was Antium again," Latoni said. "What does he have against us?

"He sure doesn't like Gadoni and me," Samuel said with a chuckle. "We'll tell you more about that later."

"Sam," Latoni said, "Oreb and Nonita have been lost for over two days. They just now were returned to camp." He smiled at his two younger children and said to them, "So where have you two little urchins been, anyway? You have had us very worried."

"We were down the mountain. We made a camp and were waiting for someone to find us, just like you always said," Oreb explained briefly, his chest puffed out with pride.

"And that is where they were when Gadoni and I found them this morning," Samuel added.

"You mean that you found them?" Latoni asked incredulously.

"Well, stumbled onto them is more like it."

"Actually, Oreb found *us*," Gadoni said lightly. "He was going to shoot me but he saw Samuel just in time. He wasn't going to take any chances on anyone hurting his little sister."

"This is unbelievable," Latoni said with a hearty laugh. "And I can't wait to hear about that cat!" he exclaimed as he watched Nonita pick up the cub. "I'll bet there's a story behind that little creature."

"You'll never believe it, Father. Let's go see Mother," Samuel said with a twinkle in his eye.

"Yes, come. All of you, come. She'll be so relieved to see the three of you—four of you. You come too, Gadoni. She's very ill, but I'm sure that the return of her children is just what she needs."

Gadoni followed but lingered near the tent flap as the others entered and approached Sarah. She slowly turned her head toward them at Latoni's voice. "Mother, there is someone here to see you."

Her pained eyes fell on Samuel. Completely stunned, she reached a frail, hot hand in his direction and he took it reverently as he knelt beside her. "God bless you, my son," she whispered. "You've come back. Oh, how I have prayed for this day." Her sunken eyes wept tears of joy.

"Mother, Oreb and Nonita are back, too," Samuel comforted her. In the dim light her eyes rested on Oreb's repentant face and then on Nonita standing beside him, equally penitent for the worry they had caused. Sarah reached for Oreb and Nonita, pulling them both close.

"I'm sorry I got lost, Mother. I didn't mean to worry you," little Nonita sobbed.

"I'm sorry, too," Oreb echoed. "I promise I won't ever worry you again. I took good care of Nonita for you, Mother. I didn't let the jaguar get her, and I killed a deer to feed her."

Surprise and love showed on Sarah's face as she listened to her son proudly recount his heroics. Happily he accepted her praise. "You are so brave. Thank you for watching over your sister. And Sam, you are here now too. I'm so grateful to have you all back."

Latoni pulled back the tent flap. "Sarah, there is someone else you'll want to see. Gadoni, come in and say hello to Sarah." Sarah's eyes opened wide at the sight of the young Lamanite who stepped shyly into the tent.

"Mother, he saved my life. We are brothers now," Samuel hastened to explain. "And he swore an oath to Captain Moroni."

Sarah studied Gadoni's dark face for a long moment then said, "If you have taken an oath of peace, you are welcome in my family." No more needed to be said. Gadoni had been accepted without reservation.

He smiled.

Latoni said, "We must all leave now and let Mother rest. We can visit later."

Around the campfire that night, the people sat up late and listened to the many stories recited by Latoni's children and by Gadoni. Samuel answered question after question. As he talked, he noticed Ophera, sitting quietly near the edge of the circle. She was more beautiful than he had remembered, and his eyes kept drifting her way. He longed to speak to her, but the words of little Nonita kept coming to his mind, triggering feelings of anger and jealousy.

Latoni was cheerful all evening. The return of his children had lifted his sagging shoulders, brought the light back into his sad eyes, smoothed the wrinkles on his brow, and even made his limp less pronounced. Samuel watched him swell with pride as each tale of courage and ingenuity unfolded.

The next morning, Latoni summoned his children early. "Your mother is not feeling any better this morning," he said, "but she seems much more at peace. She wants us all to come see her."

When they entered the tent, Samuel was conscious of Sarah's heavy and irregular breathing. She insisted on holding the hands of each child in turn and speaking of her love and gratitude for them. She spoke with difficulty, pausing frequently to draw in each ragged breath. She spoke words of comfort and advice to each of them, concluding, "Latoni, we have been truly blessed with good children. They will go far. Please take good care of them."

Samuel blinked back his tears. Sarah smiled at them all—a tender, loving smile. Her eyes slowly closed. Latoni knelt motionless at his wife's side, a single tear wending its way down a whiskered cheek. Samuel gently placed his hand on his mother's still, white cheek.

Her gently smiling face was at peace at last. Sarah had passed life's greatest tests like the queen she truly was. With unwavering faith that God would watch over her little family, she obeyed his final call and slipped quietly away.

Sarah was buried beneath a massive pine tree, far taller than its neighbors. Its impressive presence warned all that it would jealously guard the hallowed spot beneath its limbs. As Samuel looked for the last time at the little mound of dirt, a silvery beam of sunlight penetrated the branches of the great tree, illuminating the humble grave. At this, Latoni said, "Sam, we have been given a sign that your mother will be unmolested until the day that she comes forth from this sacred spot. May we always remember the beautiful example she was to us." Head bowed, he turned and limped away.

Ahead of the group of Nephites lay some of the most dangerous mountain passes in the entire wilderness. Samuel and Latoni turned their attention to safely leading the brave people of Gilead up the narrow trails and down the steep slopes as they sought a way through the wilderness. Captain Omni had wisely advised Captain Siron and Latoni to avoid paths known to the Lamanites, so they were struggling through rugged terrain.

Nonita mourned for her mother and shared her grief with Snap, wetting the little jaguar's shiny coat with hot, bitter tears. She was seldom seen far from her cub. Oreb spent much of his time with the two of them, encouraging and lifting the little girl's spirits as he bravely rose above his own hurt.

It was Oreb who took full responsibility for feeding the jaguar. Each day he carried his bow and shot rabbits, squirrels and other small game for it. The cub grew with amazing speed under the loving and constant care of the two children.

Kamina, Ophera's widowed mother, had developed a strong bond with Sarah's children during the days following the captivity in Shurr. Now she helped to care for them in every way she could: cooking meals, keeping the little ones clean, and encouraging Nonita whenever she was particularly blue.

Except for some of the soldiers, Gadoni was accepted by the people without reservation. He pitched in and helped anyone who needed it, especially the elderly. When he did come in contact with the resentful soldiers, he would simply ignore their taunts and jeers.

"You're a better man than they are, Gadoni," Samuel told him, "and you have proven it by your actions. They would do well to follow your example."

Samuel, like Gadoni, did what he could to lighten the burdens of others as they traveled. He spread cheer and encouragement through the company. His presence took much of the burden of leadership off Latoni's shoulders.

Latoni was a rock. His heart ached as he felt, each day, the bitter sting of his beloved Sarah's death, but he never broke down or showed discouragement in the presence of the people. Under his leadership, they never gave up, no matter how difficult the traveling became.

Ophera was a mystery. She seldom spoke to Samuel, and when she did, her words were impersonal, almost curt. When Samuel's family shared meals with Kamina's family, Ophera didn't seem to know Samuel was there.

Occasionally, Samuel saw her talking with Jashan although Jashan had done nothing to acknowledge Samuel beyond a mere nod. Jashan was the leader of the soldiers who taunted Gadoni, although he was careful not to do so in Ophera's presence. Samuel knew there would be trouble with Jashan sometime and hoped that when it happened it would not create a bigger gulf between Ophera and himself than already existed. When a confrontation came, he was determined to do what he had to do and not let his feelings for Ophera interfere.

CHAPTER ELEVEN

As THE NEPHITE GROUP EASED THEIR WAY AROUND THE edge of a deep ravine on a narrow, rocky trail that would defy the most able of travelers, Samuel complained, "Father, if this trail gets any steeper, we won't be able to get the people through. I just don't see how we can get the women and children across any place worse than this." They were going over the summit of the highest mountain pass, and beyond were miles of craggy peaks shrouded in clouds.

"Faith, my son—you must have faith. I'm sure this will be the most difficult part of the trip." With an encouraging smile, Latoni went on. "You must admit that this is a path not likely to be used by the Lamanite armies. So we are safe from them, anyway."

Samuel knew Latoni was right, and he paused to look out over the magnificent view below him. It nearly took his breath away. He shivered as a cold wind whipped his bare face and arms. He leaned against the rock to his back. The view made him dizzy.

"Don't look down, son," Latoni cautioned. "It can draw a man right over the edge when he looks into the depths of a steep canyon. We need to hurry past here and leave these supplies and go back to help the others."

Samuel moved cautiously forward and was relieved to see a long, sloping plateau appear beyond the next bend. "I'm glad it looks better ahead. I was afraid we would have to travel a lot farther before we got off that ledge."

"The worst is behind us, son. Now it will take us the rest of the morning to help the others. Then we will have lunch over there," he said, pointing to a grassy area at the base of a steep wall of solid grey rock that rose for hundreds of feet above the plateau.

Samuel thought about the deep canyons, long slide-rock passes and cold mountain streams they had crossed. It hadn't been all that bad for him, but he knew that the women, children, and older people had suffered. He had heard few complaints, though, except from the soldiers, who were constantly moaning about the cold and rugged conditions and their longing to rejoin their army.

It was past noon before all the people and supplies were on the rocky plateau. The morning had brought another tragedy with the loss of an elderly woman who had fallen to her death. Jashan and the other soldier who had been escorting her when it happened explained that she had slipped. Samuel, ever suspicious, wondered what had really happened.

A meager meal was served by the women while the men tended to a camp full of blistered feet, bruises, and cuts suffered during the morning's difficult trek. The soldiers, resting a short distance from the others, tended to their own needs while complaining loudly about their misfortunes.

When he had a chance to speak with him alone, Samuel remarked to Latoni, "I think we'd be better off without them, Father."

"We need their help, Sam. It would be much more difficult if we didn't have them to carry some of the small children and the supplies," Latoni responded.

"There have been many accidents," Gadoni observed somberly. His eyes met Samuel's, and though he said no more, Samuel was sure that he too suspected that the accidents were not as accidental as the soldiers would have them believe.

After a moment of reflection, Samuel said, "Father, Gadoni and I will help the elderly and children from now on. We don't need to depend on the soldiers for that."

Latoni relented. "It'll slow us down, but I'll speak to Captain Siron. The soldiers could spend their time hunting for meat and going ahead to scout out the best trails," he said.

After Latoni had talked to the captain, he explained the decision to the people. They appeared relieved and agreed with the decision. Only Ophera spoke in opposition. "I think you're being unfair," she said hotly. "They're good soldiers. I can't believe you suspect them of killing anyone."

The tension crackled in the air when Opera said plainly what had only been inferred by others. Kamina spoke up quickly. "Ophera, no one has accused them. We are just worried. And surely you can see the attitude of those men. They . . ."

"Their attitude is just fine," Ophera cut in curtly. "You don't understand them, that's all!" She stormed off.

"I don't understand what's gotten into her," Kamina said in a worried voice. "She never used to act like this. I wish I knew what to do. Oh, if only her father were here."

Oreb, observant as ever, was not one to beat around the bush. "I know what her problem is. It's Jashan. He's awful."

Attempting to put an end to the tension, Latoni said, "It's time to get on our way again. We don't want to spend the night up here. We'd all freeze. I'll ask the captain to move his men out ahead and we'll follow."

The people began preparations to continue their journey as Latoni limped off to find young Captain Siron. Nonita scampered after her young jaguar. "Come here, Snap," she shouted, her voice full of childish laughter.

Samuel watched them and chuckled when the cub outdistanced Nonita and darted through a group of the soldiers. "Snap," he heard her call. "Come here, Snap."

The cub stopped just beyond the soldiers and cocked his head, listening to the call of his mistress. Finally obeying Nonita, Snap started to trot back. As Samuel approached, unobserved, behind the soldiers, one of them pulled an arrow from his quiver, fitted it to his bow, and aimed it in the direction of the little jaguar. Samuel shouted, "Don't shoot that cat!" and charged into the midst of the soldiers.

Samuel dove against the archer just as he let his arrow fly. The arrow went wild and missed the cub. The angry soldier turned on Samuel, striking him across the chest with his bow. Samuel stumbled backward, regained his footing, and dove at his opponent's midsection. The other soldiers quickly formed a circle around the fighters and were loudly cheering their champion on.

In the urgency of the moment, Samuel had not recognized the

archer, but now as his opponent sprang toward him, bow still in his hand, he saw that it was Jashan. The thought flashed through his mind that if he would kill old people, it should be no surprise that he would kill a child's pet. Samuel stepped back as Jashan swung his bow toward him. He caught the bow with both hands, wrenching it from Jashan's grip and hurling it over the heads of the other soldiers. Relieved of his bow, Jashan began to throw punches at Samuel in earnest. Samuel fought back fiercely, righteous indignation giving force to his own fists.

Samuel soon began to dominate the fight, and the soldiers gave way as he backed Jashan down the slope, throwing punch after punch. At last Jashan stumbled backward, landing on the ground. Given a moment's reprieve, Samuel leaned over, his hands on his knees, trying to get his wind back.

Without warning, Jashan sprang to his feet and came at Samuel with a knife. Darting aside, Samuel pulled his own golden-hilted knife from its sheath and the two circled each other, their knives flashing menacingly in the sun.

The shouting of the soldiers and Nonita's screaming brought several people running to the scene. In the lead was Gadoni, followed closely by Captain Siron. They broke through the ring of cheering soldiers, the captain shouting at Jashan to put his knife away. Jashan made one last thrust at Samuel then, with a snarl, obeyed.

"You men get ready to move on. There will be no more of this. We are here to protect these people, not fight them," Captain Siron shouted.

Jashan glared at Samuel and said, "Don't ever touch me again or you're dead."

Samuel's dark eyes flashed with anger. "And don't you ever try to shoot my sister's cat again, or I'll break every bone in your body." He strode angrily from the circle, Gadoni at his side.

"What happened back there?" Gadoni asked.

"Jashan tried to kill the jaguar cub," Samuel answered, still seething. "I hit him just as he shot an arrow and made him miss, so he smashed me with his bow and the fight was on, I guess."

Latoni, limping and out of breath, caught up with them. "What's going on, Sam?" he demanded.

135

Samuel repeated what he had just told Gadoni, and Latoni said, "I am afraid that young man is going to be even more trouble from now on." He looked at Samuel, whose nose and mouth were bleeding. "Son," he went on, "you've got to be very careful now. You never know what Jashan might try next."

A moment later, Samuel noticed Ophera standing by her mother. He was still caked with blood but was surprised by the look of concern that crossed her face. Without a word, he walked by her. Behind him he heard Oreb say, "Sam just beat the daylights out of Jashan. I'll bet he'll never try to shoot Snap again. And the next time he pulls his knife on Sam, I'll shoot him."

Latoni put an end to Oreb's tough talk by grabbing him at the nape of the neck and swatting him across the rear. "We do not talk like that, young man, nor do we act like that. If you don't want to lose that bow, then don't you ever let me hear you talk about shooting anyone—ever! Do you hear me?" he demanded.

"Yes, Father. I'm sorry." Oreb hung his head in embarrassment as he plodded after Samuel.

Samuel looked over his shoulder. He reddened when he caught Ophera looking at him. He wondered why he couldn't just forget about her. She was nothing but an irritation to him anymore. He had to get her out of his mind.

His resolve was not helped that evening as his family joined hers for dinner. Several times he caught her watching him; when that happened, he dropped his head.

Samuel ate quickly and finished first. He thanked Kamina and walked off into the darkness. When he was out of sight of the fire, he let the sounds and smells of the high mountain night soothe his troubled mind. The stars were shining and a clear quarter moon was approaching the gigantic peaks behind him. The bubbling sound of running water caressed his ears like music. The sound was carried by the whistling wind blowing lightly from the west, down the ridge they had traversed that afternoon. The air was clean and refreshing. He inhaled deeply, savoring its sweetness.

He thought he heard steps behind him, but when he looked back he saw only large boulders, long since rolled down from the heights above, standing like grey sentinels across the gently sloping plateau. He sought out the stream and followed it to its source. It was a clear gushing spring that erupted from the base of a large slide-rock mountainside.

He knelt beside the pool of pure water which formed below the spring. He could see the pale yellow reflection of the moon rocking rhythmically on the soft ripples. He dipped his hand in, and the reflection shattered into a thousand glittering points of light. He splashed cold water on his bruised and swollen face, numbing the pain that lingered from the fight with Jashan. A second time he thought he heard footsteps and listened intently, but heard only the gurgling spring and the whistling wind. Looking heavenward, he watched the moon float ever nearer the top of the mountain. He looked back into the pool, and saw the moon again, gently rocking on the surface of the water.

He closed his eyes and rubbed them with his hands. He saw Ophera's radiant face staring at him from the inside of his closed eyelids, and he thought of her again—of the fun she had been when they played together as children and how close they had become while in Shurr. He just couldn't understand how she could be friends now with someone as full of hate as Jashan.

Jashan's image replaced hers in his mind, and he could see the evil sneer on Jashan's face. His was a handsome face, yet it shared a sinister quality with Antium. In fact, Samuel thought, Jashan really is a lot like Antium in many ways. He felt sure Jashan would stoop to anything to get what he wanted. It saddened Samuel that many of the other soldiers in his company were like him. A few were different—more sensitive, more caring. Maybe they would tell what they knew about the old people who had died such mysterious deaths. Maybe they would help bring Jashan and his friends to justice.

Samuel opened his eyes and sought the solace of the reflected moon in his peaceful pool of water. Instead he saw a dim but real reflection of Ophera's face. Startled, he looked up. She was smiling down at him.

He forced himself to speak, trying not to choke on his words. "Hi," he began. "How long have you been standing there?"

Ophera's voice was soft and smooth, reminding him of the gentle ripples in the stream. It was the voice he had loved so long ago. "Oh, not very long," she answered evasively.

"How did you find me?" he asked as he got clumsily to his feet. "I mean, where were you going? Funny you would come to the same place that I did." His words didn't sound right, but before he could say more she answered.

"I followed you. I want to talk to you," she said so softly he almost wondered if it was just the wind he was hearing.

"Why?" he asked, his head swimming with confusion. He had never met anyone that could leave him so bewildered.

"Because I want to tell you I'm sorry. Oh, Sam, I haven't meant to be so rotten to you! What's wrong with me? You've been through so much and have helped so many people, but still I let myself believe you were making things up about Jashan," she said in a voice choked with emotion.

She paused. Samuel said nothing, looking over her shoulder at the large, lichen-covered boulders behind her. He didn't know what to say. Finally she asked, "Sam, why did he try to kill the little jaguar?"

He motioned to a nearby rock. She sat down and he sat beside her. "I know you like Jashan, and I don't want to hurt you by telling you what I think. Let's just forget it, okay?" he said.

"No, I won't forget it!" she snapped. "There must be some reason why he tried to shoot the cat, and I want to know what it is. Did you say something to make him mad?"

Samuel stood abruptly, turning away from her. Over his shoulder he said, "I never spoke a word to him until I tried to stop him from shooting Snap. I'll tell you why he did it if you really want to know. He did it for fun, that's why. He's like Antium; he doesn't need a reason to hurt an animal, *or* a person, for that matter!"

Ophera jumped to her feet and began to head toward the camp, then suddenly stopped and stomped back toward him. He knew he was going to hear from her now. He had really made her mad. He took a deep breath and prepared himself for her scolding, but in the dim moonlight he saw the fire in her eyes fade.

"I know Sam. I knew it all along. I just didn't want to admit it. You're right about him," she said, pressing closer. "That's why I wanted to talk to you. I'm sorry, Sam. Please don't be angry with me."

He felt her warm breath on his cheek and smelled the sweet fragrance of her hair. He felt dizzy and took a step backward. She took one forward, and he took two backward—one too many. He tripped on a rock and tumbled into the pool of cold water. Before he could get to his feet, Ophera was laughing and reaching for him, her face aglow in the moonlight. She gripped his hand and helped him to his feet.

She laughed easily—a happy, infectious laugh. He joined in the laughter, and before long they both had tears streaming down their faces, pain stabbing their sides. Samuel was the first to speak. "I feel like a real fool," he said. "Gadoni would never let me live it down if he'd seen that."

"Well, I'm going to tell him," she teased, turning toward the camp.

Samuel reached out and caught her arm. "No, you aren't," he said, pulling her close to him.

The laughter faded. For a long time they gazed at each other quietly. "You're really something," he said at last.

A few minutes later they walked slowly toward the tents, arm in arm. Neither saw Jashan's angry figure standing in the shadows and cursing beneath his breath as he watched them.

The next day the weary travelers descended to the bottom of a narrow canyon then struggled upward toward yet another high pass. Samuel and Gadoni made repeated trips over the rugged terrain, carefully helping the elderly travellers. By evening the Nephite group had passed over a narrow saddle and descended part way down the other side. They pitched camp on a sparsely grassed slope that lay between a towering rock wall and a treacherous, descending mountainside.

Samuel looked down uncertainly as the last light of day faded. Before him lay the most difficult terrain they had yet encountered. Not only was it steep, but it was covered with rocks and boulders of every size, some so precariously balanced that a child might send them plunging onto the rocks beneath, creating a granite avalanche. The whole mountainside could easily start rolling and sliding into the deep, wooded canyon far below.

When Samuel walked into camp a few minutes later, he heard Jashan's voice, harsh and menacing. "What's the matter, Latoni, are you and that weakling son of yours too good for us? We'll help the people. He and his savage don't need to do our job for us!" he yelled.

"You will obey orders, Jashan." Siron was speaking. The young captain's voice quivered, but he went on, attempting to speak with authority. "I told you yesterday, our mission has changed. We are to go ahead and prepare the trail for the others, and that is what we will do. Now you men get back to camp and get something to eat. We have a hard day ahead of us tomorrow."

Samuel stepped into sight as the soldiers were leaving. He watched Jashan make his way right toward Ophera. "Can we talk a moment, please," he heard him say, the harshness gone from his voice, replaced by a pleading, tender tone. Samuel bristled when she followed him from the camp.

Ophera was not going to be fooled by Jashan again. She had made her mind up firmly after enjoying Samuel's sweet company the evening before. But she was curious to hear what he had to say tonight. He had always treated *her* well, even if he was not kind to others. She had no reason to be afraid of him.

After they were out of sight and sound of the camp, he stopped. "I saw you with Sam last night," he said, not so smoothly now. "You're *my* girl, and don't you forget it! I don't want to see you with him again."

Suddenly, she was afraid. The Jashan that Samuel described was with her now. The one she had let herself get fooled into knowing and liking was an illusion. Trying to keep her voice from betraying her fear, she said, "I belong to no one, Jashan. I'll see whomever I choose and be with whomever I choose, and that will not be you, ever again. I'll find my own way back to camp," she concluded and turned to leave.

Jashan caught her, spun her violently around and slapped her hard across the face. Instinctively her fingers flew to her mouth. When she looked, she saw blood on them. "You swine!" she raged and slapped him back with all her strength.

Before she could get away, he grabbed her again and hit her in the face with a doubled fist. She fell, hitting her head on a rock. Lights flashed in her head and pain shot through her body, then blackness enfolded her. Jashan picked her up and carried her toward the large boulders that were scattered beneath the towering ledges.

Samuel became more worried and less angry with each passing minute. Darkness settled in, and only the slender crescent moon lit the somber plateau. He touched Gadoni lightly on the arm, and the two, without a word, rose and slipped out of camp. They walked quickly in the direction Samuel had seen Jashan and Ophera go. All was still except for the wind that whistled down the face of the towering rock wall. In the distance, they heard the raucous laughter that drifted from the soldiers' camp.

Gadoni's eyes searched the ground, straining in the dim light to find any sign of where Ophera and Jashan might have gone. Samuel watched him suddenly stoop and place his finger on a rock. When he stood up, he said, "Sam, this looks like blood here."

Samuel felt a sudden panic well up within. "He's hurt her!" he cried in alarm.

Gadoni was on his knees studying the ground again. "This way, Sam," he said when he stood up. "I think he's taken her among those rocks over there."

Huge boulders loomed ahead of them. The young men moved silently, but swiftly, stopping abruptly at the sound of Jashan's voice. "When you wake up, Ophera," they heard a cold voice say just beyond the rocks, "you'll find out that I'm not through with you yet! You have a lot to learn and I'm going to teach you!"

Samuel and Gadoni slipped around a massive boulder and came upon Jashan standing over the still form of Ophera. Samuel roared in anger and barreled into Jashan, catching him off guard and knocking him to the ground with a thud. Gadoni was right behind him, and it took the two of them only a minute to subdue Jashan and bind his hands and feet with the cord from his own vest.

Samuel turned his attention to Ophera, leaving Gadoni to finish tightening the knots. She lay motionless on the barren ground. He felt her neck and found a pulse. Her hair was sticky and matted with blood. One eye was puffy and swollen. Tenderly, he picked her up and carried her toward the camp.

After a couple of minutes, she stirred. Holding her close to him, Samuel could see her eyelids flicker. Her right eye opened. The left was swollen shut.

"It's Sam," he said softly.

A whimper escaped her lips, and she held him tightly. "Don't try to talk, Ophera. I'll get you back to camp. Then you can tell me what he did."

"You've got to be careful, Sam," she warned weakly. "He hit me, and he'll hurt you if he finds me with you."

"He's with Gadoni now. He won't be hitting anyone. We're taking him to Captain Siron to be dealt with."

"I shouldn't have come out here with him, but I didn't think he would hurt me. He saw us last night and he told me I better never be seen with you again. I tried to get away, but he caught me," she sobbed.

"You're going to be all right," he said tenderly.

After Samuel brought Ophera back to camp, Kamina tended to her wounds while Samuel joined Gadoni and Latoni who had taken Jashan to the captain.

Siron was furious. "Jashan, you are stripped of your rank and will remain a prisoner until we can have a hearing in Zarahemla after this assignment is completed. You will carry no weapons. You may speak to no one of this party except the soldiers," he ordered.

Jashan spat on the ground in defiance. "Ophera only got what she deserved," he lied. "She hit me and took my knife. I had to knock her down to keep from getting stabbed. She's a bad one, and you'll wish you had never taken her side in this thing before I get through," he threatened.

Sleep did not come easily to Samuel that night as he lay on the hard ground beside Gadoni. Thoughts of Jashan's defiant attitude kept him tossing and turning. The moon had disappeared over the top of the cliffs, and Samuel lay watching the stars twinkle in the sky. They didn't soothe the anger that seethed within him as he thought of Ophera, her eye swollen shut and her head bloodied. He hoped the captain would follow through with his threat to make Jashan stand trial in Zarahemla.

A slight noise startled him. A barely discernible movement at his side told him that Gadoni was also awake and had heard the sound. A dark form moved slowly forward and stopped directly above him. Samuel studied the form through partially opened eyes.

It was Jashan. He raised a knife. Samuel and Gadoni lunged almost in unison, moving swiftly, twisting and diving for Jashan's feet. Jashan fell hard, thrashing about with his knife. Samuel felt a hot, searing pain as the sharp blade sliced his forearm, forcing him to release his grip on Jashan's ankle.

Jashan struggled to his feet, knocking Gadoni into Samuel, sending both young men reeling backward. In an instant their assailant was gone. They followed him to the edge of their camp, but it was too dark to pursue him further.

As they returned to their tent, they found Latoni adding wood to the campfire. In the light of the fire, Latoni spotted a knife on the ground, picked it up, and looked at the two young men. "Is this Jashan's? Did I hear you two scuffling?"

"I thought Jashan was to be held prisoner," Samuel said, "and not to have any weapons."

"I'm afraid that some of the other soldiers are no better than he is. I think we should suggest to the captain in the morning that he send some of his better soldiers ahead of us to guard Jashan. We can't afford to have him here after what he has done. He'll stir up a full scale rebellion if he isn't removed. Are you hurt, Sam?" Latoni asked suddenly.

"It's not bad," Samuel responded. "He just got a little slice of my arm, that's all."

They bandaged his wound and they all tried to sleep.

At the first light of dawn, people were busy preparing their breakfast and getting ready for the dangerous descent that faced them that day. Samuel was anxious to find out what Jashan had done after his attack during the night.

"Sam," Gadoni said, "I don't hear the soldiers. I don't like it."

"Let's get my father and go check things out," Samuel suggested.

None of them were prepared for what they found when they walked into the soldiers' camp. It was completely silent. Several tents remained, but no soldiers were to be seen.

"Father, Captain Siron wouldn't have taken the soldiers ahead of us to work on the trail this early, would he?" Samuel asked doubtfully.

"And taken their provisions but not their tents?" Latoni asked with a scowl. "No, I'm afraid not, Sam. Let's have a look around and see if we can find a clue."

Their search led them into the large field of boulders at the base of the cliff. There they found Siron and six of his men sprawled on the bloody ground. Only two, including the young captain were alive, but their wounds were serious.

"Mutiny," Latoni said sadly after directing the burial of the dead and bringing the wounded to camp to be cared for. "I warned the captain, but he didn't believe they'd do it. These men must have been the only ones who didn't follow Jashan." He pointed toward the fresh graves.

The mutinous band of soldiers had gone ahead of them down the mountain. This was of deep concern to Samuel and the others. "We'll have to camp here until the captain and his man can travel," Latoni announced.

But by the next day, Captain Siron had revived sufficiently to care for himself and his one surviving soldier. He insisted that the rest should go on without them. "You must go on. We can rest here until we're able to go back and find Captain Moroni. He'll want to send men to find Jashan and the others and try them for their crimes," he said.

It was with reluctance that Latoni left them, but he saw that they were well provided for before continuing the difficult trek that must now be accomplished without the questionable aid of the soldiers.

CHAPTER TWELVE

THE DESCENT TO THE WARM, HUMID VALLEY WENT smoothly. No more lives were lost and no serious injuries occurred. The Nephite group camped that night near a major highway. Beyond the highway lay more uninhabited wilderness, yet another mountain range, and then miles of insect-infected jungle. The temptation to take the concrete highway leading northward to Manti was strong, but because of the Lamanite threat, Latoni announced that they would cross the highway in the darkness and travel over the next mountain range, one not nearly as rugged or high as the one they had already crossed.

Samuel and Gadoni were appointed scouts to search for a route through the jungle that lay ahead. They traveled eastward for a few miles and stumbled onto the remains of a recent battle. Bodies lay scattered in front of them, both Lamanite and Nephite. Samuel and Gadoni recognized the Nephite soldiers as those who had traveled with them. But Jashan's body was not among them.

"He probably ran from the fight," Samuel said coldly.

"Probably so," Gadoni agreed. "We better get back to our people and warn them. Whoever did this to these men might still be in the area. We better find out where the Lamanite army is." Samuel nodded, smiling to himself at the way Gadoni now referred to Samuel's people as his people. He was grateful to have found such a loyal friend.

Samuel was alarmed when they spotted the Lamanite army camped only a few miles through the jungle from the little band of Nephites. Nevertheless, he and Gadoni crawled closer to the camp through the dense foliage and determined that the army was a relatively small one of about one thousand warriors.

Determined to learn more about their enemies, the two young men remained near the army until darkness fell. They crawled past the guards toward camp where, concealed in the thick vegetation, they listened to a small band of warriors.

One guard said, "I can't understand why such a small group of soldiers would be alone. They say they were lost and had been wandering for several days. I don't know if I believe that. There must be a large Nephite army nearby. Let's ask the captain to let us scout the area to see if we can locate them. We must know their location if we are to safely deliver these supplies to the armies fighting near the East Sea."

The others agreed. "If we find they aren't strong in numbers, we'll destroy them. If there are too many, we simply avoid them and go our way."

Samuel and Gadoni listened a few more minutes, but the soldiers discussed less interesting matters. Samuel reached over to touch Gadoni as a signal that it was time to go, but his arm froze in midair at another soldier's words.

He apparently had just arrived and had information to share. "The captain thinks he can make the two captives tell the truth. They say one more escaped, but I think they lie. They're trying to make the captain believe the Nephite army is already warned of our presence. We'll soon know. Fire sticks are being prepared now to burn their skin until they tell all they know."

Samuel's mind digested what he had just heard. If the two deserters talked, it would put the people of Gilead in extreme danger. And what of the third man—the one who had escaped? Could it be Jashan, that wily fox? Where was he and what was he doing?

Samuel was anxious to get back to camp and warn the others, but he wanted to learn more. So he and Gadoni gently brushed away the mosquitos that tormented them, endured the endless buzzing of flies in their ears, and waited. The night wore slowly on. Samuel's bones ached and his muscles protested the cramped position. He knew Gadoni suffered equally. At least two hours passed before one of the warriors left to speak to the captain.

When he came back, he was bristling with excitement.

"The Nephites talked. They were easy. We didn't even have to use the fire sticks. At dawn we go in search of their people."

The soldiers questioned him eagerly, and he continued with more news.

"They weren't with an army at all. They were assigned to escort some Nephites—mostly women, children, and a few old men—from the area near the East Sea back to their home near Zarahemla. The Nephites had been prisoners of Captain Jacob and were freed by the armies of Moroni," the warrior said. "If we capture these people, we will gain much honor."

Samuel and Gadoni beat a careful but hasty retreat. When they were clear of the army encampment, they pondered how they might best protect their people. Gadoni had an idea, a disturbing idea, but one that just might work. The two young men took time to pray, then made their decision, clasped hands and parted— Gadoni moving toward the Lamanite army, Samuel toward the Nephites.

Samuel breathlessly entered camp. He sensed immediately that something was wrong. Despite the late hour, people were milling around uneasily. There was tension in the hot, muggy air. Seeking out Latoni, Samuel asked, "What is it? What is wrong?"

Latoni put his arm around his son's shoulders. "Sam," he said, his voice full of concern, "Ophera has disappeared."

"What do you mean, disappeared? She wouldn't run away. How could she just be gone?" Samuel demanded.

"We don't know. Kamina awoke to the sound of a scuffle. She got up to check on her family and Ophera wasn't there."

"Are you saying someone came right into camp and stole her away?"

"Yes, Sam, it seems that way. I can't imagine . . ."

"I can," Samuel cut in, his voice suddenly low and steady. "Jashan!"

"But Jashan is gone . . ." Latoni began.

Samuel explained angrily, "We came upon the place where all but three of the soldiers were killed by a Lamanite army. I guess Jashan and his men were lost and just wandering around. Two that survived the fight were captured but the third got away. It has to be Jashan. And he's taken Ophera! I must find them before he hurts her, Father."

"We'll begin a search as soon as it's light," Latoni said.

"But we can't do that," Samuel protested.

Latoni looked at him in surprise. "But you just said . . ."

"Father, our people must be moved, and quickly. The Lamanite army knows about us. The soldiers told them."

Latoni suddenly remembered his son's scouting partner. "Where is Gadoni?"

Samuel told him Gadoni's plan, which the two young men had irrevocably set into motion. The lines on Latoni's forehead deepened. "This is serious indeed, Sam. Unless Gadoni is successful, we will be at the mercy of the Lamanites—and I'm afraid mercy is exactly what we will *not* receive." Latoni thought a moment, then went on decisively, "We must get the people moving now. We'll go across the valley and into the closest foothills to the north. Once we're on our way, you may go alone and search for Ophera, but son, don't be surprised if you can't find her. Jashan is a desperate and cunning man. Be very, very careful."

In less than an hour the people were feeling their way through the jungle in the pre-dawn darkness, fully aware of the danger and need for haste. Samuel stayed behind. At dawn, he found signs that betrayed the direction Ophera and her captor had gone and he moved swiftly in pursuit.

Ophera had been sleeping soundly when someone clamped an iron hand tightly over her mouth, wrenching her violently to her feet. In spite of her struggles, her captor was by far the stronger. She recognized the familiar smell of Jashan's sweaty body, and it filled her with terror.

It wasn't until they were a good distance from camp that Jashan had finally spoken to her. Roughly, he said, "I don't want to hurt you, but you know I will if you don't do as you're told. You are going with me now. Come along peacefully," he had threatened, "or I'll drag you."

Knowing that he would do as he threatened, Ophera wisely decided to cooperate and look for a chance to escape later. "Okay,

Jashan, you win. I'll go with you. Where are we going?"

He ignored her question and smugly said, "That's better, Ophera. I knew you'd see it my way. We'll get along fine, just like we used to, won't we?"

Ophera decided that her survival depended on going along with him. "Of course, Jashan," she lied, adding in a meek voice, "please take good care of me." For good measure, she forced herself to put her arms around him and lay her head against his chest.

Her guise had worked well. The tension seemed to leave his body, and he had caressed her head gently and said, "We'll go to Zarahemla, but before we do, two of my friends are in trouble and we must help them. I can't tell you more than that. Come, we must be on our way."

Gadoni hesitated for a moment in the pre-dawn darkness. Finally, mustering his courage, he approached the soldier that stood guard at the perimeter of the Lamanite camp.

"I come in peace," he announced to the surprised warrior, his empty hands in front of him and his bow slung over his shoulder. "I have escaped from the Nephite army that is pursuing you. I must speak to your commander at once," he said urgently, beginning his ruse.

After the initial surprise wore off, the Lamanite sentry said, "Come and I'll take you to Captain Lahah."

The captain grumbled at being awakened before the sun had risen, but he became very alert when he heard the story Gadoni had to tell. "Do they actually know our location?" he asked Gadoni after listening quietly for several minutes.

"Yes, they sent a scouting party. The one who made it back to camp said they had been ambushed and that all but he and two others had been killed. I heard everything that dog of a Nephite said. He said you had taken the others prisoner. You have them, don't you?" Gadoni asked innocently.

"We do," Lahah responded. "But how do you, a Lamanite, know so much about the one you say returned?" Lahah asked suspiciously.

"Oh, that was easy," Gadoni answered quickly. "I had them

thinking I would join them. They trusted me. I wasn't even tied up except when I slept, although a Nephite guard followed me everywhere because I wasn't allowed to be alone."

"How did you get away?" Captain Lahah asked.

"When I decided it was time to go, I just hit my Nephite guard over the head, took his weapons, and ran. I don't think anyone saw me go."

Lahah said, "The two prisoners tell quite a different story."

Gadoni forced a chuckle and said, "I'll bet they do. Be careful. They're trying to set a trap for you, I'm sure."

"That's probably what they were trying, all right," Lahah said grimly. "They told us they left a party of escaped Nephite prisoners not far from here. We were going to find and recapture them. We're lucky you escaped. What is the strength of the Nephite army?"

"About three thousand men. More, I would guess, than you have here. And those two you captured, you should know something about them. They are experienced scouts. They always have a story planned in the event of capture." Gadoni had to prepare the captain for their reaction in the event he should have to confront them.

"What else can you tell me about them?" Lahah asked.

"They'll resist but act like cowards and give in rather easily," Gadoni explained, knowing the cowardly nature of the men.

"Yes, they did exactly that!" Lahah exclaimed.

"After that they'll try to earn your trust by giving out information they think you might believe. They may even offer to defect and assist the Lamanite armies. Be careful, Captain Lahah. Nephites are liars and these men are no exception," Gadoni said shrewdly.

"I thank you. You have been a great help. You may have just saved the lives of many brave Lamanite soldiers. By the way, I don't believe you told me your name," the captain said.

"I am Gadoni, and I'm proud to be of service to you, sir," he answered smartly, hoping that he was not overplaying his part.

"Welcome to my army, Gadoni," Lahah said. "We'll move out swiftly when there is enough light. When the Nephites get here, we'll be gone."

Preparations to break camp began immediately. Gadoni was interested in the large number of horses they had. It would make travel more difficult through the jungle for he saw that the horses were led, heavily laden with supplies, not ridden. He remembered that they were trying to get supplies to the Lamanite forces in the area of the East Sea and realized that they needed all the horses to carry the supplies.

Gadoni hoped he would not have to confront the two Nephite prisoners. They would work hard to convince Lahah who he really was, and Gadoni was uncertain who, in the end, would be believed.

Having received an assignment, Gadoni fell in with a group of warriors as the trek began. He wondered how far they would be able to travel that day in the dense jungle, filled with its winding waterways, stagnant lakes and ponds, treacherous marshes, and dense thickets. He was reasonably certain that they would avoid the concrete highway that ran the same direction they were going, only a few miles to the southeast. He hoped they would make good time though, for the sooner a safe distance lay between this army and Sam and his people, the sooner Gadoni could slip away and rejoin Sam.

Samuel was puzzled. Ophera's captor was taking her in the direction of the Lamanite army encampment. A sick feeling came over him when he considered the reasons Jashan—if indeed it was Jashan—might have for making contact with the Lamanites. The thought of Ophera falling into Lamanite hands dismayed him.

He hastened his pace, following the trail that had been so carelessly left. It led him back and forth around swampy, impassible areas but always in the army's direction. At the top of a small rise, near the place he and Gadoni had spied on the Lamanites the night before, Samuel scaled a tall palm tree and looked out over the mass of jungle. He spotted the army, slowly wending its way in an easterly direction. As he clung tightly to his precarious perch and studied the army, he spotted movement across the ravine from him. He watched closely, and saw two people entering a tiny clearing. Then they were gone again. His heart stopped—the long blonde hair, so unusual among his people, could only be Ophera's. She and her captor were about halfway between him and the Lamanites.

Samuel shinnied down the palm tree and ran down the ridge as fast as the terrain would allow. He threw caution to the wind in his haste, fear for Ophera driving him on. The tall grass and shrubbery hid a decaying log and his foot caught it, sending him sprawling headlong into a smelly bog. Pain shot through his right ankle.

He sat down, sweating profusely from the pain and the humid jungle air. He worked his hands over the injured ankle and was relieved to discover that it was not broken. After cutting strips from his vest and binding his ankle, Samuel forced himself to his feet and plodded painfully on. He used a stick to help bear his weight and spare the sprain all the punishment he could, but he made excruciatingly poor time. His heart sank. He didn't see how he could catch Jashan and Ophera before they reached the Lamanites. Still he pressed on.

The leaves and branches that whipped Ophera's face as Jashan pushed her through the jungle were a blur. She stumbled and fell often, scratching and bruising her delicate skin. She was covered with mud and her hair hung in dirty strings around her face. Her body was numb and she wondered at each step if she could take another.

"Jashan," she pleaded, "why are we in such a hurry? Zarahemla is a long way off, and I'll never make it if I don't get some rest."

"My friends need our help," he said roughly. "You may rest for a minute or so, but then we must be on our way again."

Ophera immediately collapsed and stretched her aching body full length in the tall grass. She had barely begun to relax when Jashan forced her back to her feet and on her way again. In a few minutes, Ophera thought she could hear the sound of marching feet echoing through the trees. They came to a clearing and she gasped when she saw the rear of an army of Lamanites fading into the trees on the other side.

She shot an inquiring glance at Jashan, but he forced her on. "We must get past them," he growled.

An hour passed—one that seemed like an eternity to Ophera as she was pushed and prodded to run faster—before Jashan was satisfied that they were ahead of the army. Circling to their right, he pushed Ophera along at an even more rapid pace. When he finally stopped, he caught hold of Ophera's arm and twisted it violently behind her back. She cried out softly, suppressing the impulse to scream because of her fear of the approaching army.

"What are you doing, Jashan?" she sobbed.

"I'm making sure you stay put while I pay a little visit to the Lamanites," he sneered wickedly. "You're going to be ransom for my friends!"

Ophera gasped. "I knew you were evil, but I didn't know how evil until now," she sobbed.

He began tying her hands behind her back with a leather cord. "Poor Orphera," he chanted as he worked, "is going to be a slave to the Lamanites." His cold laughter echoed through the trees.

He tied her deep inside a thicket. "You thought you had me fooled with your sweetness, didn't you? I wasn't fooled for a minute, but it was nice not having to carry you kicking and screaming all the way." His face turned sour and he said with a snarl, "You'd have stuck me in the back with a knife if I'd given you a chance, but I didn't."

He left her there, lonely and terrified. "Sam, oh Sam," she sobbed, "please help me." But only the insects buzzing around her face and a host of chattering monkeys heard her plaintive cries.

"Captain Lahah, there is a Nephite who desires to meet with you. He says he wants to talk about our prisoners," one of the captain's servants announced.

Gadoni's ears pricked up. The army was taking a brief rest, and Gadoni happened to be within earshot of Captain Lahah. He strained to hear every word.

"Bring him here but warn the men to be cautious. This is most unusual," Lahah said.

The servant left and returned in a moment. Gadoni looked up, then quickly turned away when he saw Jashan standing there. Jashan spoke. "I come in peace," he said. "I want to propose a prisoner exchange."

153

Lahah sounded surprised. "What sort of exchange?" he asked. "We have only two prisoners with us."

"I'm here to offer a very valuable person in trade for them."

"What makes you think we are interested in any kind of trade?" Lahah asked.

Jashan plunged on. "I have a beautiful blonde Nephite girl. She would be a good slave and worth far more to you than two soldiers who are already sympathetic to your cause."

Gadoni could scarcely believe his ears. Jashan could only have Ophera! He heard Lahah say, "Bring her here and let me see her."

"Oh, no," Jashan snapped quickly. "I have her hidden. How do I know you wouldn't just take us both? My plan is for you to send one of your men with my friends. I will meet them and we'll make the exchange."

Gadoni's heart was pounding. It almost sounded like Captain Lahah was considering making a deal with Jashan. But he was not ready for the captain's next words. "Bring Gadoni to me. He might know this man."

Jashan protested immediately. "Gadoni!" he said, shocked. "If he's the Gadoni I know, you'd better be on your guard, Captain. He's a defector—to the Nephites, that is."

"I'll be the judge of that," Lahah retorted.

A minute later, Gadoni and Jashan faced each other. "That's him, Captain. He's an enemy to your people!" Jashan shouted.

Lahah ignored Jashan and spoke to Gadoni. "Do you know this man?"

"Yes," Gadoni said, holding his eyes steady on Jashan's face. "This is Jashan. He's one of the Nephite spies I told you about. He has set a trap for you, Captain. You must not trust him!"

Jashan shouted again. "He lies! I come in peace. Gadoni is the one who is deceiving you. I'm no spy. Ask my friends."

Gadoni, his face like granite, called upon Lahah's instincts as a Lamanite. "Do you really believe an honorable Nephite soldier would offer to trade a beautiful girl into our hands? I warn you again. He lies. If you agree to a trade with him, our men will die," Gadoni bluffed.

"Try me," Jashan said. "I don't pretend to be an honorable Nephite. My friends and I know that the cause of the Lamanite nation is just, and we'll prove it if you'll just give us a chance."

Gadoni opened his mouth to speak again, but Lahah cut him off. "That's enough, Gadoni. I can't be any more sure of you than of this Nephite. We'll make the trade, but two men will accompany the prisoners, not just one. We'll soon know who lies."

Gadoni's heart sank. Lahah was right. He would soon know, and when he did, Gadoni would be in serious trouble. There was nothing he could do now but wait.

Jashan was all smiles. "Your men will return with the white girl in about half an hour. Her name is Ophera. She is Gadoni's friend," he sneered.

Gadoni winced at the mention of her name. He knew Samuel would be doing everything he could to find Ophera. Was Samuel walking into a trap, too?

Even though his ankle was throbbing, Samuel forced himself to continue, making the best time he could. He was puzzled why Ophera had been taken past the Lamanite army. Samuel was beyond the army himself now, but he could no longer hear the steady beat of marching feet. The soldiers must be resting, he decided. Suddenly, voices drifted through the trees. He stopped and listened carefully as he fitted an arrow to his bow, ready to fight if necessary. Jashan's unmistakable, cocky voice came to him clearly. "You men wait here. I'll send the girl across. When she starts toward you, you send my friends across, too. Then we'll each go our own way," he instructed.

A Lamanite voice grunted in agreement. Samuel crawled forward and found himself at the edge of a marshy clearing. He could see someone partially concealed in the trees on the other side.

He waited several minutes. Finally, only a few feet to his right, Jashan appeared with Ophera. He shoved her roughly into the clearing and faded back into the trees. The lump in Samuel's throat nearly choked him when he saw Ophera, caked with mud and sobbing. She stumbled and fell to her knees. He wanted to leap from his hiding place and gather her up in his arms, but he forced himself to wait.

Jashan shouted at Ophera, threatening to shoot her with an

arrow if she didn't get up and go. Slowly she got to her feet. She had only gone a few steps when the two Nephite traitors stepped into the clearing on the other side and started toward her. Two Lamanite warriors eased forward, watching the three Nephites as they approached each other through the marsh.

Samuel pulled the string on his bow tight, took careful aim, and let an arrow fly. One of the Lamanites stumbled backward. "Trap!" he cried as he fell to the ground, Samuel's arrow protruding from his chest. Before Samuel could get another arrow ready, the other Lamanite shot an arrow at one of Jashan's friends and fled.

Ophera, in fear and bewilderment, sank to the ground. The other Nephite ran to grab her, and Samuel loosed another arrow, dropping him. He swiftly fitted yet another in his bow and listened for Jashan. Samuel was not surprised to hear Jashan's cowardly footsteps pounding a hasty retreat.

Samuel rushed to Ophera but as he tried to lift her from the ground, she scratched at him, her eyes blurred with tears.

"Ophera, stop it!" Samuel urged gently. "It's me. Sam."

At the sound of his voice she relaxed and let him carry her into the trees. There he sank to the ground, placing Ophera beside him. "Sam," she sobbed, "where did you come from?"

"You didn't think I'd let them get away with kidnapping the prettiest girl in the land, did you, Ophera?" he teased in spite of his weariness.

"I prayed that you would come," she sighed, her tired eyes smiling at him. "But I didn't know if you'd be able to. I'm so glad you came. And Gadoni? I thought he'd be with you."

"He's with the Lamanite army. He . . ."

Before Samuel could finish, Ophera moaned, "Oh, no. You mean he went back to them? I thought he'd never . . ."

Samuel laughed. "Ophera, it was our plan. I'll explain, but we better get out of here first, in case the Lamanites come looking for Jashan."

He helped her to her feet and then, limping badly, led her away from the Lamanite camp. She noticed his limp. "Sam, what's wrong? You can hardly walk!"

"Oh, it hurts a bit now, but with a little rest, it'll be okay. I just sprained my ankle a little. The army is behind us and will be coming this way. We'll have to hide in the foothills to the south and wait for them to get out of the area."

The two travel-weary young people made slow progress. After a grueling hour, they came to a stream which they followed until it led them to some small waterfalls in the foothills. The jungle vegetation was dense, and they had little strength to cut their way through. They crawled deep into the heavy growth to a small, mossy ledge and rested there, feeling quite safe.

"Tell me what Gadoni is doing," Ophera asked after a while. Samuel propped himself on his elbow and related to Ophera all that had taken place over the past day.

"So now," he concluded, "Gadoni should be heading southeast with them again. Maybe my shooting one of the warriors will get them moving even faster. Gadoni will slip away when it's safe."

The two ate a meager meal, and then, lulled by the soothing sounds of falling water and rustling leaves, they slept.

Gadoni had learned to pray, and he did so fervently as he waited for the return of the two warriors who would bring Ophera. Jashan had said half an hour, but it hadn't been that long when one of the men ran into camp like he was being chased by a wild beast.

"Captain Lahah," he screamed, "it was a trap! Gadoni speaks the truth. We must flee or we'll all be killed!"

Gadoni jumped to his feet with the others. Good old Sam, he thought, he came through. How could I have doubted?

Lahah, upon learning of the warrior's death, ordered the army to flee eastward. The fear of death drove them through the jungle like wild animals before a raging fire. Many of the provisions they carried were lost in their senseless flight, and some of their horses were left to die in bogs the careless Lamanites should have avoided.

Gadoni stayed with the army until dark the following day. He had planned to crawl from the encampment under the cover of darkness and leave on foot, but a better idea occurred to him. Late that night, he crawled to the edge of camp where the Lamanites had tethered their remaining horses.

Two men guarded the horses. Gadoni was happy to see each

guard standing alone, far enough from each other that he was able to silently overpower first one, then the other. He chose four of the best animals, loaded three of them lightly with Lamanite provisions, mounted the fourth, and rode into the night.

Samuel awoke when something brushed his face. He opened his eyes and grinned at a round-eyed little monkey who was examining him closely. The monkey scampered away and, chattering a stream of sounds that only his kind could understand, swung quickly into the branches overhead. Samuel laughed, and Ophera, also waking up, rubbed the sleep from her eyes and looked around.

"What is it, Sam?" she asked.

"We have company," he said with a grin.

"What!" she exclaimed, her startled eyes darting around.

"Not people," Samuel said with a laugh, "monkeys." He pointed into the trees.

Ophera looked up and saw a dozen or so of the curious creatures staring at them. "Aren't they cute?" she said after watching them for a few minutes.

"I guess," Samuel said with a wry grin and pulled himself to his feet. "Ow!" he cried, discovering that his swollen ankle was more tender than ever. "Ophera, we may have to stay here a bit longer. I'm afraid I can't walk."

She smiled at him. "I don't mind. I rather enjoy the company. Why don't you sit back down, and I'll pick some wild fruit. There must be some nearby."

He started to protest but obeyed meekly when she gave him a determined glance. "You've done a lot for me. Let me do something for you now."

Ophera disappeared and was soon back with a large bundle of ripe yellow bananas and a large, tempting mushroom. "Here, eat something besides that tiresome jerky," she said, handing him a banana.

They ate and lounged in the silence which was broken only by the pleasant rush of falling water, the cheerful chatter of the monkeys, and the constant chirping and singing of a dozen varieties of gaily colored birds. He admired Ophera, sitting cross-legged against the moss covered rock ledge, her faded skirt pulled modestly across her bare knees. Even with her hair dirty, her face streaked with grime and her clothes torn, she was a picture to behold. She was a mystery he hoped someday he could completely unravel.

Ophera blushed under his gaze. "I'm so dirty, Sam. I must look awful."

"You never look awful, Ophera, but you *are* dirty. Jashan must have taken you through every mud hole in the jungle." He grinned at her.

"Thanks a lot, Sam! You don't look so clean yourself," she said, fussing nevertheless with her badly snarled hair.

"Well, let's explore the stream," Samuel suggested. "Maybe we can find a place where we can get rid of some of this filth. A good soaking might help my ankle feel better, too."

Leaning on Ophera for support, Samuel pointed to where the stream widened into an inviting pool. They slipped into the water, clothes and all.

For the next few minutes they soaked in the pool, schools of sparkling fish darting daringly around them. Afterward, they found a sunny rock and stretched out while the hot rays dried their clothes. The sun made Ophera's skin glow as she brushed her hair, now shining and clean, with a stiff pine bristle.

The following morning, Samuel's ankle was stronger but still too sore to support him. "We must get started back," he told Ophera. "Our families must be terribly worried."

"I'll help you," Ophera offered.

They made very little progress that day and were forced to make camp early. That evening Samuel shot a small deer that wandered into the clearing where they had stopped. Ophera was roasting part of the deer when she asked, "Do you think Gadoni has left the Lamanite army yet?"

"Maybe. I hope he hasn't had any problems. If he's not back with Father and the others when we catch up with them, I . . ."

Ophera stiffened and Samuel jumped to his feet in mid-sentence, stifling a cry of pain. Something was crashing through the trees toward them. Samuel signaled for Ophera to help him, and they slid into the dense foliage where Samuel fitted an arrow to

159

his bowstring and waited. His fingers twitched and tensed, the bow held firmly in his strong hands. As the trees rustled, he braced himself to let the arrow fly.

"Sam!" the loud voice startled him. It was Gadoni! Samuel grinned at the sight of his dark friend on a tall, black horse, leading three more horses behind him. "Hey, Sam," he shouted as he jumped to the ground. "You can come out now. You're safe."

Samuel and Ophera stumbled from the thicket. "Gadoni! Am I glad to see you. I wasn't sure how you'd escape from that army. And I would have really worried if I'd known that you were out stealing horses, too," Samuel said with a chuckle.

"You looked like you were worrying, all right," Gadoni teased. "I sat right over there and watched you two for several minutes," he said, pointing back the way he had come.

"How did you find us, Gadoni?" Ophera asked.

"Saw a little smoke and thought I'd take a closer look. I figured it might be you," he said and grinned. "How about sharing that meat?" he asked.

"You can have all you want, Gadoni," Ophera said as she proceeded to cut a juicy piece from the sizzling roast.

CHAPTER THIRTEEN

THE LITTLE CITY OF GILEAD WAS IN A SHAMBLES WHEN THE people finally returned. Although Latoni had expected a mess, he was not prepared for the sight that met his eyes when he entered the city. Many homes had been burned, others were badly ravaged. Gardens were overgrown, and the streets were so full of grass and weeds that it was difficult to walk through them. Weeks of work would be required to comfortably situate all the people in houses and to make the streets passable.

The people elected Latoni as judge and he began immediately to direct work on the synagogue in the center of town. To provide a place to worship was of utmost importance to him. He also spent a lot of time in his blacksmith shop. Already, people from Zarahemla were calling on him to tend to their horses. No one in the land did better work.

But all his hard work governing the people did not fill the gnawing emptiness inside him. Everything served to remind him of his beloved Sarah, and his heart ached with loneliness. His children were a great comfort to him, but he knew they, too, grieved for Sarah. He ached when he saw his little Nonita without a mother. For some time she had taken solace in her little jaguar cub, but it soon outgrew her and chose to spend most of its time with the ever-active Oreb.

Latoni kept Samuel, Gadoni, and Oreb busy hunting. The boys were assigned to keep the town provided with fresh meat so that others could tend to the chores of growing gardens, cleaning the yards, caring for the children and the elderly, and tending to the flocks of sheep and goats. The boys spent most of their time away from Gilead, and whenever they were hunting, Snap was with them.

During one of their visits home, however, Latoni realized that the young jaguar could be a problem. The boys had been home for several days between hunting expeditions, and Oreb had been playing with Josh, Ophera's little brother, and with one of the bigger boys of the village. From his shop window, Latoni could see the older boy teasing Josh until he was in tears, but he decided to let the boys work out their own problem. He even began to chuckle a little when Oreb stepped in and tried to stop the other fellow's bullying. But when the boy angrily hit Oreb, knocking him to the ground, Latoni started toward them.

Before he had gone three steps, Snap bounded from his napping place under a nearby sprawling tree and wedged himself firmly between Oreb and his friend. The cat did not do any harm, and Latoni turned away, but he saw Kamina watching from the door of her house across the street. The stern look on her face told him that she did not approve of the cat.

Latoni tried to escape into the shop, but Kamina had seen him and followed. "Latoni," she said, "I don't mean to cause any hurt to your children, but I think that jaguar may be a danger to the young people of the town. Did you see what he did a minute ago?"

He knew that she knew he had but asked anyway, "You mean when he ran to Oreb?"

"Yes, that's what I mean. I know the animal was only looking out for Oreb and that Oreb was looking out for my Josh, but someone could have been hurt."

"I'm sure you're right," he answered meekly. "The cat is getting quite large, and by birth, it is an animal of the wild."

"That's right, and we never know when the wild in him could come out. I think you had better find a way to get rid of it," she said.

"Couldn't we just tie it up while it's here in town. It can't do any harm when it's out hunting with the boys. I'll build a strong collar and a cage, too, if that would help." Latoni was thinking about how hurt Oreb and Nonita would be if he were to have the tawny animal destroyed.

"Latoni, I'm sorry," Kamina said, her soft blue eyes watching him sympathetically. "That animal really does frighten me."

162

"I understand," he said as she walked toward the door.

She stopped and looked back. "I haven't been very thoughtful lately," she said with a smile. "Would you and your family like to join us for dinner tonight? We would all like that very much."

"I hate to be a bother, Kamina. We . . ." he began.

"It's no bother and you know it. Besides it's lonely without a man around the house. And I know Ophera would like an excuse to see that handsome son of yours. Will you come?"

Latoni looked at her for a moment before responding. There had never been another woman in his life except Sarah, and he felt guilty for what he was feeling now. Suddenly Kamina appeared to him as a vibrant, soft, appealing woman, not just a friend. "I'd love to . . . I mean we'd love to, if you insist."

The blood rushed to his face. He couldn't remember the last time he had blushed, but Kamina laughed as well and said, "And I . . . I mean *we* will be looking forward to this evening." She left before he could say another word, and he was glad. He didn't trust his tangled tongue.

Without thinking, Latoni followed her to the door and stood watching her walk across the street. She was indeed a beautiful woman. Her hair, darker, but not unlike Ophera's, hung loosely down her back, waving in the breeze and reflecting the golden rays of the noonday sun. She was a little shorter than Sarah had been but moved with similar flawless grace and charm.

He smiled to himself in anticipation of the evening ahead then was suddenly embarrassed again when Kamina turned unexpectedly, flashed a warm smile and waved to him. He half lifted his hand then stomped back into the shop, angry at himself for his awkwardness, but enjoying the strange stirring he felt and savoring Kamina's image in his mind.

"We're having dinner with Kamina tonight," Nonita announced to Samuel that afternoon, her little face all aglow.

"That's nice," he said, patting her on the head.

"And Gadoni's invited, too," she added.

"And why wouldn't he be?" Samuel asked. "He's part of the family now."

"I know," she said primly and skipped away.

Samuel sat next to Ophera that evening. He hadn't had much time with her since they had returned to Gilead. There had just been too much to do and he had been gone a lot. She smiled warmly, and his heart raced.

As they enjoyed Kamina's meal, Samuel felt Ophera nudge his leg with her knee. When he looked at her, she was grinning and flicked her head toward his father, who was at one end of the table, and then toward her mother, who was sitting near him.

What Samuel saw caught him by surprise. They were chatting and gazing at each other as if no one else were in the room. Ophera giggled and that got Samuel laughing. Gadoni's restrained chuckle blended in. Laughter is contagious, and before long, the younger children were hooting and carrying on, though they had no idea what they were laughing about.

Latoni looked seriously at Samuel and asked, "Is something funny, son?"

"No," he said quickly. "We were just laughing at a private joke. I don't know what the little ones are laughing about. What's so funny, Nonita?" he asked slyly.

She shrugged her little shoulders and went on laughing. That seemed to satisfy Latoni and he went on with his meal, apparently not noticing the wink Kamina sent Ophera.

After they had finished, Samuel and Ophera stood outside in the warm breeze until Samuel awkwardly asked if she'd like to take a walk. After a few moments of silence, he asked, "What's going on between our folks?"

Ophera smiled and said, "I think my mother is falling for your father. She talks about him quite a bit lately. She even told me she wished that he'd pay more attention to her. She's been very lonely since Father was killed."

"I'm sure my father's been lonely, too," Samuel said, "but I didn't think he'd ever fall for someone else."

"Why not?" Ophera asked. "He's not all that old and my mother is a pretty woman for her age, don't you think?"

"Yes, I guess so. But I don't think Father really looks at her *that* way," he said, trying to convince himself that what he had seen at the dinner table wasn't what it appeared to be.

"You saw them, Sam," Ophera pressed. "Don't tell me your

father isn't falling for her. It's all over his face."

"Oh you think so, do you? Well, I don't!" he countered with such force that the two walked on in strained silence.

The next few weeks brought many more invitations from Kamina to dinner. Kamina and Latoni frequently walked around the town after dinner, and soon the whole town began to talk about their budding romance. Samuel refused to be a part of such conversations, even with Ophera. In fact, he avoided her so the subject wouldn't come up between them.

One day, when Samuel had returned from a hunting trip, Latoni approached him as the three boys were removing the carcasses from the horses' backs. "Sam," Latoni said, "these fellows can finish this work. I need to talk with you."

Samuel followed his father into the musty blacksmith shop. Latoni sat down on a wooden bench, motioning for Samuel to join him. Samuel felt uneasy—as though he were about to have a father and son chat that was different than those they usually enjoyed.

"You fellows brought in quite a lot of game this trip," Latoni began.

"Yes, we had a good hunt. Oreb is really getting to be a good hunter, you know. And Snap actually leads us to some of the game. He's some jaguar. I just wish he didn't have to be caged or tied up all the time he's in town. He would never hurt anyone," he said, hoping to steer this conversation away from what he feared was coming.

"I know you boys all feel that way, but we just can't take any chances with him. It's best this way, but that's not why I asked to speak with you. There's something I want to talk to you about— that I need your blessing for," Latoni said. "I want to ask Kamina to marry me."

Samuel was stunned. Hearing this was more disturbing than he had thought. He studied the far wall of the shop until his father went on. "Well, what do you say, Sam? Do I have your blessing? This is not a light decision, you know. There's more involved here than just the love that Kamina and I have for each other. There are the needs of the children, too. Nonita needs a mother. So does Oreb, for that matter. And little Josh needs a father.

Kamina and I could provide for those needs while we fill our own," he said. "I want you to feel all right about it before I ask her, though."

Samuel wanted to scream out in protest. He knew that Ophera thought that her mother and his father would make a nice match. He also knew the other children would approve. What bothered him was that such a marriage would make Ophera his stepsister! The two of them would be living in the same house as part of the same family!

He opened his mouth to speak, but the words that came out were not the ones he had in his heart. "That would be fine, Father. If it will make you happy, then I wouldn't want to have you do anything else," he said, knowing as he spoke that he could never speak otherwise, for to do so would hurt his father.

"Thank you, son. I'm glad you agree. I was afraid that with your feelings for Ophera this might make you uncomfortable," Latoni said. Samuel squirmed at his father's perceptiveness.

"When do you plan to get married?" he asked.

"Well, I haven't even asked Kamina yet, but I hope she'll agree to be married soon."

"Father, there's also something I need to talk with you about. I've been thinking—for quite a while actually," Samuel began, careful not to let his father know that he had only been thinking about what he was going to say for a few seconds.

"Thinking about what, son?" his father prodded.

"Well, I've been thinking about going away for awhile." The words almost caught in his throat, but he had committed himself, so he went on. "I think the town could get by without me now, and I'd like to go to Zarahemla for awhile."

"What would you do there, son?"

"You know Pachor?"

"You mean the man who was in the village with some horses just a few days ago. The one who lives on a large estate outside of Zarahemla? Yes. A very good man, Pachor."

"I was helping him with his horses while he was here and he told me that if I ever wanted a job working with his horses, all I had to do was show up at his estate," Samuel said, recalling the conversation. At the time he had merely passed it off, but now it was inviting.

"What about Gadoni? What would he do?"

"Pachor said he could go to work there, too."

"Does he want to, though?"

"I don't know, but I plan to ask him. I think he'd want to go if I did. What do you think about us going?" Samuel asked.

"If that's what you want, then do it. You're old enough to make your own decisions now. You'd be missed a lot here, but then I suppose you'd return often to visit," his father said.

"Of course, Father."

"What about Ophera? Does she know what you're planning?"

Samuel took a deep breath. "No, and please don't mention it to her, or anyone else, Father. I'll tell her. I just don't want her to hear it from someone else," he said, not relishing the thought of breaking the news of his rashly made plan. He was not sure that she would like it at all, but, he told himself, it would be best under the circumstances.

"Whatever you say, son. I appreciate your being so understanding. I think if I searched the entire land, I could not find anyone whom I could love as I have come to love Kamina. No, she'll never replace your mother. No one could, and I can't replace Ophera's father to Kamina. We will always hold a special place in our hearts for them alone. Love is like that, son. There's always sufficient love for someone new, yet the love we already feel for others is never diminished."

"Father, I understand and I'm happy for you. I'm happy for Oreb and Nonita, too. But for me, I belong elsewhere for now, and when I'm ready, I'll probably come back for Ophera—if she wants me," he said.

The wedding took place in two weeks. The whole town celebrated. Even the birds and animals seemed pleased, for the town was alive with sweet songs from the trees and the delighted chatter of monkeys and baaing of goats and sheep. It was a beautiful, sunny day with just enough breeze to offset the muggy heat.

Ophera bubbled with excitement. Samuel had seen little of her the past two weeks and the times he was with her dared not mention his plans. He was afraid it would spoil the wedding for her. He and Gadoni had agreed to leave the day after the wedding, so

Samuel could not put off breaking the news to Ophera any longer. She willingly accepted Samuel's invitation to go for a walk that afternoon.

A constant, happy stream of prattle rolled from Ophera's lips as they strolled down the main street of town and beyond. "Where are we going?" she asked when he left the road and started into the trees.

"To the lake," he said. The lake he referred to was only about a mile from Gilead. It was not a large lake and was surrounded on all sides by dense forest. Samuel had spent many contented hours as a boy, fishing and swimming in its warm, shimmering waters. It had become to him a place of solace—a retreat from the pressures of growing up.

"Wonderful," she said. "I haven't been there for a long time."

Ophera chattered on, but Samuel found it hard to talk. His feet were like rocks. His head felt numb. He didn't like what he was doing, but he could see no other way. Gradually, his mood affected Ophera and she grew silent. As they walked the last half mile to the lake, neither said a word.

Samuel's heavy heart lightened slightly when he walked out of the forest to the shores of the lake. The afternoon sun reflected off the clear blue water, throwing rays of light deep into the dark woods. Fish jumped, breaking the perfect smoothness of the water, leaving ripples that grew in ever-widening circles before gradually fading away. Birds of all sizes and colors flew above and swam on the lake. Monkeys and squirrels filled the trees around the shore, and across the lake a little herd of deer grazed lazily on the grass that swept from the water's edge to the moss-covered rocks twenty feet beyond.

Samuel found a fallen tree that lay near the rocky shore, only a few feet from the water. There he invited Ophera to sit down. Sitting beside her, he gazed over the serene lake, taking in its undisturbed beauty. He watched a bright yellow butterfly as it played above the lake. He hoped it didn't get too close and find itself floundering helplessly on the water, much as he was doing at that moment on the shore. Unlike him, however, it seemed to know exactly what it was doing as it rose, then dove, then rose again, playing until it disappeared from his view.

The sun was sinking toward the majestic mountains that towered over the forest to the west. As Samuel watched, his spirits sank along with the sun. The pretty girl at his side had turned seventeen just a few days ago. It wouldn't be many months before he himself was eighteen. It was not uncommon among the Nephites for young couples to begin their lives together at that age or earlier, and Samuel felt sure that if he were to ask, Ophera would say yes. However, he was determined to go through with his own plans.

Mustering his waning courage, he stood up, swung one leg over the tree trunk, and sat facing Ophera. When she turned toward him, his courage nearly failed. Never had she looked more beautiful. The setting sun cast a reddish hue to her glowing face and made her hair appear to burn with a mysterious crimson fire. Her eyes seemed darker than usual, and from their depths came a spell that enveloped him.

With an effort, he shook himself and said at last, "Ophera, what I have to say is not going to be easy, but please listen."

He paused. She said nothing but her eyes grew moist as if she knew what was coming. He swallowed hard and took her hand. "I'm happy for Father and for your mother. He loves her and she'll make him very happy. I'm glad about that, and I know that you are happy for your mother, aren't you?"

"Yes," she whispered.

"In a way, their marriage makes you my sister—little sister," he said, forcing a grin. "I'll never be able to think of you as a sister." The grin faded. "And I could never live in the same house with you as my sister. It just doesn't seem right." He paused for a moment. She gazed steadily into his eyes. "I've never known anyone who made me feel as good as you do or whom I would rather be with than you."

When her eyes became hopeful, Samuel quickly plunged on, not wanting to deceive her. "Ophera, I can't make this easy, so I'll just say it. I've decided to leave Gilead and go to Zarahemla for awhile. Gadoni and I have both been offered jobs there, and we're going to leave tomorrow to work there. Please don't be angry."

Ophera pulled her hand from Samuel's to wipe away the tears that had begun at his words, but more just came to take their place.

"Ophera, let me explain. It's not you. It's me. I need time to work out some things. I'll be back—if that's okay with you," he said softly.

She dabbed her eyes and nodded but didn't look up. Samuel felt his own eyes grow damp as he reached toward her and placed an arm around her neck. She didn't resist, so he pulled her close and let her head rest against his shoulder. For several minutes neither of them spoke. Then Ophera took a deep breath, brushed away her last tears, and pulled away. She stepped near the water's edge and stared out across its glossy surface, now fiery red as it reflected the richness of the sunset.

Without turning, she spoke. "What about me, Sam? You have your plans, but what about me? What am I to do?" Her voice rose slightly, and she trembled as she spoke. "You say you'll be back, but when? Am I to wait for you forever?"

He stepped toward her but stopped when she turned. Her eyes were flashing with anger. "How can you do this, Sam?" she asked in a hard voice.

"I'm . . ."

Her voice grew softer, pleading. "Sam, please don't go. I need you here."

His eyes met hers briefly, then he looked away.

"You're going anyway, aren't you?" she said so softly he could scarcely hear her. "Very well then," she went on. "You go ahead and leave and come back when you're ready. I love you Sam, and you know it, but I'll make you no promises. I may be here waiting when you return, and I may not." Her voice was controlled but full of the hurt he had just inflicted.

Sam stepped closer and took her hand. She resisted slightly, then let him pull her close. He leaned forward and kissed her gently, holding her for a moment. Then, with a sob, she wrenched herself from his arms and began to run toward Gilead.

He didn't follow but stood there until the color was gone from the dying sky. He walked around the lake shore as darkness closed in, listening to the somber sounds of the night that had replaced the cheerful singing and chattering of the day.

The forces that drove him defied his understanding. He knew only that they were more powerful than the tender feelings he felt for Ophera. He longed to chase after her, take her again in his arms, tell her he loved her, and beg her forgiveness, but he could not. He was led by a longing to move on, to seek whatever adventures or dangers awaited him.

The sun was still several minutes from its triumphant appearance in the east when Samuel and Gadoni mounted their horses and waved good-bye to Latoni, Kamina, Oreb, Josh, and Nonita, who stood at the doorway of Latoni's house watching them. Kicking their horses lightly, they whirled and trotted down the main street of Gilead. Samuel looked back just once and caught a glimpse of a girl at the door of Kamina's house. One hand waved, almost imperceptibly. He waved back and rode on, a picture etched in his mind of Ophera's wistful wave as she leaned against the doorpost.

Shortly after noon, Samuel and Gadoni rode through the gates of Zarahemla. Samuel had always been fascinated by the sights and sounds of this great capital city. The main streets were filled with open-front shops and merchants selling and trading goods of an infinite variety. Clothing, jewelry, weapons, furniture, breastplates, shields, cooking utensils, tools of all sorts, fruits, vegetables, grains, and even animals were being traded in noisy confusion.

The streets in the marketplace were filled with people going this way and that, some slowly, others rushing about. Some were pulling carts, others carried baskets on their heads. Many were on horseback, and some rode wagons of every sort and size, pulled by oxen or horses. Still others were leading pack animals, most commonly horses and llamas.

The smell, both rich and repugnant, was unnoticed by all but the unaccustomed visitor. Shouting and laughter filled the air, and occasionally fights broke out among the patrons as they argued over the price of goods. The heat in the city was oppressive, with little shade anywhere.

Unlike the smaller surrounding cities, many of the streets of Zarahemla were paved with stone, and the main highways into and through the city were made of hard, high-quality concrete. The highways were choked with people during the busier hours of the day, the slower traffic keeping to the outer edges while the chariots and galloping horses moved swiftly in the center. Men rode in stout chariots, and Samuel saw an array of fine covered-top carriages carrying the more wealthy people of the city.

Samuel and Gadoni rode slowly down the main route, passing through the very center of town. They stopped while Gadoni admired the great temple there. Surrounding the large stone edifice were several other impressive stone buildings. "Those house the government of our people," Samuel explained to Gadoni.

Some distance beyond the temple, streets lined with trees and shrubs ran in parallel, orderly fashion. Homes had been built close together on both sides of each street, making it possible for thousands of people to live within the protection of the imposing rock walls of Zarahemla. The young men rode west out of the city and several miles beyond. There they found the sprawling estate of Pachor, one of the most wealthy men in all the land of Zarahemla.

Pachor greeted them warmly. "You have come to help care for my horses, I hope," he said. Samuel and Gadoni nodded.

"The son of Latoni, the best blacksmith in all the land, is welcome at my place anytime. So is any friend of his," he said, smiling warmly at Gadoni. "Someday, maybe you'll be as good with the iron as your father, Samuel, but for now, I already know about your skill with animals, and your help is welcome here."

"Thank you, Pachor," Samuel said sincerely, flattered by his compliments.

"Come, I'll show you to your rooms. You'll work and live together. Not everyone shares my love for your people, Gadoni," he said, his bearded face suddenly serious. "But as long as you are with Sam, I trust you will not have problems with any of my servants."

They were led to a long stone structure that housed many men, all servants of Pachor. Samuel and Gadoni were given adjoining rooms, spacious, well-lighted, and furnished. "Over there is the dining hall," Pachor said, pointing to another building that was connected by a stone walk to the living quarters. "Meals are served three times a day. In the morning I'll introduce you to Teor, my foreman. He'll assign you your duties."

"It's so good to have you here. Good help is hard to find these days with so many of the men off fighting with the armies of Captain Moroni."

The next day, they did indeed meet Teor. He did not seem very glad to see them. He put them to work cleaning stables during the morning then brushing and caring for horses in the afternoon. As they worked that day, Samuel was received warmly by the servants. Gadoni was generally ignored. No one was openly rude, but Samuel could hear comments behind their backs. As for the young Lamanite, he pretended not to notice, instead cheerfully greeting those he met and doing more than his share of the work.

"It'll be only a matter of time, Gadoni, until they all like you and respect you just as the people in Gilead do," Samuel told him.

"I hope so," was Gadoni's only reply.

Over the next few weeks they fell into a routine. Before long, one day was like the next and the time passed quickly. They both worked hard, but Samuel soon discovered that he would never be content to spend his whole life working at this kind of labor. He was not lazy, but his heart yearned for excitement and adventure.

One day Samuel said to Gadoni, "Our money is beginning to add up. I think we should stick with it here for a few more months then perhaps move on." Gadoni smiled and agreed.

And so the two young friends were content for the time being to tend Pachor's spirited horses, day after day.

CHAPTER FOURTEEN

"WE HAVE THREE DAYS OFF, GADONI," SAMUEL REMARKED to his friend one morning, trying to appear casual. "Should we visit Gilead?"

Gadoni grinned. "I think Ophera would like that. I'll bet she's getting lonely by now."

"She's probably been too busy to notice—like I have," Samuel said in a matter-of-fact way, unwilling to admit the loneliness he had felt during the weeks he and Gadoni had spent working on Pachor's rambling estate.

It was the middle of a muggy afternoon when they arrived in Gilead and rode their horses down the grass-lined main street. Samuel strolled into the blacksmith shop and informed Latoni that Pachor had sent two horses he wanted re-shod. "It's good to see you two," Latoni said. "How do you like working for Pachor?"

"It's not too bad, Father," Samuel said, choosing not to expound.

"And how about you, Gadoni? How do the people there treat you?" Latoni asked.

"Not too badly. They're not like the people here in Gilead, though. Pachor does have some beautiful horses. I've never worked with finer ones." Gadoni did not expound either.

"How are the children?" Samuel asked.

"They're fine. Oreb and Josh have become the best of friends. They are truly like brothers. They spend a lot of time hunting nearby. They do very well, too."

"And how's the jaguar?" Samuel was nervous and barely heard his father's response to his questions.

"Snap's almost grown now and has become quite an animal. He does whatever Oreb tells him to. I've never seen anything quite like it. Kamina still insists that we keep him caged or locked up when he's in town, but I still don't believe he would hurt anyone," Latoni said with a smile.

"Well, I guess I'll go find Ophera," Samuel said. He was itching to see her, but he tried to speak very casually.

"Oh, that may be a problem." Latoni looked away as he spoke.

"A problem? What do you mean, Father?" Samuel's stomach flip-flopped.

"Well, she decided to go away for awhile, too. She's with her cousin over in Shaloam," he said, still looking away.

"But she said she had no place to go! I thought she'd be here." Samuel was suddenly embarrassed. He hadn't meant to let others see how much he missed her. The disappointment he felt was very bitter indeed.

"I'm sorry, son, but . . ." Latoni began.

"Oh, I just thought if she was around I might see how she was doing," Samuel said, forcing casualness again, then he changed the subject. "So how is Nonita these days?"

Samuel decided not to mention Ophera again. He tried to act like everything was all right the next two days as he visited with his family and helped Latoni catch up on some work, but his heart ached the whole time. It was with relief that he and Gadoni rode out of town the third day. He was not sure how soon he would visit again.

That evening, back at Pachor's, Samuel sensed unrest. He sought out his employer and asked, "Is something wrong? Some of the servants seem agitated."

Pachor wearily invited Samuel to be seated. They were alone. Pachor's brow was creased and his brown eyes troubled.

"Is it about Gadoni? Don't the other servants want him around?" Samuel asked.

"No, no, I wish it were something that simple. The problem is not a new one, but it is serious. A large number of people in Zarahemla want a king. They're becoming quite defiant. With

Moroni so far away fighting the Lamanites, an uprising would be hard for Judge Pahoran to handle."

"The servants, are they . . ."

"They're fine, Sam. I have only good, loyal people here. They are worried like I am about the unrest in the city." The look in Pachor's eye and the tone of his voice left no room for doubt; Pachor trusted his people.

"Do you think it would be best if Gadoni and I left?"

"No. You're two of my best workers, and everyone likes you. Anyway, you're safe here. Even if there is a revolt, and I don't really think it will go that far, we won't be bothered here." Despite Pachor's assurance, Samuel couldn't help but wonder how well Pachor really knew the hearts of all his servants. Samuel knew that some did not approve of Gadoni, and probably not of him, either, because of his friendship with Gadoni.

Later that evening Samuel was able to be alone with Gadoni to tell him what he had learned. Gadoni had something to report as well. "I overheard Teor and several other men talking while I was rubbing down the horses. Teor didn't sound like someone who supports his government. Now that you tell me there's a rebellion brewing, I can't help but think that Teor may be part of it."

The two took a long walk near the border of the estate, seeking privacy from prying ears and eyes. "I don't feel good about staying," Samuel told Gadoni as he looked into the dense jungle that stretched to the south. "I get the urge to move on." The disappointment over not seeing Ophera, coupled with the tension on the estate, made the urge to roam almost irresistible.

"I'd like to go to the land of Melek," Gadoni said.

Samuel wondered why he hadn't thought of the land of Melek himself. Most of the people there had come from the land of Jershon just a few years ago. They were Lamanites by birth, but after being converted by the sons of Mosiah, the last Nephite king, they had sought asylum among the Nephites. Originally they had been given the land of Jershon, but Lamanite invasions made it unsafe there, so they had gone to Melek. Two thousand of their sons, all valiant young men, were fighting under the leadership of the prophet Helaman, now a captain under Moroni.

"Do you think they would accept me?" Gadoni asked.

"Accept you! They'd see you as their own. Better people don't live, my father tells me."

"Let's do it then, Sam. When should we leave?"

"Let's tell Pachor soon so he can find someone to take our places. He's a little shorthanded lately, and I hate to leave him in a bind when he's been so good to us." Samuel turned his back on the beckoning jungle and started back through the fields.

"How far is it to Melek, Sam?"

"It's not too far, about a day's ride to the west," he said, pointing. "There are no armies in that direction or any fighting that I know of. We could take our time and enjoy ourselves. I can hardly wait to get on our way."

The next morning they explained their plans to Pachor, who said, "I didn't expect you two to stay long when you first came. In fact, you've stayed longer than I expected already. I hope the tension in the land isn't the only reason you're going."

Truthfully, Samuel said, "It has a lot to do with it, but we would have gone before long, anyway."

Pachor told them that Teor's cousin was coming to work for him. They could leave as soon as he arrived. "Remember," he said smiling, "you both have a job here anytime you want one and for however long you want to work. I have never employed men who worked harder."

Samuel couldn't help but notice how cold Teor acted that day. He spoke to Samuel only long enough to say that his cousin would start working in two days. Excited, Samuel and Gadoni packed their belongings and their savings and prepared to depart as soon as the new man arrived.

To celebrate their new adventure, Samuel suggested a visit to Zarahemla. "I hear there will be some festivities in the center of town. It'll be our last chance to have some fun before we leave for Melek," Samuel said as he brushed the dark brown coat of a handsome gelding.

Gadoni agreed. "I'd rather not sit around here tonight, anyway. Teor makes me nervous."

"It's settled then. Let's skip dinner and ride in as soon as we're finished. If we're lucky, there may be some pretty girls there."

Gadoni looked up in surprise when Samuel said that. "What

about Ophera?"

"It won't hurt me to get to know a few others. After all, I'm not married to her, you know." Samuel was determined to get her off his mind.

A dance was in process when Samuel and Gadoni arrived at the park near the synagogue where the festivities were being held. "Let's eat first," Samuel said, his stomach reminding him that they had skipped dinner. "Then we'll dance."

"I don't know how to dance," Gadoni said.

Samuel glanced at him and laughed lightly. "Well, my friend, there is no time like the present to learn. If you're going to live among the Nephites, you need to be able to dance like the Nephites."

By the time they had eaten, darkness had settled over the city. Bright torches lit the area with frolicking orange flames, and the sound of many happy voices, drums, and crude string instruments filled the night air. Samuel led Gadoni near the dancers where they lounged for a few minutes, watching the people come and go. None of the reported tension in the city could be felt there that night. Everyone was enjoying the festivities.

Having decided to forget Ophera for the time being, Samuel scanned the crowd and his eyes focused on two attractive girls who were standing under a tall, sprawling tree. As he drifted toward them, one looked up at him. She was short and dark, with long black hair and a pleasing figure. Her dark eyes flashed a friendly greeting.

"I'm Sam, and this is my friend, Gadoni. We were thinking about dancing." He didn't know what else to say, suddenly feeling awkward and out of place.

"I'm Laishita, and I want to dance, too. Where are you from, Sam? I don't remember seeing you around here before." She had taken his arm and her friend, although not introduced, wasted no time in taking Gadoni's. With little break in her friendly, nonstop chatter, Laishita guided Samuel into the dancing throng.

"My father told me about another Samuel," she said, after catching her breath between sentences. "He's some kind of hero, he said. My father was injured badly in the fighting near the city of Bountiful and was sent home by Captain Moroni. He told me that this boy Samuel was given a Medal of Valor by Moroni himself, and the boy wasn't even a soldier."

Intrigued by her story, Samuel asked with a smile, "Did your father say what Samuel did to earn the medal?"

"Rescued some prisoners from a city the Lamanites had taken, I think. But I want to talk about you. You never did tell me where you're from."

Samuel laughed. Up to now she hadn't given him the opportunity. She paused in her chatter to wait for his answer, an unusual occurrence, he guessed. "Gilead," he said.

"Gilead!" she exclaimed. "I bet you'd know the boy Father told me about. He was from Gilead. Have you heard of him? Of course you have, Gilead isn't very big, is it, although I've never been there. He had a friend, a Lamanite who took an oath of peace with Moroni." She looked up at Samuel, her dark round eyes questioning.

Her vitality and vibrancy had caught him up and he was surprised when she stopped dancing. "What's the matter, Laishita? Did I step on your toe or something?" he asked sheepishly.

"What did you say your friend's name is? You know—*him*." She pointed at Gadoni who was trying to dance with Laishita's attractive friend and looking most uncomfortable.

"Gadoni."

"That's what I thought you said. He's a Lamanite, too. This is really strange, you know," she said. "And you're Sam! You're not…?"

Before she could finish, Gadoni and his partner joined them. "Sam, tell this girl I don't know how to dance. She doesn't believe me."

"He doesn't know how to dance, but he's a fast learner. I'll bet you can soon teach him," Samuel said with a grin.

"But Sam, I'm too clumsy," Gadoni protested. "We didn't dance in Gilead. Why do we have to dance here?"

"We would have gotten around to it, Gadoni. We were too busy, that's all. We used to dance there, before the invasion."

The perplexed look on Laishita's face made Samuel laugh. He realized she wanted an answer and wasn't going to be put off any longer. "Are you the same Samuel?" she demanded, her round face looking up at him fiercely.

179

He couldn't resist teasing her a little. "I'm the same Sam I've always been."

Laishita stepped close to him, her face was only inches from his. She smelled so good! "You are, aren't you? Come on, Sam. Admit it."

He grinned and she let out a delighted squeal. "You are! You are," she sang. "I've never met a real war hero before." She suddenly made a fist and hit him playfully on the shoulder.

"What was that for?"

"That was for teasing me," she said. "Now, you have to tell me all about it."

He looked around for Gadoni, who was several feet away again, suffering through a dancing lesson from his persistent partner. He was not having fun. "Well, it's not really a very interesting story," Samuel began and Laishita hit him on the shoulder again. He relented and gave her a brief sketch of the events, never mentioning Ophera, of course, although he thought about her as he talked. Interestingly enough, his thoughts of Ophera weren't as painful as they had been earlier. Laishita was delightful company.

It was late before Samuel reluctantly admitted that it was time to go. Even Gadoni was reluctant. He had finally gotten into the swing of things and was beginning to enjoy himself.

Samuel and Gadoni offered to escort the girls to their homes, and they strolled through the peaceful streets of Zarahemla, pausing momentarily at Laishita's friend's house to see her safely home, then at Laishita's home. Laishita coaxed them to come in and speak with her father, who, she said, would be angry if he knew his daughter had spent the evening with a "war hero" and didn't bring him in. As she spoke, her eyes lingered on Gadoni's face, although it was Samuel she took by the hand. "Come on," she pleaded prettily. "You don't have to stay too long."

As Samuel and Gadoni tied the horses, they exchanged smiles. What rotten luck! Just when he had met this charming girl, they were leaving. He wondered if he and Gadoni should stay a few more days and get to know Laishita better.

Laishita proudly introduced Samuel and Gadoni. Laishita's father reached a hand toward them each. "I am Ethan, and this is my wife, Taritha. It's nice to meet you two."

Samuel saw the pain in Ethan's eyes and the hunching of the shoulders. He wondered what injuries he had suffered in the war. Seeing Laishita's mother, Samuel could easily see how the girl came by her striking good looks.

"Father, these are the young men you told us about. Samuel got the Medal of Valor from Captain Moroni, and Gadoni is his best friend." Ethan's eyes lit up with surprise.

"Well, can you beat that? You're very famous, both of you. It's an honor to have you in my home. And how's Latoni doing?" Ethan asked.

"Quite well, sir. His leg is still numb and he limps badly, but other than that, he's all right. You know him, do you?" Samuel asked, surprised.

"Know him! Why Latoni and I were best of friends. He talked of you often, and of your mother and little brother and sister, too. How are they?"

Samuel's throat tightened. Mention of his mother brought back a flood of memories, and he had trouble finding words. He was grateful when Gadoni came to his rescue and said, "Oreb and Nonita are fine. Sarah, Sam's mother, died of the fever before we ever got to Gilead."

"I'm sorry, Samuel. Your father must have suffered greatly. He did love her so. We talked of Sarah and Taritha often," he said, nodding at his pretty wife. "By the way, Gadoni," Ethan went on, shifting the attention away from Samuel, "Taritha is part Lamanite, too."

Samuel realized then the reason for Laishita's dark beauty and Gadoni brightened. Before long, Taritha and Gadoni were deep in conversation.

For over an hour, with Laishita at his side every moment, Samuel visited with Ethan and Laishita. Gadoni and Taritha eventually joined in, and Samuel was reluctant to say they had to leave. He and Gadoni still had a good ride tonight just getting back to Pachor's estate, and they had work to do in the morning.

Laishita stepped outside the door with them, clinging to Samuel's arm as if she feared to let go. As he said goodnight, Samuel was already feeling the return of the loneliness he had lived with for so many weeks.

Laishita asked him softly, "Will I see you again?"

Samuel's chest tightened. First Ophera, now Laishita. Why did he always have to be going away? Again, he entertained doubts about leaving for Melek so soon. "I hope so," he finally answered.

Laishita returned to the house and Samuel followed Gadoni toward their horses.

"They're gone!" Gadoni exclaimed.

"Who's gone?"

"The horses! They aren't where we left them!"

"That can't be. We tied them tightly." Samuel darted around the dense clump of small trees that hid the hitching rack. They were indeed gone!

Gadoni bent and studied the ground for a moment. "This way, I think," he said, beckoning Samuel to follow. The tracks led behind Ethan's neighbor's house. "Sam, look. I think someone's leading them. They've been stolen!"

Samuel studied the ground for a moment. He could see tracks but was not sure how Gadoni had come to his conclusion. However, there was no questioning his judgement. Someone *had* taken their horses. They followed the tracks for over a mile, cutting behind houses and through groves of trees. The thieves had tried hard to avoid being seen, not that discovery was very likely; the streets were deserted—almost deserted, anyway. Samuel froze when he heard angry shouts and a scuffle beyond a stone wall that surrounded a very large home. At the same moment they heard a familiar horse whinney. "Gadoni, go after our horses. I'll have a quick look over here then join you," Samuel said.

He ran to the wall and hurried to the corner where he dropped to his knees and peeked around. Just a few feet away, three men struggled in the street. There was something familiar about two of them, he thought. Then the third, an unfamiliar man, dropped to the ground. In the light of the moon, Samuel saw clearly an ugly scar over one man's right eye, an arm that was held crookedly. . . . No, thought Samuel, it couldn't be. But, it was . . .

Antium!

And the second man . . . he turned his head and Samuel could see the smug smile on an otherwise handsome face.

Jashan!

That his two worst enemies could be here in Zarahemla, together, was an unthinkable nightmare. Antium should have been dead! How could he have escaped the justice of Captain Moroni? And how had he found Jashan? It was impossible, but here they were. Grim evidence of their evil ways lay almost motionless in the street.

Impulsively, Samuel rushed headlong into the street as Jashan and Antium fled. He gathered the man up in his strong arms and ran back to the secure shadow of the wall. A quick examination of the victim revealed several stab wounds—serious ones, bleeding profusely.

The man, whose life was fading in his arms, spoke, his voice rattling from deep in his throat. "I am Jarohah, a chief judge." There was a pause. Samuel felt helpless. "Those men are part of a rebellion that will overthrow the government." His voice faded and he was quiet again except for the rasping of labored breathing. His body jerked.

He spoke again. "Please . . . get help . . ." He coughed, his body wrenching violently, his face creased with pain. Then his body relaxed, his head dropping at an awkward angle onto Samuel's blood-drenched arm.

Jarohah was dead.

Samuel laid him carefully on the ground, straightening his long blood stained robe—he didn't know why. Then he ran back in the direction they had heard the horses. Gadoni wasn't there! A horse snorted, and Samuel dove behind a tree. A second later, Gadoni emerged from the shadows, leading his black gelding.

"Where did you find him?" Samuel asked in a forced whisper. Before Gadoni could answer, he went on, "The rebellion has begun and a chief judge was just murdered by Antium and . . ."

"Jashan," Gadoni finished. "He has your horse. I spotted both horses tied to a tree and had just untied them when Jashan and Antium spotted me. They frightened the horses and yours got away from me. Jashan caught it and he and Antium rode away on it."

"Did they recognize you?" Samuel asked, alarmed.

"I don't know, but I doubt it. They would have come after me if they had, but they just seemed to want to get away."

"That's what we better do," Samuel said. Gadoni mounted his horse and Samuel scrambled on behind him and spoke in Gadoni's ear. "Let's return to Ethan's house. He'll know what to do."

In a few minutes, Samuel was at the door, pounding loudly. He paced nervously as he waited, then pounded again. "Who is it and what do you want at my house this time of night?" It was Ethan's voice.

"It's Sam. I need to talk to you." His voice trembled. Ethan appeared from the shrubbery, a sword in his hand.

Ethan pushed the door open with effort. He was not very strong. Taritha, Laishita, and her little brother emerged from a back room when Ethan called out, "It's all right. It's just Sam." He turned to Samuel and said, "I'm sorry about the sword. I hope I didn't frighten you. I had no idea who it could be pounding on my door so late at night."

"There's trouble in the city." Samuel was still shaken by the ghostly reappearance of Antium and Jashan.

"Sam, you're covered with blood," Laishita cried out as she rushed to him. "Are you hurt?"

The wide, glistening eyes looking up at him were almost enough to make him forget what he was there for. "No," he said, "but I just saw a man killed."

"Who?" Ethan asked grimly.

"Jarohah."

"He's one of the chief judges. But how do you know it was Jarohah?" Ethan asked.

"He told me his name. I know who killed him. I saw them do it."

"Slow down, Sam, " Ethan said calmly, " and start at the beginning. Laishita, get some water so you can wash some of the blood off the poor boy."

When Samuel had finished, Ethan paced the floor, into the moonlight and out of it. Finally, he stopped and said, "You and Gadoni better ride for Pachor's place, but be careful at the walls of the city. They may try to stop you there. I'll take over from here. Don't worry, there are others who will help. We have dreaded the very thing that has happened tonight. I just hope that Judge Pahoran, our righteous Chief Judge, is still alive."

Samuel started for the door, but Ethan stopped him. "Out the back, Sam. There's a stable there. Take one of my horses. And hurry!" Samuel hesitated. "Do it!" Ethan ordered. "One horse can't carry the two of you with the speed you will need tonight."

The tone in Ethan's voice sent Samuel scurrying through the dark house with Laishita. She swung the back door open and said, "Be careful, Sam." Before he knew what was happening, she had kissed his cheek and shoved him outside. He and Gadoni were mounted and riding in seconds.

At the gate of the city, several men stepped out to block their way, but the two young men leaned low on their horses and pushed them at breakneck speed through the scrambling men and out of the city. Several arrows soared past them, but in a moment their horses had carried them beyond the range of the weapons and into the forest at the side of the road.

The next morning, after a grueling ride home and very little sleep, Samuel and Gadoni headed to the dining room for breakfast. Samuel stopped so abruptly at the door that Gadoni ran into him. Without speaking a word, Samuel motioned Gadoni back. They didn't stop until they reached Samuel's room.

"What did you see in there, Sam? " Gadoni asked.

"Teor had a breakfast guest. It was Jashan!" He paused a second while the full impact of the statement hit Gadoni and then he said, "He must be Teor's cousin."

"So Teor is part of the rebellion," Gadoni mused. "Don't you think we better tell Pachor? And then we better make ourselves scarce around here."

Pachor's wife ushered them into the big house. They were surprised to see the spacious front room full of men with worried faces. "Welcome, boys," Pachor said. "We were just discussing the state of affairs in the city." He turned to the men in the room and said, "This is Sam and his friend, Gadoni. Sam is the young man I told you about who was awarded the Medal of Valor by Captain Moroni."

Samuel nodded politely and then said, "Pachor, there's something you need to know and then Gadoni and I must leave."

"Well, go ahead. What is it?"

"Could we talk in private please. It's about the uprising."

"These men are loyal, Sam. What you have to say to me, they

should hear, too," Pachor said, inviting the young men to sit down. "We know about the rebellion. The city is in the hands of men calling themselves Kingmen. Many of the judges have been murdered. Now, what do you know?"

"I know who committed one of the murders." He immediately had the full attention of everyone. "One of them is in the servant's dining room right now. He's having breakfast with Teor."

"Oh! that's Teor's cousin. He's starting work today. Teor brought him to the house earlier."

"His name is Jashan. He murdered some of his own company of soldiers in the wilderness while they were escorting my people back to Gilead. And I saw him, along with a wicked one-eyed man named Antium, a white Lamanite captain, stab Judge Jarohah last night! They stole my horse, too. It's probably in the stables now if you were to look." Samuel's face was serious and Pachor paid attention.

"Boys, you're in grave danger. We must get you out of here at once. You can leave through the back of my property. Let's get your things together. I'll get your horses." He paused, pulling at his beard, then went on. "I guess you'll need another horse. We best not let Teor know we're onto him just yet."

"I have another horse," Samuel said quickly. "It's a bay mare. We put it in the stable with Gadoni's black gelding." He chose not to mention Ethan's role in this drama.

"Fine. Gadoni, you go in the kitchen with my wife to get some food for the trip while Sam and I get your things. We'll meet you out back in a minute." Pachor opened the door and ushered Samuel out ahead of him. Too late, they saw armed men coming up the rock walkway.

"That's the one," Jashan shouted. "I saw him kill poor Judge Jarohah." Samuel was stunned. "He dropped his knife and left his horse. I took both of them as proof. Antium saw him, too. And he had a Lamanite with him—Gadoni. They got away on Gadoni's horse. Where is he?" Jashan demanded.

Pachor was standing firmly between Samuel and the angry men. "Gadoni is gone. He left during the night."

"Arrest Sam," an older, evil-looking man ordered.

Pachor protested, but they shoved him to the ground and

carried Samuel, kicking and shouting, down the walk.

"What about the Lamanite?" Jashan cried. "Aren't you going to get him?"

"You find him and we'll arrest him," the older man said, a murderous look in his eye.

"Let's look in the house," Jashan shouted, starting for the door.

"You get off my property! You, too, Teor," Pachor, who was already back on his feet, thundered with authority.

"We'll be back with a warrant," the leader countered.

"You do that," Pachor challenged him.

A moment later, Samuel was dumped head first into a wagon. His mind was a whirlwind of confusion. He should have realized what was happening. He knew Jashan hadn't seen him at the scene of the murder, but he and Antium had obviously recognized Gadoni after all. They would have assumed that Samuel was near. At least Gadoni was free for now, and Samuel hoped that he could remain so, but he also had frightening doubts about that.

Back in Zarahemla, Samuel was locked in a clammy, smelly cell, crowded with Nephites. It was dark, the only light coming from a barred window high in the south wall. For several hours, he sat hunched on the floor in one corner, fighting back the tears and frustration. If only he and Gadoni had kept riding the night before, he wouldn't be in this mess. And what a mess it was. His captors told him he would get a trial, but Jashan and Antium wanted him dead, and Samuel feared they were going to get their way. A sinking hopelessness drifted over him.

He gradually became more aware of the others in the musty cell and listened to them speak quietly to each other. It was apparent that they were all in the same kind of fix he was, accused by the Kingmen of one crime or another and facing futile trials.

More and more men were shoved into the jail during the long day and evening. Samuel expected to see Gadoni each time the door clanged open, but it was always another stranger. He began to have hope that Gadoni had managed to get away, a thought which sustained him during the long days that followed.

From the prisoners who came later, Samuel and the others learned another thing that gave them hope. Chief Judge Pahoran had escaped with some of his men and fled to parts unknown. They all cheered and prayed that he would somehow be able to overthrow the traitorous Kingmen before it was too late.

Day after day when no other news reached the dismal prison Samuel became more and more depressed. The food the prisoners were fed made the food he had received in Shurr seem like fine dining. Samuel grew weak, but the older men fared much worse than he. It was actually a relief when they were told their trials would soon begin.

"You can have lawyers to defend you—if you have the money," the prisoners were informed. "And you will be tried by fair, open-minded judges." Samuel had grave doubts about the fairness of any judges the rebels appointed.

One afternoon, his name was finally called along with several others. They were all ushered up the narrow, dark stairway and into a large, drab room above the cells.

"Samuel, this is Sebul. He'll be your lawyer," one of the guards said, to Samuel's astonishment.

"Samuel, it's nice to meet you," his new lawyer said in a strong, deep voice that contrasted remarkably with his thin frame and narrow, pointed face.

"But, I didn't . . . I mean, I can't . . ." Samuel stuttered.

"I have been hired by Pachor to defend you on a charge of murder. You are accused of killing a judge. What have you to say for yourself?" Sebul asked sternly.

"I did not do it, sir, but I saw it happen and I know the guilty men. It's not the first time they've murdered, either." Samuel was unsure of this strange man who sat across the table from him, but if he had been hired by Pachor, Samuel told himself, he must be all right. He would have to put his trust in him.

"I will do all I can to help you, but, as you know, we may not have a judge who will listen to the truth, for the Kingmen hastily appointed men from their own ranks. It may not mean much, Samuel, but I believe you."

Samuel's knotted stomach cinched tighter at the discouraging words about the Kingmen. Still, there was some comfort in the knowledge that his lawyer was honest with him and intent on doing his best.

Sebul thought deeply for a moment then said, "Sam, I'll tell you what I believe they will use as evidence against you. Then you tell me what actually happened."

Samuel listened nervously as Sebul outlined the case against him. When he was done, Samuel recited the events of that fateful night. He left out the names of Laishita and Ethan. When he had finished, Sebul looked him hard in the eye. Samuel squirmed, wondering what was going through the strange man's mind.

"Sam, I can't help you if you aren't completely honest with me. That means I need the names of everyone who was involved that night. You failed to say who the friends were you were with that evening and whose house you were in when your horses were stolen." His deep voice rumbled his rebuke.

"But, sir, I don't want to get them hurt. They didn't see the murder, I did. Isn't it enough to tell you what I did and what I saw?" Samuel begged. He could picture Laishita, vivacious but so innocent, being drawn into this mess and getting hurt. He could hardly bear the thought of it.

"If you want any chance at all of coming out of this affair with your life, you better help me all you can. Obviously, Gadoni is not available to testify, so who else can back up your account of that evening?"

"Do I have to say?" Samuel pleaded.

"Yes, it's your only chance," his lawyer answered firmly.

Samuel looked around. No one in the room seemed even remotely interested in their conversation. He leaned across the table and tensely provided the missing names. Sebul blinked, then smiled. "I know them," he said. "Ethan is still recovering from some bad wounds he received in battle." A broad grin spread across Sebul's thin face, revealing an over-abundance of superb white teeth, and his protruding eyes twinkled. "I can certainly understand how a young man might end up at that house. Why, his daughter . . . Laishita, is it?"

"Yes."

"Why, she certainly is a most attractive young lady—most attractive." He chuckled a deep, throaty chuckle, then went on. "I'm glad you told me about them. They could be a great deal of help. Yes, yes, a great deal of help if they are willing, and I'm sure they will be."

Samuel watched Sebul as a brilliant legal mind churned inside his peaked, hairless skull. All the while his teeth were reflecting rays of the sun that shined through the south window. Finally, the gaunt lawyer stood and said, "You have been a great help, Sam. I'll return soon."

The next day, Samuel was again ushered from the dark, putrid cell and brought to the visiting room. When his eyes had adjusted to the light, he was surprised to see a very sober Laishita waiting, head down, at one of the little tables. This was the first time he had seen her in the light of day, and she was even prettier than he remembered.

He sat down across the table from her. She looked up and tried to smile; her mouth cooperated, but her eyes did not. She reached across the table and took his hands in hers. "Sam, what are they . . ." She started to sob.

"Laishita, I'm sorry. I didn't want to get you involved in this. It could be very dangerous for you and your family. You shouldn't have come."

"But I wanted to!" she said. "Everything's dangerous right now. They've driven Judge Pahoran out, and some man is calling himself our king. If we don't help each other, who will help us? Anyway, it's all my fault."

"Your fault?" Sam was speechless.

"I insisted that you take me home, and then I pressed you to come inside to meet my father, and then your horses were stolen and you had to try to find them, and . . ."

Samuel cut her off, smiling despite himself. "Now you wait a minute, Laishita. I didn't have to do anything. I took you home because I wanted to."

"Well," Laishita said, squeezing Samuel's hand and sending pleasant little chills the full length of his body, "I'm going to help you. I promised Sebul I would testify, and so will Father. You promised you'd call on me again some day, and I intend to hold you to that promise." She smiled and the chills started all over again. He wondered what it was about a pretty girl that could cause such curious feelings in a fellow.

Sweat was pouring off Latoni's face as he bent over his anvil, carefully pounding a red-hot piece of iron into the shape of a horseshoe. He was startled when he finished and straightened his aching back, for there, in the wide doorway, stood Pachor.

"Oh, you frightened me, Pachor. I didn't hear you come in. How long have you been standing there?" Latoni pulled off his heavy leather gloves as he spoke and extended a hand to his old friend and longtime customer. "What are you doing here? Do you need a horse shod?" he asked.

"No, Latoni. I'm afraid I have some bad news about your son. Let's go out and sit on the bench. This is going to take a few minutes," Pachor said, stepping into the sunshine.

After they were seated, Pachor said, "I suppose you've heard about the rebellion in Zarahemla?" Latoni nodded soberly and Pachor continued. "Well, I'm afraid Sam's in jail. I've hired him a good lawyer, one of the best in the land, in fact. But I'm worried about the judge. The Kingmen have already replaced the old judges with corrupt men," he said, evading Latoni's question.

"Pachor, what is Sam charged with?" Latoni asked firmly as he looked his friend squarely in the eye.

"He's not guilty, I can assure you of that," Pachor said, before finally coming to the point. "They have accused him of murdering Judge Jarohah on the night of the overthrow."

"How did they manage to come up with that?" Latoni rose to his feet and limped painfully back and forth in front of the shop.

Pachor explained briefly about Teor and his part in the uprising . . . and about Jashan and Antium.

"What about Gadoni? Have they got him, too?" Latoni asked, suddenly remembering that nothing had been said about Samuel's loyal friend.

"No, he got away. The Kingmen came to my house after Sam and Gadoni. Sam stepped outside with me before we realized that they were there, but Gadoni was still inside. We managed to get him out the back door and away on his horse," Pachor explained.

"Where did he go? He hasn't shown up here. This is the first place I would have thought he'd come," Latoni said, scratching his head.

"He mentioned the land of Melek. He may have gone there. I

suspect he's trying to figure out a way to help Sam. Then again, he may have gone in search of Moroni." Pachor wiped the sweat off his brow with the back of his hand, then continued. "It's all my fault. I realize that now as I think about it. They knew and warned me that Teor was up to no good, but I was too hardheaded to listen."

Latoni sat down again, his head in his hands. "Sit down, Pachor, and tell me the whole story—everything you know. Then, I can decide what to do."

"You can't help your son if you get thrown in jail yourself, and that is very likely what would happen if you go to Zarahemla. You're a judge, remember? You would not be welcome in Zarahemla if you were recognized. Now let me tell you what happened." Pachor began to unfold the strange string of events that had landed Samuel in jail.

"This is like a bad dream," Latoni lamented when Pachor was done. "What chance does the boy have?" He got to his feet slowly and started across the street, but suddenly stopped and said. "Pachor, I don't know where my manners are. You are welcome to stay the night with us and get a fresh start back tomorrow. I do appreciate all you're doing for my son."

When Latoni told Kamina that Pachor was staying the night, Ophera looked up quickly from her mending. "What's happened to Sam?" she asked. Latoni was not ready to talk about Samuel.

Kamina could tell from his face that something was wrong and she spoke for him. "Ophera, don't jump to conclusions. Pachor can visit without having to bring some kind of bad news. Why don't you fix a place for our guest to stay."

Ophera turned away in frustration when Latoni decided to get it over with. Waiting was not going to make it any easier. "Not so fast, Ophera. You're right. Something has happened to Sam. He is in jail, charged with a crime, but not for anything he actually did. A lot of men have been arrested on trumped-up charges by the Kingmen. Pachor has already hired a good lawyer for Sam."

Ophera's blue eyes were filled with pain. She had gone to visit her cousin hoping to forget Sam, but had not succeeded. "Well, I guess if he's gotten himself into trouble, he'll just have to get himself out of it," she said, her voice breaking.

"What about Gadoni?" Oreb asked. "Is he in trouble, too?"

"No, he got away."

"Latoni, what have they accused Sam of?" Kamina asked. Oreb pressed his father as well.

"He didn't *do* anything, but they have accused him of murder," Latoni said, reluctantly.

Ophera gasped, threw a hand over her mouth and ran across the street, and into her mother's old house. "I'll talk with her," Kamina said. "But before I do, tell me the rest of the story."

Latoni recited what he had learned from Pachor, wisely omitting the part about the pretty, dark-haired girl in Zarahemla. When Latoni and Pachor had answered the last of Oreb's questions—and the boy had a lot of them—Kamina went in search of her troubled daughter.

CHAPTER FIFTEEN

ONE BY ONE, THE PRISONERS WERE TRIED, CONVICTED, and sentenced. Some received long prison terms, but most were condemned to die. Samuel noted that all the condemned men had held high and distinguished positions in the government of Chief Judge Pahoran. Samuel alone stood accused of murder, the most serious of all offenses.

Each day, Samuel tried to find renewed hope, but each night brought further despair as stories circulated among the prisoners of yet another crooked judge, in the pay of the Kingmen, who failed to give fair consideration to an innocent defendant. Samuel's only hope, he felt, lay in Gadoni although what Gadoni could do to help him he had no idea. Still Samuel prayed Gadoni could do something.

The only bright spots of Samuel's shrouded existence were Laishita's visits. At first, he was puzzled why he was allowed her frequent visits, but he found his answer in the lustful eyes of the guards. Laishita spread her charm amongst them like honey on fry-bread and as a result she was allowed to visit every time she asked. It worried Samuel that the men gaped openly at her while she was there.

"Laishita," he said one day, "I don't like the way these men stare at you. You need to be more careful. The way you flirt with them may give some of them the wrong idea, and that could be very dangerous for you."

Laishita only teased him. "I didn't mean to make you jealous. I only . . ."

"I'm not jealous," he said defensively, blushing.

"Then why are you so red?" she asked, but then smiled demurely. "I don't have any interest in any of them. You're the one I come to see, and I do it because I've become quite fond of you." More seriously, she added, "I know you're right, Sam, but I have to give them a little attention or they won't let me see you. How would you feel if I wasn't allowed to come anymore?"

She had him there. Her visits kept him going, and the thought of not being able to see her devastated him. "I wouldn't want you to stop coming, but please be careful. Don't let any of them try to follow you home or something."

"I won't, you silly boy. And I will keep coming. I look forward to our little visits as much as you do. Maybe even more." Her dark brown eyes sparkled and she quickly changed the subject without even pausing for breath. "Sebul was over this morning. He said your trial will begin soon."

At Samuel's alert look, she continued. "In a day or two, I think. Father and I will be there the whole time although Sebul's not sure when he'll have us testify. And even when we've given testimony, we'll stay in case he needs us again. He doesn't know who the judge will be, but he's afraid there aren't any honest ones." Her eyes lit up and she smiled impishly. "Maybe I can use my charm on the judge, too."

Samuel was captivated by the way the light shined from Laishita's dark eyes and her quickly changing facial expressions, although he found it hard to break in if he wanted to say something. When she paused for an overdue breath, Samuel jumped in quickly. "I'll need more than that to save me, I'm afraid. From what everyone says, I'm already as good as finished."

"Not if I can help it, Sam," Laishita responded bravely. "And what about Gadoni? He'll do something, I'll bet. Do you know where he is, Sam? Or what he's going to do?

"No," Samuel said flatly. "I don't know the answer to any of your questions including the ones you haven't asked yet, but I know that if he can, Gadoni will do something. He's that kind of friend."

"What's he like?" Laishita asked, looking expectantly at Samuel and actually pausing to listen.

Samuel found it hard to describe Gadoni. "Well, he's the best friend I have, but it hasn't always been that way. At first, he was rather frightening, but I've learned that his heart is true and strong." Samuel went on talking of Gadoni, and Laishita listened, her dark round eyes never leaving his face until the guards came to escort him down the musty stairway back to his cell.

"Samuel." A loud voice broke into his dreams of Gadoni and Laishita rescuing him from the Kingmen. He rolled onto his side and sat up. A guard stood on the other side of the bars. "You are to come with me," he announced.

It was early. The guards hadn't yet brought the unthinkable offering that was to be his breakfast. Painfully, he rose to his feet, trying to ease the aches caused by sleeping on the rough, hard floor. "Hurry!" the guard commanded. "Your trial begins this morning. Your lawyer is waiting for you."

As usual, when Samuel saw the strange little man who was to defend him, he felt as though he were in the presence of a fool—until Sebul spoke. Then the feeling changed to one of confidence and awe. The exceptionally deep voice and articulate speech clearly evidenced a man of superior wisdom and knowledge.

He led Samuel to a spacious courtroom and pointed to a small table near the front. To his right was another small table, similar to the first, made of well-polished hardwood. "That's where the prosecutor will sit," Sebul said, pointing to the second table.

"Will people be here?" Samuel asked, looking over the rows of well-crafted hardwood seats behind them. "Other than Ethan and Laishita, I mean."

"Anyone who wants to may come and listen. There haven't been many spectators in the other trials, I'm told. People are afraid, and common Nephite citizens would rather not be seen here in these chambers because they are controlled by the Kingmen." A few people began filing into the room. Sebul signaled for Samuel to turn and face the front of the room. "It's time," he whispered.

The judge's bench, a massive, elevated table, also made of dark wood, stood at the front of the room. Behind it was a large blue velvet chair into which a heavily obese man was lowering himself. His dark robe was of rich fabric, and contrasted severely with the man himself. Long, unkempt strings of grey hair hung around his large ears. His matted beard still held crumbs from his breakfast. He viewed the courtroom and its human contents through dark, deep-set eyes that blinked rapidly beneath dark, heavy eyebrows.

Samuel turned a frightened look toward Sebul and whispered, "Do you know this man? He looks worse than I ever expected. He doesn't even look like a judge."

The little confidence that Sebul had managed to instill in Samuel this morning vanished instantly in the presence of the grisly judge who presided. Sebul shook his head and whispered, "The kingmen are a sorry lot. Distinguished and honorable men are not involved with them. This man—his name is Elam—is a lawyer, but not a good one. I suppose he was appointed judge because he will do whatever he is bid by the new king. We're ready to begin."

"Samuel, stand up," the judge ordered in a high-pitched, nasal voice.

As Samuel stood he broke into a cold sweat, suddenly feeling very faint. His knees shook. He grabbed the rim of the table and squeezed until his knuckles were white. Samuel had faced fierce Lamanite warriors, the evil Antium, the strong and agile Jashan, and fierce creatures of the wild, but never had anyone cast such a spell of doom and fear on him as Judge Elam did.

"Samuel, you are charged with the high crime of murder," the judge whined nasally, over the sound of people filing into the the rear of the courtroom. "The case against you will now be presented, after which you will have an opportunity to present your defense, if you have one."

When the judge finished speaking, Samuel was in a daze and Sebul had to pull him into his chair. He had no idea what the judge's final words had been. "Get hold of yourself, Sam," Sebul whispered. "This is going to be tough enough without you going to pieces on me."

A heavy, chilling voice to Samuel's right began, "Your honor, the government of the King will prove to the court that the defendant murdered in cold blood, one Jarohah, a judge of the Nephite nation."

Samuel turned his head and saw that the speaker stood at the table to his right. A short, puffy man in a long brown robe, he glanced at Samuel and frowned. "Cohor, the prosecutor for the Kingmen," Sebul whispered. "Corrupt, but intelligent."

Samuel barely heard him, because he had suddenly become aware of Laishita and her father sitting behind the prosecutor. Laishita winked at him and smiled, restoring some of his lost energy. Never had Samuel seen her look so stunning, and it occurred to him that her parents could not afford to buy her such a dress, a shimmering scarlet of the finest material. He wondered who had.

Her jewelry sparkled. She wore two blood-red stones set in gold, hanging daintily from her ears and an ornate gold headband that held her long ebony hair away from her pretty oval face. A matching ruby was set in the gold band at the very center of her forehead. On her fingers were rings, also of pure gold, with rubies sparkling from them. Around her throat she wore a gold choker necklace that contrasted strikingly with her smooth, olive skin.

A glance at Ethan surprised him even more. He, too, was dressed in rich clothing and wore expensive rings on his fingers and jewel-studded gold arm bands. He smiled nervously at Samuel, who was wondering where the expensive jewelry had come from. Only the most wealthy people in the land wore such splendid adornments.

Sebul prodded Samuel in the ribs and whispered, "Pay attention—and not to her." On his lips was a faint smile that puzzled Samuel.

Samuel listened to the prosecutor who continued to elaborate on Samuel's heinous crime, but already Samuel felt better; Laishita had provided the catalyst needed to boost his spirits. He watched Judge Elam with renewed interest, surprised to see that the old man was not looking at the prosecutor at all. His deep-set eyes peered from beneath his huge eyebrows and focused on none other than Laishita, who had cast her spell on him as she had predicted. Samuel stole another glance in her direction. Her eyes were on the judge, a tantalizing smile caressing her rich red lips.

Pulling his eyes away from her, Samuel looked to his left and caught his breath. There, side by side, sat Jashan and Antium, looking smug and self-confident in the dim light of the court-room. Seated beside them, glaring at Samuel with potent hatred, was Teor although both Jashan and Antium were eyeing the enchanting vision in red at the right side of the room.

Sebul poked Samuel again. "She's doing her job, Sam. I need you to do yours," he whispered, "by paying attention to the testimony given and helping me keep track of lies and inconsistencies."

"Yes, sir," Samuel said quietly and tried to listen to every word that was being spoken, only occasionally sneaking a peek past Sebul at Laishita. She made the terrible proceeding bearable—almost fun, if it hadn't been so serious.

This was a matter of life and death for Samuel, and sauntering to the witness chair to the right of the judge's bench was a man who had for many months wanted to end the young man's life. Antium was the first witness for the Kingmen.

Ophera wiped the sweat from her forehead and leaned back over the fireplace where she was stirring a thick stew when a knock at the front door startled her. She hooked her ladle to the side of the large black pot and walked to the door. After wiping her hands on her apron, she opened it. A handsome young man stood there, smiling.

"I need to speak to Latoni at once," the young man said, his eyes betraying his pleasure at finding one so lovely before him.

"He took my little brothers fishing at the lake. They should be home before noon," she said, self-consciously brushing long golden strands of hair from her face. "Would you like to wait here for him? Come in please."

"Thank you," he said, "I will. I have a message from Pachor for Latoni."

"Who is it, dear?" Kamina called from the back of the house."

"It's one of Pachor's servants, Mother. He has a message for Latoni."

The stranger smiled broadly at her. "It's about your brother, Sam. His trial was to start this morning, and my father promised to keep your father posted on any major developments."

Kamina entered the room as he spoke. "I'm Kamina, Latoni's wife," she said when he had finished. "You're welcome in our home. I see you've already met my daughter, Ophera."

"I'm Zaron, the youngest son of Pachor." Ophera jumped at this news, but he kept his eyes on Kamina. "My brothers are all serving in the armies of Captain Moroni, but I'm at home, acting as a *servant* to my father." He beamed, enjoying Ophera's embarrassment.

Ophera's embarrassment shifted to anger. He was nice looking, but she didn't like being made fun of. How was she to know he was not Pachor's servant? "Well, Sam isn't my brother either!" she retorted.

Zaron appeared unshaken by his mistake. "I guess we're even. I'm sorry I jumped to an erroneous conclusion. I thought you were Sam's sister. Ma'am," the young man said, turning to Kamina, "how far is the lake where your husband is fishing?"

"It's not very far, maybe a mile or so."

"It's a while before noon yet, and I need to be getting back before too late. Maybe I could just walk out there and find Latoni, then be on my way." He smiled at Ophera. "I'd do much better with a guide. It would help me out a great deal, and I'd certainly enjoy such pretty company."

Ophera assessed him quietly. She judged him to be about twenty or so. He had light brown hair and a muscular build; he was not quite as tall as Samuel and was impertinent, she thought. However, a walk to the lake offered a welcome change.

"I'll finish the stew, Ophera, if you'd like to go." Kamina was happy to see that Ophera was interested in this young man. Interested enough, Kamina hoped, to forget Sam a little.

Outside Zaron took her hand boldly in his own and said, "You'll need to show me the way." Ophera made no attempt to pull away.

"I am Antium," the renegade answered the prosecutor's query in his gravelly voice. "It was late, and I had delivered a message to the home of the good Judge Jarohah. I had only gone a few blocks when I met Jashan. He told me that we needed to return to Jarohah's house and warn him of a threat on his life." Antium kept rubbing the ugly red scar where his right eye had once been, and his head twitched in a series of uncontrolled spasms as he talked.

"So, what did you do then?" Cohor strolled pompously back and forth before the bench in his flowing brown robe.

"We turned back toward Jarohah's house."

"And what did you find when you got there?"

"Well, sir, we never actually got back to the judge's house," Antium answered, scratching his long, hooked nose.

"And why didn't you get back?" the lawyer prodded.

Antium aimed his beady eye at Samuel and said smugly, "Because we came upon a fight."

"And what did you do at that point?"

"We ran over to break it up, but one of the men fled, and the other one fell wounded in the street. He'd been stabbed!" The expression on Antium's face was one of horror—as if he had never witnessed such a terrible thing before. He was enjoying his theatrics so much that he got ahead of the prosecutor. "I tried to help the poor man, but he was dying, and he said, 'Sam . . .'"

"I object!" cried Sebul. His booming voice shook the room.

"I sustain the objection," came the nasal whine from the bench. "Antium, you must wait for the prosecutor to ask the questions." The judge looked over at Laishita. Samuel glanced at her just as she flashed the judge a resplendent smile of approval. The puffy little prosecutor threw the judge a disgusted glance that the bearded old man missed. His eyes were elsewhere.

"Who did you find lying in the street wounded?" he proceeded.

"Judge Jarohah! He had been stabbed!" Antium thundered, as if shocking the world with some little-known fact.

"Did he say anything to you?"

"Oh, yes, sir. He said, 'Sam stabbed me!'" Antium looked down at Laishita, puffing out his chest and squaring his broad shoulders. Samuel glanced back and saw her continue to smile at the judge. He was amazed at how brave she was, but shuddered to think what could happen if she ever met one of these men alone in the dark.

"What happened next?" the lawyer asked.

"He died," Antium said blandly.

"The man who ran away, did you see him well enough that you could recognize him if you saw him again?"

"Yes, sir," Antium replied, happily showing Laishita and

everyone else in the courtroom how many teeth he was missing.

"And do you see him in this courtroom today?"

"Yes, sir," Antium answered, pointing at Samuel. "That's him!"

"What did you do after Jarohah died?" the prosecutor asked.

"Sam dropped his knife when he ran. We picked it up."

"Is this the one?" the lawyer asked, pulling a long, curved knife out of a box he had just lifted to his table. He handed it to Antium who, with his head tilted, studied it for a minute with his beady eye.

"Yes, sir, that's it, blood and all," Antium responded gleefully, smiling proudly at Laishita, vying with the judge for her attention but losing badly.

"Now, Antium, please relate to the court what you did next," the prosecutor said, turning to see what was so entertaining to Antium and the judge. He nearly tripped over himself when he saw Laishita, but she ignored him, smiling constantly at Judge Elam.

Antium answered, "I helped carry the poor dead man to the side of the street and then went for help."

"Did you meet anyone else before you went for help?"

Antium looked at Samuel with an evil glint in his dark eye. "Yes sir, we did. We ran right into a Lamanite—Sam's friend, Gadoni. He was leading their horses down the street toward us. But he got scared, so he jumped on his horse and rode off, letting the other horse go. We caught it and reported the murder to the authorities," Antium concluded.

"That's all the questions I have for this witness, Your Honor," the prosecutor said to the judge who momentarily looked away from Laishita and nodded.

The prosecutor glanced at Laishita, but she gave him a cold stare, then smiled warmly at the judge.

"Do you have anything to ask this witness?" the judge asked, scratching his wrinkled, balding head. Samuel turned and glanced at Laishita who was also watching the judge attend to his itch. He could tell she was making a monumental effort to suppress a giggle.

Sebul, unaffected by the side show that distracted Samuel and Laishita, rose slowly to his feet. As he approached Antium, he looked him up and down for a full minute. Antium withered visibly before the intense scrutiny, and his head jerked nervously. When Sebul finally spoke, his deep rumble reverberated around the room.

"Antium, the court has listened attentively to your testimony. You swore to tell the truth, did you not?" Sebul roared.

Antium's head jerked rapidly and the scar where his right eye used to be twitched in unison. "Yes, I did, and I have nothing more to say."

"Do I need to ask the judge to remind you that this is a court of law and that you are required to answer my questions as well as those directed to you by the prosecutor?" Sebul thundered, staring into Antium's remaining good eye.

"No, sir. I just meant that I had told my whole story."

Sebul led him back over the testimony he had given. To Samuel's dismay, Antium stuck to his version of the fateful night's events in almost every particular. When that was done, Sebul asked intently, "Before the night in question, had you ever seen Samuel or spoken to him?"

Antium hesitated a moment before saying, "No, sir. But I know he's the one I saw that night."

Sebul pressed his attack with force. "Isn't it true, Antium, that you lost your eye and suffered a badly broken arm at the hands of this same Samuel?"

"He tried to kill me, but he . . ." Antium cut himself short, realizing his error.

Sebul, ignoring his answer asked, "And isn't it also true that he did you serious injury with some small spears another time?"

Trying to cover his slip up, Antium said, "I don't know who it was, but someone did try to kill me. He looked like Sam."

Before Sebul could ask another question, the prosecutor popped to his feet objecting. "Please instruct the defense to stick to the events of the night in question."

Judge Elam did as he was asked. "Don't ramble, Sebul," he ordered in his nasal whine.

Sebul tried several different lines of questioning but was cut short each time by Cohor, who accused him of trying to taint Antium's good name. Finally, he said, "I have no more questions," and sat down.

Samuel leaned over and asked Sebul, "Why won't they let you ask him those questions?"

"Because we're dealing with dishonorable men, Sam. The judge couldn't help but see that Antium was lying, but does he care? We'll keep trying though," he said softly as the prosecutor called Jashan to the stand.

Samuel glanced at Laishita again. She was becoming a little discouraged, but she smiled at him hopefully and he smiled back. Jashan leered at Laishita, but she ignored him, smiling again at Judge Elam.

Ophera and Zaron strolled arm in arm as they followed Latoni and the boys through the forest, returning to Gilead. Oreb and Josh each carried several fish they had pulled from the clear waters of the lake that morning. Oreb jerked one off his line and threw it to Snap. The sleek jaguar downed it in a single gulp and begged for more. Ophera smiled at Zaron when Latoni gave his son a stern look, convincing him to save the rest of his fish.

"Why don't you come down and visit for a few days?" Zaron asked Ophera. "My parents would love to have you, I'm sure. And I know I would."

The idea had instant appeal to Ophera, but she was not sure how Latoni and Kamina would react. "Why don't you have lunch with us, Zaron? I'll ask Mother and Latoni when they've had a chance to get to know you better."

"If they worry about you being safe there, I can assure you there is no danger. Things have settled down in Zarahemla. Besides, we live outside of the city. No one would even know you're there," Zaron argued.

"You don't need to convince me," she said with a laugh.

"I'll save my arguments for your parents, then," he said, his brown eyes looking at her with admiration. "We need a bright and pretty face to liven up the mood at our estate these days. It's pretty drab around there."

Latoni and Kamina responded as expected. "It's just too dangerous, Ophera. The land is in turmoil. You're safer right here."

"I wasn't safer when the Lamanites invaded," she argued

shrewdly. She had them there, but they still resisted the pleading of both Ophera and Zaron.

Oreb, twelve now and growing like a weed, chipped in. "I'll go with them, Father, and take Snap. I'll make sure nothing happens to Ophera."

Ophera threw him an angry glance but quickly withdrew it when Latoni chuckled. He was looking his son over carefully and Oreb was gazing steadily at him. He gave in and said, "Okay then, you three may go, but only if you promise to do exactly as I ask."

"Yes, sir," Zaron said, disconcerted at the prospect of having a tag-a-long little stepbrother. Ophera caught his eye and smiled. She was sure he would rather have Oreb along than for her not to be able to go at all.

Kamina wasn't convinced but Latoni soothed her fears. "They'll be all right if they stay out of Zarahemla and return home, with Zaron as an escort, in three or four days."

"I'll make sure we don't have any trouble, Father," Oreb said confidently. "And we'll stay out of the city."

"Thank you, Latoni. I'll have them back in four days," Zaron said, capitalizing on the long end of Latoni's time frame.

Ophera did not join with Oreb and Zaron in their promise, but neither Latoni nor Kamina seemed to notice. She always kept her word, but this time she chose not to make any commitments she did not want to be bound by.

Ophera nervously noted her mother eyeing her as she prepared to leave. She had the feeling Kamina could read her mind— maybe she had noticed that Ophera had failed to promise Latoni anything. She was grateful that her mother chose to say nothing.

By early afternoon, the three young people were on their way, the tawny jaguar ambling lazily alongside the horses. Zaron's mount was skittish around Snap at first but soon took its cue from the other horses and paid Snap no further attention.

Jashan told the same lies Antium did. His testimony differed only in that he tried so hard to make himself look good. He was the one, he claimed, who was mainly responsible for identifying Sam. He claimed he had captured Sam's horse, found the knife, and spearheaded the arrest. His effort to appear heroic was no doubt for the benefit of the ravishing Laishita primarily and only secondarily for the judge. Samuel remembered how badly Jashan had treated Ophera and feared for this innocent, young girl.

A sharp pang of guilt pricked at Samuel when he thought about Ophera and looked over at Laishita. He remembered Ophera's firm declaration of love even when he was leaving her to work for Pachor. To ease his feelings of guilt, Samuel reminded himself that Ophera probably had written him off anyway.

When Teor took the stand, Samuel told himself it probably didn't matter how either girl felt toward him. Unless Gadoni, by some miracle, could rescue him, he wouldn't be around much longer to sort out the affairs of his heart.

Teor sat proudly in the witness chair and looked down on Samuel with disdain. Unlike Antium and Jashan, he did not deny knowing Samuel. "He and his friend Gadoni, the Lamanite, were troublemakers from the day they first came to work on Pachor's estate. I wouldn't have lost my job if it hadn't been for them. They told Pachor all kinds of lies about me. Sam wanted to be foreman himself, and he could never achieve that unless he got me out of the way," Teor fabricated. He too eyed Laishita with gleaming eyes and was totally ignored by her.

"Did Samuel and Gadoni have any horses when they came to work?" Cohor asked.

"They did. Pachor let them keep their horses in the stables."

"Did you ever have an occasion to see the horse that Antium and Jashan found near the place Jarohah died?"

"Yes," Teor responded with an evil grin.

"And will you tell the court whose horse it was?"

"Sam's. I'd know that horse anywhere." He looked smugly contented, knowing his testimony had the power to send Samuel to the executioner.

Sebul's voice rocked the courtroom again when he cross-examined Teor. Teor, however, firmly and consistently stuck with his lies.

The prosecutor rested his case, confident that he had presented enough evidence to more than convince the judge that Samuel had murdered Judge Jarohah. The judge, yawning, asked Sebul how many witnesses he would call.

"At least three, Your Honor," he said firmly.

"Then we'll adjourn until tomorrow morning," he announced and looked longingly at Laishita before walking out of the room. She winked at him, using one more effective weapon in her distinctly female arsenal.

Samuel glanced at Laishita. Her lips formed the word "Tomorrow" and he nodded. As she left the courtroom, every eye followed her. Her leaving was like the setting of the sun. The room was gloomy and cold without her presence.

Samuel was relieved to return to his cell. He fell to the hard floor and tried to conjure up the image of Laishita in his mind to console himself. To his consternation, Ophera's fair face appeared and lingered in his mind.

Sebul left the courtroom hurriedly and unhitched his small black filly from the hitching rack out front. His mind was preoccupied as he climbed into his little cloth-covered surrey and headed toward Pachor's estate. He had never handled a tougher case than this one, nor one more hopeless. He had tried, and continued to try as he clicked his horse faster, to think of every possible angle he might use to cause Judge Elam to let his client off.

Pachor listened somberly to Sebul's report of the day and said, "Put me on the stand first and I'll set them straight about the kind of attitudes Samuel and Gadoni had. I want the court to know how completely false Teor's testimony was."

When Sebul tried to point out the danger to his family, Pachor said, "I must take that chance. Look at the danger young Samuel is in. I cannot, in good conscience, put my own safety ahead of his," Pachor said firmly.

Sebul agreed reluctantly then laughed as he described Laishita's performance in the courtroom. "She looked absolutely entrancing and kept the judge off his guard all day. I just hope we haven't put her in too much danger," Sebul said soberly, then quickly smiled. "I can't wait to see what she wears tomorrow. It must have cost you a bundle to outfit her like you did."

"Nothing is too expensive if it'll help. She's a good girl and surely seems taken by Sam. I just hope we can save the future for them," Pachor said, his bearded face long with worry.

On the road back to the city, Sebul was so wrapped up in his thoughts that he failed to notice a man partially concealed in the trees, waiting for him to pass by.

Standing in the trees outside Pachor's estage, Jashan thought how much he wanted to be rid of Sam once and for all. He wasn't going to let Pachor or anyone else try to ruin that for him. He knew full well that Pachor would attempt to refute Teor's testimony in court. He had raced ahead of Sebul in order to reach Pachor's place unseen as soon as possible so he could trigger the trap he and his friends had set.

After Jashan had convinced Pachor of his good intentions, he would send him scurrying to Ethan's home. His eyes narrowed as he pictured Antium and Teor waiting in the shadows near the house of Ethan. Jashan knew his cohorts would see to it that the rich man would not be available for court the next day.

Jashan dismounted and tied his horse to a small tree at the end of the walk. He was puzzled at how skittish his horse became and how he fought the reins as he tied him up. Angrily, he slapped the horse on the nose and started toward the door of Pachor's house. He had no way of knowing that the horse's keen sense of smell had picked up the scent of a jaguar or that his was not the only surprise visit that Pachor was about to receive.

Pachor himself answered Jashan's knock. "What are you doing here?" he demanded. "Haven't you caused enough trouble already?"

Jashan bowed his comely head, pretending to show his shame. "Please, Pachor, hear me out. I'm sorry for what has happened. Antium and Teor have gone too far. I've come to help."

Pachor was still apprehensive, but he swung the door wide and said, "All right. I'll listen to you, but it better be good."

After the door closed behind him, Jashan said, "They plan to kidnap Ethan and his daughter tonight so that they can't testify tomorrow. You've got to help me. You don't know Antium. He's cruel and I can't bear to think of what he might do to that lovely girl. They think I'm going to help them, but I can't. It's just too much. I must stop this thing before it gets any worse."

Pachor was listening intently. Jashan was sure he was softening, so he went on. "Sam didn't kill Jarohah. Antium did. I didn't help him. You've got to believe me. I was there, but I only intended to frighten him. I didn't know Antium had orders to kill him. When he did, I was afraid they might accuse me if I didn't do what Antium wanted, so I agreed to go along with him. Ethan will never believe me, but he will believe you. In a few hours it'll be too late. Please come with me," he pleaded, wringing his hands for effect.

"I must believe you, because I can't take a chance and do anything else. Let's be on our way," Pachor said wearily.

Satisfied with his performance, Jashan opened the door and stepped out ahead of Pachor. Samuel had interfered once too often, and he would make him pay. He would see to it that Sam's little Laishita was not there to help him tomorrow.

"I'll get a horse, Jashan," Pachor called from behind him. "You wait here for me and . . . Well! Will you look at that?" he said in surprise.

Pachor's surprise was nothing compared to Jashan's when he saw Ophera, Oreb, and Pachor's son, Zaron, walk around the corner of the servant's quarters. Jashan recovered quickly. "Why look who's here. It's nice to see you, Ophera. We were just going in to Zarahemla. Sam's got himself in a spot of trouble, and Pachor and I are going to try to help him."

Her face darkened. "That man tried to kill me!" she screamed. "And he tried to sell me to the Lamanites! Pachor, he is a liar! He'll get Sam killed!" She appealed to Zaron. "Tell your father that he's got to believe me. Please."

Before Zaron could say a word, Jashan appealed to Pachor. "Sir, I was wrong about Sam. You've got to tell her. We must hurry or it'll be too late."

"Don't believe him!" Ophera cried.

In spite of his sudden anger over Ophera messing up his plan, Jashan tried to stay calm. "Please, sir, we must hurry or . . ."

"Don't listen to him!" Ophera screamed.

Pachor attempted to soothe her. "You must calm down. Jashan came here in peace. We must give him a chance to . . ."

"Peace!" Ophera stepped toward Jashan, a look of loathing on her face. "He hates peace! He tried to kill his own captain and he did kill my grandfather! He is a murderer and a traitor!"

Jashan looked back and forth between Pachor and Ophera, then at Oreb, who had the jaguar on a leash. It had matured greatly since he had tried to kill it. The animal growled at him. He knew he had to settle this situation quietly and quickly. He held up his hand. "Ophera," he said, trying to sound friendly. "I didn't do those things. Please, you have to let me explain."

"Explain! There is nothing to explain. You're a murderer, a deserter, a traitor, and a liar!" she screamed, her voice becoming hoarse from screaming.

That was all Jashan could take. Blinding anger took over and he stepped toward Ophera menacingly. "Somebody ought to slap your lying face," he shouted, drawing back his fist. He had to hit her. It was the only way to shut her up.

Oreb yelled, "Grab him! He hit her before and he'll do it again!"

Jashan swung his arm just as Pachor and Zaron dove toward him. They were too late and so was he. His fist never connected. The last thing he saw on earth was the snarling face of Snap, the jaguar he had once tried to kill.

Jashan screamed in pain as he felt his flesh tear. He tried to smash the jaguar's face with his other hand, but like lightning, it released his mangled arm and grabbed his face. Jashan screamed again, kicking and hitting at the wild beast, but to no avail. For a fleeting moment he felt his head being crushed; then he slipped into blackness.

Pachor watched in stunned silence as the big cat lifted Jashan's lifeless body, shook it like a rag doll, then dropped it to the ground, and walked sheepishly over to Ophera. Lying at her feet, he licked her trembling hand and looked up at her face as if to say, "It's okay now, Ophera. He can't ever hurt you again."

The shock of Jashan's sudden and brutal death left them all stunned. But Pachor sprang into action. The servants had gathered around and Pachor explained, "This cat just saved this girl's life. Jashan attacked her and the jaguar killed him."

None of the servants needed to hear more. These were Pachor's loyal servants, who knew already of Jashan and his evil ways. One of them spoke up and said, "We'll take care of his body, Pachor. No one will know he was here. We'll get rid of his horse, too."

"Thank you, my good and trusted friends," he said and turned to one of the maids. "See that Ophera and Oreb are taken care of. And find some food for their cat. I'll be back later."

"Father, surely you aren't going into Zarahemla? It's a trap. Ophera has told me much of this man and his friends," Zaron warned. "They are among the most dangerous in all the land."

"You're right, son, but we must ride to the city to warn Ethan," he said calmly. "We'll take two of the servants with us. Come, let's get fresh horses." A few minutes later, father, son, and faithful servants rode swiftly into the gathering darkness.

They rode straight to Ethan's house. Pachor, hoping that they weren't already too late, was counting on Jashan's cohorts leaving when they saw that Jashan did not return. He was right. He caught a glimpse of two men in the dark shadows near the house. They fled when he and his three companions arrived.

Samuel had spent a long, sleepless night replaying the events in the courtroom. As a result, the next morning he was exhausted. As the people filed into the courtroom, he rubbed his eyes, trying to drive the fatigue away. He felt sluggish and nauseated. He knew he had to shake this feeling or he would be no help to Sebul this day.

He shook his head and looked around. Although Teor and Antium were already seated, Jashan was late. Samuel wondered where he was. He also didn't see Pachor, whom Sebul had just said would be testifying this morning.

The arrogant little prosecutor in his long brown robe entered with a swagger and took his seat at the little table to the right. Six or seven other people, none of whom Samuel recognized, had taken seats behind him. Suddenly, a hush came over the courtroom. Samuel swung his head around and what he saw gave him the lift he needed. If Laishita had looked stunning the day before, she certainly gave new meaning to the word today, Samuel thought appreciatively. All eyes were upon her as she made her way toward the seat she had occupied the day before. She was wearing a beautiful, dark green dress and jewelry of glittering emeralds set in gold that accented both the dress and her dark, silky complexion. The green set off her beauty even more than the scarlet had the previous day.

So intent was Samuel upon watching Laishita's entrance that he failed to see Pachor enter, accompanied by another girl, not so richly dressed, a little taller, very blonde, and equally beautiful in a quieter way. She took a seat directly behind Samuel, while Pachor approached Sebul and knelt beside him in whispered conversation.

Samuel glanced once more at Laishita, who smiled at him before turning her attention to the old judge who was just then making his way to the bench. After taking his seat in the blue velvet chair, Judge Elam rapped on the bench with an oak gavel and said in his nasal whine, "Court is in session."

Behind Samuel, Ophera took it all in, particularly the stunning black-haired girl who wore clothing and jewelry worth more money than most people saw in a lifetime of hard work. She also noted Samuel's frequent glances in the girl's direction and her intimate smiles in return.

Ophera had been hurt deeply when Sam had abruptly left Gilead. She had been angry when she heard that during his visit he had said nothing more beyond simple inquiry as to her whereabouts. Still, she loved him. The time she had spent with Pachor's conceited son, Zaron, had only served to make her more sure of this. True, she had enjoyed Zaron's company, but merely because she had been so lonely. Her mind and heart had never left Sam and his problems.

Now she had found him, and he had eyes for no one but . . . her! One glance at the dark beauty was enough to see her power to turn the head of any man in the land. But watching Samuel, even as her anger battled with her deep hurt, Ophera prayed he would soon be free.

CHAPTER SIXTEEN

AFTER FLEEING FROM PACHOR'S ESTATE WITH A HEAVY heart, Gadoni wrestled with the decision he had to make. Where should he go? What could he do to help? He considered going to Gilead, but dared not, knowing that Jashan might send men looking for him there. He could go in search of Captain Moroni, but a lone Lamanite wandering around the battlefields in the East Sea area would be vulnerable. He could be taken captive by skeptical Nephites and be of no help to Sam at all.

He finally swung his mount toward the land of Melek. It was but a day's ride and there he would be accepted and could seek advice from good people of his own race by birth. Word of the overthrow of the government in Zarahemla had not reached the people of Melek, who were saddened to hear of the wickedness in Zarahemla. Over two thousand of their brave sons were fighting in defense of their country, serving faithfully under the leadership of the prophet Helaman. Now the people weren't sure what might happen with the Nephite armies, and they mourned.

Gadoni, whom they received with open arms, told them he was sure Moroni would try to restore the government to the people. They were glad to see someone with their own color of skin who had accepted the teachings of the Nephites but still retained hope and love for his own people.

He told them of his friend, Samuel, and they were touched by the love he had for the young Nephite. They related it to their own love for the sons of Mosiah, men who had been willing to sacrifice all they had to bring the word of God to the Lamanites.

Gadoni spoke of his desire to help Samuel and to go to Moroni, and of his fears of being taken captive by skeptical Nephites.

"There are some among us who are Nephite by birth. We will arrange for someone to accompany you who is familiar with the shortest route to the city of Bountiful where Moroni is most likely to pass through on his way back to Zarahemla," the chief judge of the land promised Gadoni.

True to his word, three men, all of whom desired to not only accompany Gadoni but also to join with Moroni in restoring the government, were ready to leave the next morning. In less than a week after his departure from Melek, Gadoni stood in front of Captain Moroni and told him of Sam's plight.

"We're moving as quickly as we can, Gadoni. I, like you, hope we can get there in time to save our young friend," Moroni said.

"Sir, several days have passed already. We may be too late now," Gadoni said, expressing his worst fear.

"I think the Kingmen will not be too hasty in bringing judgement against the citizens. They should know that they must at least appear to be giving fair trials to the people if they hope to gain the support of the masses. It'll take them a few days to get judges appointed, and the prosecution of Sam and others will take time to carry out. If we're lucky, they'll still be in jail, untried, or at least unsentenced by the time we get there and defeat their forces," Moroni reasoned.

"Sir, what can I do to help?" Gadoni asked. "May I travel with your army and be allowed to fight?"

"You're welcome to come with us, and when we're ready to attempt to free any prisoners being held, you will be part of the force assigned to carry out that mission," Moroni assured Gadoni.

Gadoni agreed, feeling that at last he was doing something for his friend. Every day the army pressed closer to Zarahemla, and every day it grew in strength as freedom-loving men joined with them and took up arms to help overthrow the rebel government of the Kingmen.

In Gideon three days later, Chief Judge Pahoran and his loyal forces joined with Moroni's army. Now just one day's march away, Moroni's scouts brought word of the status and location of the Kingmen's forces. Captain Moroni laid out his battle plan, including the part that Gadoni and a few selected men would fill in rescuing political prisoners.

Gadoni was hopeful when he heard that none of the men being held had been executed, just sentenced, but was worried to learn that the trials were proceeding rapidly and public executions would begin in a couple of days. The exact location of Samuel and a number of the other prisoners was identified, and this location was carefully mapped out for the special squad. The layout of the jail and the adjacent government building that contained the courtroom where the trials were being held was also drawn for the men.

Gadoni was anxious to make an attempt at rescuing his friend. He was ready to lay down his own life, if necessary, to free Sam of the false charges brought against him because of the lying and deceit of their common enemies, Antium and Jashan.

"Defense will call its first witness," instructed Judge Elam.

Sebul called Pachor to the stand and began by having him tell who he was and how he had come to know Samuel and his family.

"Please tell the court what kind of employee Samuel was," Sebul asked.

Pachor was happy to comply. "One of the best. He was a very hard worker. There was nothing he and his friend Gadoni wouldn't do when asked, and they did it without complaint. Samuel always found something else that needed to be done and went to work on it when his assignment was finished," Pachor said.

"Who was his supervisor?"

"Teor was in charge of the stables. He was foreman there, and Sam, because of his experience with horses, worked under him."

"Did Teor ever come to you and report any kind of problem with Sam?"

"Your Honor! Objection!" Cohor roared, drawing Judge Elam's eyes away from Laishita. He continued, "Teor's not on trial here. The defense is trying to make you think he's a liar. Please instruct Sebul to stick to the facts of the case."

Sebul explained smoothly, "Your Honor, I'm only asking for the kind of reports that Teor gave his boss. If that shows that Teor is a liar, then so be it!"

The judge, paying better attention now, indicated his interest in what Pachor had to say.

"Teor reported to me regularly, as do all my foremen. He never said a word that would indicate Samuel was anything but a loyal, hardworking employee. I do remember him saying that some of the servants were not comfortable working with Gadoni because he was a Lamanite, but when I asked him how he felt about Samuel and Gadoni, he said they did more work than any of the others."

"Is it true that the boys told you recently that they were going to leave?"

"Yes. I told them they could go as soon as Teor hired another man. I knew he had a cousin who wanted to work, so I told them it would probably be soon."

"Who was the cousin?" Sebul asked.

"Objection."

"Denied!" whined the judge after Laishita looked at him in a pleading way.

"Jashan. I understand he was here yesterday. I don't see him here now, though," Pachor said coldly.

"What would you do, Pachor, if Samuel were to ask you for another job?"

"I'd hire him without hesitation. I told him that, too. In fact, I told both Samuel and Gadoni that if they ever needed a job for just one day or permanently, I would hire them, and I meant it," he said forcefully.

"Did you ever talk to Samuel about making him foreman in Teor's place?"

"Absolutely not. Samuel is too young for that kind of responsibility, although someday he would make an excellent one, if he chose to continue in this line of work."

"Pachor, did Samuel ever come in to Zarahemla? And if so, how often?" Sebul quizzed.

"He very seldom did. The boys preferred to spend their free time riding on the estate or hunting in the jungle. They did go to Gilead once when Teor gave them three days off. Samuel seemed very lonely at times and wanted to go home," Pachor said. "They went to Zarahemla only one time that I know of. I didn't know they were going there until they were already back."

"Did Samuel, in your opinion, kill Judge Jarohah?" Sebul asked unexpectedly.

"No," Pachor answered, so quickly that the prosecutor's attempt at an objection was too late.

"That's all," Sebul said, flashing a toothy smile, and sat down.

The cross examination was brief. Pachor was firm in his position, and the prosecutor didn't want to have the judge's mind filled with good things about the boy he was portraying as a cold-blooded assassin.

Laishita was the next witness. The judge almost fell over the front of his bench when she flashed him one last smile before seating herself daintily on the very front of the polished wooden chair. She faced Sebul, her hands folded neatly in her lap. Then, as if she realized fully what was at stake, her bright smile faded as she looked around the room. When her dark eyes looked into Samuel's, he saw fear there—unmistakable, deep-rooted fear.

"Sebul, don't make her do it. It's too much," he whispered, but his gaunt lawyer dismissed him with a shake of his head and approached Laishita. Samuel gave Laishita a weak smile of encouragement, and her smile regained some of its brightness.

"Laishita, do you know the young man who is on trial here today?" Sebul's voice rumbled.

Her resilience having reasserted itself, Laishita faced Sebul resolutely. "Yes, sir, I do," she said.

"How long before the night of Judge Jarohah's death had you known him?"

"Samuel asked me to dance with him that night at a party. I had never met him before." She turned after answering and smiled at the judge, then turned back. Samuel noticed that her eyes were distracted to some unseen place behind him in the courtroom; her smile disappeared and a defiant look took its place. The urge to turn around and look was almost too much, but Samuel knew a single motion would disrupt the proceedings in the courtroom. Laishita had the full attention of the judge and that was something no other witness had managed.

"Were you with him for very long that night?" Sebul probed.

"We danced for a long time—two or three hours, at least. Then we walked home together," she said.

"Who walked home together, just you and Samuel, or were there others?"

"A friend and I had come together to the festivities that evening. Samuel had a friend with him, too. The four of us walked home together."

"Who was Samuel's friend?" Sebul asked.

Laishita hesitated before saying, "Gadoni."

"And why did you walk? There has been testimony that Samuel and Gadoni had ridden into the city that evening on horses." Sebul looked at the judge when he asked the question, but the old man had eyes only for Laishita.

"That's right," she replied, forcing another smile, "but we wanted to walk, so they led their horses."

Sebul painstakingly maneuvered Laishita through her recollections of the events of the fateful night, being careful to have her stress Samuel's actions, behavior, and the words he spoke after witnessing the murder. She answered each question perfectly, and Samuel was almost positive the judge believed her. A glimmer of hope entered his heart that maybe Sebul's tactics might work.

"And did Samuel say who it was that he saw fighting with Jarohah before the judge died?" Sebul queried.

"Objection!" roared Cohor.

"Sustained," whined Judge Elam, dashing Samuel's hopes. Laishita turned a pleading look toward the judge, but his features hardened.

"Laishita, in your opinion, did Samuel kill Judge Jarohah?"

"Objection!"

"Sustained."

"No more questions." Samuel leaned his forehead on the cool wood table and ran his fingers through his hair in anguish. He was vaguely aware of Sebul sitting down beside him. "Sam, it's not over yet. She's doing her best," he whispered.

Samuel forced himself to look up. Laishita's dark eyes were on him and he forced a smile, which seemed to give her strength to continue.

The prosecutor tried to intimidate her as he went back over her testimony, but Sebul had schooled her well, and she stuck to the facts. After listening to her tell how she stood at her front door and watched Samuel and Gadoni ride off, Samuel on her father's fleet bay mare, Cohor pressed on. "When was the next time you saw Samuel?" he asked, his voice much louder than necessary.

"I went to visit him at the jail after he was arrested."

"Oh yes," the prosecutor said slyly, "you visited him at the jail. I'll wager you visited him more than once, didn't you?"

"Yes," Laishita said, her face strained and her smiles at the judge less frequent and lacking their usual luster.

"How many times?" Cohor moved closer to her chair, his face only inches from hers. "How many times did you visit him at the jail?"

"I object, Your Honor," Sebul thundered, his voice shaking the room. "The questions the prosecutor is asking have nothing to do with the matter at hand."

"Overruled," the judge whined, then smiled at Laishita. "Please tell us how many times you visited Sam at the jail."

She tried to smile back as she answered. "I don't remember. Several, anyway."

"Several!" the prosecutor exclaimed. "Then it's true that you used that flirtatious personality and pretty face so much in evidence in this courtroom to persuade the guards to let you visit him almost every day since he's been there!" he shouted.

"It's true, I went quite often," she began, feigning a naive innocence. "When I asked to see him, they always let me. Nobody said I shouldn't be there, and Sam was lonely. I tried to cheer him up a little, that's all."

"Oh, I'll bet you did!" shouted the prosecutor. "And I'll bet you would say anything, no matter how untrue, to save him from the justice he deserves. You're only here today, testifying, to try to save his hide because you like him so well and have plans for a future together, isn't that true? You are just a spoiled little rich girl who always gets what she wants, and you want him! True?"

Samuel could see a rare anger burning in Laishita's dark eyes. She glanced at the judge and took a deep breath. The burning faded. Wryly, Samuel thought about how Ophera would have exploded under the intense questioning of this lawyer, but not Laishita. She was in perfect control when she finally answered.

"Your Honor," she said, turning to face Judge Elam, "I am here for only one reason. I know that Samuel is innocent, and I don't want to see him punished for a crime he's not guilty of." She paused for effect, then concluded, "And I'm sure that's why you're here, too."

The judge nodded, scratched his wrinkled head, and smiled at her.

"No more questions." The prosecutor sat down. The judge smiled at Laishita as she stepped down from the stand.

"The defense calls Ethan," Sebul said.

Laishita's father limped painfully to the stand. Despite the strain and discomfort of the courtroom on his still-healing body, Ethan sat with dignity, his arms folded across his chest. His testimony was brief, given in simple support of what Laishita had already said. The prosecutor railed on about his obvious wealth and tried to drive home the point that he was only there at the request of his spoiled child, but nothing he said or did upset Ethan. Like Laishita, her father maintained perfect control.

After Laishita's father was through, Sebul again addressed the judge. He wiped the perspiration away from his eyes. "Your Honor, it's been a long morning, and it's very hot in here, but I have only one more witness. Even though it's nearly noon, I would like to call him now if it's all right with you."

Laishita, back in her role again, smiled at the judge and nodded approval. "Go ahead, Sebul," Judge Elam said.

"I call Samuel, the defendant in this case."

As Samuel took his place on the stand and faced the courtroom, he felt the color drain from his face when he found himself looking into the beautiful, angry eyes of Ophera!

Outside, the sun bore down unmercifully on the great city of Zarahemla. Despite the heat, merchants hawked their wares and travelers passed continuously on the great highways. As part of an innocuous group of weary farmers carrying large vegetables to be sold or traded, Gadoni had been allowed to enter the city and mix with the throngs of people there. Other soldiers, similarly disguised, had entered the city from three different directions. Beyond the walls of Zarahemla, Captain Moroni and his army were approaching the city and would soon engage the forces of the rebel king in mortal combat. Not until the battle was in full swing would the rescue squad make its attempt to free the prisoners. After entering the city, Gadoni and his colleagues located the other squads and abandoned their burdens in the busy business district. Together they awaited the signal to go into action.

Samuel's mind froze when he saw Ophera, and he missed Sebul's opening question. Sebul repeated his question with a stern, reproving look, his eyes flashing. Samuel forced himself to take his time, answering Sebul's questions clearly, at the same time, wondering how Ophera had come to be in the courtroom. The anger wasn't hard to figure out. Her glaring looks at Laishita told Samuel the answer to that. The months since he had seen her had done nothing to diminish her exquisite beauty, and Samuel found himself caught up in her very presence here. The dour look on Laishita's face told him that his feelings for the blonde stranger had not gone unnoticed.

When Sebul asked Samuel about meeting Laishita, he tried to downplay it in an effort to ease the tension that filled the air between the two rival beauties. He had noticed the growing concern on Ophera's face as his story unfolded.

"What did you do when you saw the three men fighting?" Sebul asked him.

"I didn't do anything for a moment. When the one man fell and the others ran away, I went into the street to help the one who had fallen."

"What did you do next?"

"I carried him to the side of the road. He had been stabbed and was dying. He told me his name was Jarohah and that he was one of the chief judges. He asked me to help him." Samuel's voice filled with emotion as he remembered how helpless he had felt at the time. He paused in an effort to control his emotions. The courtroom was strangely silent.

"What did you do for Jarohah, Samuel?" Sebul prodded.

"Nothing. I just had to watch him die. There was nothing I could do." Samuel thought about mentioning the judge's expression of concern over the rebellion but decided not to.

"After Jarohah died, what did you do?"

"I left him and went to find Gadoni. I found him leading his horse. Mine was gone."

"Sam, let's go back to when the two men dropped Jarohah. Did you get a good look at either one of them?" Sebul asked.

"Yes, both of them."

"Did you recognize them, and if so, can you tell the judge who they were?"

"Antium and Jashan," he said, pointing at Antium and wondering again where Jashan was.

"Are they the men who testified against you yesterday?"

"Yes, they said I killed Jarohah."

"Can you tell us how you came to know them and why they would want to lie in court about something so serious?"

"Objection!" roared the prosecutor. "I have let this go on long enough. Samuel is on trial here, not Jashan or Antium. It's clear that he's making up lies about our splendid witnesses. The court's time is too valuable to allow such nonsense to continue."

Sebul argued vigorously but to no avail. The judge, ignoring the pleading looks from both Laishita and Ophera, who had somehow reached a silent truce, spoke. "It's clear to the court what happened that night, and there is no point in letting Samuel ramble on," he whined.

"But Your Honor, Samuel must be allowed to tell his whole story or he can't possibly have a fair defense," Sebul argued, unable to hide his anger.

Samuel closed his eyes. Sebul tried to ask several other questions, but the prosecutor, smelling victory, objected each time, and the judge went along with him. Finally, Sebul sat down and Cohor started in on Samuel with a vengeance, but to everyone's surprise, old Judge Elam stopped him.

"I've heard enough. As I said a moment ago, it's clear to me what happened. I don't need to have you drag Samuel through it all again," the old man said, clearing his throat as he spoke.

The smirk on the prosecutor's face told Samuel that his chances, if there had ever been any, were gone now. Samuel wanted to cry but wouldn't let himself, not with Ophera and Laishita looking on. He glanced at Laishita, who was making a final effort to win over the judge with her dazzling smile. In contrast, Ophera's eyes were alive with fire. Samuel was afraid she would jump right out of her seat. Only Pachor's calm, reassuring hand on her shoulder kept her in her place. He whispered something to her, and she sat back on her bench, the burning anger against the injustice she was witnessing still seething in her eyes.

The judge asked Sebul if he had anything more. "No, Your Honor. We have stated our case. Samuel is wrongly accused of the crime of murder, and I urge you to find him not guilty and let him get on with his life. He is young and has much to live for. Please order his release," Sebul said, confidence clearly lacking from his deep voice.

"Do you have anything further to state to the court?" the judge asked Cohor.

"Your Honor, the King's case against Samuel is solid, as you can see for yourself. This young man did, in cold blood, take the life of one of the good judges of the city and should be required to pay for his crime with his life. I know that you will make the only right decision," he concluded, the confident smirk on his face undiminished.

"Samuel," came the high nasal whine, "please stand and face this court. I have made my decision."

A silent prayer ran through Samuel's mind as he faced the grisly old man who held the power of life or death over his head. Silence filled the courtroom as Samuel, young though he was, masked his fear with a face of dignity and awaited the fateful words of the judge.

The unmistakable sounds of battle reached the ears of Gadoni and the rest of the rescue squad. Confusion broke out in the marketplace, and people began to gather their wares together and flee. It was time to act. The captain of the squad gave the order, and, armed only with long knives, Gadoni and the others moved swiftly toward the city center where the prisoners were being held.

"I'm coming, Sam," Gadoni cried softly as he ran, head bent, feet pounding the cobbles.

"I believe that the testimony of the King's witnesses is very clear," the old judge said severely. "I have no reason to doubt the word of men of the caliber of Antium, Jashan, and Teor."

Samuel felt faint, but anger surged through his veins, and he pulled himself to his full, impressive height when he heard a wicked chuckle from Antium. Judge Elam glanced at Laishita and then at Antium.

"Jarohah, who has been portrayed by the prosecutor as a good judge, was personally known to me. I tried to serve in his court-room, but he was an enemy of the people!" the judge screamed, his eyes glistening from beneath the dark shrubbery of his eye-brows. "I detested him!"

Samuel was confused. In fact, everyone in the courtroom wore puzzled expressions on their faces. The judge continued. "Samuel," he said, "you stand accused of killing a man, but that man was not an innocent man. He deserved to die. I find you not guilty of murder and commend you for your invaluable service to the Kingmen. You are free to go. This court is adjourned."

Intense shock froze the courtroom. The judge swept out, with a final longing look at Laishita. Suddenly pandemonium broke out. Antium and Teor could be heard, cursing loudly. The huffy little prosecutor, his face a dark, dangerous, angry purple, charged after the judge. Pachor grabbed Sebul, nearly crushing him in a grate-ful embrace. Ethan wiped happy tears from his eyes. Laishita and Ophera, both squealing with delight, swept into Samuel's arms, crying and hugging him, each oblivious to the other.

From the corner of his eye, Samuel saw Antium and Teor leave the room, promising vengeance against everyone there. Ethan took his beautiful daughter by the hand and said, "Come, Laishita. It is finished. We must go now."

Samuel followed them to the door, Ophera following closely. Ethan's harnessed horses waited patiently beside the hitching post, a large, ancient, weatherworn carriage attached behind them. Samuel felt a lump rise in his throat when Laishita looked toward him and waved, then wiped the tears from her face with the sleeve of her extravagant green dress.

Ethan had just begun to untie the horses when suddenly, a fig-ure darted from behind a tree and clubbed him on the head, sending him sprawling to the ground. A moment later, Laishita was torn from the carriage and thrown like a sack of corn onto the back of a horse. Samuel took off at a run, his shouts mingling with her cries for help. But Teor, already on the horse with the struggling girl, only laughed and cursed as he rode off. Antium quickly followed. A moment later they disappeared around the corner of the sturdy rock building in a cloud of dust, Laishita's plaintive screams for help hanging in the hot, heavy air.

CHAPTER SEVENTEEN

FRANTICALLY SAMUEL UNHITCHED THE CARRIAGE FROM Ethan's horses while Pachor and Sebul tended to Ethan. "He's unconscious, Sam, but he'll be okay. You go after Laishita," Pachor urged, his bearded face pale and drawn.

"Sam, take me," Ophera shouted to Samuel as he untied the horse from the rail and scrambled aboard.

"Sam, stop! What's going on here?" a familiar voice shouted. Samuel piled off the horse as fast as he had mounted and bolted to meet his best friend.

"Gadoni! What are you . . ."

Gadoni cut Samuel off. "We're here to free you," he said, looking confused.

"I'm free now, but Teor and Antium have Laishita. I'm going after them."

Gadoni looked in anguish toward his captain, who quickly sized up the situation. "Go with your friend, Gadoni." Samuel looked at the farmer who was giving orders to Gadoni. It was his turn to be confused. The farmer continued, "We'll tend to the other prisoners."

Samuel's face cleared up with Gadoni's next words, "Thank you, Captain sir."

Pachor motioned for Gadoni to take his horse and Samuel remounted on Ethan's carriage horse.

"I'm coming too, Sam," Ophera shouted, unhitching Ethan's other horse as Samuel dug his heels into his mount's side, and thundered away beside Gadoni.

"No, Ophera, don't . . ." Pachor shouted, coming to his feet, but Ophera swiftly climbed the horse and swerved around him.

Samuel looked back and saw her riding hard, her dress pulled up high on her legs as she frantically kicked the galloping horse.

Despite his good intentions, Oreb had broken his promise to his father. He had been angry at Ophera when she had gone to the city to Samuel's trial. "I made no promises, Oreb. I'm going to see Sam, and that's all there is to it," she had told him that morning.

For an hour he had stomped around the estate muttering to himself. Finally, he made up his mind. "I'm going too, Snap. I promised I wouldn't, but I also promised to take care of Ophera. She might need me, so I'm going."

The jaguar stretched his spotted back and looked up at Oreb expectantly. "All right, you can come, too," Oreb said impulsively as he gathered up his bow and arrows and headed out. He had been to Zarahemla with his father many times and was sure he would not get lost, and with the cat along, he felt quite safe.

One thing Oreb hadn't counted on was the fighting that he came upon as he neared the city. Seeing Nephites in combat against other Nephites, Oreb realized it could mean only one thing—that Moroni had arrived to drive out the Kingmen. He hurried into the safety of the trees and scurried high up into the leafy branches of a tall mangrove. Snap bounded gracefully up behind him. From the thick, sturdy branches near the top, Oreb watched the battle.

Even though he was some distance away, he could tell that Captain Moroni's men were dealing death on every side as they drove the forces of the wicked Kingmen back toward the city. He imagined himself as a brave warrior, fighting to restore freedom to the people of Zarahemla. For an hour, he watched and daydreamed as the battle moved farther and farther away.

"Hey, Snap, we better get closer or we're going to miss the rest of the fight. We'll find another tree," he said, forgetting all about Ophera and his promise to take care of her. He had barely started to inch his way back along his high branch when a horse whinnied beneath the tree. Two horses trotted into view. He expected to see soldiers, but instead, he saw a man holding a struggling black-haired girl in front of him on one horse and an ugly, one-eyed man on the other one.

The horses stomped and snorted wildly. One man shouted, "I don't know what's the matter with these horses. They act like they're crazy or something."

"They're spooked," the other one said.

Oreb pressed against his big cat and put his arms around Snap's neck when he realized it was jaguar scent that had frightened the horses. One horse reared and tossed its one-eyed rider to the ground. The man stood up, cursing, his hand still clinging tightly to the reins. Oreb studied the man carefully. The scar where his right eye should have been, the bent arm, a hook nose . . . he seemed very familiar. Then it hit him. This was Antium! He was free and right there below the very tree Oreb was sitting in.

Over the noisy stomping of the horses, Oreb caught a few words. "Your boyfriend Sam is going to get a little surprise we've prepared for him."

"Why can't you just leave him alone?" the struggling girl pleaded.

"Silence, Laishita!" This time it was Antium who spoke. "Give me your jewelry."

"Not now, Antium," Teor said. "We've got to get moving. If I know Sam, he'll be coming soon. We want to be far from the fighting and the city before we let him catch up with us." Teor laughed.

"But what if he doesn't find us?" Antium asked doubtfully.

"We'll send him a message he can't ignore."

With that, they rode out of sight, their horses still stamping and snorting in fear. Oreb clung to his branch, digesting the information he had just overheard. It must be his brother Samuel they spoke of, but Samuel was in jail.

He thought about the girl they called Laishita. Sam must have a new girlfriend, he decided. But what about Ophera? Oh, no! He had forgotten about her. He better find out where she was and . . . He began to sob. It was all too much for him. He didn't know what to do, so he stayed in the tree, crying until the tears wouldn't come anymore.

Oreb had no idea how much time had passed when he heard another horse snort and whinny. A horse came into view, and he recognized Gadoni instantly. The Lamanite was studying the ground in front of him.

"I can't see anything here, Sam," Gadoni called out. "Let's go back a little ways and look more carefully."

"No, don't, Gadoni," Oreb tried to shout but his voice was thick with tears and the rustling of the leaves and branches covered the sound. He tried to call out louder but Gadoni was talking to Samuel who had just ridden from the trees, followed by Ophera. They were all oblivious to the small voice in the tree above.

Samuel and Gadoni both dismounted and began pacing back and forth with their heads bent to the ground. The horses, upwind from Oreb and Snap, had not picked up the jaguar's scent and stood calmly awaiting the will of their masters.

Oreb shouted once more, but his voice was carried away by the breeze. He was up so high that it would take him several minutes to reach the ground and by then they might be gone. In desperation, he reached for his bow and quiver on the branch above him. Snap sat stiffly behind him. He was sure the cat had picked up the familiar scent of the three people out there, but he showed no inclination to scramble down from the tree and let them know of Oreb's presence.

Oreb strung an arrow and, balancing precariously on his limb, he let it fly. Samuel and Gadoni both saw the arrow at their feet and reacted swiftly, pulling Ophera to the ground and slipping behind the horses for cover. Having succeeded in getting their attention, Oreb let a second arrow fly, hoping that Sam would recognize the arrow by its color.

Oreb started to descend from the tree. Impatient at his slow progress, Snap bounded to the ground and ran to Sam, frightening the horses. By the time they had calmed the animals, Oreb was down and streaking toward them. "Oreb, what are you doing here?" Ophera scolded.

"I was looking for you. I promised Father I'd look after you, remember?" he replied then turned to Samuel. "Antium and Teor went *that* way with some girl," he said and pointed in the direction they had ridden, a wide grin on his face. "They said something about setting a trap for you."

"Oreb," Samuel said with a grin, "I don't know where you came from, but let's ride. You can get on with me."

The sky grew darker as the afternoon wore on. Gadoni had been able to track Antium's and Teor's horses fairly well, but he feared he would lose the trail if it rained. The dense jungle ahead would be a perfect place for Antium and Teor's trap.

Samuel's days of imprisonment were telling on him, and coupled with the worry over Laishita, it was a strain to keep going. He was also worried about Oreb and Ophera and thought about leaving them behind but discarded the thought almost as quickly as it had come. It was too easy for an inexperienced person to get lost.

For several hours they rode deeper and deeper into the wilderness. Gadoni took the lead with Snap at his side. Samuel knew that the big Jaguar with his keen nose was their best protection against ambush. Samuel followed with Ophera next and Oreb taking up the rear.

With Ophera so near, Samuel's tender feelings were returning, and the way she looked at him told him she still felt the same toward him. He tried not to think about the confrontation that was almost sure to come between Ophera and Laishita. He had strong feelings for the spunky, dark beauty, too. And she had sacrificed so much for him. So difficult was his dilemma that Samuel forced it from his mind.

Gadoni stopped as darkness settled in. He signaled for the others to come closer. "We'll have to go a lot slower now," he said, because of the darkness, "but I think we're close to them. I don't want to stop."

Progress was slow, but a full moon rose an hour later, enabling Gadoni, on foot now, to follow the path Antium and Teor had made. Several hours later, Oreb said, "I can smell smoke."

Samuel tested the wind currents. "You're right, little brother," he said, feeling renewed strength.

Following the pungent odor of a smokey fire, they found the camp of Teor and Antium easily. Overly confident, the two villains had stopped and built a small fire, one which put out little light and a lot of smoke. They lounged with their backs against a ledge, their weapons on their laps. Their frightened captive sat, securely bound, a few feet in front of them.

"Let's get them right now," Gadoni, usually the cool head, whispered angrily to Samuel from behind the trees that separated them from the two men who had killed before and would happily kill again. "We can't let them treat her like that and get away with it."

Samuel was surprised at the anger in Gadoni's voice. He was angry himself, and his heart went out to the suffering girl, but he feared that her captors had placed her in that position for a purpose. It would be best not to charge blindly in. He motioned Gadoni to retreat with him until they were a safe distance away where they argued about how to attack.

Gadoni still wanted to go in immediately and snatch the girl up and take her to safety. "But Gadoni," Samuel warned, "don't you think that's exactly what they'd be expecting me to do? We have the advantage. They don't know you're here. We need to use that advantage wisely. Now . . ."

Reluctantly, Gadoni listened to the idea Samuel proposed. An hour later, Samuel and Gadoni slipped cautiously back to Teor and Antium's camp. Ophera and Oreb waited a short distance behind them. The horses were tethered far enough away that their scent wouldn't alert the horses of Teor and Antium.

As Samuel peered through the trees, he was relieved to see that things hadn't changed much. Both men were still near the fire, weapons in hand. Laishita appeared to be dozing, her head slumped on her knees, which were drawn tightly to her chest. Her once fine dress was torn and muddy from the hard ride through the jungle. Her valuable jewelry was gone, and her captives had even taken her sandals, leaving her small brown feet bare. Her hair hung in matted curls around her knees.

At Samuel's signal Gadoni scurried to the right while Samuel crawled to the left. Ophera and Oreb waited in the trees. Oreb had his bow strung, ready to use if needed.

Suddenly, the outlaws' horses broke the still of the night with terrified neighing as they fought their ropes wildly. Samuel was dismayed. So quiet and unnoticed had Snap been, that he and Gadoni, their minds on the problem of Laishita's rescue, had not thought about his presence. Unfortunately, the wind had shifted, and the horses had picked up his scent.

Reacting swiftly, Teor grabbed the terrified horses while Antium jerked Laishita to her feet. Using her trembling body as a shield, he backed around the edge of the mossy rock ledge and joined Teor. They tried to mount the horses, but the nearness of the jaguar had driven the animals mad with fear. Samuel and Gadoni both tried to safely launch an arrow without endangering Laishita, but neither one could. However, with the aid of the bright moon, little Oreb sent an arrow sailing toward Antium's rearing horse. The arrow grazed its neck, adding fury to its fright, and the crazed animal plunged down the slope past the fire, in the direction Samuel had crawled. Antium, the reins wrapped tightly around his hand, was dragged along.

Samuel, in the path of the charging horse, tried again to get a shot off, but he slipped on the wet grass and the horse ran into him, knocking him violently into a tree. Bright flashes exploded in his head before he slipped into unconsciousness.

Oreb, ever alert, sent his jaguar after Antium's fleeing horse and the cat wasted no time in catching up with the crazed animal. Sinking its teeth in its neck, the jaguar dragged the horse to the ground. Antium, finally able to unwind the reins, rolled free, found his bow and quiver of arrows and awkwardly fitted an arrow to the string. When Snap looked up from the now dead horse, Antium let his arrow fly. The arrow found its mark and Snap stumbled to the ground just as Oreb raced toward Antium. But he was too late.

His eyes blurred with tears, Oreb did not see Antium flee into the woods. He ran to his beloved pet and kneeled down at its side. Gently he eased the arrow from the jaguar's muscular chest. With a heavy heart, he broke the bloody stick over his knee and threw it as far as he could. Then he buried his head in the great beast's neck and sobbed. Forgetting the brave warrior he had been just moments ago, he was a little boy again, grieving over his fallen pet. Even the thought of Antium, and the deadly danger he presented, was swept from his mind by his grief.

Ophera had seen Samuel fall and rushed to his aid. His head

was bleeding, but he was still alive. She cradled his bloody head on her lap and felt him stir. "It's all right, Sam. I'm here," she said gently.

"Ophera, help me up. We've got to find the others!" Samuel said, desperation in his weak voice. He struggled to his feet only to topple over again.

"Sam, lie still for a minute," Ophera said. "You've had a bad bump on the head. It'll take a little while before you can walk."

He didn't resist, and she again cradled his head in her lap. All the tender feelings she had ever felt for him came flooding back. In a few minutes, she helped him to his feet.

"Sam, we've got to find Oreb," she said and headed him toward where she had last seen the boy. "He sent his jaguar after Antium and his horse. They haven't come back."

Overcome by pain and exhaustion, he passed out in her arms. She lowered him to the ground again. He would awaken again soon and maybe he could stand the pain and they could go in pursuit of Oreb, if he hadn't returned by then.

Gadoni had pursued Teor and Laishita through the moonlit jungle. Even though they were on Teor's horse, Gadoni was able to keep pace as the horse could not make good time through the dense foliage and boggy ground.

For several minutes Gadoni ran in pursuit, unobserved by Teor, staying far enough behind to avoid discovery and yet close enough to spot them periodically. Each time he caught sight of Laishita struggling behind Teor, her long black hair reflecting the moonlight, his determination and anger grew.

Teor finally allowed his charging mount to slow down to rest. His energy nearly spent but his gallant spirit undaunted, Gadoni made a great, final effort. He leaped, reaching past the surprised Teor, and tore Laishita from his grasp, the impact causing them both to fall to the ground.

Before he could regain his feet, Teor was off his horse. His powerful kick into Gadoni's side sent the young Lamanite rolling in pain through the wet grass, then coming to rest against a thick clump of flowering fern. From the corner of his eye he saw Teor deliver an angry slap to Laishita's face. Her scream brought him surging to his feet in rage. Despite the pain in his side, he lowered his head and with an angry roar dove into Teor's midsection.

Both men went to the ground, Gadoni beating Teor viciously about the head. Teor ducked and pulled a knife from its sheath at his side, stabbing swiftly at Gadoni, who received a gash across the cheek. But before Teor could use the knife again, Laishita's ear-splitting scream filled the jungle night, and Teor's head was suddenly jerked violently back onto the ground. Like a mother cat fighting for her young, Laishita clawed at Teor's eyes and bit the arm holding the deadly knife, causing Teor to drop his weapon. Gadoni deftly pulled his own knife from its sheath and held it to Teor's exposed throat.

Within minutes Teor lay tightly bound. Neither Gadoni nor Laishita moved, so great was their fatigue and physical pain, until Laishita noticed the blood oozing from the cut on Gadoni's cheek. Soon her once beautiful dress had yet another tear, the piece of fine cloth now applied to Gadoni's wound, his head cradled tenderly in her lap.

Samuel came to and struggled to his feet. "Ophera, I'm going to look for Oreb. If anything has happened to him . . ." He let his words trail off.

"He went this way," Ophera said, leading the way.

Samuel felt a tremendous surge of relief when he spotted Oreb across a small clearing, his arms around the thick neck of his jaguar. "I think something's wrong with Snap," Ophera said.

"Oh no," Samuel said softly. "Is he dead? There's blood all over him." Samuel felt sorrow and relief at the same time. "At least Oreb's all right."

But his next emotion was one of terror when the hideous face of Antium arose from the bushes, only a few feet from Oreb. The moon gleamed menacingly off the blade of a long knife he was wielding in his hand. "Oreb, look out!" Samuel shouted, charging into the marshy clearing.

Oreb's reddened eyes opened wide with fear. He felt a movement beneath him as the great jaguar suddenly gathered its feet beneath it and flew swiftly through the air toward the man who threatened his master. Antium's knife fell to the ground as he was violently knocked backward by the jaguar. His arm snapped in the cat's powerful jaws and his terrified scream resounded through the jungle.

Oreb scrambled to his feet. "Snap!" he cried, as he jumped up and down in his excitement. The cat let go of the mangled arm, turned away from his victim and crawled toward Oreb, who once again threw his arms around the thick spotted neck of his pal. "You old faker, you," Oreb was saying. "You made me think you were dead, but all the time you were just resting until I needed you."

Samuel and Ophera soon had Antium securely bound, his newly broken and mangled arm tied tightly to his crooked one. Then Ophera joined Oreb at Snap's side and tenderly stroked the jaguar on the head with one hand while she reached around the boy's shoulders with the other. "We both owe our lives to him now, Oreb, don't we?"

"We sure do, Ophera," Oreb said proudly.

"What do you mean, you both owe your lives to him?" Samuel asked.

Before Ophera could answer, Oreb spilled out the story of how the jaguar ended Jashan's life. Hearing of his partner's death, Antium cursed and threatened the lives of the young people even more angrily.

"Antium," Samuel said patiently. "You keep trying but you keep failing. You don't frighten me. Anyway, if your broken arm heals crooked like the other one, you won't be able to do anything to anybody."

"You talk smart, Sam, but you forget one thing. Teor still has your dark little filly, and you'll never see her again unless you deliver me to Teor," Antium said with a sinister chuckle. "Have you told Ophera about your little Laishita. She would be interested to know exactly . . ."

"I know all about her, Antium!" Ophera broke in hotly. "Sam's a big boy. He can do as he pleases. Nobody owns *him* like the devil owns you!"

"Gadoni will be back with Laishita any time now," Samuel told

Antium, hoping he was right. He prodded Antium to his feet, herding him across the marsh. Ophera joined Samuel, and Oreb followed, his hand on Snap's head. The jaguar was walking slowly, obviously in pain, but at least he was alive.

Gadoni left Laishita watching a securely bound Teor while he went in search of the horse, which was grazing in a clearing not far away. "You'd better ride the horse," he said to Laishita, whose eyes had a new sparkle in them. "Teor and I will walk."

He prodded Teor to his feet and pushed him ahead while Laishita followed on the gelding. Gadoni's side hurt terribly. He knew that Teor must have broken some of his ribs when he kicked him. Laishita noticed that he favored his left side as she rode alongside of him. "You can't walk. There's room for both of us up here, Gadoni. Let's just tie a long vine to Teor and he will have to follow along."

Gadoni didn't argue. After he had Teor secured, he struggled on to the horse behind Laishita and they started out again. Every few minutes, Laishita turned her head and asked Gadoni how he felt. He tried to be gallant, but he was in a lot of pain. Even though Laishita had carefully cleaned and dressed the knife wound on his face, the throbbing reminded him constantly of its presence.

"It hurts, doesn't it?" Laishita asked.

"What?" he asked, playing dumb.

"That cut, silly. I know it hurts even if you won't admit it. Well, one thing about it, when it gets better, you'll have a handsome scar for life," she giggled.

Gadoni, his arms around her slim waist, smiled, even though it hurt to do so. He was pleasantly aware of a strange stirring inside. He could see why Samuel had been attracted to this spirited young girl. He felt a pang of jealousy but fought it off out of loyalty to his friend. Gadoni could never take anything that Samuel had laid claim to, no matter how much he wanted it.

As if reading his thoughts, Laishita said, "I owe my life to you, Gadoni. Thank you." She turned her head and gave him one of her captivating smiles. "You just don't give up do you?" she went on. "I thought for sure Teor had gotten away with me again. I was so surprised when you pulled me off the horse. I've never been so glad to see a man in my life." To keep Gadoni's mind off his pain, Laishita continued. "I'm hungry, Gadoni, aren't you? I wonder how the others are. Let's hurry faster. I don't care if Teor can't keep up. We'll drag him. I . . ."

On and on she went. Gadoni smiled and subconsciously tightened his arms around her. He was intoxicated by the smooth, cheery sound of her voice. He didn't care if this ride never ended; he had never experienced such pleasant feelings. He kept trying to ignore them, thinking again of Samuel, but it was impossible. This girl had, in a matter of a few hours, taken control of his heart.

Samuel had fallen asleep, and Ophera was fighting to not do the same thing. Oreb was wide awake. "Someone's coming," he announced, whipping his bow from his shoulder and expertly fitting an arrow. "If it's Teor, he'll wish . . . Gadoni!" he cried, mid-sentence, as Teor's big gelding came out of the trees.

Samuel woke up, lifted himself painfully to his feet, and went to meet them. He grabbed Teor, allowing Gadoni to drop the vine and slide off the horse. Samuel noticed, with a flood of relief, the tender look Laishita gave Gadoni when he helped her to the ground and the way she clung to him after Oreb took the horse's reins and led it away to be tethered.

Samuel knew Ophera was watching him, measuring his reaction. He also noticed how self-conscious Gadoni was. "Hey, you two, welcome back. I figured Gadoni would find you. He seemed so determined." Samuel smiled at Laishita and winked at Gadoni, surprised but happy to see their obvious mutual interest.

Samuel glanced at Ophera who gave him a smile as bright as a bed of daisies. All uncertainty and jealousy vanished. *I owe you again, Gadoni,* he thought to himself. *I really owe you for getting me out of this little mess.*

Late in the morning, after killing some small game and eating, the five young people prepared their horses for the trip back to Zarahemla. Antium and Teor grumbled loudly as they were forced to walk along behind with their hands tied, while the others rode the horses.

Pachor ran eagerly to meet the group that now stood in front of his house. "You are safe," he exclaimed over and over.

When questioned about the state of affairs in Zarahemla, he responded, "Pahoran has been restored to the judgement seat. Moroni scored a swift and decisive victory yesterday. His army crushed the Kingmen before dark. Now, what do we have here?" he asked, turning toward Teor and Antium, who for once were silent, their tongues swollen after the long and tiring march.

"Teor and Antium bit off more than they could chew," Samuel said evenly. "Do you think some of your men could deliver them to Pahoran? I've seen about all I can stand of these two."

CHAPTER EIGHTEEN

"ANTIUM IS A WICKED AND DESPERATE MAN, AND AT TIMES he seems like . . . well, a ghost," Captain Moroni said as he sat in Pachor's house visiting with Samuel and Gadoni before he left with his army for the city of Bountiful.

"Yes, sir. I understand. He just keeps appearing in my life and causing me misery," Samuel said. "I sure have wondered how he got away from you."

"Well, it's like this, Sam," Moroni said, his brow creased. "We had him bound and under heavy guard. There was to be a trial the next day, but that night we were attacked by a large Lamanite force. We fought a terrible battle, losing many good men, but we drove the Lamanites to the edge of the sea where they finally surrendered.

"When we returned to our camp, the men I'd left to watch Antium were gone, and so was he. Now, you know as much as I do. I haven't seen any of those men since. I suppose he talked them into deserting. I wouldn't be surprised if they were all part of the Kingmen."

The burden of doubt clouding Samuel's mind lifted. A breeze, light but refreshing, blew in through the open window. He shifted nervously. "I hear he's to be tried soon in Zarahemla. Will he be brought to justice this time?" Samuel asked, not intending for his question to sound so bold.

"I accept the scolding," Moroni said pleasantly. "I do believe he'll get his just rewards at last. You young men shouldn't have to bring an enemy of the people in more than once—more than twice, anyway," he chuckled. Moroni got to his feet. "We leave at dawn for the battlefront," he said. "I almost wish I could be here for Antium's and Teor's trials, but I have no doubt that justice will finally be served. I'm sorry that you and . . ." Moroni stopped and grinned. "You and those two pretty girls have to go through another trial."

Antium's trial started two days later. Antium was charged with treason, desertion, kidnapping and murder. The desertion charge went back to the days before he was a captain in the Lamanite army. The charge of treason was directly related to his involvement in the recent uprising. The kidnapping was for his part in Laishita's abduction. And finally, murder, the most serious charge of all, was for the death of Judge Jarohah. So, to his chagrin, Samuel found himself back in the same courtroom where he himself had so recently been on trial.

Sebul, dressed in a flowing robe, entered, seated himself at the prosecutor's table and flashed his perfect teeth at the young people. Struck as always by the contrast between Sebul's gleaming smile and his strange, narrow face, Samuel smiled easily at him.

Antium was seated in Samuel's old chair, next to a defense lawyer. His most recently broken arm hung in a sling. He looked neither to the left nor to the right but only stared straight ahead.

Samuel was mildly surprised when the judge entered. He had pictured the wicked old judge who had acquitted him, not the tall, stately gentleman who walked confidently to the bench and took his seat in the blue velvet chair. His black robe was clean and neat, his face clean shaven, his hair neatly trimmed. His brown eyes radiated intelligence and his dark face was honest, reassuring Samuel that in this trial the truth would be sought.

Sebul's deep voice rumbled through the courtroom as he outlined Antium's deceit, treachery, and murder. Antium's defense lawyer told a much different story, one full of half-truths and lies. The judge listened to every word before ordering Sebul to call his first witness.

The day wore on, long and hot, as witnesses testified of Antium's desertion. Samuel was anxious to get his part over with. Even though he was not on trial here, the feelings and emotions that he had experienced earlier in this courtroom kept flooding over him. The day ended before Samuel was called to testify.

That evening Samuel and the others were guests of Ethan and his family where they had accepted lodging until the trial was over. Laishita, who had been more sober than usual all day, sat quietly as the others talked and laughed. Samuel finally asked, "Laishita, I've never known you to have so little to say."

Gadoni sat next to her. He took her small hand in his and said, "What is the trouble? You really are not yourself today."

She hesitated. "Come on, tell us," Ophera coaxed. "We're all friends."

"Well, you'll think this is silly, but I had a dream last night, and it frightened me. I saw Teor's face in my dreams. He was trying to kill you, Gadoni. He frightens me, you know. Promise me you'll be careful."

"I know he dislikes me, but he's locked up and can't hurt anyone, Laishita. But, I will be careful. You just put your mind at ease and quit worrying." Gadoni smiled at her.

Samuel glanced at Ophera. Her face was creased with lines of worry, too. She smiled when she caught him looking at her, but not before he got the feeling that she shared some dreadful premonition with Laishita.

The next morning as Sebul launched his case against Antium, Samuel jumped when his name thundered through the courtroom. Gingerly, he made his way to the witness chair and sat down. He looked up, determined not to let anything distract him from telling his story. Ironically, the first thing he saw was Antium's evil, glaring eye, piercing him with hatred and contempt. He was instantly unnerved. He shifted his eyes to the pleasing face of Ophera but shuddered when he recognized in her eyes the worried look of the night before.

"Sam," Sebul's voice boomed, "tell the court about your first meeting with the defendant, Antium."

Samuel did so, describing in detail his captivity in Antium's Lamanite army. As he told what had occurred there, the judge gave Antium a stern look of disgust. Next, Sebul led Samuel into the encounter with Antium in the wilderness. Samuel painted a vivid description of Antium trying to shoot him as he swam with

Gadoni in the deep, clear pool, and he brought a smile to the judge's face when he described how he and Gadoni had outwitted Antium and knocked him into the stream.

Next Samuel described the encounter in the cave that led to Antium's subsequent capture. He tried to avoid looking at Antium as he spoke, still feeling uneasy and a little frightened at the appearance of the man Moroni described as a ghost.

Finally, Samuel recounted the murder of Judge Jarohah. He had a difficult time, not because he couldn't remember the details of that night vividly, but because of frequent objections by Antium's lawyer.

Samuel finished with the story of Laishita's abduction and Antium's attempts to take the life of his little brother, Oreb, as well as his own. By the time he was through, his clothes were soaking with perspiration. In contrast, his mouth was so dry that he could hardly speak.

Antium's lawyer attacked Samuel with venom, but to no avail. Try as he might, he could not trip Samuel up in any part of his testimony. Samuel left the witness chair exhausted but relieved. At last he had been able to tell the horrible tale of Antium's crimes to someone who would see that justice was carried out.

Gadoni was the next to testify, and he solidly backed Samuel's story. The tactics of the defense, to paint Gadoni as a traitor to his own people, did not seem to impress the judge.

After Gadoni sat down, Sebul signaled for Samuel to join him at the prosecutor's table. "I hadn't planned to call Laishita, but since she's here, do you think she'd mind testifying about Antium's part in her abduction?"

"I'm sure she'd do it. Do you want me to ask her?"

"Please do."

Samuel slipped back and whispered briefly to Gadoni and Laishita. She smiled and nodded her head. Sebul stood and said, "I'd like to call Laishita."

Laishita told her story in a straightforward manner, looking very relaxed and pretty. A sparkle was in her eyes and a smile on her lips. The defense attorney stood to cross-examine, studied her innocent face, and sat down without a word.

The final witnesses told of Antium's involvement with the

Kingmen, and late in the afternoon, Sebul rested his case. The judge instructed the defense to be ready to proceed the next morning.

Teor was present when the four young people walked into the courtroom the following day. A husky Nephite guard sat next to him. His presence increased the tension in the room. He glared menacingly at them as they waited for the day's proceedings to begin. The air was damp and heavy that morning, and the sun was hidden by heavy clouds. Samuel was depressed and gloomy but was not sure why. It had not been this way the day before. He reminded himself that the case against Antium was airtight, as was the one against Teor, who would stand trial soon, but the thought did little to cheer him up.

The judge had called the court to order and Antium's lawyer was on his feet. "The defense calls Teor," he announced.

Teor was unbound to take the stand. He seemed cocky and self-assured. He glanced at Gadoni with a wicked sneer, his hatred clearly evident. Samuel wished the judge could see that look, but Teor was too smooth to allow that. His look of hate swiftly vanished, although it lurked behind his eyes.

The first few questions from the defense related not at all to the case, serving only to make Teor appear as an upstanding, loyal citizen. Samuel was shocked when the lawyer asked Teor, "Teor, do you know who killed Judge Jarohah?"

"Yes, I do," Teor crooned.

"Was it Antium?"

"Oh, no. He tried to prevent it."

"And how do you know that?"

"I was there," Teor lied blatantly.

"Would you tell the court what you saw? Can you name the actual killer?" the lawyer asked, no emotion on his stony face.

"Objection, Your Honor," Sebul thundered.

"I want to hear what this witness has to say," the judge said firmly. "Please answer the questions truthfully," the judge cautioned Teor.

"I was with my cousin, Jashan, that night. He and Antium had been asked to warn Jarohah of a threat on his life. We came upon a fight in the street in front of the judge's home. Sam stabbed him with a knife, dropped it and ran." Teor gave a sorrowful look at the judge, then turned and grinned wickedly at Samuel.

"Teor, you were with Antium when the two of you and Laishita left this building and went into the wilderness together, were you not?" Samuel could not believe his ears.

Even more surprising than the question was Teor's answer. "Yes, she approached and asked if she could go with us."

"Objection!" Sebul's voice made the building shake.

"Overruled."

Samuel glanced at Gadoni who mirrored his look of disbelief and dismay. The defense lawyer continued to question Teor. "Did you say she asked to go with you? Do you mean that Antium couldn't have been involved in kidnapping because the young woman went of her own free will and choice?"

"That's right."

Laishita squealed in protest. "That's not true! He lies!"

"That will be all, young lady," the judge admonished. "This witness may tell his story, and I will not tolerate further outbursts from you."

Samuel studied the judge. He still looked as kind and honest as ever, but now Samuel found himself seriously doubting the man's integrity.

"Teor, please explain exactly what happened," the lawyer said.

"Well, she ran up to us outside this building and said, 'Please take me with you. I hate Sam and I'm afraid of him. My father trusts him, but he's a killer, and I must get away.' So I said, 'Well, it's up to you. You better tell your father, though.' I could hardly believe what she did then. Her father was busy untying his carriage horse from the hitching rack. Laishita picked up a stick and hit him over the head with it. Then she climbed on my horse behind me. I know I should have just thrown her on the ground then, but I didn't think that fast. So we rode off together."

Laishita moaned in disbelief.

Teor went on to tell the judge that Gadoni had pulled Laishita from his horse and proceeded to knock her around. "I tried to intervene because we were only trying to escape with our lives, but my horse jumped and I fell. Gadoni kicked me in the head. It didn't knock me out, but I was so stunned that I couldn't move. I did see Laishita make one last effort to get away, though. She pulled Gadoni's knife from his side and cut his face. He beat her badly then and tied us both up and took us back to where Sam was waiting."

Laishita gritted her teeth and listened. Sebul spent several minutes trying to get Teor to contradict himself and was successful to a small degree, but for the most part, Teor stuck to his preposterous story.

When Teor returned to his seat, the judge looked sternly at him and then at Antium's lawyer. "I allowed this testimony to proceed only after a stern warning about telling the truth. Teor now stands charged with perjury before this court, and if you try anymore stunts like this," he said to the lawyer, "you will be in contempt and I'll send you to jail with your client." The judge's face was red with anger and Samuel's faith in the judge was restored.

"Young lady," the judge smiled at Laishita, "I'm sorry for putting you through this. Please forgive me."

Laishita smiled, the judge was forgiven. It was at that moment, when all eyes were on Laishita, that Ophera screamed. Samuel turned in time to see Teor, a long knife in his hand, curse Gadoni and charge toward him, murder in his eyes. His guard was on his knees, clutching his stomach. Antium's guard tried to stop him but stumbled over a bench and sprawled on the floor. Samuel and Gadoni tried to push the girls out of harm's way, then jerked knives out of their sheaths. Teor stopped uncertainly when he saw their knives, then in a desperate effort threw his knife at Gadoni, striking him in the left shoulder. Lunging through the stunned crowd, he fled to freedom out the back door, followed moments later by the men who regained their senses enough to go in pursuit.

Samuel and Sebul laid Gadoni gently on the floor and pulled the knife from his shoulder. Laishita held his hand, weeping with fear. Gadoni made no sound, bravely enduring the pain. Frozen and silent, everyone gathered around Gadoni and the injured guard.

Suddenly Samuel looked around, and his heart sank when he discovered that the old ghost, Antium, was gone too! A search of the area was ordered, but after an hour, when no one had been able to locate the defendant or his witness, the judge called the court back to order.

Gadoni and Laishita had been taken to Ethan's home but Samuel and Ophera stayed in the courtroom. The lawyer for the defense said, "Your Honor, I would respectfully request that the charges against my client be dismissed since he is not available to testify in his own defense."

The judge half rose behind his bench and said harshly, "That is his fault! This trial will go on! Call your next witness!"

"But I can't. My client isn't here and I have no other witnesses," the lawyer pleaded.

"Then we'll proceed with the evidence already before the court. Do either of you have anything to add," the judge asked both lawyers.

Neither did, and he went on, "I find the defendant, Antium, guilty of murder, treason, desertion, and kidnapping. And I order that as soon as he is found, he be hanged until he is dead!" He paused while a murmur passed through the room. He concluded with, "And I also order Teor returned to stand before this court as soon as he can be found. I will not tolerate the kind of display that we have endured today. This court is adjourned."

The spirit of gloom that Samuel had felt in the courtroom that morning filled Ethan's house that afternoon. Gadoni, in pain but not seriously wounded, rested while Laishita paced the floor. "Teor will be back," she moaned. "He's coming after Gadoni. We've got to do something. I can't believe he got away—and Antium, too. They must both be captured or we'll never be safe."

Samuel stopped her gently. "Now, Laishita, don't worry. They'll soon be caught. In the meantime, we'll be extra careful." He hoped he sounded more confident than he felt.

Ophera led Laishita to find Taritha where the three women could comfort one another. Alone with Gadoni, Samuel said, "We've got to do something. Those two will stop at nothing. Laishita is right. We are in danger."

"They won't try anything here, will they?" Gadoni asked hopefully. "They'll try to ambush us on the road to Pachor's estate or something like that, don't you think?"

"I wish I knew. One thing is for sure, though. We've got to get out of Zarahemla," Samuel said as he stood looking out the window at the dark clouds that cast a somber shadow over the city.

"We can't leave Laishita here!" Gadoni said in alarm.

"We'll take her, too. And her family, if they'll go. How's your shoulder feeling?"

"It's not too bad."

Ethan joined them and they agreed that one would keep watch while the others slept. They would leave the city the next day.

Samuel took the first shift and prowled around the house, feeling uneasy, but hearing and seeing nothing unusual. The crickets and frogs kept the night alive, but other than that, all was quiet and peaceful.

After being relieved by Ethan, Samuel drifted into a deep but troubled sleep. He slept on a mat in the main room of the house, beneath a window where the cool evening breeze drove away the heat of the night. He awoke with a start, thinking at first that he was dreaming. Gadoni's voice was calling urgently, "Sam, wake up. The house is on fire!"

Samuel sat up, rubbing the sleep vigorously from his eyes, and was immediately aware of the pungent odor of heavy smoke. He thrust his head out the window only to withdraw it rapidly when he saw bright yellow flames licking hungrily at the old wood on the side of the house.

"Where are the others?" he shouted.

"I don't know where Ethan is. The rest are asleep. Let's get them out of here," Gadoni cried urgently.

Samuel dashed one way, Gadoni another. Samuel woke Taritha and her young son, who were in one room. Flames leaped through the bedroom window and licked hungrily at the ceiling. Smoke filled the room, and Samuel made them crawl, keeping their heads near the floor where fresh air could still be found. They crawled through the living room and out the front door.

Flames enveloped most of the house, but Samuel, not seeing Gadoni and the girls, rushed back inside. He found them in Laishita's room where Ophera lay still on the floor. Gadoni and Laishita were trying to pull her out, coughing and choking as smoke filled their lungs. Samuel felt heat in the floor and realized the fire was under the house, too.

He helped pull Ophera from the room. As they struggled through the door, a bed near the far wall crashed through the floor and flames exploded from the hole, filling the room almost instantly. Laishita was trying to guide them through the heavy smoke but had a difficult time finding the doors. Keeping close to the floor, they crawled desperately, their lungs burning and the heat singeing their hair.

Finally Laishita cried, "This way!" and led them in a mad rush through the burning doorway to safety outside. Samuel carried Ophera the last few steps.

Miraculously, none of them had any serious burns. A short time in the fresh air was all it took to revive Ophera, who sat up, wide-eyed and coughing. "Watch her," Samuel shouted to Taritha and Laishita. He grabbed Gadoni's arm and led him around the burning house. "Ethan must be out here somewhere. I'm sure he wasn't inside," Samuel said, gesturing with his sword.

They found him behind the house, sprawled on the ground and unconscious, a bump on the back of his head. They carried Ethan around the house where the neighbors were gathering and Ethan's wife—relieved to see him alive—tended to him. Samuel watched the bright inferno, feeling totally helpless.

His eyes drifted to the stables behind Ethan's house. He thought he saw a movement in the shadows. He inched toward Gadoni and nudged him on the arm. "Gadoni," he whispered, "there's some-one in the stables. Do you feel up to having a look?"

"Let's go," Gadoni said, following Samuel.

They were just a few feet from the corral gate when it burst open and a horse and rider bolted through. Gadoni, moving like lightning, snagged the horse's halter and planted his feet, pulling for all he was worth. The horse's head came around fast and its knees buckled, pitching it to the ground.

Samuel saw the rider tumble beyond the horse. In a flash he was on him, pounding his face. Gadoni joined and they both fought hard. Once the rider was subdued, they rolled him over, and there, his scowling face lighted by the flames of the burning house, was Teor.

Samuel spoke to Gadoni as several men hauled their old boss off to prison. "Antium must be close. Teor wasn't alone. Let's check the stable."

They passed together through the gate and into the dark stable. Samuel and Gadoni's horses were there along with Ethan's. The horses stomped and threw their heads as Samuel and Gadoni felt their way around the wall. Samuel, who was in the lead, felt the presence of evil, as if a vile ghost were mingling with the snorting horses.

They held their swords in their hands as they continued around the wall. The strong odor of horse flesh mixed with stable dust made it hard to breathe, and their progress was slow. A couple of horses broke free and ran frantically into the corral. The young men reached the halfway point and had encountered no one, when they suddenly spotted the ghost whose presence they had felt. He appeared as if by magic and stood illuminated in the stable door as light from the burning house cavorted about his silhouette. His beady eye glared at them. His broken arm hung in a sling while a long, gleaming sword waved from his crooked arm.

For a second, Antium stood there. Then, with a smile on his repulsive face, he slowly turned before charging through the tunnel of dancing light and into the corral. Samuel and Gadoni pushed through the milling horses and out the door after him, but the ghost had vanished. They checked all around the corrals to no avail. Finally, defeated, they joined the crowd at the house.

Teor was on his way to jail again and Ethan had regained consciousness. "I heard something outside," Ethan explained to Samuel, "and went out to check. I was walking around the house when I heard footsteps behind me. The next thing I knew, I was waking up with my wife leaning over me, her face reflecting firelight and the air filled with smoke."

"I'm sorry about your house," Samuel said. "Come, let's get you to one of the neighbor's to rest."

"No, you and Gadoni go with the others. I want to stay here. My father and I built this house with our own hands, and I can't leave until it's gone."

Samuel and Gadoni stayed with him through the rest of the long night. The three of them sat with their backs against the huge trunk of a sprawling tree and watched until Ethan's house was nothing but a glowing pile of embers.

Dawn found the two young men leading their horses from the stable. Ophera and Laishita joined them there. The girls had not yet cleaned up, and their faces were black from the fire. "Where are you going?" Ophera asked.

"A search of the city for Antium is starting in a few minutes. We're going to help," Samuel said, matter-of-factly.

Ophera, less than enthusiastic, took hold of Samuel's hand and pleaded, "Please don't go. You've done enough. Let the others find him. You're tired and . . ." She choked, her voice full of emotion as tears began eroding small black trails on her smoky cheeks. She tried again, saying, "And . . . and Sam, I don't want to lose you again. Please stay." Her deep blue eyes glistened as she pleaded.

He felt the desire to give in, to throw his arms around her neck and never leave her sight again, but there was another fire burning in him that wouldn't go out. He had the unconquerable need to rid his life of the ghost that haunted him and tormented his soul. He had to help catch Antium, and even though he had tender feelings for this bedraggled but beautiful girl who pled with him so fervently, he could not change the course to which he was committed.

"No, Ophera, you won't be safe until Antium is caught or driven from the land, nor will I. Please don't ask me not to do this thing," he said gently.

Anger flashed briefly across her face, and then it was gone, replaced by a look of pride and respect. Samuel saw in her eyes a new understanding of him.

"You go then, Sam. I'll be waiting with Laishita when you return," she said softly, burying her head against his shoulder and stifling a sob.

He kissed her lightly on the forehead and turned to Gadoni who still held the hand of a tearful and subdued Laishita.

"Ready?" he asked.

"Ready," Gadoni replied.

"Then let's ride. We have a ghost to find," Samuel said with a laugh, his heart made lighter and his confidence strengthened by the love and respect of a beautiful, blonde-haired girl.

CHAPTER NINETEEN

ANTIUM COULD NOT BE FOUND. SAMUEL'S PRIDE WAS HURT. "How can I explain to Ophera that I failed?" he moaned to Gadoni as they rode in the twilight along the road to Pachor's estate.

"What is there to explain? He's gone, that's all. We really didn't have much hope of finding him anyway, did we?" Gadoni reasoned.

"I suppose not, but now we must live with the threat of his reappearance hanging over our heads. Not a pretty thought, is it?"

"No, not at all," Gadoni agreed glumly, "but there's nothing more we can do about it."

"There they are," Samuel shouted, pointing up the road and urging his horse into a trot.

Ophera and Laishita, out for a walk, squealed and ran to meet them. "Was Antium captured?" Ophera asked expectantly.

Samuel hung his head. "We failed, Ophera. The search for Antium has been called off. Tomorrow Teor will be tried, though. After that we can leave Zarahemla."

"Good," Ophera responded brightly, masking her concern for the sake of Samuel's feelings. "Care to give a girl a lift?"

Teor's trial took only a few hours. He was convicted of the charges against him and condemned to die. The next morning at dawn his rebellion was cut short at the end of a long rope in a tree outside of the towering walls of Zarahemla.

At Latoni's invitation, Ethan and his family moved to Gilead and life soon settled into a comfortable and peaceful routine.

Samuel and Gadoni resumed hunting to provide meat for the residents of the city. They were determined to put the fear and worry of Antium out of their minds.

Several uneventful weeks passed. The young men returned one day with an abundant supply of meat. They were met by a small, wiry man as they rode up to Latoni's shop. He was well-dressed but carried the dust of a long ride. He introduced himself as Himni.

"I bring greetings from Captain Moroni," Himni said with a tired smile.

"How is the war going? Will it soon be over?" Sam asked.

"How interesting that you should ask," Himni said, still smiling. "Captain Moroni is hoping to drive the enemy from the land and bring the war to an end soon, but he needs more men. That is why I am here."

Samuel's chest tightened involuntarily. He was aware of Ophera and Laishita watching from across the street. "He wants me to come," Samuel suggested slowly, knowing how Ophera would hate for him to go.

"That's right. Gadoni, too, if he would like to."

Samuel hesitated before saying, "I guess I knew I would be called to fight. I was just hoping the war would be over before ..."

Himni did not seem to be listening. He interrupted. "Oh, and Moroni said to tell you that he knows where Antium went."

"Where?" Samuel and Gadoni asked in surprised unison.

"Back to the Lamanite army. He has gained command of 3000 men. He has stirred them up until they have become feared by our soldiers. They are a bloodthirsty, ferocious lot."

"I'm going, Gadoni," Samuel said with sudden resolution. "Why don't you stay here and keep . . ."

"I'm going, too," his friend interrupted fiercely.

"Excellent," Himni said smugly. "You will be assigned to Moroni's own force. They are moving in the direction Antium and his warriors were last seen."

After a tearful and strained parting from Ophera and Laishita and a long and tiring trek through the wilderness with thousands of other men, Samuel and Gadoni stood in front of their old friend, Captain Moroni.

"It is good to have you men with us," Moroni said sincerely. "There is much fighting ahead, and I need brave, faithful men in my army if we are to prevail. You have both proven yourselves on the field of battle and will be a great strength to my army."

During the long weeks that followed, Moroni's words proved to be prophetic. Several bloody battles were fought and won by the courageous Nephite soldiers and none fought harder or with more skill and courage than Samuel and Gadoni. City after city was retaken as they drove the Lamanites out. Still, the two friends constantly thought of Antium and wondered if and when they would face him again.

"Captain Antium, sir, it is them. They are fighting for Captain Moroni, just like you heard."

Antium's beady eye squinted at the young man who was addressing him. A Nephite traitor like himself, Migan had followed Antium's orders and spied on Captain Moroni's army. Rumors from the Lamanite ranks that Antium's personal enemies, Samuel and Gadoni, had joined the fierce fighting in the region had prompted his actions.

His evil mind was already plotting the deaths of his young foes. "Did you meet Samuel and Gadoni?" he asked.

"I did."

"Did they suspect you?"

"No."

"Excellent." Antium fingered the scar where his other eye used to be. "You will return immediately. You must gain their confidence quickly, for I want Samuel and Gadoni dead before we engage Captain Moroni and his army in combat. Does Moroni know where we are?"

"He does not, Captain. Do you want me to kill your two enemies in their sleep tonight?"

"No!" Antium thundered. "They are mine! Your job is to lure them from Moroni's camp before the full moon rises tomorrow night. I will be waiting with some of my best men where this river," he motioned at the water in front of him, "meets the one to the west. If you succeed, there will be a great reward for you— men of your own to command."

253

Clair Poulson

For the first time, Migan's broad face broke into a smile. "Fifty men," he said.

"Fifty men," Antium agreed. "Go now."

There was no fighting the next day. Samuel and Gadoni spent the afternoon honing the edges of their swords and pounding out dents in their breastplates and shields. "Captain Moroni has announced that one final, coordinated offensive will bring victory," a junior captain informed the group of men they were with. "Every Lamanite army in the region has been located and defeated except one."

Samuel looked up. "Antium's," he said bitterly.

"That's right. We are now in the general area where they were last known to be camped," the captain said. "Get plenty of rest, for we will be back in battle soon."

After he had left, Samuel said, "Antium is near, Gadoni. I can feel it."

Gadoni nodded in agreement, but before he could speak, another soldier spoke in a whisper so he could not be overheard. "I am Migan. Do you remember me?"

"Yes," Samuel muttered, annoyed by the interruption.

"I slipped out during the night," he said, yawning. "That's why I'm so sleepy today. I think I know where this Captain Antium and his army are hiding."

Samuel looked at him in surprise. "Have you told Captain Moroni?"

"No, but if you two will help me tonight, I'm sure we can find Antium and report his army's exact location to the captain in the morning. He would be . . ."

"They are that near?" Samuel cut in.

"Yes. Will you help me? There will be a full moon tonight and . . ."

"I will speak to Captain Moroni," Samuel said.

"No, please don't. He might send someone else with me and I trust only you two. We can do it. I know we can."

Samuel and Gadoni exchanged glances. "All right," Samuel agreed reluctantly.

During the rest of the afternoon, he tried to get a moment alone

254

with Gadoni but Migan stuck with him like a leech. Samuel did not feel right about the young soldier or his request. Finally, in the hour of darkness before the silver moon arose, the three of them slipped past the guards and out of camp.

For an hour they traveled through the forest as the moon rose and cast shadows all about them. The farther they followed Migan, the worse Sam felt. He had a feeling much like the one he had felt in the cave when the Spirit had warned him to go back. Disregarding that prompting had nearly cost him and Gadoni their lives.

Suddenly he stopped dead in his tracks. He had been given another chance! He would not continue to ignore the powerful prompting of the Spirit *this* night. Gadoni stopped beside him. "We've got to go back," he whispered to his friend.

"I'm with you," whispered Gadoni. "Something is wrong. I don't trust . . ."

"Hey, you two. Hurry up," Migan said with an icy edge to his voice.

"No, Migan," Samuel said, drawing his sword. Moonlight filtered through the leafy branches overhead and reflected from the razor-sharp steel of the blade. "This is as far as we go. Who are you, anyway, and what are you up to?"

A brief flicker of fear crossed Migan's broad face, confirming Samuel's suspicions. Without another word, Migan turned and fled. Samuel and Gadoni pursued him and Migan died in the fight that followed.

Breathless, Samuel said, "He was working for Antium. Quickly, let's return and get some help. I suspect that Antium is waiting at the fork of the river where Migan said the army is camped."

Two hours later, a force of fifty men, led by Samuel and Gadoni, crept through the silent forest. They found the river and followed it to where it split. There they flushed a small band of ferocious Lamanites out from the foliage near the bank. Though they were outnumbered, the Lamanites engaged the small band of Nephites in a fierce battle.

Suddenly Samuel caught a brief glimpse of a ghostly face with a hook-nose and one eye as the man turned tail and left his men to die. "Gadoni," Samuel called to his friend who was fighting at his side. "Let's follow him," he pointed quickly with his sword.

"Antium?" Gadoni shouted as he warded off a blow from an enemy sword and sent another Lamanite on an eternal journey.

"Who else? Once again he flees. Let's get him."

For several minutes they pursued Antium through the forest, leaping over fallen logs, dodging low branches, and stumbling over hidden rocks. They finally succeeded in overtaking their old foe and cornered him at the edge of the murky, meandering river.

"It's all over, Antium," Samuel shouted. "Give yourself up."

Antium, his sword drawn, shouted an oath and threw the weapon at Samuel who dodged deftly as the sword sailed harmlessly by. The two of them closed in on him. Antium turned, and with his mouth spewing out curses, hurled himself into the moonlit water.

"Come on, Gadoni. We can't let him get away again," Samuel said, stripping off his armor and dropping his weapons on the ground.

Antium was swimming fiercely across the river, his arms tossing up a shower of water that glittered like diamonds in the moonlight. Gadoni and Samuel swam after him, gaining rapidly, but before they could get to him, Antium reached a leafless tree that had fallen into the water and began to pull himself onto its trunk.

Gadoni stopped and shouted, "Look, Sam!"

A monstrous snake was stretched out on the fallen tree between Antium and the shore. Antium, apparently feeling a kinship with the serpent world, paid the snake no attention and attempted to crawl past it. The snake, however, showed no mutual kinship with the hook-nosed intruder. With lightning speed, it wrapped its long, brown and yellow body around Antium and tumbled him off the trunk and into the reeds on the bank. Antium screamed, a familiar long, blood-curdling wail. Then the snake wrapped itself around the old ghost's neck like a hangman's noose and began to squeeze. Antium's eye bugged out and his rough, red face turned purple.

Gadoni and Samuel watched in fascinated horror as the judge's sentence of death was carried out by one of Antium's kin: a ruthless serpent. The snake seemed to know when the life had left its victim, for it relaxed and slowly uncoiled its long, scaly body from Antium's corpse and slithered into the reeds. Samuel and Gadoni gave the snake plenty of time to get away before clawing a hole in the wet ground and forever hiding Antium's hideous face in a crude grave.

"Gadoni," Samuel said after their task was finished. "Antium's army must be close by. Surely he was running back to it."

They swam back across the river, recovered their weapons and armor and proceeded cautiously upstream. "I hear something," Gadoni whispered after a strenuous half-hour.

On their bellies in the tall grass and thick foliage, they worked their way forward until they could confirm the position of the hidden Lamanite army. They slipped away and returned to their waiting companions with the news crucial to the final Nephite conquest.

"Oh, there you two are," the captain said. "Where have you been?"

Samuel explained. "Antium's army is not far upstream. If we surround them tonight, we can claim victory before noon tomorrow," he predicted.

Following a swift and decisive victory over Antium's ruthless warriors the next morning, the armies of Moroni swept the remaining Lamanite aggressors from the land. Captain Moroni himself released Samuel and Gadoni from the army with a special commendation for their help in bringing peace once again to the Nephite nation.

"And now you may return to Gilead without having to look over your shoulders to see if old Antium is after you," Moroni said with a chuckle.

"Yes, and I hope his ghost doesn't haunt us, either," Samuel joked as he accepted the captain's firm handshake.

CHAPTER TWENTY

"I WONDER WHEN THEY'LL START TALKING OF MARRIAGE?" Laishita ventured just a few weeks after the triumphant return of Samuel and Gadoni.

"Soon, I hope," Ophera said dreamily. "Ever since Samuel returned from the war I have been expecting him to propose, but, even though he's very romantic, he never brings it up."

"Gadoni's the same way. I wish he'd hurry. I'm ready. I don't want to be old and grey before I become a wife. Anyway, Mother says that being a parent is a job for young people, not old ones. I wonder what they're waiting for? Oh, here they come now," Laishita said with an excited giggle.

"Care to take a little stroll out to the lake?" Samuel asked Ophera.

"Sure," she said, and cast Laishita a hopeful look.

Samuel and Ophera strolled arm in arm toward the lake, bright splashes of color flitting among the trees as a multitude of beautiful birds played an accompaniment to the song in Ophera's heart. Monkeys swung from low-hanging branches, chattering a friendly greeting. At the lakeshore, a herd of tiny deer fed on the lush grass and flowers growing there. They looked up briefly, their large, soft eyes blinking slowly, then they resumed their feeding, their ears flickering and their short tails beating a happy tune.

"It's never been so alive and cheerful here before," Samuel said as he led Ophera to a large rock that jutted over the shimmering water. A clump of small flowers poked through a crack at their feet. He plucked a bright blue blossom and poked its stem gently into her hair, just above her right ear. "There," he said, admiring his artistry, "doesn't that look pretty?"

Ophera leaned out over the clear water of the lake and saw her face reflected there. The blue of the flower did look nice in her long, golden hair. "Thank you, Sam," she murmured. "Do you know why it's so beautiful here today?" she asked him.

"Why?"

"Because we're so happy."

"I hope it stays beautiful." Samuel held her away from him and gazed at her for a long moment, his face serious. "There is something I need to say, and I hope you're ready to hear it." Her heart beat wildly in anticipation. "I have had more than my share of close calls and wild experiences the past few years," he continued. "I should be ready to settle down and live a quiet, peaceful life here in Gilead, I suppose," he said.

The wild beating stopped abruptly. He wasn't saying the words she longed to hear. But Ophera waited patiently. This was a time to listen.

"I've learned what a fragile but special gift freedom is, Ophera. We've both been deprived it, and we've seen men die in its defense. But I've also come to know that there's another kind of freedom that some men crave—an elusive, personal kind of freedom. It's the freedom to do what is right and best for that person, not tying himself down but seeking growth and fulfillment wherever he can find it."

He stood up and stepped to the edge of the rocky ledge, gazing over the lake with its tiny, uniform ripples, whipped up by a sudden breeze. Ophera stood but did not speak or approach him, wondering where this conversation was headed. Everything she had felt and seen of him these past weeks told her he still loved her, but now she wondered if there was something wrong.

When he turned and faced her, a smile creased his sunburned lips. "You're wondering if you really know me anymore, aren't you?"

"Yes," she whispered.

"Well, I wonder, too. I've been trying to figure myself out. What do I want in life? Where do I want to go? I haven't been sure, even though I've thought about it a lot since the war ended." He paused and she forced a smile. "I think I know now, Ophera.

259

I'm not like most men and don't want to be too soon tied down. I need my own personal freedom."

Ophera felt like a thunderbolt had struck her. Her knees shook and threatened to collapse. She stumbled closer to Samuel, unable to speak. He was staring beyond her—seemed not to see her discomfort.

"Ophera," he spoke again, "you must understand how I feel. I may never be able to settle down, at least not for many years, and live the quiet life my father has always preferred. Do you understand what I'm saying?"

His piercing eyes fell on her face and she felt him searching for the feelings of her heart. She fought the impulse to turn and flee.

"Well, do you?" he pressed.

"Yes, I think so, Sam. And I'm afraid that I've fallen in love with a wanderer. Stupid of me, isn't it?"

"You've been very patient with me, Ophera. I know it hasn't been easy for you, and I love you so much for accepting the pain I have inflicted. I'm a lucky man, and I hope my luck continues." He paused, then asked, "You're confused, aren't you?"

"Yes. You say you love me, but you can't settle down. Where does that leave me? I love you, Samuel."

"Having told you this, there is something I want to ask you. It is very important."

"All right," she said fearfully.

"Will you marry me and be my companion wherever life's road leads me?"

Ophera was completely taken back by his sudden proposal when she thought he had been saying that he wanted to stay single. She stepped toward him, relieved that she had misunderstood. Playfully, she reached over and poked him in the chest. He laughed and took a step back. There was nothing beneath his feet. His eyes registered surprise for a brief moment as his arms thrashed wildly, in an attempt to regain his balance. He failed and fell clumsily into the warm water of the lake, laughing at this replay of a long-ago situation.

Ophera stood dumbfounded for a moment, then with a squeal of delight, she kicked off her sandals and plunged in after him. Giggling and splashing water on each other, they swam beyond the ledges and Samuel helped her back onto the steep, rocky bank.

"Did that mean, no?" he asked after he had followed her out of the water and stood dripping on the lichen-covered rocks.

She laughed as he gazed at her, his dripping hair plastered against his head. "No, that meant yes!" she cried and threw her arms around him.

Samuel pulled her close to him. "Do you really mean that, Ophera?" he asked softly.

"Yes. Oh, yes I do!" Ophera smiled and his eyes smiled back at her. "I've always dreamed of settling down in a quiet town with a loving, hard-working husband and raising a family. My dreams included flowers in the yard, a garden, and friends nearby. Yes, I always wanted to do the things that families and friends do. But today my dream has changed. It changed because I love a man who isn't ready to settle down, but who wants to include me in all his crazy dreams, whatever they are and wherever they lead. All I want is to be with him, to support and love and . . ."

"Now listen, Ophera. I still want children," Samuel teased. Then in a more serious tone he added, "I want to worship and have friends, but I want to see far off places and do other things as well."

"What do Gadoni and Laishita plan to do?" she asked.

He said nothing for a moment, his eyes drifting out over the deep blue of the lake. She followed his gaze and spotted the other young couple on the far shore. "Gadoni and I think a lot the same. I don't know about Laishita, though."

"She will feel as I do," Ophera said confidently.

Samuel pulled her close again and kissed her tenderly. She melted in his strong arms. Ophera knew she was where she belonged.

Samuel had never seen the mountains more beautiful. Maybe it was the company, he decided as he caught a glimpse of his pretty wife from the corner of his eye.

"How much farther is it, Sam?"

He twisted around on the bay stallion he rode. "Not far."

She smiled. Ever since their wedding two weeks ago, he

marveled when he saw her. Long golden strands of hair whipped about her smooth, tan face. She sat erect on her glossy white mount, like an angel, Samuel thought, placed on the earth just for me. The sound of iron on rock pulled his attention from her and he turned in time to see Gadoni and Laishita ride up beside them.

"Just as pretty as I remembered it," Gadoni said, looking out over the rugged sea of green that stretched below them as far as they could behold.

Samuel had laughed with delight when Ophera suggested they spend their honeymoon in the wilderness. The time he and Gadoni had spent in these mountains had etched their magnificent picture indelibly into his memory, and, difficult though it had been to get here, the beauty, wildness, and privacy were worth it.

Later that afternoon, the two happy couples stood overlooking the very pool where Antium had first tried to take Samuel's life. He grinned when he heard Ophera take a deep breath. "Do you mean you jumped into the water from here?" she asked, her mouth open in surprise.

"Yes, of course. The water is pretty deep down there," Samuel assured her.

Gadoni was already tying his black gelding to a small tree and getting ready to jump.

"Are you sure it's safe, Sam?" Ophera asked doubtfully.

"Watch Gadoni," he said in answer as the bronze Lamanite dove with a piercing shout of delight and descended gracefully to the sparkling pool.

Samuel followed a moment later. It took several minutes before they finally returned to stand beside their quivering wives, who preferred to watch rather than participate. Not until the next day did Ophera finally bolster enough nerve to jump. Her enthusiasm, however, was contagious, and she soon talked Laishita into taking the plunge as well.

For several days the cares of the world were forgotten for the two young couples as they lounged and played, enjoying the creations of God. At length, Samuel suggested they move on. "Maybe someday we can return," he said with a grin.

"One last dive?" Ophera asked, her dazzling smile inviting Samuel.

"Why not?" he said.

"Together," she said.

"Together," he agreed.

Hand in hand, Samuel and Ophera stood at the edge of the ledge, studying the pool far below. "Ready?" he asked.

"Ready," she said, turning her face to him. He kissed her light-ly. Then together they dove, their glistening bodies reflecting the morning sun as they descended in a graceful arc and were trans-formed into speeding shadows beneath the shimmering surface of the sparkling blue water.

About the Author

Clair M. Poulson has spent most of his adult life patrolling the highways and enforcing the law in his native Duchesne County, in the state of Utah. After his retirement as Duchesne County Sheriff, Clair became a part-time judge for the justice court and finally had time to seriously pursue his life-long interest in writing. For many years he has kept a journal and has a wealth of recorded experience to draw from. However, when he sat down to write, he decided that fiction would be more fun than autobiographical writing and would also be of more interest to the reading public.

Clair's interest in fiction actually found its beginning many years ago when he would tell bedtime stories to his small children. They would beg for just one more "make up story" before going to sleep. He wishes he had recorded those stories for his grandchildren!

His current schedule allows him to come home each day after spending a few hours handling the business of the justice court and work on his writing where he is limited only by his own imagination. He finds writing fiction to be as immensely satisfying as was creating bedtime fiction for his little ones.

The Church has always been an important part of Clair's life and he has served in many positions. He is currently serving as High Priest Group Leader. He and Ruth, his wife and sweetheart of nearly twenty-four years, are the parents of five children. Nothing is more important to him than his family, and even as the children loved his stories when they were little, he hopes to provide them uplifting entertainment and encouragement through his writing today.

The son of a librarian, Clair still reads from fifty to one hundred books a year—an interest his children share. His favorite book, and one from which he feasts daily, is the Book of Mormon—so it was natural that he would choose a Book of Mormon setting for his first novel.

Clair loves the out-of-doors. He still farms with his brother, as he has for many years, and raises a variety of livestock including cattle, sheep, and pigs. He spends many hours running on the back-roads and remote areas behind his rural home. When he is running he finds time to think, and many of his best ideas for writing come to him when he is alone with nature.